Hugo

Olive Township
Book 2

Jennifer Millikin

Copyright © 2025 by Jennifer Millikin
All rights reserved.

This book or any portion thereof
may not be reproduced or used in any manner whatsoever
without the express written permission of the publisher except for the
use of brief quotations in a book review. This book is a work of fiction.
Names, characters, and incidents are products of the author's
imagination or are used fictitiously. Any resemblance to actual events,
or locales, or persons, living or dead, is entirely coincidental.
JNM, LLC

ISBN: 979-8-9909048-5-9
www.jennifermillikinwrites.com
Cover by Okay Creations
Editing by Emerald Edits
Proofreading by Sisters Get Lit.erary

*For those who like stories
that feel like cozy hugs you can settle into.*

Chapter 1

Olive Township

I SHOULD LOVE ALL MY INHABITANTS IN EQUAL measure.

But that's not the case. I cannot love the wicked as I do the saint.

The moment Simon De la Vega left this world, I felt it. A stuttering in my heartbeats. A pain from which I could not recover. I've taken extra care with his children, doing what I can to bring them warmth and love. But their broken hearts, I cannot heal.

Something looms on the horizon. I feel it, a rumbling around me.

Someone is coming.

So is change.

Both are desperately needed.

Chapter 2

Mallory

To: Hugo De la Vega
From: Mallory Hawkins

Hello,

I'm following up on my most recent email to see if you've given any thought to meeting me. I'm sincerely sorry for what you and your family have experienced, and I'd love to give you a voice. I understand this is unconventional, and not something people usually find enjoyable, but it has tremendously helped others to speak about their experience. I'm including a link to my podcast below. If you listen to it, you'll see how deeply I care about giving voice to unfinished stories.

Best,
Mallory Hawkins
Host of *Case Files*

Hugo

"Hugo hasn't responded. Not to your first email, your second, your third, or, shockingly, your fourth." Jolene levels me with a maternal stare as she leans over our kitchen table. Gently she closes my open laptop, and the string of unanswered emails disappears from my sight. Her fingers traipse across the closed computer, finding their way to my cup of fruit. She snatches a red grape and pops it into her mouth.

"I never should have made you my best friend," I gripe, snaking a hand around the white porcelain fruit bowl and curling it into my chest. "Or my producer."

"Face it, toots," Jolene says, settling into the chair opposite me. Her reddish-brown hair is wound in a perfect bun on top of her head, giving her the look of a regal ballerina. "Hugo De la *whatever* his last name is—"

"De la Vega," I supply, glancing at the closed computer as I say his name. When I open it again, it will show that same name, and all those unanswered emails. Jolene may have interrupted my fixation on the gold medal Olympian and his non-response, but it's waiting for me where I left it.

She extends a flattened palm between us, nodding. "Hugo De la Vega wants nothing to do with you. Or your quest."

I sit back, selecting a pineapple chunk and nibbling at

the end. Disappointment courses through me, but it's nothing new. Months have passed since I sent that first email. Every time I check my inbox, a tiny *what if* thrill presses at me. It's short-lived, because so far, Hugo De la Vega is incomunicado.

Choosing to be gentle in my initial approach, I'd emailed him a basic query letter. I introduced myself, my true crime podcast, and my mission. I spent hours crafting that email, revising and editing and choosing words that conveyed the depth of my condolences over what he and his family had endured. If there was one thing I knew, it was that the pain from a murdered family member, especially one still unsolved, was endless. And, oh, how it tormented the soul. The heart.

"It's rude of him to ignore you," Jolene says, uncapping a yellow highlighter. She's on hour three of sifting through phone records, highlighting calls that took place during certain times. Jolene moonlights as my *Case Files* producer, but by day she's an assistant at a law office.

"One could argue it was presumptuous of me to email him." There is a pinprick of defensiveness in my tone. Hugo's not being rude. He's protecting himself. And probably his family, too.

It's what I would do, if somebody cold-called me about my little sister's murder. If I wasn't a true crime podcaster, didn't know what I know, understand how, sometimes, cases are solved and hearts are healed because of podcasts like mine. "If he would email me back and tell me *no,* I could put this to bed."

Jolene's eyebrows arch. "Could you?"

Hugo

A reluctant smile curves my lips. My stubbornness lives in infamy. "No."

"Do you want to hear what I think?"

"Aren't you already telling me what you think?" I blow her a kiss, and she pretends to bat it away.

She holds up a finger, saying *hold please*. Her hand swipes over her phone, and a moment later, she Airdrops a link to my phone. I tap on the notification, and it opens my internet browser. The page loads, showing a serene space, teak furniture, a woman wrapped in a plush white towel lying in a sauna. The image is replaced by a different woman receiving a massage.

"Sagewood Spa?" I ask, confused. "What about it?"

"It's in Olive Township."

"Correct." Olive Township is also where the De la Vegas live, at their locally famous Summerhill Olive Mill. "So?"

Jolene sits back, regarding me with a thoughtful look. "I can't get away anytime soon, but you? You, my friend, are long overdue for a spa day."

"I can't show up in his town, Jolene. Talk about stalker vibes."

"You have the same right as everybody else to use the spa. Come on. It's not weird. That place is basically famous. There are articles written about the Sacred Prickly Pear red clay body treatment. It's listed as a destination spa in travel magazines." She adjusts the sleeve of her button-down blouse. "It's a two-hour drive. Make it your *destination*."

"Maybe," I say, toying with my lower lip. Should I go

to Olive Township? Scope out the place? I've read about the eclectic small town online enough that, by now, it feels like I already know it. The popular places to eat, the speakeasy with the secret entrance, the store that operates on an honor system. I know all about the Italian family who runs a gelato shop, touted as making a fior de latte that can transport you straight to a piazza in Florence. I know all this because I've been fascinated by the juxtaposition. How can a seemingly senseless murder have occurred in such an idyllic location?

It's the same question that has haunted me every day since I was fourteen, and my little sister was killed at a water park. Years later, the thought manages to steal my breath. The grief is never far, ebbing and flowing like the tide, sweeping over me then leaving me bereft. Powerful enough to drown me on some days.

"Mallory?" Jolene waves a hand in the air. "Where did you go?"

"Memory lane," I respond.

Jolene frowns. "You looked upset. Are you sure all this is a good idea?"

For years, I've been driven by the need to bring my sister's killer to justice. Nothing will bring her back, though I'd give anything for it. My sister's smile could light up a dark room, and ever since that day, I've been living in perpetual darkness. How can I ignore the possibility that the two cases could be linked?

"Yes," I say, with confidence I feel to my bones.

"We can scrap it," Jolene presses.

Hugo

I shake my head. "No way. Not if there's a chance they could be connected."

"The chance is slim," Jolene warns. Maternal again. I'll have to ask her for tips on how to do that. She's not a mom, but for her, it's natural. An instinct. I certainly won't be asking my own mother. Or my father, not that I ever knew him. He left my mom before I spoke my first word.

"If I have the opportunity to make this world a tiny bit safer, I should take it. I owe him." My hand slides over my slightly swollen midsection, a bump that is barely there. "Or, her."

Jolene eyes me. "What do you plan to do?"

I hold up my phone, scrolling to the button that says *Book a service*. "Spa weekend."

Jolene attempts a smile. "For both your sakes, I hope you get what you're after." She opens a note on her phone, begins typing. "Fresh notebooks, sharp pencils, felt-tip pens."

"What are you doing?"

"Making a shopping list for your getaway weekend. I know how you like to take notes the old-fashioned way. You need to write down everything you see. Hear. Whatever strikes your fancy. Remember, the end goal is to get *Case Files* picked up by a podcast network. Foundry," she says dreamily, referring to the network she's had designs on since the moment *Case Files* was born.

"The end goal is to figure out who killed my sister, and then figure out if it's the same person who killed

Simon De la Vega," I remind her. "We are healing hearts. Seeking justice."

Jolene blows out a hard breath. "Yes, of course. Consider Foundry an ancillary goal. Never mind that the show is struggling, and Foundry would be its savior."

"There are dips and swells," I tell her. "It's a natural part of every business."

Even if I truly believe my words, there's still a part of me that worries. What if one day, the dip will be too low to come back from?

It's Jolene's big dream to be picked up by a podcast network. Like so many people, Jolene graduated law school and began practicing, only to be slapped in the face with the reality of the long hours, and how little time she'd have left to have a personal life. Producing *Case Files* is her passion, and she'd be thrilled to make it her only job.

It's not that it's not my dream, too, but my singular focus was recently interrupted. Getting pregnant was a personal development that left me gobsmacked. So was the realization that I'll be raising this baby on my own.

But, if there is one thing I know for certain, it's that I can't stand the idea of bringing a child into a world where my sister's killer roams free.

I'll do almost anything to get to the bottom of what happened to Maggie, and it starts with a trip to Olive Township.

Chapter 3

Hugo

THERE ARE PLACES IN THE UNITED STATES WHERE March is a winter month. Here in the Sonoran Desert, March signals the beginning of spring. And, on warmer days, the start of summer. Not the real summer the desert is known for, but a taste. An *amuse-bouche*, as my sister Vivi would say. The chef in her is always thinking about food, or something food-adjacent.

The climate here in my little corner of the world is hardly something to complain about. If it weren't for the arid desert and its relatively mild winters, my family wouldn't have an olive mill. I wouldn't have had a profession to fall back on following the close of my fencing career.

I swing my truck bearing the Summerhill Olive Mill name and logo into an empty spot in front of Sammich. Unaccustomed to the size of the truck, I end up bumping the curb with my front tires. I have a personal vehicle, a cherry red Audi R8. It's sexy and sleek and smooth, all adjectives I should ascribe to a woman. Despite that, they fit the car perfectly. I don't usually pass up the chance to drive my car, but I'm not clean enough to sit in her today.

Pruning olive trees is an arduous, dirty, and oftentimes boring task, and all morning I've been thinking about lunch. Days like today, when I wake up before the sun and make my way to the room I've turned into a home gym, leave me famished. It would've been easier to stop in at the big house, where my mom lives with my aunt on the Summerhill property, and grab something to eat there. But for hours now I've had my heart set on a double meat Bellamy sandwich, named after my best friend Penn's mom. She passed away last year, and Margaret, the owner of Sammich, promptly added her favorite sandwich to the menu. The double meat order is my twist on it.

The familiar yeasty scent of fresh bread envelops me as I walk through the swinging door. Margaret, positioned behind the cash register, beams when she sees me.

"I was wondering if you were going to mosey in here today," she says, planting one hand on her hip as she leans on the counter. Her gaze roves over me, taking in my dirty jeans, my equally filthy shirt.

"Oh yeah?" I ask, stepping up to the counter. "Why is that?"

"Pruning time always makes you hungry." A pleased twinkle makes its way into her eyes.

"You like to think you know me," I joke, crossing my arms and leaning back on my heels.

Hugo

She makes a noise like *hmph*. "I've known you since you were running down Olive Avenue in diapers."

The corners of my lips turn down at her exaggeration. "I was always clothed."

Margaret grins, and I groan. I played right into her 'old embarrassing stories about Hugo' trap. "Except," she says, "that one time you unzipped your fly and tried to pee on a cactus."

Laughter sounds from a few feet away, and I turn. A woman I hadn't noticed when I walked in sits alone at one of the pub tables against the wall. She's turned away, her shoulder up, like she's trying to muffle her laugh.

I've never seen this woman before, not that I know everybody in town. Olive Township has grown exponentially in the last few years. All those restless Phoenicians, fleeing the bustle of a city that has also seen tremendous growth. I don't blame them. If I didn't live here, I'd want to.

I turn back to Margaret, exasperated.

She winks. "The next time I tell you that story, I'll be sure to say it quietly. Now, do you want your usual, double meat?"

I place my order, adding an iced tea and a white chocolate macadamia nut cookie, and settle at a table closer to the front of the place. At first I try not to stare at the woman, but soon give up. She's making it a point not to look up from her phone, or whatever else it is that has her attention, so I am free to stare at her back as much as I please.

Her chocolate brown hair draws the overhead light,

shining under its harsh glare. It's the color that captures my attention first, followed by her shoulders and the skin left bare by her thin-strapped top. I'm a sucker for a set of shoulders, and hers are as perfect as they come. A feminine curve, a delicate climb up to the creamy skin of her neck. Shoulders are underrated, and unsung. I love them.

She shifts on her stool, crossing one leg over the other and tucking her shoes under the footrail at the bottom. As much as I'd love to let my gaze drop, wander over other parts of her, I force it away. A long, appreciative stare is one thing, but I don't need to be a creep about it.

Ventura, one of Margaret's granddaughters, approaches the woman. The young girl holds out a sandwich and fries, reciting the order as she sets it down. The woman glances left to speak to Ventura, and her facial profile comes into view.

A sound steals up my throat, the very opposite of a gasp, the sound I'd make if I were playfully punched in the gut.

That's how I feel, in a way. Like I've been punched in the gut. This woman is gorgeous.

Stop-traffic, chin-droppingly stunning. Straight nose, full lips, a Grecian goddess. In so many other instances I'd be on my feet, headed her way, snatching her up before another man could make a move. But here, in a sandwich shop in a small town, where it happens to be only the two of us eating in the middle of the afternoon, I stow my impatience. She's just received her lunch, and I don't want to interrupt her. My gaze falls to my jeans, caked with that persistent Arizona dust. It's probably not

Hugo

a great time to talk to a beautiful woman. My back pockets bulge with thick work gloves and pruning shears, and I'm sure I smell of sweat and the bitter smokiness of olive leaves.

I grab my iced tea and suck it down, nodding my thanks as Ventura slides my lunch in front of me. I tuck in, being very purposeful about where I place my eyeballs.

It takes me all of five minutes to polish off my sandwich, house-made chile-dusted chips, and cookie. I wipe my mouth with my napkin, balling up the paper and tossing it on my empty plate. And then it happens. I look up, just in time to catch the beautiful woman's eye.

She was staring at me.

A thrill steals through me.

A tourist, for certain. The only type of woman I want anything to do with. They don't know my history, the story of my dad. They don't pity me, or feel bad for me, the way the local single women do. They don't know about my time competing in the Olympics, or my gold medal. Tourists are safe. Never a chance I'll have to dip below the surface with them.

I offer her a small smile, tentative. Her eyebrows lift, the corners of her lips turned up playfully.

Blood courses through my veins, hot and heavy. It's been a long damn time since I was with a woman, in any capacity. It would be nice to spend time with a female who isn't my sister, mom, or aunt. Or my employees. Or Penn's wife, Daisy.

A simple date is all I'm after.

Her gaze remains planted on me, only three-fourths of her face visible because of the angles of our tables. She looks expectant, waiting for me to approach. Inviting me with her eyes, her fingertips drumming the tabletop like she's counting the seconds.

I push back from my table, the scrape of my chair competing with the soft rock playing over the small restaurant's speakers. A group of four older men walk in, followed by four older women. Their lively conversations fill the space. Good. I don't need Margaret eavesdropping on whatever it is I'm about to say to this woman. Which is what, exactly? I don't know. My brain sifts through options, rapid fire, but in the end it's she who speaks first.

"I hope the story about you peeing on a cactus didn't happen recently." Her lips curve, more flirtatious smirk than smile.

I laugh. A genuine laugh I wasn't expecting, shaking my head. I round her table, stopping when I'm on the other side. It's the first time I've seen her full-on, and she's dazzling. Deep brown eyes to match her hair, full and rosy cheeks, plump lips slicked with red lipstick.

"Yesterday," I say, and her eyes widen. "Kidding," I add. She huffs a relieved laugh, hand pressing at the front of her top. The fabric is red, to match her lips. And her nails.

I offer a hand over a plate empty but for the crusts of the bread. "Hugo De la Vega."

She shakes my hand, and for the shortest second I get the feeling she already knows my name. Something in her eyes. The brief look of knowing disappears, and maybe it was never there. Maybe I'm paranoid. Used to women in this town knowing who I am, because of my family. Summerhill. My father. Tragedy.

Her delicate hand nestles in mine, palm warm and soft. "Mallory Hawkins."

The blip of unease dissipates. Of course she doesn't know who I am. "It's nice to meet you, Mallory. May I take this seat?"

"Please," she answers, voice smooth and supple, honey over warm bread.

I pull out the leather-topped stool, settling in. The edge of the table meets my sternum.

Why did she choose a pub table when she had the choice of the place?

"So, Mallory, what brings you to Olive Township?"

She shakes her head at me, a twinkle gleaming in her deep brown eyes. "You can do better than that."

My teeth capture the inside of my lower lip to keep from laughing. "Sorry," I say, rubbing a hand over the back of my neck. I don't embarrass easily, but I'm finding my neck warming beneath my palm. "I'm out of practice."

Her pleased look tells me she likes that. "I prefer that over a man who says the right thing too easily."

I open my mouth to say something, *anything*, but my ability to think has left my body.

There's no way she'll believe me if I say she's so pretty it's robbed me of my ability to think. Somehow I don't think that's any better than asking her what's brought her to my small town, even if it's the truth.

I glance down at my forearms, noting a smear of dried dirt. "Do you see this?" I point at the mess on my skin.

She nods, gaze roaming my arm.

"I spent the morning pruning olive trees. Have you ever done something like that?"

She tucks a lock of that thick, gorgeous hair behind her ear. "Can't say I have. Honestly, I didn't know pruning olive trees was a thing."

"Like any other plant, olive trees require care. I take care of them, and they reward me with the best olive oil in the southwest."

She toys with the chain of her gold necklace. "You're an olive farmer?" Her tone conveys genuine interest, and honestly, that excites me.

I sit back, collaring the enthusiasm for now. Nothing scares a woman away faster than waxing poetic about olives. "Something like that."

There's a long pause. Her eyes dance, and there's something about them I've never seen before. Mischief, maybe? Intelligence, for sure. I like what I see, that much I know.

"I came for the spa," she finally says, answering my first question. One corner of her lips curves. A slow, sly, sexy grin that has my own lips peeling apart in anticipation. "But now I'm hoping to try the best olive oil in the southwest."

Blame it on my brain short-circuiting in the presence of unparalleled beauty, but my stupid lips say, "Chances are you will, if you order food from the spa restaurant. Their dressings are made with my oil."

Hugo

My oil. What a nerd. Who talks like that? I am leaving here and going straight to Penn's house to insist he punch me in the mouth.

I seem to have fallen in favor with Cupid, because Mallory smiles. Again, she appears to like how unpolished I am. Dusted in Arizona dirt. Gloves and pruning shears tucked in my back pockets.

It boosts my confidence enough that I say, "If you decide you've had enough eucalyptus and zen rock gardens, I'd love to take you out for a drink." My eyebrows lift. "Assuming secret speakeasy's are your thing."

Mallory moves to cross one leg over the other, her shoulder disrupting the purse straps she has wound over the back of her chair. The purse tumbles to the ground, contents spilling over the floor. I'm out of my seat quickly, picking up a pack of gum, a wallet, her phone, retrieving a bottle that has rolled under a nearby table.

"Oh my gosh, thank you," she says, breathless. Worry slides in along her eyebrows. She's off the stool now, holding open her purse so I can toss everything inside.

It's at this moment I happen to glance down, and as the plastic bottle I'm holding rolls off my open palm and into the brown leather purse, I see the label.

Prenatal vitamins?

My stomach sinks.

I look into her eyes. Guilt floods those pretty brown irises.

"You're expecting?" Disappointment swings through me. I'd been so attracted to her. Still am, given the way my body's wanting to lean in closer, touch her soft-looking skin. Drop my nose to the top of her head, find out what she smells like.

Her spine straightens, chin lifting. "Yes," she says, voice clear. Resolute, and also a little challenging.

As if she is challenging me to challenge her. About what, I do not know.

Dammit. My hand rakes over my face, irritation finding space beside the overwhelming disappointment. Was I seriously hitting on a pregnant woman? Even if I didn't know it, I feel a little foolish. "Let me guess. You're taking a weekend for yourself and thought it'd be fun to flirt with a local. Did you leave your wedding ring behind in the hotel room?"

She's nonplussed by my accusatory question. Secret revealed, she moves her purse from in front of her abdomen. The bump of her stomach is small, something I'd never notice and would certainly never comment on, but now that I know it's there, it's all I see.

"Hugo," she says my name softly, eyes watching me with care. Too much care for someone who should be ashamed they were caught flirting with another man. She takes a deep breath, steeling herself.

And then, like an anvil, it hits me. Her name. I've seen it before, barely registering it when hastily sending the emails to the trash bin.

I see it now in my mind, the email signature. And below it, *Host of Case Files.* "Mallory Hawkins." A thick exhale slides between my lips, appalled by her audacity. My stomach pitches, back teeth grinding. "This is so wrong."

Hugo

"Please," she says, arms shooting out to stop me, though I haven't gone anywhere. I step back, and her seeking arms drop. "I only want to speak with you."

My arms cross. "I got that from your emails."

"The ones you ignored?"

"Deleted."

She winces. "Listen, I know that—"

I hold up a hand, stopping her. "We're not talking."

Her eyes widen, worry in those brown irises. "I think—"

My work boots protest the tile floor with the swiftness of my turn. I want nothing to do with this conversation. Or the beautiful woman trying to have it.

I stride from the restaurant, well aware I have drawn plenty of attention to myself. The small town gossip mill will be churning in no time.

Chapter 4

Mallory

It wasn't the way I would've chosen to meet Hugo, if given the choice.

I was sitting at the table, minding my own business in the quiet shop, when he breezed in. He didn't notice me, not at first. It was all I could do to hold back my gasp as my eyes swept over him. Possibilities buzzed through me, but in the end, it was *he* who approached *me*.

I should have been upfront in the beginning, I know that. Something kept me from total honesty. I'm not sure yet what it was, only that I didn't want to show him my hand. It wasn't fair because he wasn't aware of who he was playing against, but some cards I need to keep close to my chest.

More than likely, I have ruined any chance of ever gaining Hugo's trust, at least enough for him to talk to me about his dad. I'm disappointed in myself, and in the situation as a whole.

Having very possibly just signed the death certificate

Hugo

on all the work I've been doing for years, I force myself through the small restaurant. I feel the gazes of the men and women who walked in, and Margaret, the lovely owner who introduced herself to me.

The relentless sun assails my eyes as I step from Sammich. Tenting my hand across my eyebrows, I—

Hugo?

The man I have probably pissed off for life stands on the edge of the sidewalk in front of me. His eyebrows cinch with his angry stare, his jaw taut. His arms cross in front of his chest, his weight rolling back on his heels.

God was very, very heavy-handed when He created this man's physical attributes. From his head of thick, shiny brown-black hair to his olive skin and arched eyebrows, forearms roped with muscle, and shoulders a woman could hold onto, there's a lot to look at. Don't let me get started on that angular jawline. He must have some physical abnormality to make up for the unfair generosity. Six fingers, perhaps?

I already know he doesn't. I've spent plenty of time learning about him on the Internet, poking through photos of him fencing, standing on the podium at the Olympics, accepting his gold medal. I came to Olive Township knowing exactly what Hugo De la Vega looks like.

Hugo's eyebrows are raised, like he's waiting for me to say something. Only, I don't know what to say. How can I make this any better? Angry doesn't begin to describe him. Anger's second cousin, hurt feelings, has joined our twosome. And quite possibly embarrassment, a third cousin twice removed.

Not that I blame the guy. What was I thinking, letting him talk to me like that? Letting him think I was available? It's just that, well, he's so handsome it makes my stomach turn in on itself. It actually hurts to look at him.

And yet.

Nothing could've prepared me for the real thing. Because he's nothing like the photos. The Hugo I met today is warm. Genuine. Modest. Funny. He became a real person to me in a way the photos hadn't allowed him to be.

And yes, I feel guilty.

And ok, he's insanely attractive. I didn't know I had a thing for men in dirty work clothes with tools tucked into a great pair of ass-hugging jeans.

New kink unlocked. Or maybe just pregnancy hormones.

Sweet relief sweeps through me. Yes, that's how I feel. Not attracted to him, and that great smile with one corner of his mouth rising higher than the other. It's the pesky cascade of extra hormones wreaking havoc.

Hugo leans back, his backside coming to rest on the front of a white truck. His, I presume.

Now that I don't have to worry about him seeing my (admittedly small) baby bump, I haul my purse higher around my shoulder and stand up straight. His gaze remains locked on mine.

Excitement bubbles. He might be mad, but does he

want to talk? Might this be the moment where I finally get to tell him everything I've been trying to say? Stowing my eagerness, I say as calmly as possible, "Would you like to talk?"

"Not even a little." His voice is cold, and his eyes are cool.

"Did you wait for me to come out just so you can tell me what an awful person I am?"

"Awful?" He scrunches one eyebrow, scratching at it with his thumb. "That depends. Does pretending to flirt with somebody just so you can satisfy your personal curiosity make you an awful person?"

I open my mouth to respond, but he continues.

"Or, does traveling to a small town and interrupting somebody's peace, after they've given you no indication you are welcome, make you an awful person?"

I look down at my cute low-heeled boots. Heat burns at the backs of my eyes. My vision blurs.

No no no no no.

I've never been a crier, but this pregnancy has turned me into an unreliable, manic faucet. I cry at nothing. I cry at everything. I cry at puppies. Not puppies being hurt, or uncared for, or malnourished, because that might actually make sense. Puppies simply existing is enough to send little balls of salted water rolling down my cheeks.

It's mortifying. But so far, nothing is more mortifying than standing here in front of an impossibly handsome man who despises me, trying my best to keep the faucet from turning on.

Hugo's dirty brown boots step into my line of sight.

"Are you...*ok?*" Reluctance colors his tone. I'm sure he wishes he were anywhere but here in this moment.

"I'm fine," I whisper, and though I've managed to rein it in and not go on a real crying jag right here and now, my nose has begun running. A sniffle is all it takes for Hugo to ask with horror, "Are you *crying?*"

"It's not you," I say, face flaming.

"I'm not sure how it could be me," he answers, perplexed.

Ugh. Of course. It couldn't be him, because he's done nothing wrong. I'm the one with the audacity to show up here. Though, to be fair, I wasn't expecting to run into him. It's not like I sought him out. It would be one thing if I'd booked a tour at Summerhill Olive Mill in hopes of seeing him there, but I didn't. I was in Sammich, *minding my own business*.

He stepped in, and the opportunity presented itself. I'd waited so long, hoped and hoped for him to respond to one of my emails, only for that hope to be dashed. I had to take the opportunity. I just had to.

What I did not have to do was allow him to flirt with me. Or, to flirt back.

But how do you stop an avalanche once it gets started? One look at his handsome face and mesmerizing eyes, and it was like all my nerve endings plucked up to the surface of my skin.

None of our banter was fake, but I won't be telling him that. Certainly not with this baby growing inside me, or the fact I'm a host of a podcast he wants nothing to do with.

Swiping at my eyes, I look up. Immediately, I recognize my mistake. He's too close. Too handsome. The physical pull, the desire to step closer, is irrelevant to who he is, or the possible connection between my sister and his father.

A flash cuts across his eyes. He feels it, too. Even angry with me, hurt and embarrassed, he knows something is there.

"Come on," he says, pushing off his truck. "I'll walk you to your car."

"Why?" I ask, staying rooted in place.

"Because it's the nice thing to do. And it'll allow me to make sure you get inside and drive west."

"What's west?"

"The road out of Olive Township."

I can't help the laugh that burbles out of me. "Jokes on you, buddy. I have a massage tomorrow morning at ten, followed by a facial at two." There's no chance I'll be skipping out on the pampering. I need it.

"You're here for the spa?" His eyes narrow. He doesn't believe me.

"Yep." I nod. Any trace of my near sob episode has gone away, and for that I'm extremely grateful. "The spa, and a taste of olive oil."

One side of his mouth quirks up, and a small part of me rejoices. I know that's the closest I'm going to get to a smile.

"Where are you staying?" Hugo asks. He finally uncrosses his arms for the first time since I exited

Sammich. His voice isn't nice, exactly, but it's not as acerbic. I'll take what I can get for now.

"The Olive Inn."

Hugo makes a face. "I'm surprised you're not staying at the hotel connected to the spa."

I shrug. "Booked."

He nods. "Well, let's go." He turns, starting off down the street.

Despite how good he looks in those jeans, I won't be backing down. "There's no way I'm giving up a massage and a facial just because you want me to leave town."

Hugo stops, turning around to face me. "The Olive Inn is this way."

We stare at each other, a three-second standoff. It would be nice to know what he's thinking, but he has mastered an unbelievably good poker face.

"Fine," I answer, "but I need my bag from my car." Which, as luck would have it, is parked beside his truck.

I pop the trunk with my key fob, and when I get to the back of my car, Hugo is already there, lifting my small suitcase and setting it on the ground. Without a word, he heads for the sidewalk and sets off.

"So, what do you—"

"This is a silent walk," he clips, cutting me off.

Silent walk? What kind of horseshit is that?

I want to talk. Ask all the questions. I'm brimming with queries. Dying to hear him speak about almost anything, because there is so much to be gleaned from idle chatter.

But, no. The guy is a fortress.

Hugo

One block down and to the right, sits the Olive Inn. I pause when we reach it, but not Hugo. He pivots, begins retracing his steps. I take a deep breath, knowing this might be my final opportunity, and I have to exhaust every last option.

"Hugo," I call after him.

He stops. Turns around slowly. Looks me in the eyes.

With finality, he says, "No, Mallory."

Hugo leaves me in front of the small hotel with little more than a gesture at the place and a terse *goodbye*. Our first in-person meeting was only marginally better than all those deleted emails.

THE CHECK-IN PROCESS IS SMOOTH, consisting of little more than producing a driver's license and credit card. Olive Inn is quaint, as the name suggests, but not out of date. The lobby has gleaming wood floors, a stone fireplace, and charcoal drawings of olive branches on the wall above a plush leather couch. It's homier than a typical hotel check-in, and smells of something resinous and earthy. A peek at the candle burning on the check-in desk tells me the scent is *Desert Rain*.

The day manager, Karen, wears a warm smile and gestures with her hands as she spouts directions to my room. Her right hand lifts when she tells me to make a left, and her left hand lifts when she tells me to make a right. It's endearing. I like her immediately.

"Unfortunately, the hotel doesn't have its own restaurant," she says, like it's an afterthought as I'm stepping away. "But there's a guide to the town on the table in the room. And if you need anything, the night manager's name is Braxton. He'll be here soon."

I thank her and walk in the direction she's pointed me, hoping to find my room despite her jumbled instructions. It's a small place, maybe twenty-five rooms. Turns out, I could have found room seventeen without a single direction from anybody. I let myself in, giving my wheeled luggage a push with my foot. It's a basic room with a king bed, a nightstand, and a small desk and chair. The only thing of note is a framed original town map on the wall opposite the bed. Sidestepping my luggage where it has rolled to the middle of the room, I stand before the map.

Olive Township, 1959.

Summerhill Olive Mill stands proud in the west, peering over the rest of the town. The main road, Olive Avenue, runs through the center of town, and reminds me my car is still parked in one of the spaces on the street. A few store names buffet Olive Avenue, and a mass of house-shaped boxes designate a neighborhood. One large home takes the space of all the other houses, the scrawl beneath it reading *Hampton House*. A hotel, maybe? To the east, a farm spreads, with the words *St. James Farm*. Smaller roads crisscross the map, but are not named. Is one of these the road where Simon was murdered?

There is so little I know about what happened to Simon De la Vega, and it seems I'm not the only one. The investigation was closed following a lack of evidence. A man was strangled in broad daylight on an open road, but there was no evidence. No witnesses. The only person of interest had an alibi.

If it hadn't been for the Reddit board and my late-night phone scrolling, the cold case from twenty years ago wouldn't have caught my attention.

What Arizona murders remain unsolved?

It pulled me in. Not only because of *Case Files*, but because I was morbidly curious if my sister would be on it. She was all over the news for so long, the shy smile of a twelve-year-old girl who still had baby fat in her pink cheeks.

It made my chest ache to think of her, but I kept scrolling. Halfway down the list, I saw her name. And then, in another comment, was Simon De la Vega. The person called him an *Olive King*. I was curious, my mind running. Was he killed for money? His land? Was it something less nefarious? A crime of opportunity?

A quick type of his name in my internet search bar revealed story after story, all variations of the same report. But then, on a true crime message board, was the dissection of the case. The anonymous poster had details that weren't included in the bland news reports.

Details that were consistent with my sister's cause of death.

There had been nothing to go on with Maggie. No cameras in that area of the water park, especially not in the bathroom where she'd been killed. Because of all the parkgoers, there was no way to separate one set of footprints from any other. No signs of struggle. It was a well-used public space and the cleaning staff had neglected the bathroom the night before, there was no way to connect the various DNA lifted from the scene to the murder.

Whoever killed my sister walked away, and here I am fourteen years later, sitting on a hotel bed in Olive Township, chasing a lead that might turn out to be futile.

But I have to try. For so many people, I need to see this through. My mother, for starters. Maybe if I can bring her healing, she'll get her life back. I'll get my mom back. For Maggie. For me. For this little peanut in my belly.

Chapter 5

Hugo

FRIDAY NIGHT FAMILY DINNERS HAVE BEEN A STAPLE of the De la Vega family as long as I can remember. At one time they were loud and bustling, a cacophony of forks scraping plates and excited voices talking over one another. Our numbers have dwindled over time. The first departure was my dad's, followed by my grandparents over the next ten years. My dad's parents were the glue that kept our family together, and with them gone, the connections withered. Aunts and uncles began to move away, and cousins, too. For jobs, for love. Now it is only me and my sister, Vivi, and her two kids. My mom and my aunt.

It's sad, really. There used to be a running joke in Olive Township that a person couldn't throw an olive pit without hitting a De la Vega. That joke expired a while ago.

"Who needs the others?" Vivi likes to scoff, adding, "The cream rose."

My sister, thirteen months my junior, is known for saying the most unbelievable things.

Stepping through my front door into the waning late afternoon sun, I take the extra ten seconds to fish my keys from my pocket, waiting for the thudded slide of the deadbolt.

Plenty of people wouldn't think to lock their front door all the way out here, ensconced in desert and olive orchards. But not me. I've never been able to shake the fear, ever-present and ugly, that coils low in my stomach. The person who murdered my dad was never caught.

You'd think nearly twenty years would be enough time to dull the fear, but it's not. It serves as a reminder that justice is a gift, and it's not given to everyone.

My dad's murder took more than his life. It stole a nine-year-old's innocence and naïveté. Made me jaded, paving the road for the distance I keep between myself and women. Arm's length is about where I can stand them.

The thought causes a certain chestnut-haired beauty to materialize in my mind. The way she tilted her head and smiled. Flirted. Using those feminine wiles on me for a story. Those tears though...were they real? Because they looked it. She's either a good actress, or... *No.* She wasn't genuine. It was an act, all for the purpose of getting my guard down. Not that my guard is all that visible to most people. I am talented in the art of being Happy Hugo. Carefree. Nice. It's not an act, but it is a wall. I know it's there, I know it's unhealthy, but it's not something I've

Hugo

managed to scale. I keep it there, because who am I without it?

Nobody, especially a showstopper with ulterior motives, is getting through.

I push across the field of short grass, cutting over the dirt road that leads to the looming big house. It's an imposing structure, big enough to house my family comfortably, and host the extended family when they visit.

I let myself in the back door, toeing off my work boots and stowing them on the shoe rack. My mother is a very relaxed person, but not when it comes to work boots in the house. She was always shooing my dad back with her hands, frowning with a furrowed brow until he deposited the shoes where they belonged.

Smells of oregano and chili powder lure me to the kitchen. Vivi stands at the stove, dark hair gathered in a ponytail high on her head. In one hand she holds a glass of red wine, in the other, an olive wood spatula.

"Smells good," I comment, walking up behind her and peeking into the cast-iron pan.

"I should hope so," she sasses, giving me a look.

Vivi's restaurant, Dama Oliva, is the best and nicest restaurant in town. Open only for dinner, and booked out for a month. She's the owner and head chef, and I'm proud of her. Usually it's the younger sibling looking up to the older, but I admire the hell out of her. She's the opposite of me, marrying her first boyfriend and making a home. It's not her fault the asshole turned out to have a problem keeping his pants up when his administrative assistant was present.

"Where are the kids?" I ask, reaching around my sister and plucking a beefy crumble of finished taco meat from the pan. Vivi moves to smack my hand, but I'm too fast, popping the extremely hot meat into my mouth as I duck out of her reach. It's too hot and I end up wincing.

"Serves you right," she says, taking a slow sip of her wine while I suck air into my mouth in an attempt to cool down the food. "Everly and Knox are being spoiled by Grammy and Auntie Carmen. Where else would they be?"

"Running wild through the orchard."

"As children should."

Elbowing her gently until she gives me her wine, I grumble, "I almost whacked Knox in the head with a shovel." Scared me half to death, the way Knox appeared out of nowhere. Little guy had no idea what almost happened, but he loved the way I dropped the shovel and gathered him up into my arms. I snorted into his neck to make him laugh, and relished in the sound.

Drinking half of Vivi's wine in one gulp, I offer her the glass, but she waves it off. "I'm not drinking after you. You have—"

"Cooties?" I pull a face. "Really?"

She sniffs. "I was going to say syphilis."

I laugh as I watch her pour herself a fresh glass from a half full bottle. She swirls the ruby liquid, scrutinizing the way it clings to the sides of the glass.

"Does it have legs?" My lips widen with pride at my

use of the term she taught me. *Legs* are the droplets on the sides of the glass after swirling.

"Yes," she answers, giving the meat in the pan a quick stir. "I'll talk to Mom. Ask her not to let the kids run around the grove."

"She wasn't far off. But they're faster than her. She either needs to learn how to roller-skate or keep them out of the fields during the week when everyone is working."

It's not like it was when we were kids, and we both know it. My mom on the other hand, not so much. She still sees Summerhill as a family-run small operation, and remembers the way our dad trekked through the trees with us taking turns sitting on his shoulders. And then, when we were older, the way Vivi and I pelted each other with fallen olives.

Since I took Summerhill over two years ago after I retired from fencing, it's grown nearly as fast as Olive Township. I'm not done yet, either. I've pushed into creating a wedding venue, and agrotourism. It's going to be everything my dad never thought to dream of. Everything he didn't know was possible, because his life was cut short.

A stampede of little footfalls announces my niece and nephew's impending arrival. They blow into the room, a whirlwind of chaos and euphoric smiles.

"Uncle Hugo!" Everly, who turned six last week, launches herself at me. She's a wild child, emotional and loud. Whether she's happy, mad, or sad, the whole room knows it.

I catch her one-handed, holding out my wineglass so

she doesn't knock it out of my hand. Vivi helpfully takes it from me, setting it down on the kitchen counter.

Burying my face in Everly's dark hair, I make a show out of sniffing her. "Why do you smell like"—I pause for dramatic effect, and Everly giggles—"a rhinoceros?"

Everly leans away from me, nose wrinkled, and palms my cheeks with her tiny hands. "I do *not* smell like a rhino," she informs me with utter seriousness.

"Oh sorry, I meant to say you smell like a warthog."

Everly leans sideways, looking at her mother over my shoulder. "Mommy, your brother is hopeless."

Laughter erupts around the room, including from my mom and Aunt Carmen, who entered the kitchen in time to hear Everly.

"Sor-ry," Aunt Carmen singsongs the apology. "I accidentally taught her that today."

"Whose brother were you calling hopeless?" I ask. Everly shimmies and twists in my arms, telling me she wants down without saying the words.

"Obit," Aunt Carmen explains, sliding into her favorite chair at the kitchen table.

Nobody ever believes Aunt Carmen when she tells them what she does for work. She writes funny and irreverent obituaries, and she's typically hired by people before they pass away.

It's an odd job, one she didn't get into until after my dad died. She hated her brother's obituary, saying it was the equivalent of the color of dirt. *Boring. Read like a grocery list.* She later rewrote it, and my mother had it printed and framed. To this day, it sits on a bookshelf in the living room, reminding us that his pursuits in the olive grove were more successful than the time he tried out for the town play, and how he never met a coupon he didn't clip.

I was a teenager when she rewrote it, and I was temperamental and full of grief, and I told her I hated it. Now, I love it. It keeps him alive, reminds me that he was more than an olive farmer who was preceded in death by his older brother, Jack, and his great uncle, Martin.

Crouching down, I open my arms for three-year-old Knox. He's the opposite of his sister, measured and thoughtful. He'll be four in a month, and takes after his father with his sandy brown hair and fairer skin.

Knox's little legs carry him into my embrace, his small head resting against my chest. He is the calm to his sister's storm.

"Hey, buddy," I say, pressing my cheek to the top of his head. The kid gives a great hug, and truth be told, I need it. I'm still reeling from my run-in with the podcaster earlier today.

"Hi," comes his tiny voice.

I wrap my arms around him, gathering him into me and standing. He resets himself, resting his head on my shoulder and tucking his arms between his body and my chest.

My mom sends me a wistful look. I know what it means. I'll be thirty soon, and I haven't given her grandchildren. She reminds me of this far too often.

"Please don't say it, Mom."

She rolls her eyes at me and rounds the counter,

opening up a cupboard and taking down dinner plates. The sound of their stacking fills the air as she says, "You look good with a child in your arms, Hugo."

I feel good with a child in my arms too, but I'm not about to tell her that. My mother does not need any additional ammunition to use against me.

Mallory Hawkins' face flashes to the front of my mind, maybe because we're talking about children and she's the only person I know of who's expecting. Vivi knows a podcaster has been emailing me, but I haven't told my mother.

"Mom," I start, stepping back so she and Vivi can move freely around the kitchen. "A while back I got an email from a woman who hosts a podcast. Case Files."

Vivi's knife, tip poised above a head of purple cabbage, freezes. She looks at me with a mixture of curiosity and dread. We agreed not to tell our mom, but with Mallory in Olive Township, it feels like I should say something. What if somebody asks Mallory why she's here, and she tells them the truth, and then the truth gets back to my mom? It's a small town, gossip is more like currency. She should hear it from me, not the old hens who cut their teeth on idle chatter.

"Case Files?" Mom holds the stack of plates in one hand, adding folded dinner napkins on top. "What does she talk about? Crime, I'm guessing?"

I nod, rubbing a hand over Knox's back. He's content where he is, and I'm happy to have him. It's as if he is soothing me. "True crime."

Something flashes across my mother's eyes, but it's

hard to decipher what it is she's feeling. "And? What did you say in response?"

"I haven't responded. She's emailed me four times."

My mother says nothing, and Vivi leads the way to the dining room table, holding the ceramic bowl of heavenly smelling ground beef. My mom follows with the plates and napkins, and Aunt Carmen comes up behind her, parading in with a platter of taco fixings.

I get Knox situated in his chair, and on the other side of me, Everly is using crayons to draw a picture on a piece of paper.

Everyone is quiet as they process this information, and I start to feel bad. I hope I didn't ruin family dinner. Vivi makes one more trip to the kitchen for the warmed taco shells, and on her way by me, she flicks my ear with her middle finger.

I sigh, hating that I'm having to bring this up, but I know I have to get all the words out, so my mother understands why I've said anything. And Vivi, too.

"The host, Mallory Hawkins, claims she only wants to have a conversation with me about Dad. According to her, her show has helped family members work through their grief about unsolved cases, and in some instances, has helped solve a few." This is from her most recent email, verbatim. The one I read, then promptly deleted.

My mother's hands are in her lap, her eyes on me. "But you've ignored her?"

I nod.

"Why?"

"Because I don't see the point of talking with her. The past is in the past. Why drag it back up?"

"Exactly," Vivi snaps, losing her patience. "Why are you telling Mom all this?"

"Because she's here, in Olive Township." At Vivi's obvious confusion, I add, "The host, I mean. Mallory." My elbows meet the table, my chin resting on fisted hands. I might appear calm on the outside, but on the inside, I'm a wreck, trying to reconcile the person who wrote those emails with the person I met today in Sammich. *Before* I knew who she really was.

Vivi blows out a harsh breath. "Of course she is. Apparently you ignoring her for months wasn't enough of a message." Vivi grabs a taco shell, roughly spooning beef inside. The hard shell cracks in two, and she drops it onto her plate.

"Mommy's making her taco into a tostada," Everly comments. She picks up a piece of diced tomato, removes the seed, and eats it. I hand her a napkin, but she wipes her hand bearing the seed on her pants, grinning at me.

I shake my head in warning, fighting an indulgent smile.

"Why can't she leave us alone?" Vivi moves forward with fixing her plate. "What is her interest in Dad's case, specifically?"

"I don't know if it extends beyond basic curiosity." There have been people over the years, true crime junkies who have shown up at Summerhill. Mostly, they pretend to be here for one of the tours we offer, or meander through the store on our property. They pretend to be interested in the olive mill, but inevitably conversation and questions take a turn to Simon De la Vega. It's exhausting, and a poke at a wound that will never fully heal. In these moments, I would love more than anything to knock the overly curious people onto their asses, but I think of my dad and how he would want Summerhill to be represented. And then I shake my head and politely say, *"That topic is not up for discussion. I hope you enjoyed your tour."*

I understand the allure. It's the same reason people slow down to look at car accidents. Part morbid fascination, part learning opportunity. *What did they do wrong, so I don't make the same mistake?* Only, my dad didn't error. He did nothing wrong that day. The best the detectives could tell, it was a crime of opportunity. Someone depraved.

It sickens me to think of it, a repugnance that hasn't faded with time. I cannot comprehend taking someone's life, especially when they are unarmed, and non-threatening.

Hurting nothing, and nobody.

Only once in my life have I hit somebody, and it was to defend a woman from unwanted advances. Even the sport I chose was civilized. As the saying goes, I'm a lover, not a fighter.

But on nights when I can't sleep, my mind drifts, and I envision meeting the person who killed my dad. In my imagination, I become somebody I don't know if I could ever be. The violence I'm capable of in my fantasy is frightening.

"Find out why she's here." My mother speaks with a calmness that unnerves me.

"Mom, are you sure?"

We've never given interviews, or spoken with anybody about my dad. As a family, we decided enough was enough. All the so-called journalists invading our town, the true crime shows, the amateur sleuths, we've said no to them all. There's only so much mud a person can stand to be dragged through, and bringing it up time and time again was stunting us. You can't heal from such a horror if you constantly relive it.

I glance at Aunt Carmen, attempting to get a read on her reaction. She might be my dad's sister, but she's my mom's best friend. She's the reason my parents met. Her face is blank now, watching my mom carefully.

"If she has emailed you four times, it's more than typical curiosity," my mom points out. "And then for her to come here?" She ends her sentence with raised eyebrows.

"She says she's here for the spa." It could be a lie, but it's one that is easily verifiable. I know the owners, and the girl who works the front desk. Vivi knows the kitchen staff who work at the on-site café.

Vivi gives me a *come on* look. "'That cannot be true."

I shrug. "She claims to have a massage and a facial scheduled for tomorrow."

Vivi crosses her arms.

"Mommy is mad." Everly giggles.

I welcome the dose of six-year-old humor into the

Hugo

conversation. It keeps everything from being too tense, too awful.

Mom changes the topic, asking Everly how her week was at school. I say nothing, listening as Everly recounts an altercation near the swing set, and how she overheard the principal say a bad word. Vivi tells us she's doubling down on efforts to source as many local ingredients as possible, and in doing so has cut a deal with the Hayden Cattle Company. She will exclusively use their beef, in exchange for a discount off her cost. Aunt Carmen reads us her latest obituary, further lightening the mood (as weird as that sounds). Knox and Everly don't understand any of it, but they know to laugh when we do, one second late and somehow still on time. I love these family dinners, but despite how bright and fun they are, there's always a bit of a shadow. A dark lining around the picture we make, reminding us who is missing.

After dinner is over and I've cleaned up the kitchen, I snag a bottle of beer from the fridge. I pass through the living room on the way to the back porch, where Vivi is snuggled up on the couch watching a movie with Knox and Everly. Everly takes notice of the bottle and promptly informs me, "My dad says beer is bad for you."

Tell your dad it also wasn't a good idea to poke his admin in the whiskers while he was married.

"Thank you for letting me know," I respond diplomatically, then continue on my way.

The back porch has a spectacular west-facing view, and this time of year, the sky holds onto the sunset with a fierce grip. Tonight it's showing off an expanse of magenta and orange, a fiery red around the edges.

I settle in one of the outdoor chairs, take it all in. How the grove goes as far as the eye can see. Olive trees, rows upon rows, acres upon acres of gnarled trunks and rounded crowns.

Home. I missed this place while I was gone. First to college, and then after to train for the Olympics, staying with my coach in Denver, and then San Diego. I enjoyed the other places while I was there, the majesty of the Rocky Mountains, the sparkling blue Pacific Ocean. But little compares to the riotous colors of a setting sun filtered through the olive branches.

The screen door snaps shut, breaking my reverie. My mother sinks into the open seat beside me. She holds a glass of Vivi's red wine.

"What has your eyebrows pinched?" she asks.

"They aren't pinched," I argue.

She reaches over, smoothes them out with two fingers like she's zooming in on a phone screen. "Not anymore."

"Just appreciating the beauty," I say, gesturing straight out with the bottom of my bottle.

Mom looks out with me. "And considering how your mother could possibly want to open up a dialogue with a true crime podcaster?"

I breathe a laugh, tapping the side of my bottle against the arm of my chair. "I suppose."

"All these years I've been saying no, but I'm not sure if that was a mistake."

Hugo

I look up sharply, trying to understand how she could say that. Back then she was protecting us, and herself.

"It's been a long time since everything happened." She sits back, adjusting her long, flowing skirt. "I see now what I couldn't then. I tried hard to shield you as best I could, not understanding no matter what I did, the effects of what happened to your father would be far reaching."

I shake my head at her, digging through her words to uncover what it is she's really saying.

She continues. "Your sister married her first boyfriend, even though he was all wrong for her. She wanted to create a home like the one she had lost. And you?" Her eyebrows lift.

"You are busy achieving great things, and keeping every woman you meet at arm's length."

My mouth drops open in surprise.

"Oh yes," my mother says, chuckling softly to herself. "I pay attention."

"Mom," I start, needing to defend myself at least a little. "It's damn near impossible for me to have a relationship. Confiding in a woman about what happened to Dad is a recipe for relationship disaster. Some of them are too curious, and for others it kicks in an odd kind of maternal instinct, and they start wanting to take care of me. Fix me." I'm not broken, and I don't need to be fixed, thank you very much.

My mother has always been a good listener, an attribute she still has to this day. Her head nodded along while I was speaking, and even now she says nothing, gazing out over the land.

When enough time has passed that I think maybe she will drop it, she says, "Talk to this woman, for me."

"Mom—"

Her hand covers mine, silencing me. "It's been a long time, Hugo. Maybe it's ok to talk about him. About what happened." She sighs into the open spring air. "Maybe I never should have silenced you."

I shake my head. "Don't do that, Mom. Don't blame your past self. You can't change any of it."

"Fine," she answers, sipping her wine. "I won't blame my past self, if you agree to step into the future with me."

I eye her warily. "And the future consists of talking to a nosy podcaster?"

"For now, yes."

Chapter 6

Mallory

My first morning in Olive Township, and I awake early. I'd been hoping to sleep in, but my body knew I was in an unfamiliar space, pulling me from slumber too soon.

Or, more likely, it's this incessant and insistent need to pee. Four months pregnant, and I'm still not accustomed to the number of bathroom breaks I require in a day.

Rolling over in the passable but not amazing bed, I stare at the ceiling. I'd done the same thing before falling asleep last night, sifting through the day, replaying the moment I realized I was in the same restaurant as Hugo. His easy, lopsided grin, the way his tan work boots were partially unlaced. His unhurried walk, his casual, familiar banter with the owner.

Then the shuttering when he saw the vitamins, plucking my name from the recesses of his memory bank. Still, he walked me here. An ingrained kindness.

Yesterday, I felt embarrassed, and guilty. Today, I feel sad. Sad to have misled him. Sad to have misled myself, even for the briefest of moments. I can't shake the feeling I'm missing out on him.

Stupid of me.

I get up from the bed, exerting just a little more force than I used to. My baby bump is slight, but it still requires a little more effort than before I was pregnant.

Pregnant.

My stomach stares back at me in the bathroom mirror. Some days, I haven't yet accepted I'm pregnant. Other days, I feel that spark of excitement. Nerves, too, plenty of those, but also a feeling of kismet. The man may not have stuck around, but this baby and I? We're meant to be.

I finish in the bathroom, padding over to my suitcase, thrown open on the small desk. I select a pair of leggings, a tank top, and an oversized sweatshirt. My stomach lets out a growl that would mortify me if I were with anybody right now.

"Sorry," I say, patting my belly. I didn't eat the best dinner last night, making do with the snacks I had left from the drive. Slipping my feet into my shoes, I retrace my steps to the lobby, hoping to snag a bottle of water. I'm not particularly thirsty, but it never hurts to have a bottle, especially in the desert.

A head of greasy, black, stick-straight hair greets me.

"Hello," I say, slowing down.

The person looks up without hurry, eyes meeting mine as his unkempt hair falls in curtains around his face.

Hugo

"Good morning," he says evenly. No smile or show of welcome. "How can I help you?"

The name tag clipped to his shirt reads *Braxton*. His cheeks are pocked with acne scars, eyes faintly bloodshot. I would put him in his mid-thirties, maybe younger if not for his poor posture. My muscles tense, near-flinching, but I school my reaction.

Objectively, his appearance is off-putting, not to mention his overall demeanor.

I snap on a smile and say, "Are there any breakfast places you'd recommend around here?"

He takes a glossy tri-fold paper from a rack, sliding it over the desk with one finger. And then he says nothing. *Nothing.* The silence stretches on, growing more and more uncomfortable.

"Ok, then," I murmur, taking the paper. "Thanks."

I have the urge to be gone from there as fast as possible, but I hate the idea of him seeing he's rattled me. Forcing myself into a steady pace, I walk from the lobby and out into the fresh Olive Township morning air.

I feel his eyes on me the whole time.

"Thank you." I smile up at the young woman as she places my breakfast down on the table in front of me. Cherry pie pancakes.

Fluffy and warm, a crackle of sugar in the air. I take a

bite, nearly groaning. I need these calories. Me, and Peanut.

Very few people know I'm expecting. Jolene, of course. My mom and stepdad, whose reactions were not great after finding out I'd be raising the baby alone. The father, obviously, though I'd like to forget about him. *I will* forget about him.

And Hugo knows. Not that it matters. He, and Olive Township, will be in my rearview after this weekend. Hugo has made it clear he wants nothing to do with me.

Despite my hunger, I only make it through half the serving of pancakes. I push the plate away, sitting back and wrapping my hands around my mug of honey chamomile tea. One of my favorite activities in life is finding a cozy spot from which to people-watch. Tucked in this back corner booth at Good Thyme Café, there is no better vantage point.

People are fascinating. I once read that when we watch others, certain parts of our brains fire up. The temporal lobe, and the amygdala, helping with facial recognition, social processing, and interpreting emotions based on expressions and body language.

For example, the man sitting a few tables over from me. He drinks a coffee, black, and scribbles in what looks to be a well-loved journal. He writes aggressively, ballpoint pen scratching over the paper, but every so often he pauses to stare out the window, gaze thoughtful and far-off. He wears a starched white shirt, faintly yellowing around the under arms. The sport coat slung over the

Hugo

back of his seat is a cheap material, the lapels curling. Even his—

"Is this seat taken?"

I startle at the deep voice, the way a man has seemingly materialized out of nowhere. My gaze lifts, trailing over a broad chest, finding their way to a familiar face.

"Why? Trying to make certain I leave town?"

Hugo smirks, taking the seat opposite me without waiting for me to approve. He settles in the booth, an open palm propped on his right thigh, elbow stuck out. He looks casual, comfortable, but somehow princely. Like he owns this place. Like he belongs here. This is his turf.

Now that I know I won't be getting anywhere with him, I feel punchy. When he doesn't say anything right away, I say, "You are the opposite of a Welcome Wagon. You're like...like..." I search my brain. "The Ciao Chariot."

A short laugh bursts from his chest. "Not gonna lie, Mallory, I did not take you for funny."

"What did you take me for?" He's going to give it to me now, I just know it. And why wouldn't he? I've served him up with the perfect opportunity to remind me how underhanded I was.

He props a forearm on the table, leans forward. Brown eyes, deep and thoughtful. Finally, he says, "Tenacious."

I blink against the surprise I'm feeling. Tenacious? That word is very, very far from the litany of adjectives he could have used to describe me.

"I wasn't expecting you to say that."

"I know."

The server sidles up to the table, offering Hugo a friendly smile. "Hey, Hugo. Cappuccino?"

"Please," he nods. "Thanks, Annie."

When she's gone, he looks back to me. "You jumped out of your skin when I walked up. What were you staring at?" He accompanies his question with a look around the space.

"I like to people-watch." My fingers press into my teacup, the warmth seeping through. "I find there's a lot you can learn about a person by watching them. And what you can't learn, your brain fills in."

Hugo's eyebrows, thick and dark, raise. "When your brain fills in information about somebody, is it fiction?"

"Until it's verified, yes."

"And you were watching…?"

I give a slight nod of my head. "The man sitting alone with his journal."

Hugo surreptitiously clocks him. "And? What did you determine?"

"He writes with gusto. He drinks black coffee, because it gets free refills. His shirt needs to either be replaced, or have the underarms scrubbed with stain remover. His jacket has seen better days. He's stuck in a job he hates, and he has the soul of a dreamer."

Hugo blinks. Hard. "You figured all that out just by looking at him?"

I shrug. "It could all be wrong. Unverified, remember?"

Hugo thanks the server as she drops off his cappuccino, declining her offer to place a breakfast order. "The man you've been watching is named Cliff, though he goes by Crazy Cliff, a name he's given himself. He's not all there, but he's not all gone, either. He lives in a small house on the edge of the east side of town, and he's a used car salesman. That notebook goes everywhere with him, but nobody knows what he writes in it."

"Hmm." My lips purse. "I wasn't that far off."

"No, you were not."

I glance at my watch. The free time before my first appointment at the spa is slipping away. I need Hugo to tell me why he's here. "Are you going to tell me why you've sought me out?"

Hugo sighs, rubbing a hand over the back of his neck. "My mom wants to know your story. Why you're in Olive Township."

Anticipation starts in my belly, trickling out into my limbs. I've waited so long for even the slightest nod of interest in my direction. This is huge.

"For the record, this is all her idea. If it were up to me, I'd be escorting you from town on the—"

"—Caio Chariot."

He nods. "Exactly."

I keep my tone calm. Flat. I'm worried if I show too much excitement, I'll spook him. "Does she want to speak with me directly?"

"Consider me the *Mallory's reason for being here* filtration system."

I resist the urge to roll my eyes. He's acting like I'm a true crime sycophant, as if I harbor an unhealthy obsession with murder.

I've envisioned this so many times, conferring with the De la Vega family, comparing notes, and in the end, we are victorious. I don't know who, with what detail we uncover, but we always do, and in the end, the killer is brought to justice.

In my imagination, we are never in a bright and bustling café, a half eaten plate of pancakes between us. We're in a dining room at Summerhill, a space I've filled in with that fiction-supplying brain of mine. We're making discoveries, gasping at breakthroughs.

It was Professor Plum in the library with a candlestick.

Good Thyme Café's sugary air fills my lungs with my deep breath. Here we go.

"I told you in my email I wanted to give you a voice. And I meant it." A chill creeps into my fingers, and it doesn't matter how hard I press into the sides of my teacup. It persists. My sister's sweet face swims in front of me, the way her cheeks clung to her baby fat. "Your dad and my twelve-year-old little sister were murdered the same way."

Hugo's whole body stills, except for his eyes. Compassion sweeps through them. Few people know what it's like to be the survivor of a murdered loved one.

The air between us shifts. In an instant, I get the feeling we are friends, or at least an approximation of friendship. Allies. We are on the same team, us against everyone who hasn't known loss at the hands of another.

"Mallory," Hugo rasps, voice low and apologetic and soft. "I'm sorry."

Hugo

My lips purse as I nod my acceptance of his apology. "It was fourteen years ago, but it doesn't get easier."

"No. It doesn't." Something he knows too well. "I... I want to ask you questions, but I don't know how. Or where to start. This...," he falters, searches for his words, "wasn't at all what I was expecting you to say."

"You should know that I rarely tell the people I'm interviewing about Maggie." I'm not interested in trauma bonding with strangers.

"Maggie," Hugo repeats. "Maggie Hawkins?"

"Maggie Atwood. Different dads." Just saying her name makes my throat constrict, but I fight my way through it. I'm still holding onto the teacup, as if it were a talisman. The cup is nearly empty, only the gritty dregs remain.

"And when you say they were murdered the same way, you mean..." His voice trails off, as if he cannot bear to release the words.

My teeth sink into my lower lip, a streak of pain to halt the sob gathering in my throat. "Strangled from behind." Oh. My heart. It twists and curves in my chest, possessed. My baby sister, the way someone kept from her the very thing she needed to survive. Oxygen.

"Fuck," Hugo mutters, pinching the bridge of his nose as his eyes fall closed. There's a sheen to his eyes when he opens them, his hand dropping to his lap. "A child?"

I won't tell him I saw her that way. That it was my fault.

Hugo's arms slide across the wooden table top, buffeting the plate of cold pancakes. His fingers reach for my hands, skating over my skin in the softest of touches. He exerts a gentle pressure, peeling my fingers from the teacup.

I look down, examine where his skin touches mine.

"You were gripping it so hard, I thought you might break it." He releases me, his touch retreating to his half of the table. "I didn't want you to cut yourself."

"Sorry," I whisper, embarrassed.

"Don't be," he whispers back.

There it is again, that feeling. Allies. People who have lived through the fallout of atrocity.

Hugo glances at his watch. "You have a massage at ten, right?"

I squint at him, confused. "Yes, but how—"

"Yesterday," he answers. "When I offered to escort you from town, and you told me the joke was on me because you have a massage at ten and a facial at two."

A faint smile ghosts my lips. "Offered to escort me from town? That's a nice way of saying *don't let the door hit you where the good Lord split you.*"

Hugo scrunches his eyes like he's in pain. "Sorry about that. I default to asshole when I think my or my family's peace is being threatened."

"Understandable."

The server, Annie, stops by with the check. Hugo snatches it up, motioning with two fingers for Annie to come closer to him. She bends slightly at the waist, her eyes flickering over to me when Hugo whispers something in her ear.

Hugo

"You got it," she says, sending me a second look of interest before leaving to take care of her other tables.

"What did you say to her?"

"That I was taking care of your check today."

My eyes narrow at him. "That's it?"

He nods solemnly.

"Then what was with the cloak and dagger?"

He shrugs, nonchalant. "That's between me and Annie."

"Thank you for breakfast," I say, letting it drop because I'm learning Hugo can be strong-willed.

I stand from the table, winding my purse around my body. Hugo steps aside, motioning for me to go first. He waves at a few people on our way through the restaurant, and I don't miss their curious looks. I've heard about small towns being nosy, but I didn't stop to think about what that really means. The way people are in your business, always knowing things.

Might there be some people here who know details that are important to the day Hugo's dad died? People who were watching, listening, keeping tabs on others, not realizing the significance of a seemingly unimportant detail?

It doesn't seem like the right time to bring it up to Hugo. I've only just begun to make an intro with him, and still the connection is tenuous. Easy does it.

"I'll drive you to Sagewood," Hugo says as we spill out into the bright Saturday morning.

People mill about, waiting for shops to open, holding

white paper coffee cups with the words Sweet Nothings printed on the side.

"It's not in walking distance?" Another thing I've always heard about small towns, everything is within walking distance.

"Depends on how froggy you're feeling." Hugo motions with his head for me to follow him down the sidewalk.

"Froggy?"

"It's something my friend Penn says. He's a former SEAL."

"Gotcha."

Hugo steps off the curb beside a low-slung, obviously expensive bright red car. He reaches for the passenger door, opening it and gesturing for me to get in.

"Yesterday you were driving a truck."

"That's a mill truck. This is my car."

I step around Hugo, into the open space of the car door. He watches me over the doorframe. Pausing, I press a hand to my hip and squint up at him. "Are you having some sort of midlife crisis?"

He grunts a laugh. "No. Why?"

I drag a single fingertip over the roof of the car. "This is a crisis car."

He smirks. "I thought it was a Ciao Chariot."

A laugh bubbles up as I slide into the car. "If it is, you've officially rounded me up." Hugo produces a pair of sunglasses from his jacket pocket. Sliding them on, he says, "Don't worry, Gumshoe. I'm taking you to the spa."

Chapter 7

Mallory

GUMSHOE.

He meant it in a friendly way. Teasing, even.

I can't help the flicker of warmth it puts in my chest.

"Are you blissed out?" Jolene's image is outside her phone's frame, but I hear her voice, and the hard close of a cabinet.

"It was incredible," I answer, adjusting myself on the hotel bed. "You missed out."

"I'll make it there eventually." Jolene steps into the frame, a microwave dinner balanced in her hand.

"Chicken marsala or burrito bowl?" I ask. I'm hungry again. The fare at the spa was delicious, but I need more than a harvest salad with salmon. As Hugo promised, the dressing was delicious.

"Burrito bowl." She takes a bite, then says, "Tell me more about Hugo."

"What else is there to tell?" We've already covered

what happened at Sammich, and this morning at breakfast.

She shakes her head, chewing. "Less recitation of events. More personal observations."

"Personal observations?" I reach behind myself, adjusting the pillows. The reel in my brain rolls back, serving up what little time I've spent with Hugo. "He's nice. Funny. Irreverent." The way he gently touched my hands, peeling my fingers off the teacup. "He's kind."

Jolene's nodding and chewing, so I keep talking. "I'm looking forward to meeting his mom."

"I still can't believe he asked you to come over." She pops the top on a ginger flavored soda water. "What kind of voodoo magic did you work on him? Are we sure this is the same person who ignored all your emails?" She gasps, eyes wide. "You showed him your boobs, didn't you? You hussy."

"He seemed apathetic toward my boobs, but when I showed him my pregnant belly, that's what did the trick."

Jolene laughs as she's taking a drink, and now she's sputtering. "Some dudes get turned on by pregnancy."

I run a hand over my belly. "He hasn't asked me anything about the baby since he saw my prenatal vitamins."

"Yeah, because he thinks you have a husband. Or partner. Or whatever. He assumes the person who got you pregnant is in the picture."

Something tells me if I told Hugo my situation, he'd be furious. I don't know him well, but a part of me understands he would never make the same choice as Peanut's father.

I can't dwell on that, though. It's me and Peanut, and that's it.

"I'll see if I can book this room for one more night. Go to Summerhill tomorrow evening and speak with Mrs. De la Vega."

"Will you take the recorder?"

I consider her question, but immediately reject it. "No. I want the tone of tomorrow evening to have a friendly vibe. Unassuming. If Hugo's mother is anything like him, she'll be hesitant." I need to be respectful of the various feelings she might have, while gaining her trust.

We talk for a few minutes, and Jolene tells me about a new client she's seeing this week. "A chic little marketing firm in Scottsdale."

"Ooh, sounds fun. You should take them out for a client lunch at Obstinate Daughter. You know I can't get enough of their food." Mediterranean is my favorite, closely followed by Mexican. I could eat souvlaki right now. Maybe a gyro. Followed by baklava.

Yeah, I'm hungry.

Jolene finishes her bite. "Anything beats this frozen dinner." She frowns and pushes away the food. "Eat some olives for me tomorrow."

I promise her I will, and we hang up.

I spend the next two hours poring over every piece of information I've gathered about the De la Vegas. Tomorrow is a big deal, and although I'm shooting for casual vibes, I won't bring anything less than my A game.

When dinnertime rolls around, I take a break and venture out. I spend a little time acquainting myself with Olive Avenue, the heart of the town, before heading back to Good Thyme Café. I'm a creature of habit, and when I find something I like, I stick with it.

Annie, my server from this morning, is still working. She spots me as she's refilling waters at a table, sending me a wave. When my to-go order is ready, she's the person who brings it to me.

"Are you working a double?" I ask, the restaurant shorthand coming back to me. I put myself through college waiting tables at a restaurant in Phoenix.

"Short-staffed," she shrugs. "Plus, I need the money."

A guy at one of Annie's other tables waves a hand her direction, like he needs something. She gives him a signal for *one moment* and turns back to me, giving me a look that says *did you need anything else?*

"I'll pay my bill and be out of your hair," I remind her. "I'm sure you have a million things to do."

"Oh!" Her eyes are wide. "I forgot you don't know."

"Know what?"

"Hugo said you don't have a bill here." Annie grins, like Hugo's sly move makes her happy. "Everything goes on his tab."

Shock flutters through me. And then something warm, and a little fuzzy. Hugo was taking care of me. And Peanut.

"Have a nice night," Annie adds, pivoting on her heel and hurrying back to her section.

Hugo

I don't have Hugo's phone number, so I send him an email as soon as I'm back in my room.

To: Hugo De la Vega
   From: Mallory Hawkins

Thank you for dinner.

Mallory & Peanut

Chapter 8

Mallory

THE RISE IN ELEVATION ON THE DRIVE OUT TO Summerhill delivers a spectacular view of Olive Township. A mountain range towers to the east, and west, past the acres upon acres of olive trees, is nothing but desert. Eventually that barren desert gives way to Phoenix city limits. Out here, it feels like another world.

The romance of the orchard makes it hard to imagine the patriarch of the De la Vega family could be taken so violently.

Around the bend in the road, the main buildings of the olive mill come into view. From my reading, and copious time spent on the Summerhill website, I know these first buildings are the agrotourism side of the business. A cute little store selling flavored olive oil and other goods, a new wedding venue, a restaurant. Beyond these structures, set back in the distance, is the De la Vega household.

As instructed, I wind my way around the commercial

buildings. I let off the gas pedal, trying not to kick up dust, but it's useless. This is still the desert, after all. Dust is inevitable.

Still, I go slowly. An odd feeling bubbles up in my belly, a nausea I know doesn't truly have bite.

Nerves.

I'm not usually nervous when speaking with friends or family of the victims, but this is different. This is personal.

Sonya De la Vega may have thought she was ready to speak about her husband, but what if she answers the door, takes one look at me and feels the weight of what she thought she could do, and changes her mind?

I take a deep breath as I steel myself, rolling to a stop in front of the home.

A large two-story, the home is a creamy mixture of warm ivory paint and burnt red roof tiles. The lower half of the front features a stone façade in varying neutral shades of tan. Windows framed in black match the color of the garage doors. Arizona ash trees reach high and run parallel to the home, providing it with shade from the morning sun.

The vibe is warm, and inviting, and deepens my feeling that the person who was a part of all this was too kind to be treated in such a way.

The same is true of Maggie.

A second deep breath fortifies me, and I step from my car. I stride toward the front door, taking the two stone steps to the landing. An oversized wreath of faux eucalyptus hangs on the door, and well-groomed flowering topiaries sit on either side in cedar boxes.

Cozy. Appealing. A place that practically screams *I have a pot of flavorful soup on the stove and a warm hearth.*

My hand is poised to knock when a figure steps around the corner.

Brown work boots, laces undone. Dark wash jeans, a crisp white shirt. Tan skin, a jaw darkened by five-o'clock shadow.

Hugo has all the makings of my personal physical kryptonite. Tall, dark, and unbelievably sexy.

My hand drops to my side.

He looks like he wants to say something, so I wait. And wait. The seconds, slow and torturous, pass. He runs two knuckles along his jaw, and finally says, "I'm nervous."

His honesty brings me up short. It's the last thing I expected him to say, and it sets an ease to my galloping heartbeats.

"I am, too," I admit, feeling the corners of my lips turn up in a tentative smile.

Hugo studies me, dark eyebrows tugging. I wish I knew what he was thinking.

As if he's decided something, he nods in the direction he came from. "Follow me."

He starts off, and I listen, assuming he's leading me around the house to a different entrance. But then he stops at a massive porch swing, settling back onto it.

I hadn't noticed the swing when I arrived, but there's

really no way I could have. Green vines grow thick through a trellis, blocking the swing from view.

"This looks more like a bed suspended in the air than a porch swing." I step closer, holding tight to the arm as I lower myself down. Hugo's feet are planted firmly on the ground, keeping the swing in place for me. Using the palm of my hand to hold my weight, I reverse until I've met the back frame.

"It's actually called a swing bed," Hugo replies, settling back against the yellow and white striped cushions. "I have one at my place, too."

He's close to me now. So close, his thick, muscled thigh presses against mine. Heat radiates off him, an electric warmth, my nose invaded by the scent of him: rich, earthy, spicy.

Be professional.

A furtive shift of my leg, giving myself an inch of needed space from him.

"You're making that up because of what I just said." I force the joke, desperately grasping for levity. Anything to keep me from spiraling into a tornado of hormones.

Hugo's head shakes back-and-forth slowly, one arm extending across the back frame as his other arm settles on the armrest. "Cross my heart."

The following line to that childhood rhyme sinks between us, heavy. *Hope to die.*

Hugo grimaces. "That was...unfortunate."

It's the perfect sentence to break through the thick tension of the moment. "You can do better."

Hugo's brown eyes find mine, his gaze strong, meaningful, as if he is trying to convey something. Is he thinking what I'm thinking? Remembering how that was what I said to him two days ago, the first time we met? Before he knew who I was, and our flirtation was happy and innocent and unencumbered by the truth.

"I'm sure I could," he says quietly. His gaze leaves me, travels out east where the sky grows ever darker.

I'm resisting the urge to really settle all the way back on these plush pillows, tuck my legs up at an angle, and take a nap. This swing bed would be an excellent choice for afternoon napping.

Hugo is quiet again, and I wait patiently. When I'm hosting a podcast, it is my job to lead the conversation. But now, sitting out here with Hugo, it is imperative I go at his speed.

It's not too much longer before he asks, "Are you usually nervous to talk with people you're hoping to interview?"

"No," I answer. "But in the spirit of transparency, I've never worked so hard to have a conversation that could *possibly* lead to an interview."

A terse breath streams from his nose. "Everybody can't wait to run their mouths, huh?"

Disdain drips from his words. My heart hurts for him. For the way he grows prickly in an instant. The thought of talking about his father pains him, hardens his tone and possibly his heart.

I want to make this as easy as possible for him. "Oftentimes, it's simply people talking about someone they loved, and when they do that, there's a certain..." I search for the right word. "Resurrection, if you will. Their loved one is alive again, even if it's only in a memory shared."

"We've never talked about what happened." Hugo eyes me meaningfully. "My mom tried, in the beginning. When it was all fresh. New. But the journalists, reporters, whatever they were, they sensationalized it." He shakes his head regretfully, and that dark hair of his swipes his forehead. "I was young when it happened, but I knew they were making my hero into a headline. It tore me up, and I didn't think it was possible to hurt more at that point. My sister, too. So, my mom stopped giving interviews. We talked about him at home instead." A smile crests Hugo's lips, and a small celebration erupts in my chest. I feel his pain all too well. "We did what we could to keep him as alive as possible. And we worked to remember him as the man he was, not the victim someone forced him to be."

Hot tears assail the backs of my eyes. Everything Hugo's saying, every emotion he's describing, it all hits home for me. As much as I want to give in and cry, I swallow it down. I'm here in a professional capacity. "I promise to be very respectful, Hugo."

My right foot is beginning to fall asleep, and I adjust my stance. Hugo takes it as me getting up, probably assuming I'm growing antsy. His arm shoots out, cups my elbow.

"Please," he says, eyes burning with intensity. "Please don't make my dad into a victim. I can't bear it."

At the end of the day, his father and my sister were

victims of a crime, but I understand the nuance of what it is he's saying. "Hugo, I will not reduce either of our loved ones to simply being victims."

Relief sweeps over his face. Gratitude.

His grasp leaves my elbow, only to extend across me, pinky finger offered. "Pinky promise, Gumshoe?"

I laugh. Hugo has a talent for introducing levity to difficult moments.

Hooking a pinky around his, I say, "Pinky promise, Swordsman."

"Aren't you a pretty thing?" Sonya De la Vega declares, wrapping me up in a cinnamon and sugar scented hug.

And it's...well, it's *nice*. Something I could relax into. When was the last time my own mother held me so tenderly? The answer hits me square in the chest. *A long time.*

"Mom," Hugo warns, playful but slightly parental. "You're supposed to ask people you've never met if it's ok to hug them."

"Pshh," Sonya scoffs, releasing me. She takes a step back and waves at my face. "Look into those eyes and tell me she's not starving for a hug."

"It's true," I agree, winking at Hugo to let him know I'm good. In truth, I'm better than good. I needed that hug, and I didn't realize how much. Sometimes, a person yearns to sink into someone else's arms, and be held. I swear, certain people's hugs contain medicinal properties. Sonya De la Vega is one of them.

She's not what I was expecting. The only photos I've seen of her were from nearly twenty years ago. Online photos of Hugo are almost completely from the lens of him fencing, and he doesn't keep a current personal social media. Or, at least not an account I've been able to find. Without realizing it, I'd been picturing Sonya as a grieving woman in a black veil. Permanent frown. Grief hanging heavy around her like a shroud.

I couldn't have been more wrong. Her dark hair shines, her olive skin beautiful. Tonight she wears loose yellow linen pants, flowing over espadrilles. A white blouse with fabric-covered buttons. It's a happy ensemble.

"Come, come," she says, motioning us to follow her. "Hugo, take off those boots." The instruction zooms over her shoulder in a practiced way that speaks of years giving that directive.

"Already on it, Ma." Hugo stops to toe off his boots, but I go on ahead into a kitchen with green cabinets and a black tile backsplash.

"I baked snickerdoodle cookies," Sonya says, pointing to a white ceramic tray with rows and rows of freshly baked cookies.

I sniff the air appreciatively. "I assumed you naturally smelled like sugar and cinnamon."

"Wouldn't that be great if that were the case?" Sonya

turns to a wine rack built into the wall, selecting a bottle of red. "What scent would you choose if you could choose any?"

This cordial, silly conversation is upsetting the expectations I had for this meeting, but I roll with it.

"Spiced apples," I answer.

"What about them?" Hugo asks, walking barefoot into the kitchen. Normally, I would never find a man's feet attractive, but something about Hugo's ease in this home, the way his jeans skim the floor, and the soft swish of the material, is really doing it for me.

I've got to get that under control. How does a pregnant woman rein in her hormones?

"How funny," Sonya says, grinning pointedly at Hugo. "Spiced apples are Hugo's favorite."

Of course they are.

"What about them?" Hugo repeats.

Sonya pulls a wineglass from a shelf. "Mallory was saying that if she could choose a natural scent, she'd pick spiced apples."

Hugo's eyes meet mine, then skitter away. "Hmm." It's half growl, half polite disinterest.

"Can I pour a glass of wine for you?" Sonya asks me.

A second look from Hugo, and a question behind his eyes. "No, thank you," I answer. "Water is fine, please."

I'm wearing a T-shirt dress, one of those that are casual and don't hug the body. My baby bump is hardly noticeable, but I didn't want to take a chance Sonya would notice, and inevitably the conversation would become about me, and the baby. At which point it would be nearly impossible not to overshare. Despite how friendly Sonya is, I need to maintain a level of professionalism. Telling her my ex signed away his rights to our child and I'm staring down life as a single mother does not achieve that.

Hugo strides for the fridge, coming away with a beer. For the briefest moment, his gaze falls to my stomach. He looks into my eyes, and when he sees I'm looking at him, he looks away quickly.

Did you leave your wedding ring behind in the hotel room?

He'd said it with disgust. Disappointment. But now this is the third time we've seen each other. That means this is his third opportunity to notice I don't wear a wedding ring.

Ridiculous.

He's not looking. Why would he?

Brushing off the foolish desire, I thank him for the bottle of water he's holding out for me.

"Take a seat," Sonya offers as she sits in a round-backed stool at the far end of the kitchen island.

Sitting beside her, I take one of the cookies off the plate she pushes my way. Hugo remains stationary on the other side of the island, arms crossed and hips pushed forward slightly.

"Well," she says, waiting for me to take a bite. It's charming, the way she wants to make sure I'm eating. Very motherly, and it twists my heart. My own mother stopped parenting the day Maggie died. It was as if she quit existing, and left behind was nothing but a husk of the mother I once knew. Maggie's dad, my stepfather, has always been a quiet man. I think after my dad left her with an infant, she was looking for his polar opposite. She got it, but I don't know if that was a good thing. "Let's get to the nitty gritty," Sonya says. "Why did you come to Olive Township?"

I glance up at Hugo. Did he tell her nothing after our breakfast yesterday? Nothing about my sister, or the real reason I'm here? He's looking at me with patient expectance, and I don't know why, but I feel an emotional tug in the center of my chest. *He didn't tell his mom about Maggie. He saved it for me.*

Taking a small sip from my water, I begin. "I host a true crime podcast called *Case Files*. My best friend from college is the producer. We spend time learning the cases, interviewing friends and family, trying to create a fuller picture than what is available just by reading articles. For the most part we've given loved ones an opportunity to talk about the person and share with others, but we've had two instances where tiny details shared on the show were what solved unsolved murders." I hesitate, choosing my next words carefully. "I'm not saying I expect that to happen where your husband is concerned. I can't promise that. But," I hesitate again, searching out Hugo. For strength, perhaps? To get a nod of his head, urging me forward? Somehow, he seems to understand this is what I'm seeking. With a dip of his chin, he gives me the go-ahead. "My twelve-year-old little sister was murdered in the same manner as Simon."

Sonya inhales sharply, her hand covering her mouth

as her eyes widen. "That's *evil*." The words slip through the spaces between her fingers.

"Truly," I agree. "And it doesn't automatically mean it was at the hands of the same person. But what if it was? That question is what has kept me up at night. What spurred me to write Hugo my first email. What if it was?"

Sonya's gaze falls down to her hands, now folded in her lap. She doesn't speak, and I meet her silence with patience because I expect it. But then the silence stretches on, and I look to Hugo. He's watching his mom, concern etched on the plains of his face.

"Mom?"

She looks up, first to him, and then to me. "It's been a long time since I talked to anybody about Simon."

"Hugo said as much." My voice is low. Gentle.

Sonya spins a simple gold band she wears on her ring finger. "Did Hugo also tell you he doesn't have relationships because the women he's met have odd reactions when they learn about Simon?"

My lips press together to stop my chuckle. "Uh, no. He didn't mention that."

Wherever Sonya went in her mind a few moments ago, she is back. Her humor has returned.

Hugo rolls his eyes. He reaches for a cookie, shoving the entire thing in his mouth, probably to keep himself from saying anything.

Sonya takes a cookie, too, breaking it in half over her plate. "That's one of the reasons I think it might be time, Mallory. Time to talk about Simon. Rip off the Band-Aid.

Maybe, if the wound is exposed to air, it can heal. Lives can be lived in healthier ways."

Hugo, still chewing, doesn't say anything. But I'm nodding along, thinking of how true those words are. How this might be an opportunity for me to heal from what happened to Maggie. To do my best to mend an old wound so I can be a whole person for my baby. A single mother, doing the job of two. Not quite what I pictured for myself, but here we are.

"I think that's a lovely idea, Sonya. And if you're willing to have me, I would love to help facilitate that." I glance at Hugo, doing my best not to smirk. "Not sure I can help with Hugo's problem, though."

Sonya adopts an expression of innocence. "Oh, I think you might be able to."

Oh.

Is she...*playing matchmaker?*

I open my mouth, ready to tell her there's a tiny human growing inside me, but Sonya glances at her watch. She jumps from her seat, saying, "I completely forgot I'm meeting friends for a movie tonight. Thank goodness for this new watch where I can get my text messages on my wrist. I probably wouldn't have looked at my phone for hours."

I slide from my seat, too, ready to be on my way, but her arm shoots out. "Please stay for the sunset from the back patio. It was Simon's favorite view." Her eyes light up. "In fact, can you stay in town a little longer? The Olive Festival starts in a few days. Maybe the best way for you to tell Simon's story is to get to know him through the town." Her eyebrows raise, hope shining bright in her eyes.

"Yes," I say, no hesitation. Can I extend my stay at the Olive Inn? No clue. Is Jolene game to water my plants? No idea. I don't know if it's ok for me to reschedule my sixteen-week appointment at the OB-GYN, and I most certainly did not pack enough extra underwear for this long of a stay, but *YES!*

I try not to appear too elated. No happy dancing for me. Just a covert squeeze of my fisted hands in my dress pockets.

Sonya smiles. She doesn't necessarily look happy, but maybe it's a combination of various emotions in varying levels of intensity. She glances between me and Hugo for a long moment before announcing, "Well, I'm off. Enjoy the sunset."

Sonya disappears around the corner with a final fluttering of her fingers, and a moment later, the front door closes.

"Umm." I look at Hugo.

He's grimacing. Palming the back of his neck, he says, "Sorry about that. My mom can be a lot."

"Don't worry about it." I shrug. "She's worried about you." It must be nice, having a mom who cares like Sonya.

"I'm not sure why." He scrunches his face like her concern confounds him. "I'm fine."

"The words of every person who is not, in fact, fine."

Hugo leans his forearms on the counter, hands grasped. He nudges the tray of cookies toward me. "Take another cookie. You are eating for two, right?"

Talk about an abrupt subject change. Did I hit a nerve?

Gently, I run a hand over my belly. "You already know the answer to that." I take another cookie, because they're delicious, and I'm hungry. I'm always hungry.

Hugo is quiet, but his eyes are on me. I know he has questions, but he's too polite to ask them.

Besides, we both know my pregnancy is none of his business, and is not relevant to why I'm here.

Hugo straightens, pointing beyond my head with his beer bottle. "I do believe there's a sunset waiting for us outside."

Chapter 9

Hugo

I REPEAT IT TO MYSELF, A MANTRA.

You don't know her situation.

I say it twice more. A chastisement.

Mallory passes in front of me, sailing through the door I'm holding open for her. She says thank you with her eyes as she goes, and I dip my chin at her gratitude.

She finds her way to the railing, gripping it tightly with both hands. She looks out, her chest swelling with a quiet, deep breath.

I step close to her. Fingers wrapped around my beer bottle, the other hand resting on the wooden rail. My pinkie finger, so near to her dainty one. A subtle stretch of my finger and I'd touch her. Makes me think of the moment she hooked her delicate finger around me, promising me she'd do right by our departed loved ones.

"It's remarkable," she says, after a slow exhale, absorbing the land I love. "I can see why it was your dad's favorite spot on the property."

The olive trees stand proud, the grove thick and running long, following the gentle slope of the hills. A pink and orange sky blends into the tops of the trees, putting on a show. As if Olive Township and the sunset sky have conspired to give Mallory a glimpse of what my father loved.

The breeze lifts her hair off her shoulders. Her face is soft, almost dreamy, and I know she's saying something nice about my dad right now, but I'm finding it hard to process her words. She's beautiful.

She peers at me, and I snap my gaze back to the olive grove. "My dad could work the fields all day long, and still, this is where he wanted to be every evening. He never got used to this view. Never tired of it, or took it for granted."

"I think that's what happens when you love something. When it becomes woven into the fabric of your soul."

I clear my throat, push away the desire to openly admire the straight edge of her nose, the way her lips puff out in the prettiest shade of pink. *Am I lusting after another man's woman? Is this how Penn felt when he found out Daisy was engaged to Duke, but he couldn't help the way he wanted her anyway?*

"Is that how you feel about true crime?" I ask, banishing my amorous thoughts. "Or podcasting about true crime?"

Her mouth opens with an immediate response, but she catches herself and snaps it shut.

"What?" I press.

She shakes her head. "Nothing."

I squint at her. "Try again. Your response was definitely something."

She directs a clear gaze my way. There's an honesty in her eyes. Like she's realizing something in real time.

She turns west, letting the burnt shades of the last of the sun wash over her face. "Solving Maggie's murder is the reason I wake up in the morning. It's the reason I took psychology courses in college."

I catch this detail, tucking it away for later. It makes sense. Learning what makes people tick is probably helpful to her job now.

She continues. "But I don't know if I want it to be a thread in a tapestry that represents my soul. It's what motivates me, but it's dark." Her hand dips to her belly, fingers spreading over her dress as if palming a basketball, curling and flexing tenderly. Protectively.

Something about it makes me...*happy?* Not quite. Relieved, I guess. Mallory seems tough, but I like this stroke of vulnerability.

"I want the fabric of my soul to be light. Airy. Pastels." She looks down at her stomach, at her hand splayed across it. "Not dark. I want my baby to only know light."

My baby. No mention of a father.

"That's understandable," I say, and she looks at me. Reluctant. She's waiting for me to ask about the baby's father. Steeling herself.

I'm dying to ask, dying to know. The truth is, I feel a spark with her. Sounds crazy though. Probably is.

We're in the oddest of circumstances, but I feel the

beginning of a buzz in my fingertips. It's not the beer I've been sipping on.

It's Mallory. There's something about her. She's different. A stranger, but she doesn't feel like one. Not when I'm talking to her, or looking in her eyes. Most women I have to tell about my dad, but not her. She already knew. She sought me out. I didn't have to watch the information transform her expression.

I bet if I told Penn, or my other best friend, Ambrose, about Mallory, they'd tell me I like her because she's not available. Not because I want what I can't have, but because I wouldn't have to worry about getting in too deep. She's so full of roadblocks, I wouldn't have to worry about getting too far down the path. Safe.

Ugh. How pathetic can I get? Standing here beside the pregnant true crime podcaster who wants to explore my dad's case and thinking of her in a way that's not professional.

Forget that we met and immediately began flirting. Mallory is pregnant with another man's child, and there has been no confirmation if he is or is not in the picture. Not to mention the tiny little fact that *I don't do relationships.*

Given these two very important reasons, I'll be keeping my thoughts and questions to myself.

"I'm sure all parents want the best for their kids." It's such a bland response, I almost cringe.

She raps her knuckles on the railing, only twice. "I'm sure."

Her tone is forlorn. Sad, even.

Hugo

Together, we watch the sun sink below the horizon.

"There it goes," Mallory says. She turns for the door. "Please tell your mother I said thank you for inviting me to stay and watch something your dad loved."

"Let me walk you out." I point around the side of the house. "You're parked right over there."

She walks beside me. Even if somebody removed my sense of sight or hearing, I'd still know she was there. I feel her energy, as if it radiates off her skin. I'm hyperaware of this woman, but I don't understand why.

Is it because she's the first woman I've had out to the grove? She's not here in a romantic capacity, not in the slightest, but her being here brings to stark relief the fact that I've never brought a woman home.

That's...*odd*. And probably unhealthy.

And also not something I want to look too deeply into right now.

Talking to Mallory, opening up the possibility of having her look into my father's murder, that's about all I can take.

"So you're staying in Olive Township for a few more days?" We've arrived at the driver's side of her car. I know Mallory already told my mother yes, but I'm sure there are logistics she needs to work out.

"I plan to," she responds. "First, I need to see if I can extend my stay at the inn, and make sure some things get taken care of in Phoenix." She pats her stomach. "Reschedule an appointment."

"Check in with your husband?"

Did...I...just say that?

83

The back of my neck heats like somebody is holding a lighter to it. *What a dumbass.*

Mallory's lips purse, as if she wants to laugh, but instead she shakes her head slowly back-and-forth. She doesn't make a face like she's offended, and that encourages me. Maybe I'll dip my toes in the dumbass pool one more time.

"Check in with your *boyfriend*?"

Her lips twitch again. Another slow shake of her head. *No.* Then she says, "The only person I have to worry about is the guy chained up in my basement. He should be ok for a few more days though. He has enough length of chain to reach a rusty pipe that drips dirty water." She immediately makes a face, laughing awkwardly. "Sorry about the macabre humor. Hazard of the job."

I wave it off. I should probably be more concerned about the fact I was thinking it might not be the worst thing in the world to be chained up in Mallory's basement.

Ok, what's wrong with me? Why am I thinking this way? Maybe I should call Ambrose and tell him. It might be good to be on the receiving end of his thoughtful listening. Or I could call Penn and ask him to meet me for a beer. When I tell him the nonsense running through my mind, he'll deliver an open palm *thwack* on the side of my head.

Maybe that's what I need.

"Poor bastard," I choke out, smiling to show her I don't mind her morbid joke.

Hugo

Mallory wiggles her eyebrows. "Maybe he likes it."

This time, I really do laugh. I can't contain it. This woman is funny.

"I'll see you later this week at the Olive Festival," she says, climbing into her driver's seat.

On a whim, I pull my phone from my pocket. "We should exchange numbers. In case you need something."

She nods like she agrees, reciting her phone number. I key it in, calling her so she has my number, too.

With a single wave I watch her drive down the dirt lane, rounding the outbuildings. She disappears from sight, but still I stand in place, watching the dust plume.

In the end, I don't call Ambrose, or Penn. I walk my ass home to my house, where I spend the rest of the evening prepping for the meeting I have tomorrow with an olive oil sommelier, and internet stalking Mallory.

Her only social media is related to her podcast, and it's not up to date. There is not a single mention of her sister, her pregnancy, or her personal life at all.

It seems Mallory is a lot like me.

Two people who had a piece of them stolen, and do their best every day to live with a heart that is not whole.

Chapter 10

Mallory

THE OLIVE FESTIVAL IS STILL A FEW DAYS AWAY, BUT I'm not waiting until then to get started. I want to know all there is to know about this town. Its history. Its inhabitants.

Normally I'd say one of the best places to go to reach that goal is the local bar. A hole in the wall kind of place with peanut shells on the floor and something sticky on the countertop no matter how many times it's wiped down.

It's too early in the day for that, so I'll try my luck at the next best place. A spot where the gossip is sure to be fresh and flowing.

The Rowdy Mermaid hair salon. I'm not in need of a trim, but I think I'll be getting one today anyhow.

Lucky for me, Rowdy Mermaid accepts walk-ins. There's one stylist available, a round-faced young girl who looks like she cannot be older than eighteen years old. Her name tag reads *Miranda*.

She is shy and a little nervous with hands that shake. Her jitters don't worry me. It would be hard to mess up my long layers and no framing around my face. My hairstylist in Phoenix is always joking she's basically robbing me blind because of how expensive her haircuts are and how simple my preference is. That may be true, but she's the only person who has ever put color in my hair, and I trust her completely. When a brunette finds a hairstylist who can give her dimension without making her brassy, it essentially means they mate for life.

Miranda leads me to her station at the back of the room. All the other chairs are full, and the conversation slows as I walk through. Their eyes are on me and I don't only feel it, I see it reflected in the individual mirrors in each station. If this were Phoenix, I'd be uncomfortable, fearing I was suffering an embarrassing wardrobe malfunction. But this is a small town, and newcomers are noteworthy, warranting a slowdown in the pace of chatter.

I say nothing. My plan is to keep a low profile, stay quiet with ears open. I'm listening and learning.

Miranda guides me into her chair. "What can I do for you today?"

"A simple trim, please."

Relief cascades over her young features. "I've only been out of school for a few weeks," she admits. "I hope that's ok."

"Of course it's ok," I tell her. "Everybody has to start somewhere."

Her shoulders relax. The chatter in the salon picks

back up. Miranda leads me to a row of basins and begins to wash my hair. I've been in salons where they have a dedicated person to do the washing, but the Rowdy Mermaid is small. Intimate.

"Is the water temperature ok for you?" Miranda asks, running the back of her hand through the water to test it.

"It's a little bit hot," I confess. I'm the type of person who would've grinned and beared it, not wanting to complain, but one of my goals this year is to feel more comfortable with asserting myself. Even if it's as simple as admitting the water temperature is too hot for my comfort.

The new life growing inside me is the reason for my goal. Suddenly, there's this pressing need to be all the things I've always wanted to be, but did not feel incentivized to go after or change about myself. I want to be an assertive woman, a mom who says what she likes and what she doesn't like. I don't want my child to grow up with someone who doesn't know how to draw boundaries. If I want my child to be a person with firm boundaries, I have to draw them for myself.

Miranda finishes the wash and settles me back into the chair in front of her station. She tries to engage me in small talk, the usual *where are you from? How long are you in town? What do you do for a living?* I do my best to give short answers that don't lead to follow up questions, and when she asked what I do for a living, I outright lie. *I'm in grad school.*

People tend to be very interested in true crime, and

podcasting, and when those two things are put together, the questions are endless. Right now, I'm focused on listening in on conversations, so I can't be engaged in one myself.

The women getting their hair done today are older than me by quite a bit. Fifties, maybe sixties. The chatter volleys around the small room as they interrupt and talk over one another. They must be familiar with each other, because that's not the behavior of strangers. With strangers you take your turn and appear to listen politely, but really you're planning what you're going to say next.

There is one woman, perpendicular to me, and in the seat as far away as possible, who acts a little differently than the other women. She has a refined air about her, despite being covered in the same unbecoming smock as the rest of us. I'd say she's haughty, though she's trying to come off as regal.

"Who is the woman in that first chair?" I ask under my breath. "The one closest to the window?"

Miranda, face set in determination as she gives my haircut her undivided attention, whispers, "Liane Rooney. The mayor's wife."

My first inclination is to nod, but I have to keep my head still. "Gotcha," I say. Now it makes sense, the way she acts like she is a part of the conversation, but above it.

"My mom doesn't like her," Miranda says, sectioning off the hair near the front of my face and combing it down over my nose. She compares the length, then uses her scissors.

Snip snip.

"Why not?" I ask, matching Miranda's hushed tone, taking care not to glance at the woman.

I find it interesting that she's trusting me, gossiping in that way young people do.

Miranda shrugs. "She calls her a wolf in sheep's clothing. I know what it means"—she shrugs again—"but I don't understand why. They serve on the school board together, and they've been on a shit ton of committees together over the years. My mom is kind of quiet, she's not a take charge kind of person. But Liane is." A third shrug. "I think it's more that my mom doesn't like being around that personality type. It overwhelms her."

I absorb the information, but try not to stay on one topic too long. "You seem to know your mom pretty well."

Unlike me, Miranda has the ability to nod, and she does so vigorously. "We're, like, best friends."

"That's sweet," I say. "Being best friends with your mom."

Miranda holds a section of my hair out to the side, trimming at an angle. "Are you close with your mom?"

No matter how easily the lie slips out, it pinches my chest. Hurts something fierce. "Yes."

Though I live in the same city as my mom, I haven't seen her in months. My mom's best excuse is that her broken heart never healed. That's the one that sits on the surface anyway. Deep down, in an ugly dark place where nobody wants to look too closely, is where she holds her blame, and it's all pointed at me. She hates that she blames me, resents that there's anybody to blame at all. Instead, she ignores me.

I steal a glance at the woman across the room from me one more time. My guess is that she's at least ten years younger than the other women in the salon. "So, I guess whether or not you like Liane is dependent upon your personality type?"

Miranda huffs a laugh. "I suppose, but most people seem to like her. Or pretend to like her." Miranda's neck is bent, focused on her task. I'm grateful for that. Just because I have an easy hairstyle doesn't mean I want to walk out of here looking like Edward Scissorhands.

Miranda continues. "I think she's one of those people it's better to have with you than against you, you know? Not that she would do anything bad to somebody, but life is probably easier if she likes you."

Miranda's astute observation takes me by surprise. "How old are you?"

"Twenty-one," she answers, but the way she says it makes it seem like she thinks she's a grown-up. "I know, I know, I look sixteen with this round face and dimpled cheeks."

"One day you'll be very happy for that baby face," I comment, surreptitiously watching Liane Rooney from the corner of my eye. Her hairstylist removes her smock, revealing Liane's pale blue dress pants and white silk blouse. Liane leans forward in her chair, peering into the mirror. She fluffs her smart blonde bob, adding a smidge of volume on top. Her eyes shift in the mirror, finding my gaze. I keep my eyes focused on hers, but like most people my first instinct is to look away. Instead, I offer her a small smile, one that is just friendly enough without being too enthusiastic.

Something tells me Liane knows everything about this town. It's entirely possible that spending one afternoon bending her ear would prove almost as informational as thumbing through old police reports.

Our eye contact is broken as Liane spins in her chair. She loops a gold chain purse over her shoulder and marches my way. I would prefer to meet her with hair that's not wet and hanging in my face, but those aren't the cards I was dealt today.

Liane stops a foot from my chair, blonde bob bouncing, smile warm and expectant. The expression of somebody who is always well-received. To her face, at least. "I may not have a photographic memory, but I'm almost positive I've never met you before." She extends a hand. "Liane Rooney."

"Mallory Hawkins." I shake her hand, smiling at her through the mirror. "You are correct. I'm from Phoenix. Came for the spa, and decided to stay for the Olive Festival."

Liane's meticulously drawn-in eyebrows raise. "A young lady all by herself?"

Miranda drops the hair dryer on the tile floor, frowning sheepishly at the loud noise it makes.

"I have to go it alone sometimes," I respond, keeping my smile in place.

"I suppose I'm being silly," Liane says, waving a hand.

"No safer place than Olive Township. Especially coming from the big city."

"It certainly feels safe here."

Liane presses a palm to her chest. "I'm the mayor's wife, and every year I run the lemonade stand at the festival. It's tradition. Promise me you'll stop by for a cup?"

"Wouldn't miss it," I answer.

Liane sails from the salon with a final wave at everyone. There is a collective sigh around the place, as if Liane raises the frequency wherever she goes.

"Famous in a small town," Miranda mutters, and it makes me laugh.

Jolene: What exactly is an Olive Festival?

Mallory: I...don't know.

Jolene: Hold please.

Jolene: Ok I'm back with answers. The Olive Township Olive Festival is a one-day event that started as a way for the Summerhill Olive Mill to showcase its goods to the townspeople, but has grown over the years to include all local vendors.

Jolene: It goes on from there, but you get the gist.

Jolene: Per our old pal, the Internet.

Mallory: Love that guy.

Mallory: Sometimes, anyway.

Jolene: Do you miss me?

Mallory: It's been six days since I've seen you.

Jolene: Not the question I was asking.

Mallory: I miss you.

Jolene: Want to know what I really miss? The appointment I was going to with you. You know, the one where we were going to find out if you're having a boy or a girl?

Mallory: I only pushed it out to next week.

Jolene: STILL.

Mallory: I have to get going. The Olive Festival waits for no woman.

Jolene: Nooo I want to hear more about Hugo.

Mallory: I already told you, he's kind and obviously still very wounded.

Jolene: Like you.

Hugo

Jolene: I want to hear you describe how gorgeous he is. How all that olive farming and fencing has worked in his favor.

Mallory: You don't need me for that. Consult your old pal, the Internet.

Chapter 11

Mallory

From my research, I learned Simon was murdered on the day of the eighth annual Olive Festival.

He'd left Summerhill earlier than his wife and kids, with plans to help his employees set up the Summerhill booth. When Sonya and their children showed up at the booth and learned nobody had seen Simon, Sonya located a rookie police officer put in place for crowd control and told him. Using his radio, he'd alerted the officers at the station. According to an interview given by Sonya at the time, this is when her heart sank. She knew something was very wrong.

Simon was found lying beside his car on Six Digit Road, not too far from where the festival was taking place. The investigation went on for months, and the family went quiet. The police exhausted their resources, and for the next two years, the Olive Festival was shuttered. Nobody wanted to gather on that day for any reason other than to remember one of their beloved townsmen, a man whose family had been a fixture of Olive Township, and even the reason for its name.

Though I searched, I couldn't find online when the festival had resurrected, or who was responsible for bringing it back to life.

The park where the event is held isn't too far from the inn, and I'm on foot. Yesterday I'd gone on a bit of a shopping spree, picking up two new sundresses, a cute pair of court-style tennis shoes, and a few loose tops. I'd also stopped for more toiletries, and snacks and water to keep in my room. I'd forgotten to refill my water bottle before I left, and I'm regretting that now. Pregnancy makes me thirstier, makes physical exertion more tiring. Growing a human is hard work.

Is that perspiration I feel gathering at my hairline? I've only been walking ten minutes. I either need to exercise more, or never exercise again. Right now I'm leaning toward the latter. Good thing I chose to wear one of my new tank tops, and a pair of linen shorts. Any more fabric and I'd be roasting.

The park that holds the festival gets bigger and bigger the closer I get. The faint offbeat of a song reaches me, the lonesome sound of bluegrass.

Hugo's face pops into my mind. I've known him less than a week, and already I've seen him wear numerous expressions. Flirtatious, surprised, tense, angry, resigned, sorrowful. The many faces of Hugo De la Vega.

For a man so guarded, he's easy to be around. Does he do that on purpose? Make being around him effortless so nobody knows how deeply he's hurting inside?

Takes one to know one.

An old defense mechanism I didn't know I had until I began taking psychology classes in college. I've met plenty of people who've experienced tragedy, but none who chose to deal with it the way I did.

Until now.

Hugo, and the way he palms the back of his neck, how he looks down at the ground when he's weighing his response.

Hugo, and—

"Hey."

Stumbling, I smack a hand to my chest. Hugo's arm shoots out, catching me by the elbow.

Fun fact: that bony little point is the least sexual part of the body. *Unless you're pregnant.*

Hugo's hand still grips me, his thumb rubbing over the inside of my upper arm. Does he know he's doing that? It's making me lose sense. Making me want to lean into him, allow my hands to peruse his chest.

The tenderness in his dark-eyed gaze fades, replaced with mirth. "How did I manage to startle the true crime podcaster? Shouldn't you be impervious to surprise?"

I pull my arm away from his touch, ignoring the indignant woman inside me who wants nothing more than to continue to be touched by Hugo. My reaction to him needs a leash.

Possibly an ice bath.

"I'm not a ninja," I respond, adjusting my shirt.

Hugo watches my hands as they move my straps to

the appropriate place on my shoulders. "No kung fu for you, then?" Hugo turns for the festival.

I fall in step beside him. "Hardly. I tried karate when I was ten but I was terrible." A smile breaks over my face. "Maggie, though, she was—"

What am I doing?

Talking about Maggie with ease, remembering her as if I were telling a funny story that held no pain? The memory brought with it nothing that hurt, only an effervescent bubble of happiness.

Since the moment Maggie left this world, I have not thought of her without an underlying sadness, longing, regret. The list goes on and on.

It's as if somehow, with Hugo, I slipped into another realm. A place where pain is not a prerequisite to my memories of Maggie.

Hugo touches me again, lightly on my non-sexual elbow. "Mallory?" He says my name softly, neither of us breaking stride. "Maggie was...?" He trails off, eyebrows raised, urging me to continue.

My lips press together as I take a deep breath, composing myself. "She was naturally good at karate. When it came time to break a board for her belt test, her 'hiya'"—I slice through the air with my palm to demonstrate—"was high-pitched. Childlike. She wore her hair in a ponytail, and she had the cutest little bangs. She pushed the bangs out of her face right before she broke the board. And after she did it, she looked at me first."

The memory grabs me by the throat. Chokes me.

In a move that takes me by surprise, but soothes me

all the same, Hugo's hand slides down my arm, slips into my palm. His squeeze is gentle, reassuring. "Your little sister was proud of herself, and she wanted to share that with you."

Gratitude fills me. Not only for his kind words, but for his ability to remain here with me in this. This situation, these feelings. He's staying in the storm with me. I squeeze his hand back. "How do you know that?"

I'm certain I already know the answer.

"Because every time I won a fencing match, I'd look for my dad. No matter how old I was. No matter how many years had passed."

He walks us forward with purpose, his strong jaw and carved cheekbones not giving away a single sliver of the emotions coursing through him. But I see it. In the very places he hides it, are the same places he gives it away. A person need only know what to look for to discover it.

We arrive at the edge of the park. The music slips over us, closer now, and the scents of fried dough and sugar permeate the air.

"Come meet my friends," Hugo says, tugging me sideways.

I follow along, looking down at my hand in his.

Does he realize it's still there?

Chapter 12

Hugo

HER HAND IN MINE FEELS RIGHT.

Who am I right now?

Every ounce of her vulnerability draws out my own. It's terrifying, but I've never felt more awake. Her grasp, her straightforward acquiescence, calms and energizes me at the same time.

Under the shade of a bright blue canopy sit my sister and my friends, not attempting to hide their shock as we approach.

Penn is the first to wave a hand. I return the gesture, greeting my lifelong best friend. Daisy, his wife and Vivi's best friend, smiles happily from her perch beside Penn. My sister, however, narrows her hawk eyes at our clasped hands.

Mallory releases me, and I fight the urge to hold on tighter. At this point, I'm not certain I recognize myself.

"This is Mallory," I say, pulling up to the group. They sit in folding chairs, Vivi beside Daisy, and Penn with his long legs extended. "Mallory is the true crime podcaster I've told you about."

I guess it's accurate that married people start to look like one another, because Penn and Daisy wear identical expressions of shock.

"I thought you were..." Penn trails off, glancing from me to Mallory.

"Ignoring me?" Mallory supplies, amusement in her tone.

Penn purses his lips, head dropping in a single decisive nod. "Exactly."

"Turns out it's more difficult to ignore someone when they show up in your favorite sandwich shop." I look at Mallory, biting back a smile.

She lays an open palm on her chest. "In my defense, I was already there when you walked in."

We look at each other, trading memories of the moment we met.

Me asking *What brings you to Olive Township?*

Her smirking. *You can do better than that.*

Penn and Daisy are the first to jump into action. Penn stands up to shake Mallory's hand, and Daisy, sweet as usual, pulls Mallory in for a hug.

Leaning around Penn's back, I give Vivi a hard-eyed stare that says *Get your ass up and introduce yourself.* She narrows her eyes at me, but stands up.

"This is my sister," I say, annoyance rising in me at Vivi's blank face.

Mallory nods. "Vivienne."

"I guess you did your research," Vivi says flatly.

Vivi doesn't know about Mallory's little sister yet, doesn't understand why Mallory's really here. Vivi was busy at the restaurant on Sunday and couldn't make it out to Summerhill when Mallory came to meet my mom. Vivi might be in the dark, but she should know that if I have Mallory with me, it means something. I wouldn't be bringing her around people if the situation hadn't evolved.

Daisy's foot glides across the grass, delivering a sly kick to Vivi's shin. Vivi's expression does not change. I'm not sure if she felt her best friend's physical *tsk*.

The air under this canopy is thick, and my annoyance only grows. "Vivi, knock it off. I've had a chance to get to know Mallory. It's not what you think." Vivi's attitude toward Mallory is largely my fault, so I gentle my voice and add, "It's not what *I* thought."

Vivi's gaze shifts to me. Her arms are crossed, her eyes steely, but I know my sister. She's trying to understand why we are no longer on the same team when it comes to Mallory.

To her, Mallory is still a true crime podcaster looking to rustle up unpleasant memories.

To me, Mallory has become *Mallory*. A person with a backstory. A life. Pain and regret that propels her through every day. In the span of a week, she has gone from one dimensional, to multifaceted.

And I'm not loving the way my sister is treating her. Vivi can have a pass because she doesn't know Mallory's true reason for being here, but once she knows, an attitude like this won't work for me.

"Well," Penn says, cutting through the silence. "This is fucking awkward."

A grin tugs up one corner of Daisy's mouth, and she leans into her husband's arm. "You're awfully good at stating the obvious, Sailor."

He winks at her, eyes radiating unadulterated love. "Just continuing my service to our country, Sunshine."

I bite the side of my lip and try to pretend like their loving interaction doesn't feel like tiny spikes inside my chest cavity. I've never had that. Ever. Nobody has ever looked at me with such longing, an equal mixture of *I love every part of you* combined with *I will rip off your clothes right here and right now*.

I want that someday. The problem is, I don't know if that's in the cards for me. It's entirely possible I will never have that.

"Hey, beautiful people," a male voice says from behind.

Duke swoops around my seat, dragging a chair of his own.

Vivi's shoulders slump as she attempts to retreat further back into her chair. "Is it too much to ask to be struck by lightning?" she grumps.

Duke drops quickly into his chair, not looking her way when he says, "There isn't a cloud in the sky, but keep wishing."

Vivi sends him a middle finger he doesn't see. "Heads up," he says, the words forceful and under his breath. "Overzealous mayoress incoming."

On cue, Liane Rooney's cloying voice filters from two

tents over. I can't make out what she's saying, only that inauthentic tone.

Vivi cuts a razor sharp glare at Duke. "If you brought her over here with you I will tear off your arm and beat you with it."

Mallory sits taller, craning her neck. "I met her a couple days ago when I got my hair cut."

"Did you get a cavity?" Vivi asks.

Mallory's dark eyebrows draw together. "No. Why?"

I answer for Vivi. "My sister, who apparently woke up on the wrong side of every bed in the world today, is saying that the woman is so sweet she might give you a cavity."

"Nauseatingly sugary. Fake." Vivi doubles down on her assessment. She dips her chin Liane's direction, saying, "She specialty orders those heels she wears. Can't trust a bitch that bougie."

A burst of raucous laughter comes from Penn, but Daisy frowns. "Vivi, you are being a pill right now. Liane Rooney is just *nice*. She always has been."

Vivi shoots Daisy a withering look. "Daisy, you of all people should know it's impossible to be that *nice*"—air quotes—"all the time. You yourself got so caught up in being this town's sweetheart you almost married someone you didn't love."

Mallory jerks forward, eyes bright and hands gripping the arms of her chair. "Wait, what?" Her curiosity turns to confusion as she glances at Penn. "Who?"

Penn, that fucker, smirks. He doesn't usually rub it in Duke's face that he's the one who ended up with Daisy after all, but he's not above sprinkling a little salt in the wound either.

Not that there's much of a wound where it concerns Duke. He loved Daisy as a friend, and still does, but he wasn't in love with her.

"Duke The Twat," Penn says, at the same time I say, "Paper Towel Duke."

Duke, bless his heart, simply points back at himself while saying, "Yours truly." He looks nonplussed at the less-than-kind nicknames Penn made for him, but then he pretends to pull guns from holsters on his hips, transitioning to middle fingers mid-air.

Vivi gasps dramatically, miming a pearl clutch. "Not the extra-spicy finger guns."

Duke ignores her and blows on the ends of his fingers, miming holstering them.

Mallory's wide brown eyes are on me as she tries to understand. I lean over the fabric arm of my chair, and Mallory meets me. Her nearness sets off alarm bells in my head, and she has me wishing I could inhale, loud and long, taking in her sweet scent.

Getting control of myself, I say, "There's too much to explain, so I'll sum it up. Duke and Daisy were engaged but they weren't in love, and then Penn came back to town after being gone for a long time. The rest is sort of history, I guess, except that it's worth mentioning Penn showed up to crash their wedding."

Mallory's mouth forms a wide O. She blinks several times, long dark lashes sweeping the delicate skin beneath her eyes. "It's like a soap opera."

Hugo

Penn is suddenly there, in our conversation. "You should know," he starts, looking at me conspiratorially, "that it was Hugo's idea for me to break up the wedding. He told me to, and I quote, *"Storm the castle."*" Penn claps me on the shoulder. Hard. "A real romantic, this one."

I open my mouth, ready to tell Penn that somebody had to stop him from being an angsty whiner about the whole thing, when a shrill voice rings out from two feet away.

"Good afternoon, ladies and gentleman." Liane Rooney offers the greeting with pomp, as if we are her benevolent subjects.

"Good afternoon, Mayoress Rooney," we all chorus, except for Mallory. It's on purpose, this singsong, meant to make her feel like a school teacher we dread seeing.

Her careful smile falters for only a second. She knows what we're doing, and she doesn't appreciate it, but she'll never tell us.

Liane turns her attention on Mallory. "You're the young lady I met at the hair salon."

"Yes," Mallory says with a smile. She sounds far more genuine than any of us. I catch my sister's gaze behind Liane's back, and she rolls her eyes. Vivi is usually no-nonsense, but this is extreme. Maybe something happened with her ex? I wouldn't be surprised. Though he was the one who was unfaithful in their marriage, he does everything he can to absolve himself of the guilt by trying to make Vivi feel like she caused him to step out. My sister might talk a tough game, but on the inside, she's sensitive.

Liane is saying something to Mallory about coming by her booth later for prickly pear lemonade. Then she turns to Duke. "Duke, make sure you call the mayor and schedule some time with him. He'd like to talk to you about a new hotel chain looking to build here in the next few years. Just some due diligence."

Duke nods dutifully. "Yes, ma'am."

Liane spends a minute asking Daisy how things are going on her parents' thoroughbred farm. Daisy smiles her trademark warm and winning grin, and answers politely. Despite finally putting herself first and following her heart by choosing Penn, she remains the town golden girl.

"Well, I just wanted to thank you all for coming today," Liane says, walking off on her bougie heels to torture another group of people.

"It's as if she believes she is hosting this event," Vivi gripes, watching Liane's retreating form.

"You know that's how she is," Duke says. "She mother hen's the whole town."

Vivi's arms cross. "I don't like it."

"We couldn't tell," Penn mutters.

Vivi points at him. "Don't sass me."

Suddenly, I have the urge to walk away, to take Mallory and be on my own with her. I love sitting with my friends and bullshitting, but that's not why we're here.

Tipping my head Mallory's direction, I ask, "You ready to explore?"

She glances around the group, eyes landing back on mine. "I think I'm done absorbing."

I stand up, offering her my hand. She doesn't need the assistance, not in any real physical capacity.

I like the idea of treating her well. Given that she's pregnant, without a partner, tells me somebody recently treated her poorly. I don't like thinking any woman was mistreated, but it's especially upsetting when it comes to Mallory.

"I'm going to take Mallory around the festival," I inform the group, thumbing behind myself.

I await Vivi's snide remark, but mercifully, she stays quiet.

"It was nice to meet you," Mallory says to everyone.

We make it a few feet away when I hear Duke say, "Somebody please tell me who that woman is."

Mallory chuckles, and I sigh in apology. "Sorry about that. I never bring women around. I think my friends are in shock."

"No apology necessary. I like observing, and there was a lot to soak in."

Her comment piques my interest. "Tell me more."

"Well," Mallory says, stopping at a homemade soap vendor. "Your sister isn't open to talking about your dad. Not with me, at least."

"She doesn't know your history yet. Or why you're here."

Mallory selects a cube of sample soap from the tray, the one with a thin slice of lemon poking out of the top and leaves of rosemary inside. She lifts it to her nose, inhaling. "You can tell her. Or I can. I'd rather have her on board."

"Me, too. I've seen mules less stubborn than my sister." Mallory offers me the soap, and I take it. "I have this in my kitchen. The owner uses cold-pressed olive oil in her recipe."

"Your olive oil?" Mallory asks, eyebrows raised.

I nod. Carley, the shop owner, comes to say hello. Mallory introduces herself, explaining she's in Olive Township for a visit. She doesn't seem interested in telling people the real reason she's here, so I follow her lead and introduce her this way as we walk throughout the festival.

The sun burns hotter in the sky as the day progresses. Mallory seems to enjoy meeting people, shaking their hands and asking questions relevant to their products. I already know everybody, so I stand back and watch her. She's a natural people person, with a warm smile and eyes that hold authentic interest.

With a light touch on Mallory's lower back, I say, "I don't know about you, but I'm about ready for food and drink."

"Same," she agrees. "And a bathroom." She points at her belly. "I probably reach my step goal every day walking to and from the bathroom, thanks to the baby."

Her hand hovers over her midsection as if she wants to caress it, but won't allow herself to. Her reason for being in town isn't the only thing she's keeping a secret from everybody. If I hadn't seen her prenatal vitamins fall from her purse, she probably wouldn't have told me, either.

I want to know why that is, but that feels like a lot to

unpack, and we're in the middle of a crowded public space. Another time, then.

"Do you have five minutes to swing by and see my mom at the Summerhill booth? I promise we'll find a bathroom right after that."

"And food and drink?" she adds hopefully.

"All the things," I assure her, grabbing her hand and weaving her around the back of a row of white tents. We come out the other side and head for the Summerhill tent at the end of the row. Despite being the most commercially successful vendor here by a mile, my mother has insisted we keep our tent modest. *Everybody knows who we are and what we offer*, she says. She's right, of course, but I managed to sneak a stack of tri-fold glossy pamphlets on the table this year. I'm doing what I can to revamp our website and bring it into modern times, but until the new site goes live, paper marketing and word-of-mouth are the best ways for me to make people aware of all the new experiences being offered at Summerhill.

Employees of Summerhill usually sign up for time slots to run the booth throughout the day. My time slot isn't for a few more hours, but Vivi and my mom are running it now. Everly and Knox stand beside Vivi, helping her in ways that don't look very helpful.

"Mallory," my mom says when she catches sight of us walking up.

"Mrs. De la Vega," Mallory greets.

My mom crooks an eyebrow, and Mallory laughs. "Sonya," she amends, and my mom gives a swift nod of approval.

"Hello again," Mallory says to Vivi.

In my opinion, it's more of a greeting than my sister deserves after her behavior earlier.

Vivi's expression is cool, but my mom knows better and she is having none of it.

"Vivienne Alexandra De la Vega I am going to rename you Petty Betty." My mom reaches out, pinching the delicate skin on the underside of Vivi's arm.

Vivi snatches her arm back. "I am looking out for you, Mom," she argues. Her gaze runs over her kids, playing at her feet. "I am looking out for everybody."

"My daughter, I love you deeply, but I am a grown ass woman. If I've decided it's time to open up about your father's murder, then that's what I've decided."

"Grown ass woman," Everly parrots, head popping up and leaning on Vivi's mid-thigh. "What is murder?" she asks, the childlike voice at a juxtaposition to the ugliness of the word.

Vivi brushes a hand over Everly's hair. "I will tell you later."

"You better promise," Everly demands, one hand propped on her hip. "Sometimes you say you'll tell me somethin' later, but you don't." The word *sometimes* comes out like *sun-tines*, and the innocence and sweetness of it makes me chuckle.

"Hey Everly, if she forgets, you tell me." I point back at myself. "I'm the big brother. I'll deal with her."

Vivi likely has numerous hand gestures and various expletives ready to fling, but she's stuck being a good

Hugo

example in front of her kids. The most she can do now is narrow her eyes.

Beside me, Mallory shifts. The movement draws Vivi's attention to her, and Vivi says, "You've earned the trust of my mom and my brother."

Mallory is nodding, but she stays quiet, as if she knows Vivi is working through something.

"Hugo said it's not what we thought, so..."

Mallory leans forward, gripping the edge of the rectangular table, where everything is set up. She must be having a hard time hearing Vivi with the sounds of the festival in the background.

"...I'm willing to listen, too, and"—Vivi's eyebrows suddenly cinch—"Mallory, are you ok?"

My head whips to Mallory, standing only inches from me. Face pale. Lips lacking her natural rosy shade. As if compressed by the air above her and the packed earth below her, she crumples.

But I'm there, arms out, sinking to my knees and catching her.

Mallory slumps in my arms, unconscious.

"Get the medic," I bark to Vivi.

Vivi rounds the table. "I'll be right back," she says as she passes me. My mom gathers her grandkids in her arms.

"Vivi," I call out, as Vivi continues on. "She's pregnant."

Chapter 13
Mallory

My eyes flutter open.

Bright sun, relentlessly filtering through the thick green canvas above my head. Voices nearby. Beneath me, something hard and unforgiving.

What happened?

Scanning through my mind, I try to pull up my most recent memory.

I was talking to Vivi. I was so hungry and thirsty, and hot. Her voice began to feel far away, and my vision tunneled.

I passed out.

My hands fly to my bump, feeling the small roundness, wishing I could see inside. Peanut's ok, right?

"Hey, there," a relieved voice says, curling around me like a hug. Hugo appears in the air above my head. His thumb brushes my cheek, and he murmurs, "You got your color back."

Embarrassment creeps over me. I've never passed out

before, but here I am, doing it in front of someone I'm supposed to be in an (admittedly unconventional) working relationship with. I'm gearing up to apologize when a playful light filters into Hugo's eyes, and he says, "What brings you to the medic tent?"

My breath of laughter is a relief, sweeping away my embarrassment. "You can do better than that."

Hugo takes a knee beside what I've decided is a cot. I shift, pressing my palms into the hard material and slowly pushing myself to a seated position.

"How about," Hugo says, looking up at me earnestly, gaze laden with remorse, "I do better by apologizing for not making your food and drink needs a priority?"

My hair falls across my face as I shake my head. "I should have remembered to bring one of my snacks." They are all there at the hotel, sitting on the side table where they aren't doing me any good.

"If you don't mind, I'm going to go ahead and take the blame for this one. I led you around the whole damn place without remembering you're eating and drinking for two."

My stomach rumbles. "Speaking of, is there something to get my blood sugar back up?"

Hugo hops up, reaching into the back pocket of his jeans. "You weren't out for long," he says, producing a large bright red cylinder wrapped in plastic. "Just a minute until I got you here and propped your feet up. But Vivi snagged a popsicle from a cart. It's"—he pushes on the bottom of the frozen treat, forcing the top open —"cherry. I hope that's ok."

"It's perfect," I say gratefully, accepting the popsicle. It's one of those enormous popsicles, the kind that looks pornographic.

But sugar is what I'm after, and this is available, so I don't have a choice. I try not to make it too sensual, too much like the real thing, but a phallic shape entering the mouth can't look any other way.

I avert my eyes, but my peripheral vision works just fine, and I don't miss the tense pull of Hugo's jaw, the way his throat undulates with a gulp.

He crosses his arms and angles his upper half away from me, like he's glancing out of the tent. "I should probably tell Jerry you're looking better."

"Jerry?" The cold sugar is hitting my system now, bringing me back to life.

"The medic." Hugo's still looking away. "He went to see if old man Murray is still here."

"And old man Murray is?"

"A doctor."

I frown. "I don't think I need a doctor." I feel better every second that passes.

"Jerry insisted when I told him you're pregnant."

Ahh. That makes sense. My hand grazes my belly. "I'm sure me and the baby are fine."

Hugo finally turns his gaze on me. "I need to make certain of it."

He says it with authority, but I detect a chord of worry.

"Well, then," I say, sticking the popsicle in my mouth, "I promise to be a good patient."

Hugo

A man strides into the medic tent and introduces himself as Murray. I can't help but gape. "When Hugo called you old man Murray, he meant—"

"I have a baby face," Murray says with an easy smile.

The guy looks like he should be sitting on phone books to see over the steering wheel in his vehicle. "Whatever you say, Doogie."

Murray doesn't react to the nickname. At all.

"You've heard that before, haven't you?" I ask as he directs me to lie back on the uncomfortable cot. Hugo takes the popsicle from me.

"Only every time I see a new patient," Murray says. He pulls a stethoscope from a genuine Gladstone bag.

"Look at that bag. Now I definitely believe you're a doctor."

Hugo coughs, but I know he's covering up a laugh.

Murray presses his stethoscope to my belly, and a hush falls over the three of us. The seconds stretch, each one growing, and then he sits taller, taking the piece from his ears.

"A strong heartbeat," he announces.

A tenuous string inside me snaps. I didn't realize how worried I was until this moment. My subconscious was hiding my fear, even from me. A lone tear trickles from my right eye, and when I reach up to wipe it away, I find Hugo watching me.

I cannot read the expression on his face. Sympathetic maybe, but no. That's not right. *Relieved.*

I need to make certain of it. Hugo was worried about

us. Me and Peanut. A second tear leaks from the corner of my eye.

Damn hormones.

Murray listens to my heart, and declares me healthy. "Vasovagal syncope," he announces. "Fancy way of saying your blood pressure dropped and you hit the deck." He glances at Hugo. "Almost, anyway. I hear this guy caught you."

Hugo nods once in agreement. He stands back, hands in his pockets, while old man Murray gets ready to leave.

"Any other problems, please come to my office," he says to me. I thank him, and he ducks from the tent.

I sit up again, feeling remarkably better thanks to the hit of sugar from the popsicle. My stomach, though, has other ideas. Needs. A loud, insistent rumble roars audibly.

Hugo offers his free hand, as if he wants to help me up. "Time to feed you two."

You two. Me and Peanut. A duo. Just the two of us. From the moment Dylan signed away his rights to this baby, I'd known we were on our own. But it's not until now that I'm realizing quite what that means. What it all entails.

For starters, I'm going to need to step up. Peanut depends on me. I can't run around without food and water for hours on end. And I can't expect a chivalrous man like Hugo to come riding in on his white horse and save me. He does know how to wield a sword though, so if there were any man who would be capable of such, it would be the tall, dark and mind-bendingly handsome man standing in front of me.

It would be rude to ignore his offered hand, so I place my palm in his. His fingers curl around me, and I shove away the jolt of electricity at his touch. As soon as I'm standing, I break the connection. Hugo hands me the softening popsicle. "I'll grab food on my walk back to the inn."

"I'm happy to take you somewhere," Hugo says. His expression is open, honest. He's a good man who wants to do a good thing.

"Sammich is around the corner from here." I thumb over my shoulder, though I have no idea what direction I'm indicating. "I'll grab whatever it was you ordered that day." The day we met, when he didn't know who I was. When his eyes crinkled at the corners, and he flirted with me.

He nods solemnly, but he looks conflicted.

"Thank you for introducing me to people today."

"You're welcome." He motions with his head. "Order the Bellamy sandwich, Hugo style." He narrows his eyes at the popsicle in my hand. "And finish that."

Cherry red melted popsicle drips off the end, sliding down my thumb. "I will. I was waiting because—"

"Yeah, yeah. I know." He shakes his head quickly, as if clearing it. "Go."

I listen, sidestepping him on my way out of the tent. Skirting the edge of the festival, I find my way to the sidewalk of Olive Avenue. I finish my popsicle in no time, enjoying the burn of the cold and licking the melted juice from my hands because I don't have a napkin.

Neither of the ladies I met on my first day in Olive Township are working in Sammich today. I order the way Hugo instructed, requesting they package it for takeaway. I also buy a bag of chips and a cookie at the counter, scarfing them down as I wait for my order to be ready.

It seems everybody is at the festival today, locals and tourists alike. Sammich is a ghost town. Even Olive Avenue is quiet, only a handful of people coming in and out of the shops that buffet the road. I'm sitting at a table next to the front window, brushing chip and cookie crumbs from my lap, when I spot Liane across the street. She's stepping from a shop that says Sweet Nothings in white on a large lavender sign. Glancing right, and then left, and apparently appeased by whatever she sees or does not see, Liane dips her hand in her large purse. She comes away with something small, and metal. A flask, I think. My guess is confirmed when she twists off the top and splashes whatever is inside into what appears to be a to-go cup of coffee.

She stashes the flask back in her purse, blows across the top of the hot liquid, and takes a sip. Her gaze lifts as she's drinking, landing squarely on mine as if magnetized. She flinches, then looks abashed, like she's been caught doing something wrong. I don't care that she's spicing up her coffee in the middle of the day, and I doubt anybody else would either. To communicate this, I wave and smile.

Liane charges across the street. She looks like a

rushing bull, but without the crazed look of vengeful indignation.

As I watch, she clears the curb of the sidewalk in her *bougie heels*. For a brief moment I think maybe I am not her destination, but it's wishful thinking. It's not that I don't want to talk with her, but also, I don't want to talk with her. I want to eat my sandwich and write down every interaction I had today in the notebook in my hotel room. I need to list all the people I met, the businesses they run. Nobody struck me as suspicious, but it's good to get a clear picture of the town.

Liane yanks on the Sammich door handle, and unless she had a sudden hankering for a sandwich, I am her goal.

She slows when she enters, approaching me. Her golden bob is perfectly styled, artfully cut so she can tuck one side behind her ear and still have the ends curve forward to fall against her neck.

"You didn't see that," she says coyly, pulling out the seat opposite me.

"See what?" I ask, winking at her.

Elbows on the table and hands clasped, she leans forward conspiratorially. "Between you and me, events like these can be exhausting. When your husband is the mayor, you're always"—she pauses to create air quotes—"on." She sits back, her hands moving to rest in her lap.

"That sounds like it could get tiring after a while," I respond diplomatically. She must have no idea that people can hear it in her voice, the way she forces herself to be this way.

The Sammich cashier appears at the table, setting down my order wrapped in a white paper bag. I thank her, and she asks if she can get anything for Liane. "I'm ok with my coffee, but thank you."

Liane peers at the bag on the table in front of me. "Eat," she instructs. "I heard what happened to you."

I'm too hungry to wait on Liane to decide she needs to move on from this impromptu visit, so I remove the sandwich and take a bite. It's heavenly, this sandwich, piled high with fresh turkey and the best crunch from the layer of potato chips.

Liane taps a pink painted nail on the table between us. "I also heard you're expecting."

It's not a big deal if people find out, but I didn't want to advertise it either. I'm in Olive Township for a very specific reason, which has nothing to do with expecting a child.

Except, it does. It has everything to do with this baby, and simultaneously nothing at all.

"Sixteen weeks," I answer. "Seventeen, actually." The smile that appears on my face when I say it is still new to me. The announcement was not joyous for other people, and so I felt it could not be joyous for me. The feeling is fading, thankfully.

Liane beams. "Do you know what you're having?"

"Not yet." I take a small bite of my sandwich, chewing and swallowing it down. "I missed the appointment this week where I would've learned."

"You know what? It doesn't matter." Liane sips her coffee. "You'll love that baby more than anything." Her eyes grow soft, far away and fond, like she's remembering. "Nursing them through an illness, wiping away their tears, you'll do anything in the world for them."

Liane's words are kind, but a sting accompanies them. Maybe my own mother felt this way once upon a time, but it stopped. One day she was my mom, and the next, it was over for us.

I'm swallowing another bite when Liane asks how I know Hugo. "I met him last week, in this shop, actually." As I'm talking, an idea forms in my mind. "How long have you been Mayoress?" The title is superficial and silly, but she seems to prefer it, and I have a feeling appealing to her ego will get me where I want to go.

"A very long time," she answers. "Probably about as long as you've been alive. Nobody else in this town seems to want the job. Every time Alan runs, he's uncontested."

Perfect.

"Then I bet you know all there is to know about this place."

A twinkle sparks in her eye. "Not a lot gets by me." She pats my arm. "Which is why I don't buy your story that you're here for a visit. If that were true, you'd be at the spa."

"Busted." I laugh lightly, giving a playful show of having been caught. I don't enjoy lying, but telling the truth about why I'm here isn't the best choice either. I've already told Miranda the hairstylist that I'm a student, and staying with one story is safest. "But to be fair, I did go to the spa. I'm getting my master's degree in criminal justice, and for my final project I'm supposed to examine an unsolved case. So I chose—"

"Simon De la Vega."

I nod somberly. "Yes."

Her hands wrap around her paper cup. "Quite a case you've chosen."

"I'm supposed to gather as much information as I can, learn what happened and what I would have done differently, if anything."

Without me asking, Liane starts in. "We were devastated by what happened. My husband was a fairly new mayor at the time, and it was difficult to rally the town. And those kids? Poor babies. It's obvious how the loss shaped them." I nod and listen, finishing my sandwich while she speaks. "Just awful what happened to their dad. In the middle of the day, no less. How somebody gets away with a crime like that, I have no idea."

"Do you know if the detectives who worked on the case are still on the force?"

"There were two," Liane answers. "One retired and moved to Alaska. The other is still working."

"Name?"

"Ricardo Towles." Liane points at my purse. "Write his name down in your phone."

"Good idea," I say, taking her suggestion. She doesn't know I'm great with names, and remembering what people say. Back in the day, before my family unit imploded, I dominated in the game of Memory, to the point where my family refused to play me anymore.

"What about David Boylan? I saw his name in newspaper articles from the time."

Liane sighs. "David Boylan. I haven't heard that name in a long time."

"He was the—"

"Postal worker who was the only suspect in the case. Let me tell you about that man."

Liane points at my dark phone screen. "You can take notes."

I nod like I'm eager to take notes, but really what I'm doing is tempering my excitement at having stumbled upon the loosest lips in this town.

"David Boylan was a bit of an odd duck. I've never seen a man so excited about rare coins."

I type *rare coins*.

Liane keeps going. "He was quiet and kept to himself. In this town, that makes you odd. I don't know if you've noticed, Mallory, but everybody here is very friendly."

"I've noticed," I assure, as she expects me to. There's no need to argue, to tell her about Braxton the night manager. He most definitely does not fit her profile of an Olive Township denizen.

"Of course, sometimes people are just different, and that's ok," she rushes to make the caveat. "But on the day Simon died, David had been delivering mail. He was on Six Digit Road when he got a flat tire." My eyes widen as I furiously tap my phone's keyboard. I'd known there was a person of interest, but none of these details.

Liane continues. "Now, I happen to know a detail that was not released to the public at the time. Not only were David Boylan's tire tracks found at the scene of the crime, but so was his blood."

Liane pauses, letting that sink in. She's a masterful storyteller.

"But the police didn't have enough to arrest him?"

Her head shakes back-and-forth. "It was the Olive Festival that day. Too many witnesses were able to place him at the event at the same time the coroner said Simon was attacked."

Excitement bubbles up inside me. Not the good kind that leads to something happy, but the kind that accompanies a shot of adrenaline. "So he had an accomplice?"

"That was the theory, but they could never find evidence of it. Between a lack of evidence, no motive, and a handful of people on the record saying they saw him, Boylan was released. The whole thing ruined his life though. He moved away immediately, and nobody has heard from him since."

"Hmm," I say, like I'm mulling over the facts, feeling only the curiosity of your average, everyday true crime podcaster. I know better than to take what I hear or see at face value. Isn't there always more to the story? But damn if there isn't a twinge of a little something in the center of my chest. Hope.

"Well," Liane says, tipping her coffee cup left to right over the table. "My coffee is finished, and I should be getting back to the festival. My husband always delivers a speech to close out the day's events, and he prefers when I stand beside him."

Together we throw away our trash, and I send a goodbye wave in the direction of the cashier. She's leaning against the counter, on her phone, and doesn't see me.

"Congrats on your bun in the oven," Liane says when we step into the sunshine. It's not as bright now as it was earlier, the rays less direct. "If you need anything, please don't hesitate to ask. As long as you're in town, I'm happy to be helpful."

She hustles back across the street and down the sidewalk, bougie heels snapping the pavement.

The woman has me baffled, a position in which I don't often find myself. She wants to be the queenly mayoress, but inside there's a woman who wants to gossip and spice up her coffee. I feel bad for her, even if it appears she's constructed the gilded cage and put herself in it.

Belly full, I make it back to Olive Inn. Braxton is at the front desk, folded over his phone. I've seen him a handful of times since that first day, and he doesn't get less creepy.

I walk quickly across the small lobby, and although he didn't look up when I walked in, I feel his eyes on me as I go. Maybe I should check one of the other hotels in town, see if they have room for me. Maybe people will leave now that the Olive Festival is over.

I spend the evening writing down everything I can remember from today in my notebook, and then begin using my trusty search bar to learn more about those individuals. The day at the hair salon was more fruitful than I could've imagined. I had a feeling Liane was full of information, and I was right.

Chapter 14

Hugo

Penn: So. You brought the true crime podcaster to the festival.

Hugo: If this is a news report, it's very boring.

Penn: You do know you were holding her hand when you walked up, right?

Hugo: I wasn't holding her hand so much as leading her over.

Penn: Was her hand in yours?

Penn: No answer necessary. We both already know it.

Hugo: Do you have a point to this? It's late.

Penn: I'm giving you shit because there's something else I want to say, and I'm not sure how to say it.

> Hugo: Use your words SAILOR.

Penn: Hi, Hugo. It's Daisy. I took the phone from SAILOR. What he wants to say is

Penn: I wrestled the phone back from my wife. What I want to say is, are you aware the podcaster is pregnant?

> Hugo: MALLORY

Penn: ??

> Hugo: Stop calling her podcaster. She has a name.

> Hugo: And yes, I'm aware.

Penn: You were holding a pregnant woman's hand? Do you think her boyfriend/spouse/partner would love to see you do that?

> Hugo: She doesn't have any of the above.

> Hugo: Also, fuck right off. You came back to town and PRETENDED NOT TO BE YOURSELF. I have carte blanche to do whatever I want for the rest of time.

Penn: This is a 'do as I say, not as I do' situation.

> Hugo: Convenient.

Penn: You're letting Mallory look into your dad?

Hugo

> Hugo: Yep.

Penn: Why?

> Hugo: For one, it's a free country and she could look into my dad with or without my blessing. For two, she has a good reason for wanting to.

Penn: Which is?

> Hugo: I'm going to let her fill you in on that.

Chapter 15

Hugo

"Are you fully recovered from your fainting spell yesterday?" I ask Mallory as I pour myself a cup of coffee. Her name flashed on my phone a moment ago, and I swear I've never answered a call so quickly.

"Yes, thanks to a certain someone's heroics." Mallory's voice wafts into my kitchen through my phone, lying on the counter on speaker. "And sandwich recommendations. I ordered the Bellamy, Hugo style."

"I know what I'm doing when it comes to sandwiches," I reply, stirring half and half into the dark liquid.

"And popsicles," she adds. Do I detect a hint of a smile in her voice?

"Those, too." Holding my coffee in one hand, I grab the phone and push out the screen door into the morning sun. "It would be fine if you were calling me only to compliment my sandwich and popsicle prowess, but is there something else on your mind?"

Hugo

"Liane Rooney," Mallory says, matter of fact.

I situate myself in a chair, setting my coffee on a side table shaped like a drum. Like my father, this is one of my favorite spots in my house. It's around the corner from the morning sun, but allows me full view of the orchard, the way the sun's rays reach out, slipping through the olive grove like a caress.

"What about her?" I ask.

"Put a splash of liquor in that woman's coffee and she sings like a canary."

"You liquored up the mayoress?" I joke, reaching for my cup. Mallory isn't physically present, so I don't have to wipe off the stupid grin I'm wearing. There's something about the woman that fascinates me. Her sense of humor, her boldness, the way she knows when to be the speaker and when to be the listener. She's discerning.

"I saw her splash a little something in her coffee yesterday afternoon, but don't go telling anybody that."

"Your secret is safe with me." My right ankle comes up to cross over my left knee, settling in. "Tell me what the esteemed lady said."

"She talked about what happened to your dad. She mentioned a name..." Mallory trails off, sounding unsure.

"David Boylan," I fill in, because there is no other name that would carry weight. I've thought of him numerous times over the years, wondered if I should find out where he went, pay him a visit. For what, though? The police turned his life inside out and upside down in their quest for justice for a beloved member of the town, but found nothing. "His tire tracks were found on the road."

"And his blood," Mallory adds.

I'd been about to take a sip of my coffee, but now it's poised at my mouth. "How did you know that?" It's a detail that was never made public.

"The singing canary."

Liane Rooney knows about the blood? It doesn't make sense, but then again, when a small town buries something, it often festers and finds a way out. I can see the pathway the information traveled pretty clearly, the detectives to the sheriff, the sheriff to the mayor, the mayor to his wife.

"And now that I know, I was thinking of paying David Boylan a visit."

I look out over the grove, how the sun has risen higher and banished the shade on the trees. Is this what my dad would want? Exhume not only my old wounds, but somebody else's, too?

For years, I have thought of what I would do if I had the chance to see the one and only person of interest in my dad's murder case. I was a child when I saw him last, and could not articulate how I felt. He was cleared of any wrongdoing, but it's not easy to accept that. The heart wants justice, vengeance. It's not pretty, but it's true. I've lost count of the number of times I've been in a crowd, searching the faces of people passing me, thinking *Was it you?*

So long have I denied myself what I wanted, but here Mallory is, naming my desire out loud and making it feel acceptable. I know I've appeared to move on and heal on the outside, all the while living in a state of constant agony on the inside. I want to put my adult eyes on David Boylan. There is, of course, one massive roadblock.

"Nobody knows where he's gone."

Mallory's quiet for a moment, then says, "I do."

Chapter 16

Hugo

MALLORY STEPS FROM THE FRONT DOOR OF OLIVE Inn. She's gorgeous in a dress I'm certain my sister would call *baby doll*. She does this a lot, wearing clothing that is strategically loose in certain places. I'm not sure why, but she seems hell-bent on keeping her pregnancy to herself. It's her news, and her business, but is there something more behind it? Is it possible the father doesn't know about the baby?

Mallory strides down the sidewalk toward my car, looking better than any model on any runway. She wears white sneakers, her purse held loosely in her hand and bumping against her calf as she walks. This woman is a lot of things, including a conundrum.

A thought pierces my brain, my heart, and my whole damn body, has my fingers tightening on the steering wheel. Is Mallory keeping her pregnancy quiet because the father was abusive? Is she hiding?

Mallory slides into the passenger seat, and the smile I

wore when she first walked out has been stolen from my face by my maddening thought.

"What?" Mallory asks, arms crossing.

"You're wearing a dress that keeps your stomach a secret. Again."

"So?" she asks, voice clipped.

"Why are you keeping the baby a secret?"

"None of your damn business."

She's right. It's not. But I can't sit here and wonder if she's been hurt. I have to know, so I can demolish the man who did it.

I turn so I'm facing her. "Mallory, it's not my business, but I'm dying over here thinking the father hurt you and you've left town to protect your baby."

Mallory's jaw drops. "Hugo, no. That's not at all what happened. I haven't been chatty about my pregnancy because that's not why I'm in Olive Township. Although my reasons for being here are personal, I am still a professional. This is my job." Mallory glances down at her hands, folded in her lap. Her thumb runs the length of her knuckles. "But if I'm being honest with you and myself, I am still getting used to the idea of being pregnant. And being a single mom. This baby was a surprise, and it feels a bit like sitting in the sun beside a pool, and then suddenly being thrown into the cold water."

Relief fills me. I don't have to enlist Penn in a secret mission to track down some guy and beat the snot out of him.

I shift into Drive, appeased now. Mallory and I make a stop at Sweet Nothings for coffee and pastries. "For the two of you," I say, holding up the box in Mallory's direction.

She pats her carpet bag of a purse. "I remembered snacks today."

I shake my head. "They won't be better than Sal and Adela's homemade pop tarts."

Mallory grins over the top of my car. "I could spend the day sitting in the bakery and listening to them bicker."

"Stop in anytime," I tell her, glancing at the store. "They're always going at it."

Mallory squints at me, but I say nothing. Just the words *going at it* have my mind serving me detailed and salacious memories of a certain beautiful woman with her mouth wrapped around a popsicle. Don't let me get started on the way the coloring stained her lips an inviting shade of red.

Using an open palm, I smack the hood of my car. "Get in, Gumshoe."

She sends me a wink over the top of the car. "You got it, Swordsman."

We're only a few minutes outside of town when Mallory turns to me and says, "I'm going to tell you about my baby's father."

Involuntarily, my fingers squeeze the steering wheel. She said he didn't abuse her, but he sure as hell has abandoned her. The idea of it has me seeing red, but in an effort not to dissuade Mallory from opening up to me, I school my strong reaction and simply nod.

"Dylan was my trainer at the gym. Sounds common, right?"

Hugo

I steal a glance her way, find her grimacing. "As common as anything else, I suppose."

"We had a casual relationship. We were upfront about that, so there weren't supposed to be hurt feelings. I guess I should back up here and say that years ago my gynecologist told me I had too much scar tissue on my ovaries to ever be able to have kids. A result of endometriosis. I was told that *if* I could get pregnant—and that's a big *if*—it would require medication or surgery. Possibly both. I was careless with Dylan. And then I went for my annual checkup and my gynecologist walked in and told me I was pregnant."

So much for schooling my reaction. I'm shaking my head and blowing out a heavy exhale.

"Me, too," Mallory says. "And throw in crying and saying *Is this a joke?* at least twenty-seven times. When I told Dylan, he was horrified. Said some things he hasn't asked forgiveness for, but I've chosen to forgive because I don't want to harbor bad feelings toward him."

I'm more than happy to harbor enough bad feelings for the both of us. I don't know exactly how this story will end, but I pretty much know how this story will end.

"Dylan asked if I'd consider terminating the pregnancy, but I said no." Mallory looks down at her midsection, pressing a hand to the fabric of her dress. Her small bump is on display now, and she palms it possessively. "This might be my only chance to have a baby, and I want it. Even if that means I have to be a single mother." Mallory sighs and looks out the windshield. My car loops along the switchbacks as we climb in elevation. Dusty desert mountains rise on all sides of us. "Dylan signed away his rights as a parent. Every single one of them."

The admission, though I knew it was coming, still blows me away. I've been casual too, with literally every woman I've dated. But had she come to me and said she was pregnant, I would have said, *no we are pregnant*. Because there isn't a chance in hell I'd let my son or daughter grow up without me. As long as I'm breathing on God's green earth, I'd be in their life.

"Can I speak frankly?" I ask. She might not want to hear what I have to say.

She motions out. "The floor is yours."

"Dylan is weak."

Mallory smiles wryly, patting each of her biceps. "He's jacked, actually."

I'm shaking my head before she has finished her sentence. "Weak in character. He lacks the moral fiber to make the right choice."

I feel her looking at me, the way her eyes run over the right side of my face. This is a tricky part of the drive, acute angle turns that require two hands on the wheel and two eyes locked forward. No harm will come to Mallory or her baby on my watch.

After a moment of quiet, Mallory says, "He wouldn't have made a good father. He's not a bad person, but he had a lot of personal issues he needed to get through. It would've prevented him from being the person my baby deserves."

I'm so in awe of Mallory right now I can barely settle on what to say to her. If I weren't driving, it would be easier to focus my thoughts. It might actually be a good thing I'm driving right now, because I'm thinking things I shouldn't say out loud, thoughts that extend beyond the boundaries of a professional relationship.

That's what we're in, right? A professional relationship? Two people working toward a common goal. So I say, "Bravery is looking in the face of something scary, and doing it anyhow."

"The same could be said of stupidity."

I chuckle hard, and in my peripheral vision, I see Mallory give a pleased shrug.

"All jokes aside," she says, "I know what I'm doing is unconventional. And telling people I'm pregnant leads to questions I don't want to answer over and over. At some point, I won't be able to hide it anymore. But for now, the story is only mine. I guess I'd like to keep that going for a little longer."

"That makes sense." We climb our way out of the switchbacks, rising up in elevation until we even out. From here, it's pinion trees and desert for the next two hours. I pull a homemade pop tart from the box of pastries and devour it.

At some point, Mallory leans her head back and falls asleep. The road is mostly straight now, and I take the opportunity to steal glances at her. Her face is soft in slumber. Peaceful.

My friends were right to be stunned by the way I brought Mallory to the Olive Festival. She could have arrived by herself, could have walked around and met people on her own. But I wanted to be a part of it, and my friends immediately recognized that it was unlike me. And then I held her hand, solidifying the consternation they felt.

Mallory, and her baby, are the first real threat to the way I've been living.

Maybe that's a good thing.

Chapter 17

Mallory

DAVID BOYLAN LIVES IN THE SMALL, ALPINE TOWN of Sugar Creek, Arizona.

He has a social media profile that resembles a ghost town. That would've been a dead end, except one time, ten years ago, when he changed his relationship status. He married, and his wife is the kind of person who turns herself inside out online. Casserole recipes, crocheting patterns, illnesses, and the oddball *If you love me, pass this on* posts. And also her husband's favorite pastime, *rare coins*. David holding a rare coin. The two of them at rare coin shows.

I'm proud (kind of) to say I now know a lot about the rare coin market. After locating various websites serving as rare coin marketplaces, I narrowed my search to those in Arizona.

David could've gone anywhere, but I was hoping he'd stay within the state. It's huge, after all. Maricopa County is bigger than some states. Hours of combing through listings, and then I spotted one for a coin from a Bolivian shipwreck, and the seller's name was DaBoy.

Hugo's fancy car smoothes off the highway, cruising past the town sign. "I've been here before," he says, turning the wheel with the heel of his palm. "Only a few months ago to pick up the custom wedding arch I had made by a local guy. Daisy and Penn were the first to get married under it."

"I saw on your website that you offer weddings. That's really cool."

Hugo glances at me, eyebrows raised as he slows before a red light. "I forget you've done your research on me."

The back of my neck heats, but then he leans an inch closer to me and says, "I can give you a tour of Summerhill. Just say when."

"I'd love that."

Hugo follows the navigational directions spouting from his phone, winding his way through the most adorable small town. The vibe here is very different from Olive Township. Pine trees and cottonwood's provide shade, and the stores on the main street are made out of red brick. It has a classic feel to it, whereas Olive Township is decidedly more desert with its white stucco walls and red tile roofs dulled by persistent sun.

"Here we are," Hugo says, slowly pulling up to the home. It's small, with a tidy front yard. Brightly colored flowers spill from a hanging pot affixed to the top edge of the porch. "Are you prepared to purchase a rare coin?" He smirks.

Hugo

I pat my purse. "I came ready."

Hugo's features rearrange into a serious expression. I can't imagine what he must be thinking right now, looking at the home of the person the police questioned in the murder of his father.

"We can turn around," I say, reaching for his forearm. The muscles there are long and ropy, hewn from hard work. A light dusting of dark hair runs over his skin, and I'm trying very hard not to notice it too much. "If it's overwhelming, if it's upsetting, if you change your mind at any point, we can leave."

He looks down at my grip on his arm. With his free hand, he covers my own. "Why aren't you nervous? This affects you, too. Just as much as me."

"Because we don't know for sure if your dad and my sister are connected. I'm simply going on a hunch, and perhaps a bit of desperation. If I put too much emotional investment into every possibility, it messes with my objectivity, which in turn affects my thought process and my choices. Not that I have a lot of objectivity with this case," I add. "But I am trying to operate the way I normally do." Maintaining a clear head is the best way to bring my sister's killer to justice.

"I know this guy didn't do it," Hugo says. His fingers over my hand are still immobile, but they twitch like he wants to move them. "He couldn't have been in two places at once. But sometimes, I wish it were him. Is that terrible?"

"Not at all. You're not saying you want an innocent

man to pay, you're saying you wish the murder had been simple to solve."

"I guess, yeah." Hugo's fingers inch over my hand, and I think more than anything he wants contact. Physical touch. "Is this ok?" he asks, his fingertips feathering over my skin.

"Yes," I whisper, trying like hell to keep the breathiness out of my voice.

"Do you ever think about what you would say if there comes a day you can look at Maggie's murderer in the face?"

I'm having a hard time focusing on our conversation, so juxtaposed by the feelings his touch is setting off in my body. "I've had fantasies about it. Daydreams, whatever you want to call it. Mostly they consist of me slicing him into pieces."

Hugo's eyes widen. "I have a sword you can borrow."

This draws a smile from me. "What about you? Have you ever thought about what you would say, if given the chance?"

"Only all the time." His fingers have stilled, save for a thumb that runs circles over my skin. "I would say, 'When you murdered my father, you created the day you would die by his son's hand.'"

"Hugo," I murmur. I can't help it. That sentence could only be uttered by somebody with immense pain in their heart. My hand slips out from under his, only to reach up and lightly cup his face. Pain dances behind his eyes, and I feel a renewed sense of determination. I want to find the man who killed Simon De la Vega. I want to give Hugo, and the rest of his family, the chance to heal.

"I know it sounds dramatic, but I wish so badly that I could have been my dad's hero. That somehow, I could have saved him." Tears swim in his eyes, this big, rough man with the tanned forearms and callused hands.

"I understand," I whisper, wrapping him in a hug. His arms encircle me, and we sink into the embrace. I know we are attracted to each other, we have been since that first day, but this is the hug of two people who share a unique burden, who want to put down what we carry, if only briefly.

His chest fills, expanding, before he exhales. But he doesn't let me go. Instead, he turns his face into my hair. He's breathing me in.

I like it. It's everything I can do not to let my palm roam his back, drag my nails up his neck and over his scalp. It's a line I dare not cross, but I want to. My goodness, do I want to.

"There he is," Hugo grounds out. We let go of each other, and I look out the passenger window. The man I saw in the pictures on social media stands on the front porch, hands tucked in the pockets of his khaki pants. He lifts an uncertain hand, waving.

A thrill runs through me. Could this be a step toward understanding more about what happened that day? I hope so.

"Are you ready?" I ask Hugo. This is much more personal for him, and I want him to be ok. As ok as a person can be in this situation.

"As I'll ever be."

Hugo exits the car first, smooth and practiced. I'm not accustomed to climbing from a car so low to the ground, especially in a dress. I only make it so far as to wind my purse strap around my shoulder and place a steadying hand on the doorframe when Hugo appears, opening the door all the way and offering his hand.

There's something about the way he does it without pageantry, like it is second nature, a thing he does.

"Thank you for getting my door," I say, stepping up beside him on the sidewalk.

"I'll always get your door, Mallory."

The declaration makes me feel warm and fuzzy, but I don't have time to dwell in the feeling. We have an audience fifteen feet away.

"Mr. Boylan?" I say, walking up the driveway with Hugo. "I'm Mallory Hawkins, the woman who responded to your listing." We stop a few feet from the man standing in the same place, hands still tucked in his pockets. Gesturing beside me, I say, "This is—"

"Simon De la Vega," David Boylan wheezes the words, a touch of disbelief and horror. He stumbles back as if he's been punched.

Hugo inhales audibly. "Hugo. Simon's son." The words are a rumble, sheets of pain covering a heap of emotions.

David shakes his head rapidly back-and-forth. "You said you wanted to buy a coin." His panicked eyes find mine. "You...you." The sentence dies.

I feel bad. The police were right. This man is not a killer.

"We are here for the coin, Mr. Boylan. And anything else you can tell me about my dad."

The screen door flies open. Out steps the maker of casseroles, follower of crochet patterns. Paula Boylan. "What's going on out here?" she demands, stepping up to her husband's side.

"Olive Township found me," he mutters.

Daggers form in Paula's gaze, and she sends them our way. "David had nothing to do with what happened there. He's innocent, and you need to leave."

I curl a hand around my midsection, pressing my dress to my body, accentuating my baby bump. For good measure, I lean into my stomach, making it appear bigger than it is. Maybe it's low, using my bump this way, but I want to show David and Paula we aren't a threat. And really, there isn't much that's less threatening than a pregnant woman.

They both see my pregnancy. They both visibly soften. I push my shoulder into Hugo's rigid arm, snake my hand around his elbow and tighten my grip. Hugo looks down at me, and I watch his eyes take in the roundness of my tummy, on display. He softens, too.

Do babies soothe the savage beast? Bring healing to those who need it?

David looks at Hugo with kindness now, no fear. "I told the police everything I know. Everything that took place."

Hugo nods. "I understand that, but I was so young when it all happened. The events get confused in my mind. Sometimes I don't know what's real, or what I imagined in my nine-year-old brain."

"Iced tea," Paula says suddenly, clapping her hands together. "Why don't you two come on around back, and David will meet you out there. I'll be along shortly with drinks." She smiles graciously. "Perhaps there's more to talk about than we thought."

David looks apprehensive, but he doesn't argue.

Paula disappears inside the house, and David looks at us helplessly.

"I can invent an emergency, if you'd like," Hugo says. "We can go."

After a moment's consideration, David says no. "Your dad was always very nice to me. If there's some way I can help you, I think I should."

"I appreciate that," Hugo responds. "We'll meet you around back."

David disappears into the house. Hugo presses a hand to the small of my back, guiding me along the stone pavers laid out to make a walkway.

The way his hand feels on me, even in a place as well-meaning as the small of my back, has my stomach flipping. I'm blaming the hormones once again, because the alternative is a path I can't begin to travel.

We round the white-sided home, finding David fluffing Grecian blue outdoor pillows on a matching outdoor couch. As we get closer, he says, "Blue is Paula's favorite color. I told her it clashes with everything in this backyard, but she told me to close my eyes and picture it matching."

"I like the way she thinks," I say, because I'm not sure how else to respond.

Paula comes from the house balancing a large serving tray in one hand and a plastic pitcher in the other.

To have something to do, I meet her halfway and take the tray off her hands. In mere minutes she has managed to amass a tray of lemon cookies with lemon curd, miniature brownies, and butter crackers with a cheese ball.

I set the tray on the table between the outdoor furniture, and David helps his wife distribute drinks.

We look at each other now, no food or drinks to distract us. Paula is the first to break. "Well, come on. Dig in." She waves at the food, then points at me. "You, especially. You're eating for two now." Her wagging finger turns on Hugo. "You are, also. Go on and eat. Dad has to keep his stamina up, too."

I stiffen, prepared to correct them, but Hugo doesn't miss a beat. "Better start training myself. I hear those middle of the night feedings can be brutal."

"Middle of the night?" Paula harrumphs. "Try every couple hours like clockwork when they're newborns."

My eyes bulge.

"Don't you worry," Paula pats my arm. "Sounds like he's itching to help you, assuming you pump or use formula."

I pause, waiting for Hugo to finally say something, *anything*, remotely close to *I'm not the father*.

He doesn't.

He says, "Mallory is still deciding, but I'll support her whatever she chooses." Then he leans forward, swipes a cracker through the cheese, and hands it to me. "Time to feed you two."

It's the same thing he said to me while I was on the cot, recovering from passing out. It had made me think about how alone Peanut and I were, but now, hearing him say it a second time, it makes me wonder if we have to be alone.

The thought is almost comically stupid. Hugo is handsome, successful, single, and so kind. He doesn't want a woman who's having another man's baby.

I take the cracker from him, murmuring my thanks. It appears I'm going to have to be more careful with my thoughts around him. Rein in my heart a little bit. I don't have the luxury of fantasizing about happily ever afters and fairy tales. Peanut is already down one parent, I can't be mooning around having a crush on an unattainable man when I should be focused on my baby and what I came here to do.

"Hugo," David says, tone serious. "What is it you think I can do for you?"

"I want to hear about what happened that day, from you. My mom has told me, but it was a long time ago. We don't talk about how my dad died. Mostly we talk about how he lived."

"It's probably better that way. To talk about how he lived. He was a great man."

Hugo nods. "I agree. Except, I need more. It's"—he glances at me—"holding me back."

Hugo

What? What does he mean by that?

David nods his head like he understands.

I do, too, to a degree. I know what it's like to be held back by grief, by pain. But why did he look at me when he said it?

David lays out one arm on the back of the couch. Paula snuggles in closer to her husband. Providing him comfort.

"I'd been delivering mail that day, and I was on the way back from my route when I got a flat tire on Six Digit Road. It was a pretty straight forward flat, not like I bent the axle or anything. A quick fix and I was on my way. It was the day of the Olive Festival, and I hadn't wanted to miss it. There was a man from a couple towns over coming to show me a French Colonies New World coin he recently purchased. I remember thinking it was going to be a great day, despite the flat tire. Between my favorite prickly pear lemonade stand I knew would be at the festival and getting to see a coin like that, I was happy as a clam." He sighs. "But you know what? It shaped up to be a terrible day. The lemonade wasn't ready when I got there, the guy was a no-show, and that night police officers knocked on my door." Guilt floods his eyes. "Obviously you had it much worse that day."

"Those things can all be upsetting." Hugo offers David the kindest smile.

How does he do it? How does he extend such grace to people? He really is one of the nicest men I've ever met.

"I truly am sorry about what happened to your dad. I meant it when I said he was a good man. Summerhill was on my mail route. As you know, it's a hike from town to your mailbox, and your Dad tried to get out to the Summerhill turn-in as often as he could so I could shave off some time. I was just the mailman, and here he was this big to-do in Olive Township. He valued my time, and me as a person. And then—" David looks away, presses a fist to his mouth. Paula runs a supportive palm up and down his thigh.

I'm struck by a chord of gratitude, genuinely thankful these two found each other.

David composes himself. "They thought I had something to do with it. Declaring me a person-of-interest." He frowns, shakes his head, like even after all this time he can pluck the disbelief out of thin air, feel it anew. "Like I could ever do something so evil. I didn't get the opportunity to grieve because I was too busy defending myself."

Hugo's hand finds my fabric covered thigh, as if he, too, needs to be bolstered. Covering his hand like he did to me in the car, I give him the slightest squeeze.

I'm here.

"I'm sorry you didn't get that opportunity," Hugo says.

"I'm sorry your dad was taken from you."

The men share a sad smile. Inside the house, a telephone rings. Paula bolts upright. "That would be me. I put my ringer on full volume, I'm expecting a call from my daughter." She hustles away, yelling back over her shoulder, "If I don't see you before you leave, it was nice to meet you!"

We echo her words, and David says, "Paula has two children from her first marriage." He looks like he wants something to do with his hands, so he leans forward and takes a lemon cookie, slathering it in lemon curd. "I never did have kids. I wanted to, but the chance didn't present itself." He sighs. "Probably a good thing I didn't. I'm adopted, and I never knew about my birth parents. I worried I carried some awful genetic disease or something."

He's adopted? I don't know that it changes anything, but it's...*interesting*.

"Did you ever find anything out about your birth parents?" I ask. With a little digging, he might've been able to learn if there was any genetic reason he shouldn't have kids.

"I tried looking, once. A long time ago. I learned I have a twin sister, who was also given away at birth. But there was nothing to go on. The adoptions were closed."

Without thinking about it, I rub a hand over my stomach. "Have you ever thought about doing one of those DNA tests? Sorry"—I make a face—"I'm endlessly curious."

David doesn't seem like he minds. "I've considered it, but there's a lot that comes with the results of something like that. Some closets are better left closed, you know?"

I understand what he's saying, but I wholeheartedly disagree. I respect his opinion, though, so I drop it.

David and Hugo talk a little longer. David asks questions about Olive Township, about some of the people, including Margaret. "She still whipping up the best sandwiches in the state?"

Hugo nods. "Couldn't stop her if you tried."

The conversation lulls. It's time to leave.

We thank David for his time, his willingness to talk. He walks us around to the front of his house, pausing in front of Hugo's car.

From his pocket, he produces a small box and hands it to me. "Take this," he says. "The start of your baby's collection."

I open it, finding the coin I came here for. When I reach into my purse, David declines.

"Consider it a gift," he says.

Of course, I cry. If there were one symptom of pregnancy I could get rid of, it would be these tears with a mind of their own.

"Sorry," I apologize, shrugging and swiping at my face. And then I do the most embarrassing thing, but also possibly the most right thing. I throw my arms around him. This man lost so much being wrongly suspected.

David startles at first, but he returns the hug. When we pull apart, he looks happier. Lighter. Hugo offers him a hand, and they shake.

With a final goodbye, David retreats into his home. Hugo gets my door like he said he would.

I'm buckling my seat belt when Hugo's pinky finger slides around mine. His free hand brushes over my cheeks, swiping away any remaining moisture. Neither of us speak. The moment does not need words spoken aloud.

I'm here for you.

The air conditioning hits us on blast as Hugo starts

Hugo

the car and drives away. It's not hot outside, but I appreciate the stream of cold air against my skin.

It's a good reminder of where we are, and what it is we're doing.

Chapter 18

Hugo

"What do you think about what he said?" Mallory asks when we're a few miles outside of Sugar Creek.

It's really not what David Boylan said that was impactful, it's more the experience of putting my eyes on him that affected me. "It's not all that different from everything my mom told me. But hearing it from him felt better somehow. I don't know why."

"Now you have certainty. It's always better to hear it directly from the source." Mallory smoothes out her dress. "Thank you for driving me today. I planned on going alone."

Fat chance in hell I'd let her go alone. "There's no way I would let you go by yourself."

Her eyebrows raise, her lips making a sassy little sound. "Let me?"

I shrug, liking the way she punches back. "I said what I said."

She's shaking her head, but she can't hide the faint smile tugging at her mouth. "So we're like a team, huh?"

"Just call us Bonnie and Clyde."

She blows out a breath, lips vibrating. "You can do better than that."

"Gumshoe and Swordsman?" The nicknames aren't particularly romantic, but they're flirtatious. I'll admit to liking it.

Her lips curl into that full smile she was fighting. "Give me some time. I'll come up with a better nickname for us."

"I don't know." I tap the steering wheel. "I'm growing fond of Gumshoe and Swordsman."

She regards me with a quizzical look. As if she can't figure me out. Welcome to the club, Mallory. I can't figure me out either. What is it about this woman that makes me like her so much? I know what it is, but at the same time, I can't figure it out.

"What do you have going on tomorrow?" she asks.

I almost tell her she can do better than that, but rein it in and respond instead. "I have my second meeting with the olive oil sommelier." Her eyebrows raise dubiously. "That's a thing?"

Laughter from me. "I promise it's a thing."

She shrugs like she doesn't believe me. "If you say so."

"I know so." I reach over, give her a little pinch on the arm. She squeals and bats me away.

"Tell me about fencing," she says, digging into that box of pastries I picked up this morning at Sweet Nothings.

"What about it?" I ask, plucking the corner off a strawberry pop tart. I swear I can never get enough of these things.

"It's not your typical sport. Tell me how you got involved."

"It was after my dad died. I needed something to do. Anything, really. I needed to feel like—"

"You were in control of something."

"Exactly."

Mallory takes another bite. "Pardon the interruption. Continue."

"I welcome all interruptions from you," I say, stealing another piece of Mallory's pastry. She tears off half, and hands it over. There's some construction starting, reducing the two-lane highway down to one for a half mile. We slow to a stop. I look over to say something else, but spot a speck of strawberry jam at the corner of Mallory's mouth.

All I want to do is reach for the back of her neck, pull her in close, kiss the jam off her mouth.

Would she be receptive? Allow it?

This isn't the time, or place, but I can't help the way my eyes linger there. Mallory would taste like the most decadent treat. I can tell.

She must see the way my eyes look at her mouth, because she reaches up, thumbing away the jam. "Tell a girl instead of staring at it." And then she sticks out her tongue at me.

And I laugh.

Hugo

Funny, that's what this woman is.

The traffic lets up, and I ease off the brake.

"Keep talking," Mallory instructs.

"There happened to be a man in Olive Township who owned a gym, and he'd studied fencing. Ambrose was just becoming serious about football. We were only ten, but he had laser focus even then. So we started going to the gym."

"What was the name of the man who owned the gym?"

I like the way Mallory is curious, the way she asks questions, puts together a puzzle in her mind.

"Aaron."

"Got it." Mallory nods once. "Continue."

"Aaron taught Ambrose proper form for lifting weights. Looking back, we must have given all the other gymgoers a laugh. Two skinny pre-pubescent boys lifting weights."

"Or maybe you inspired them."

"Huh. I haven't thought of it that way."

"You're welcome," Mallory says loftily, digging in her purse and coming away with lip balm.

"So, we're going to the gym regularly. And I show an interest in the sword Aaron has in his office. I mean, it's a *sword*. Not exactly a normal item to have in an office. So Aaron tells me about fencing, asks me if I want to hold the sword. Turns out it's called a saber, by the way. Not a sword. Really, it's called a weapon, but that word is better used in the right context."

"Because anything can be a weapon," Mallory interjects. Her hands curl into fists, and she punches the air. "Including these bad bitches."

"Careful where you're swinging those," I joke, and Mallory laughs.

"So, Aaron starts teaching me everything he knows. Coaching me. I had a natural aptitude for it. The rest is history."

"Where is Aaron now?"

"Sante Fe. He met a woman online and followed his heart. It was ok, though. It was around the time I was heading to college. I was fencing in college and couldn't have outside training anyway. He recommended the man who I trained with for the Olympics."

"What was it like to win a gold medal?"

"An out-of-body experience. Years and years of training, and then it all came down to one summer."

"Two medals, right? One in teams, the other individual."

I dip my chin, confirming. "Stalker."

"Professionally curious."

"I like it."

"And now Ambrose is in the NFL?"

"Yep. Linebacker. The guy is just a smidge below a giant. He dwarfs me and Penn, and Duke."

"The day of the Olive Festival, I was doing my best to keep up with the dynamics of your friends. Daisy and Duke were engaged?"

"Yeah," I answer. That was some drama I didn't need,

or want. I hated lying to Daisy. It was like denying a kitten milk. "Duke and Daisy's families have been associated for generations, and Duke and Daisy decided to get married to please everyone. It was a big mess, honestly. And then Penn came back to Olive Township after being gone since he was thirteen, and he made things worse by hiding his true identity. He thought it was kinder to Daisy if he didn't interrupt her life. Only, he didn't know she and Duke weren't really in love." Just saying it all out loud makes me roll my eyes. You can't make this shit up.

Mallory smirks. "Is this where you came in and told him to break up their wedding?"

"I did all those assholes a favor," I insist, defending my choice.

"It looks like you did. Doesn't seem like Vivi and Duke get along."

"If push came to shove, they'd throw down for one another. They have really different personalities, though, so for the most part they stay out of each other's way."

"Does Vivi get along with Ambrose?"

I palm the scruff on my face, thinking of the last time they saw one another. To my knowledge, it's been a long time. "They get along great. He's always been like a brother to me, and that makes him a brother to her."

"Olive Township is a cute place, you know? The names of the stores are eccentric and memorable, the vibe is desert chic. It's like you drive into a magical portal on your way in."

"That's what the reporter who wrote about Sagewood

Spa said. People have been infiltrating our special bubble ever since."

"Well, then, I guess I'll go back home to Phoenix," she says tartly.

My chest constricts at the mere thought of being apart from her sass, her smile, her sense of humor. I glare at her. "Don't you dare."

Smirking, she says, "I have to at some point, you know." She grabs her phone, looks at her calendar. "Oh," she says softly, like she's just had a realization.

"What is it?"

She pinches her lower lip between two fingers. A sure sign something has affected her, and now she's thinking of it. I've noticed her doing this before. "Mallory?" I urge when she doesn't respond.

"Just some appointments I need to reschedule."

She forces a smile, but I know a brave face when I see one. With only ten minutes left of our drive, I maintain conversation, but it's not like it was before. Whatever she saw on her calendar, it has upset her.

"Here you go," I say, pulling up to the curb at Olive Inn. As pledged, I hop from the car to get Mallory's door.

She turns to face me. "Today was good, right? You're happy you went?"

The care and concern in Mallory's gaze plucks at my heartstrings. She hardly knows me compared to some, but her awareness of how I'm feeling makes it seem like we've been friends for years.

"Today was important for various reasons. Thank

you, and that inquisitive mind of yours, for making it happen."

Mallory smiles, but it doesn't quite reach high enough on her face to be genuine.

She walks up to Olive Inn, disappearing into the front door, and leaves me wondering what the hell she saw on her calendar.

Chapter 19

Mallory

I'D GROWN QUIET AT THE END OF OUR DRIVE.

Hugo was happy. Buoyant, even. What he did today was big. Something he never thought he'd get the chance to do. His relief was palpable and he was chatty, and although I joined him in that effervescent feeling, it wore off when I realized today's date. I couldn't bear to impart my personal pain on him, nor will I diminish his feeling by telling him tomorrow would've been Maggie's 26th birthday.

Chapter 20

Mallory

Jolene: Sending you the fiercest hug. Tell me if you can't find strawberry cake. I will buy some and drive it to you.

Mallory: I appreciate you. XO.

Mallory: Hi, Mom. Thinking of you today. Love you.

Mom: Thank you, Mallory.

Maggie's birthday is the hardest day of the year for me, second only to the anniversary of the day she was killed. Every year I bake her favorite strawberry cake, placing twelve candles in the thick layer of vanilla icing. I'm usually in tears, and then I double down and increase the pain by lighting the candles and singing happy birthday. It's dramatic, but it's what I need. After being forced to live in a world without Maggie, sometimes I want to spend just one day drowning in the pain of losing her. Then, and I'm not proud of this, I get drunk and pass out, knowing I will wake up with a pounding headache and self-inflicted illness. In an unhealthy way, this is punishment for how I abandoned my sister on that day.

Without my own kitchen to bake in, I set off for Sweet Nothings. I know from being here yesterday with Hugo that they don't have a strawberry cake on the menu, but I noticed they have rotating flavors. How perfect would it be if today's flavor were strawberry?

Yesterday's bickering couple is here again today. Sal and Adela.

"I told you we ran out of powdered sugar." Adela scowls at her husband.

"Bah," he says, waving her away.

I stand back from the register, surveying the treats inside the glass cases. The only thing strawberry flavored are the pop tarts Hugo purchased yesterday, and if I try and put twelve candles in one of those, I think I'll end up with an inferno.

"Hello, young lady," Sal greets me. He's wearing the cutest apron, made of forest green thick material and

Hugo

lined in green and white gingham. I bet it's homemade. "You were in here yesterday with Hugo, weren't you?"

"I sure was," I confirm with a nod.

"I've known him since he was a tiny thing."

"I'm sure he was cute."

"Sure was. Damn shame what happened to his dad. Blows my mind that they never caught the guy. Small town like this? How does somebody get away with it?"

Sal's loose lips take me aback, but it may not be out of character for him. It doesn't seem like he has much of a filter. Something about his rhetorical questions digs in. The wording, the way he insinuated a person shouldn't be able to get away with murder in a small town.

"You think it was a local? Or it's not possible because of the town's size back then?"

Sal places his age-spotted forearms on the top of the case. "I don't know what I think," he says. "It's hard for me to imagine anybody wanting to kill a man as nice as Simon. Forget having enemies, the man didn't have anybody who wasn't a friend."

A friend of Simon... Is that where I should be looking? Simon's friends?

Sal pats his fluffy white head of hair. "Anyway, what can I do for you, hon? You got a sweet tooth today? Sugar craving?" His gaze drops briefly to my stomach.

I've always heard word travels fast in a small town, but I assumed that was small town lore. Looks like I'm officially being disabused of the notion.

"I came in here hoping to find a strawberry cake. Or slice of cake. Or cupcake. A morsel, really. I'm not picky."

Sal frowns. "I hate to deliver bad news, but we don't have strawberry cake." He turns back, cups a hand around his mouth. "Adela, we gotta put strawberry cake on the menu."

Her head of long, silvery gray hair pops up in the stainless steel window separating the store from the kitchen. "I'll put strawberry cake on the menu when I feel like putting strawberry cake on the menu." She glares, waiting for his return barb.

"There's a pregnant lady who needs strawberry cake," Sal argues, thumbing at me.

Adela's gaze shifts my way. "You're the woman who passed out." The nonchalant way she says it makes it seem like she could be commenting on an odd-shaped cloud in the sky.

"Guilty."

"You're pregnant?"

Sal's lips vibrate in a dramatic sigh. "I told you this already. Woman, I swear"—his hair shimmies with the shake of his head—"you should be sent to the nuthouse."

Surely Adela heard him, but she shows no sign of it. "You want strawberry cake?" she asks me.

I nod. "Please. With vanilla icing."

"Alright," she says, gathering her hair and twisting an elastic band around the base. "I'll bake you a strawberry cake with vanilla icing."

Tears fill my eyes. At least these feel more valid than recent bouts. "Just like that? You'll make one for me?"

"Haven't seen Hugo so alive in a long time." She

winks at me. "I think that deserves strawberry cake." She disappears from the space, and me?

Tears, of course. Damn them. All I want to do is smile and thank her, but tears clog my voice.

Sal's mouth opens in horror, looking left and right like he's determining how likely he is to successfully escape the crying pregnant lady.

"We've got her, Sal," a voice says, stepping up beside me and draping an arm over my shoulders.

It's Daisy, on my right. Vivi, on my left.

Daisy's hand gently squeezes my shoulder. "Will you sit with us, Mallory?"

I sniff, dragging the back of my hand under my nose. Vivi snags a paper napkin from a nearby dispenser and hands it to me. I offer a thankful, shaky smile, and say, "I don't want to intrude."

Daisy shakes her head. "Not an intrusion. I'd be grateful." She tips her chin at Vivi. "I can't stand Vivi. The only reason I accepted her invitation to come here was because I feel bad that she doesn't have any other friends."

A straight-faced Vivi nods in the affirmative. "I've been guilting this broad into friendship since the mid-2000s."

Through the well of emotion at someone making a special cake just for me, without even asking me why, comes laughter.

"I won't take no for an answer," Daisy says, and without waiting for a response, she steers me to an empty table in the corner. "This is our table. Every week at this time, we meet. If Sal sees someone sit down anywhere close to the time when we're supposed to arrive, he shoos them away with one of those old-fashioned brooms."

More laughter. These women are kind. Vivi is still a bit of an enigma, but I think underneath that tough exterior, she's nice.

"I'll join you," I relent. "But only if you promise I'm not interrupting. You could be doing very important work, like solving world hunger."

"Nah." Vivi waves her hand. She threads her purse straps over the back of a chair and plunks down. "We judge people and talk shit."

Daisy takes her seat, and I fill the third. "We're like the early version of those old ladies you see sitting on a park bench gossiping about the town as it lives life around them."

"Tell us why you're crying," Vivi says. "You're pregnant, so it could be for anything. I once cried because I got peach ice cream and the carton said it would have real pieces of peach, but there weren't any."

"That actually makes me feel better. I know the tears are due to hormones, but they seem so...so *irrational*. I was never a crier before this."

"I wasn't a lot of things before I became a mother," Vivi states. "Welcome to becoming a person you never knew you could be. For better or worse."

"Ok, *Mallory*." Daisy sends a hard look at Vivi. I get the feeling her role in their friendship is to wrangle Vivi, be the calm to her chaos. Daisy seems to be a genuinely sweet person. "Tell us why we walked in here and found a pregnant lady in tears."

For an event that changed the trajectory of my life, I don't talk about it with new people very often. But if Hugo can be brave and have a conversation with David Boylan, I can be brave and explain to these two friendly faces why they found me in tears.

"Today would've been my little sister Maggie's twenty-sixth birthday. She died when she was twelve, and every year I bake her favorite cake and sing happy birthday to her. I'm not at home, obviously, so Adela offered to make it for me, even though they don't have the flavor on the menu."

The look on Daisy's face is one of pure sorrow, and though Vivi shares the expression, there's something else there, too. Empathy.

"My mom told me," Vivi says quietly. "I'm sorry. For your loss, and for my behavior at the festival."

"You really were quite bitchy." The words sound wrong with Daisy's sugared tone.

"I'll make up for it," Vivi promises. "With food. I can cook the pants off you."

"That's sort of how I ended up in this predicament," I joke, rubbing my belly.

Vivi howls. "I like you, Mallory."

"You have to like me. We're members of a club we didn't ask to be in."

Vivi crosses her arms, a defiant look moving over her face. "Fuck that club."

Daisy's eyebrows raise. "Not to interrupt the sisterhood vibes you two have going right now, but I don't know what you're talking about. What club?"

"The murdered loved ones club," Vivi answers, voice dull. Somebody else might flinch at Vivi's harsh language, but I know she doesn't mean it badly. It's how she guards herself against the tremendous pain. Survival. The only way to deal with the pain is to learn how to interact with it.

Daisy gasps, gaze snapping back to me. "What is Vivi talking about?"

Quickly, I fill her in. No details, just the skeleton of what happened. No muscles or sinew, no organs or skin. No heart. If I rarely disclose what happened to Maggie, then I almost never talk about the details of the day. I still can't stomach them.

"And that's why I'm here," I finish.

Daisy drums her nails on the table. "This all makes a lot more sense now. Penn told me you'd sent an email—"

"Many emails," I interject.

"And last he heard Hugo wasn't responding."

I wince. "I *miiight* have ambushed him."

Vivi shrugs. "Nobody ever moved forward by standing still."

Daisy side-eyes Vivi. "You're full of wisdom today."

Vivi winks at her in an overdone and leering way. "You tell Mama what you need, I'll make it happen."

Daisy shakes her head as she palms her forehead. "Prepare yourself for what's coming next," she mutters to me.

"Wha—"

"You gotta problem? Yo, I'll solve it." Vivi sings, deepening her voice and jutting out her chin.

Daisy eyes me. "She must like you if she's doing her Vanilla Ice routine in front of you."

Vivi looks at me, sending me the same wink. "Might as well get comfortable in front of Mallory now."

My brows pinch in suspicion. "Why is that?"

"Because Hugo's in lo-ove."

My cheeks flush with heat, my hand waving back-and-forth over the table, as if I'm declining something. "He feels bad for a pregnant lady. That's why he's being nice."

Vivi snorts. "Keep telling yourself that. I know my brother, and I've never seen him so..."

Her lips twitch as she searches for the best word. "Invested."

I laugh off Vivi's words, even as my stomach flutters. "He's indulging me."

"I don't think so," Daisy says. "It's time, if that makes sense. All of it. He's retired from a successful fencing career. He's stepped into the operation of Summerhill, a role his dad always wanted for him. It's time for Hugo to wade through all the feelings he's been running from for years." Daisy glances at Vivi. It seems Hugo isn't the only person Daisy thinks this of.

Sal arrives at the table holding a tray. "Here's your usual, ladies." With a shaky hand he sets down two large saucers and cups, holding what looks to be a latte with a heart formed in the foam.

"Mallory, I hope you don't mind, I took the liberty of

making one for you also. Decaf," he adds, sliding the dish in front of me. He's not blushing, but he seems bashful. It's probably one of the cutest things I've ever seen.

"Thank you, Sal," I say, picking up the coffee. I love the warmth of the cup, the curl of the steam. "You're so thoughtful."

"It's vanilla," he says, his voice taking on a grumble. "If you don't like vanilla, well, I don't know what to tell ya." He turns away as quickly as possible for his age, retreating with the empty tray dangling by his side.

Daisy cups a hand over her mouth to muffle her laughter. "What in the world was that?"

Vivi's laughing, too. "That's how he acts around pregnant women," she whisper-hisses. "It's the emotional equivalent of being all thumbs. He wants to treat you like you're made of glass, but he's not happy about his inclination to treat you like you're made of glass."

I'm laughing too, but my heart is doing this stretch in my chest, almost as if it's making room for the sweetness of Sal's gesture.

Vivi and Daisy settle into mundane conversation. I sip my decaf vanilla latte, listening, picking up on details. Daisy and Penn are remodeling his childhood home on the adorably named Lickety-Split Lane. Vivi is worried because recently she noticed a group of employees huddled together, and when she walked past, they stopped talking.

"They weren't looking at me with guilt, like they were talking shit about me," she says. "They were looking at me as if they felt bad for me. Kind of like they thought I was pathetic."

"You're the boss," Daisy reminds her gently. "It probably had nothing to do with you."

"Sure," Vivi says, sipping her coffee. "They were probably discussing how drunk they got last weekend, and who slept with who." Vivi looks at me. "In case you don't know, restaurants are lawless places."

"I was a server to put myself through college. The debauchery was disturbing."

Vivi nibbles her lower lip. "I'm still perturbed by the way they shut down when they saw me. I know I'm their boss, but this was different."

"Viv," Daisy says kindly, gently squeezing her best friend's forearm. "Honestly, it sounds like you are projecting."

"Do you have a magnifying glass for an eyeball?" Vivi gripes. "Stop looking at me so closely."

Vivi turns to me in a very on purpose way, signaling she's done being under Daisy's microscope. "How is your time in Olive Township going? Have you found anything?"

I know what I say next is going to add fuel to their suspicions that Hugo cares for me. Here goes.

"Yesterday, Hugo and I drove north to Sugar Creek. We visited David Boylan."

Two jaws drop. Two sets of eyes bulge.

"You should have led with that," Vivi grumbles.

Daisy tucks a lock of blonde hair behind her ear. "He left Olive Township only to move to another small town in Arizona?" She's shaking her head like she can hardly believe it. "I would have assumed he'd gone halfway around the world."

"How was Hugo when he saw the guy?" Vivi asks, concern for her brother creeping into her tone.

"I think it helped Hugo to see him." It occurs to me Vivi might be hurt she wasn't invited. She hasn't seemed interested (or even slightly approving) of my scrutiny of her dad's case, but maybe she wants to be asked, even if all she plans to do is decline. "I'm sorry we didn't ask you to go with us."

"I'll be really honest with you, I wouldn't have said yes. I'm not in the same place as Hugo. Dealing with my grief isn't where I am right now in life. I can't put my energy there quite yet." She finishes her coffee, adding, "I have babies to raise, and exes to hate. I'm swamped."

"Young lady?" Sal again. He holds a small white box. "Adela said to give this to you. No charge. We're adding it to the menu." He slides the box in front of me. "She called it the perfect spring flavor. I thought lemon and carrot cake were just fine, but what do I know?"

"Thank you, thank you," I gush. I want to wrap this sweet and salty old man into a hug, but I don't know if he's ok with it, and it might embarrass him. Adela calls out to him, something about helping her, and he shuffles away.

My fingers press into the sides of the cake box, turning it this way and that. This is the first time that I was not the person to bake this cake. It feels odd, as if there is a degree of separation to it. These ingredients did not pass through my hands. But of course, Maggie is the reason I'm in Olive Township.

"Hey," Vivi says, voice warm. "If you don't want to be alone tonight, you can come hang out with me and my kids. They sing a mean happy birthday."

"That's very kind of you, but I think I'll pass. Nobody needs to see me ugly cry." Vivi and Daisy nod. Every woman knows what it's like to need a good cry once in a while. "Typically I eat cake and get drunk." A gentle swoop over my belly with my hand. "But not this year."

"Next year," Daisy says, excitement bright in her eyes. "King's Ransom. They make a blood orange margarita that's unbelievable."

"I'm more of a tequila with soda water and a splash of grapefruit juice kind of girl."

Daisy snaps her fingers. "They can do that, too."

Vivi thumbs at Daisy. "This girl only drinks champagne."

My gaze runs over Daisy's halo of blonde hair, her pretty face and cute little sundress. "That tracks."

Vivi barks a laugh. "I told you you look like a person who drinks champagne. Or rosé, in second place."

The three of us deposit our empty cups and saucers in a dirty dish bin at the end of the counter.

"Thank you," we call on our way out, but Sal and Adela are in the kitchen, and from the looks of it, they are griping about something.

"If they weren't bitching at each other, I'd be worried," Vivi says.

Daisy pulls me in for a warm hug. Vivi hangs back

when Daisy lets me go, saying, "I usually only hug people I know well, but in a weird way I feel like I know you on an elevated level."

"Agreed. But you don't have to hug me if you don't want to. Your mom gives the greatest hugs, so I know you had a good teacher."

"Ahh fuck it," Vivi says, pulling me in. She's stiff, but her heart is in the right place.

We part ways, and I stop into a store for new pajamas because I brought only one set with me, and then pop into a drugstore for candles. My stomach rumbles, reminding me I need to eat. I snag a BLT and fries to-go from Good Thyme Café, and insist the hostess let me pay for it. It was unbelievably sweet of Hugo to instruct them not to charge me, but I need to be able to pay for my own food.

Arms full when I walk into my hotel room, my foot catches on the lip of the carpet. Thankfully, I don't go sprawling, but I drop my to-go container and it opens, the sandwich falling apart and half of the fries spilling out onto the floor.

I pat my belly, looking at the fallen fries. "Are you already making me clumsy?"

Sinking to my knees, I donkey-kick the door closed behind me and clean up my mess, reassembling the sandwich as best I can. When my dinner is finished, I decorate the cake with twelve candles and light it, softly singing to Maggie.

Forever young.

Forever twelve.

Hugo

In the center of my chest, it hits me. An unbearable pain, a tremendous guilt. It's my fault. I left her alone at the water park. A cute boy wanted to hang out with me, and I left Maggie behind.

I blow out the candles, shoulders quaking, sobs wracking my body. Though I don't want it, and can hardly stomach it, I force myself to eat a thin slice of cake. Maggie loved her birthday cake, and she's not alive to eat it, so I'll do it for her.

Eventually, I change into pajamas and lie down on the bed. I cry and I cry, until there's nothing left, and sleep overtakes me.

It's the middle of the night when I wake. Three a.m. I have a pressing urge to look at old photos of Maggie.

Slipping my phone from the nightstand, I blink against the brightness and open my photos app.

My blood runs cold. A thick gasp sticks in my throat, nausea rolling over me as I stare at the images.

My camera roll has new photos of... *me?*

Sleeping.

Photos of me sleeping.

Wearing the new pajamas I bought earlier this evening.

The same pajamas I have on right now.

Chapter 21

Hugo

THREE A.M. MY OWN PERSONAL WITCHING HOUR.

The time of nightmares, of dreams I cannot decipher and manufactured memories. Did my dad really promise to play catch with me that day before he left the house, or do I desperately want for it to have happened? Did he wear my favorite time-softened shirt, or have I dressed him in it because I can't recall the clothes he wore the day he died?

Punching at the pillow in an attempt to reinvigorate it, I flop back on my bed and place my forearm over my eyes. Just a couple more hours and I'll get up, start my day. Sometimes I fall asleep after the nightmares, but sometimes I don't. Those are extra coffee days.

Eyes closed, I think of Mallory. Glossy dark hair, straight nose, thoughtful and sharp mind. The way I feel when I'm around her is...*confusing*.

Never in my life have I been attracted to a pregnant woman. The swell of a pregnant belly is a telltale sign to a man that she is off-limits. But with Mallory, that's not the case.

I swear that sometimes, she's attracted to me, too. I've been around enough women to know what it looks like when they show outward signs of attraction, but Mallory displays none of those. She doesn't place her hand on my bicep, or tilt her head and look up at me with wide eyes like I've seen other women do. With Mallory, it's something in the air around her I can feel. Sense. Smell.

How can that be? Like I said, she has me flummoxed.

On a low groan, I roll over and reach for my phone. There's no going back to sleep now. I'm too amped up from thinking about Mallory.

I'm in my internet browser typing *Case Files* in the search query when my phone lights up with a call.

Mallory.

Adrenaline shoots through me. I slam my finger down on the screen to answer.

"Mallory," I demand, knowing she'd have no good reason to call me in the middle of the night.

"Hugo," she sobs, and something rips through my chest. Primal and raw, an instinct to defend and protect.

I haul aside the sheets, rise swiftly from my bed. "What happened?"

"I-I couldn't sleep, I—" she sobs again, and it hits me. She isn't sad. She's terrified.

"What? You what?" I ask through a jaw so clenched it aches. With my phone trapped between my shoulder and my ear, I shove my legs through my jeans.

"I need to leave this place," she whispers.

"Olive Township?" Those two words, strangled, reveal how I've come to care for her in such little time. How much I could care for her if she stayed.

"The Olive Inn," she says.

"Mallory," I say, forcing calm into my voice. I'm on quick feet down the hall, grabbing my wallet and keys off the kitchen counter. A light jacket from the hall closet. "What. The. Hell. Happened?" If somebody hurt her, I'll do things I never thought myself capable of.

It hasn't been more than a minute since her call, but I'm already in my car, driving toward town, my path lit by a full moon night. I pass the big house, and the light in my mom's bedroom turns on. No doubt she'll be calling me soon, wanting to know where the hell I'm going, and why I'm driving with such urgency.

"I couldn't sleep. Yesterday was Maggie's birthday, so I grabbed my phone to look at old photos of her." Mallory's voice is steadier now, and she takes a deep breath. "When I opened my photo app, I found photos of me sleeping."

What the fuck?

"The photos were timestamped and I'm in the same pajamas now."

Rage sweeps through me in a way I've never felt. I've spent years fencing, facing opponents in a bout, wielding objects that could fillet a man if not blunted, but with such civility. There is nothing civil about the way I feel now.

"What's the timestamp?" I ask, passing under the Summerhill sign and taking the turn for town.

"12:43," she says, voice breaking.

"Pack your things," I instruct. "I'm coming to get you. Stay on the phone." The gas pedal hits the floor.

It's a twenty-minute drive from Summerhill to town. Straight desert roads and unobstructed views allow me to arrive in far less time.

I swing my car up to the curb in front of Olive Inn, hopping out and jogging to the front door. My primary focus is getting to Mallory, but I'm halfway across the lobby when a man walks out from a set of doors behind the front desk.

"Do you need something?" he asks, glaring at me.

I change course, steering his way. "Who has access to the guest rooms? You?"

He pales. The guy is the least physically threatening person I've ever encountered, but desperate people do weird shit, so I know better than to be too aggressive.

"Only the g-guests," he stutters.

Bracing my palms on the front desk, I lean over it. "And who else?"

"The manager has a master key," he answers, fear in his eyes.

"Are you the manager?"

Reluctantly, he says, "I'm the night manager."

I'm aware that in this moment, I have no way to prove he's the person who let himself into Mallory's room and took pictures of her sleeping. Mallory's the priority now, so I push off the desk. "If I find out you're the one who did it, I'll make you wish you hadn't."

Then I'm racing on through the lobby, and behind me he yells, "Did what?"

I'm done spending time on that fuck. I need to put my eyes on Mallory, make sure she's ok. Her and Peanut. Can the baby feel her fear? The spike of her adrenaline?

I reach her room and knock on the door. "It's me," I call out.

"Hugo." Mallory's relief seeps through the cheap wood.

On the other side of the door are sounds of Mallory pulling aside the table I told her to push against the door while I was racing here.

The snick of a lock.

The dip of a door handle.

The door swings open and there she is, eyes red and puffy, but teeming with outrage. Her pajamas are a matching set, yellow like a dandelion and covered in a floral print. Her breasts spill from the low-cut top. *Somebody entered her private space, leered at her wearing a piece of clothing she felt comfortable sleeping in.* My hands ball into fists. Was it that son of a bitch night manager? Who else could it have been?

Mallory takes one look at me and her face crumples, as if she was using her fury to get her through until it was safe for her to feel her other feelings.

I'm there, stepping into the room, folding her into my chest. Her head cradles into my neck, her breath hot against the fabric of my shirt.

"Someone was in my room," she whispers. "While I was in it. Sleeping." One sob. "With my baby."

Hugo

I look down past the curtain of dark hair, watch the possessive pass of her hand over her stomach.

"What if they had hurt us?"

Closing my eyes against the thought, I run my hand down her back, all the way to the pronounced lower dip, returning. "You are both safe, and that's what matters."

Her answering nod is tiny, causing her lips to skim my chest. My heart constricts. My throat, too.

"Is your stuff packed?" I ask her.

"Yes," she answers, taking a step away.

But I don't want her to. I want to keep her in the circle of my arms, where I can make sure she and Peanut are safe.

She motions toward the bed, where there are two bags. I recognize one from that first day I accompanied her to the inn, mad as hell about her subterfuge but determined to treat her well.

I stride forward, lifting the bags from the bed. After a quick double-check of the bedroom and the bathroom, I swipe a paper grocery bag from the table. One look inside tells me it holds her collection of snacks. There's enough in there to fill a pantry, and my heart swells at that. She doesn't want a repeat of what happened at the festival.

My gaze turns to Mallory, and I watch a chill sweep over her skin. Dropping everything I'm holding to the ground, I pull off my jacket. Wordlessly she turns, sliding her arms into the jacket, allowing me to zip it. I reach behind her neck, fist her silky hair, pulling it out from where it's trapped. My jacket swallows her, and if I'm lucky, it'll absorb some of her scent.

"Thank you," she whispers.

I pick up the bags, saying, "No problem." I hear how gruff I sound.

Normally I'd guide her through the door and let her go first, but considering tonight's events, I'm walking out first. If anybody is going to encounter someone with bad intentions, it's going to be me.

No such thing occurs. We have to walk back through the lobby to leave, or use the emergency door at the end of the hall, which will set off an alarm.

Lobby it is. I take Mallory's hand, pull her in tight to my side.

The guy behind the desk stands up when we enter. Mallory's hand grips mine, her other hand coming up to grasp my arm. Her entire body grows rigid. *She suspects it was him.*

We sail through the small space, eyes forward, until he says, "If you're leaving, you need to complete the checkout process."

"Fuck off," I say clearly, never breaking my stride or looking his way.

Mallory's head turns in to me, face partially pressed to my arm. "Thank you again," she whispers.

Anytime.

Forever.

Always.

What is wrong with me?

"No problem," is what I manage to choke out.

Once she's situated in my passenger seat, she exhales, long and loud.

Hugo

"Do you think it was him?" I ask. She nibbles the side of her thumb, looking at the inn through her window.

"He's given me the creeps since I met him." She shrugs. "But I suppose there isn't a way to know for sure. I'm not sure if they have cameras, and if they do that would require reviewing footage. To do that we would need—"

"The police," I finish. "Do you want to involve them?"

She's quiet for a moment, thinking. "No. I don't want to draw attention to myself. I want to lie low."

I disagree, but I know better than to push. I've learned Mallory has a reason for doing things.

She sighs. "I guess I'll need to see if the spa hotel has a vacancy."

I turn right off the street where the inn sits, winding my way through town. I don't know if I've ever seen it like this, so sleepy and dark. Even my latest nights leaving King's Ransom were never this late. And my earliest mornings making my way to Canyon Lake to go fishing with Penn are never this early.

"What if you don't check in at the Sagewood hotel?"

Mallory chuckles, but it sounds more confused than actual laughter. "Ok, sure. I'll just break into a store and find a camping cot to sleep on."

An idea plays at my mind. Driven purely by a burning need to protect Mallory, I'd acted.

There was no consideration as to what would happen after I arrived.

I pass Sagewood. Mallory says nothing.

I pass the edge of Olive Township, where the commercial district ends. Mallory says nothing.

Now I'm on the road that skirts the town, delivering me to the road leading out to Summerhill.

"Hugo."

What is it I hear in her voice? Awareness. Exhaustion. Relief. Gratitude. "Where are you taking me?"

"Somewhere I can keep you and your baby safe."

"Home with you?"

A hot and heady mix of protectiveness and possessiveness grips me. After what happened, I can't imagine her being anywhere else. "You're coming home with me."

Mallory melts into the seat. Her face loses the look of worry. "You know what this means?"

The exhaustion in her voice mixes with a sliver of mischief. "What's that?"

"Your car is definitely not the Ciao Chariot anymore. It's the..." Her eyes squint. "Home Hooptie."

What am I doing laughing right now? The clock is well on its way to nearing five a.m. and someone I care about had their privacy violated and safety threatened. Mallory could be in tears right now. I could be raging. But I'm... *smiling*?

I scoff. "You called my precious lady a *hooptie*?"

Mallory's head lolls my direction as I follow the road leading up and around the big house. A tired grin pulls up one side of her mouth. "Good thing I didn't call her a *jalopy*. I couldn't come up with a corresponding *j* word fast enough."

"Good to know your talent with alliteration has its limits."

Mallory yawns. "Try me again when I've had sleep."

We arrive at my house and I usher her inside. "There's a guest room down the hall from my bedroom. It has its own bathroom." I lead the way, setting her things down on the ivory crushed velvet bedspread. "I'm sure you're tired. Please make yourself at home. Mi casa es su casa."

"Gracias, me siento como en cása." She waits, face expectant.

I blink. "Oh, uh, that's almost all I can say. Well, that and the curse words. My sister and I did not live up to what the De la Vega name implies."

Mallory nods, lips pursed. A secret flits across her face.

My gaze narrows. Playful. "You're fluent, aren't you?"

She grins impishly. "Sí."

All I can do is laugh. Of course she is.

Mallory pulls off my jacket, craning her neck to look into the attached bathroom.

"Anything you need, toiletries, food, whatever, we'll go get it later today, ok? I have a full day, but I'll make room. Besides, we need to get your car from the hotel. I—" My palm runs over the back of my neck. How do I explain the fear, the panic, the horror I felt at the idea of something happening to her? "I needed you out of there as fast as possible."

Mallory steps into me, her arms encircling my waist, wrapping around my back. "Thank you," she says, her face against my shirt. The press of her breasts sends my heartbeats into a thunder, but the round stomach I feel against my own reminds me Mallory is someone to be careful with.

My arms wrap around her, palms flat on her back, holding her in the friendliest way possible. I'll be honest, it fucking pains me.

We stay this way a bit longer, until she yawns again.

"You'd better get some rest," I say gently, and she breaks the embrace.

"Let's talk more tomorrow. Or, later today, I guess." She looks longingly at the bed.

"You're welcome to anything you find in the kitchen. I'll probably be gone by the time you wake up."

She nods. The adrenaline has worn off.

I retreat, pulling the door closed behind me.

Checking my phone, I see my mom's text from right around the time I was leaving Summerhill. She's probably asleep by now, but I know she keeps it on silent, so I shoot her a quick message telling her I'll explain it all later when I see her.

My bed is rumpled, sheets askew. Evidence of the way I shot from bed, panicked. I lie down, close my eyes.

She's safe now.

I say it over and over, but it makes no difference. I am too keyed up to sleep.

I take a shower, pull on the canvas pants I favor for work. Padding down the hall, I notice the light under Mallory's door is out. Good. She needs to rest.

Making a pot of coffee, I step out front with my first

cup to witness the sunrise. My father used to say he liked to watch the orchard wake up. The older I get, the more I understand what he meant. Buttery, fresh sun pours over the trees. The limbs yawn and stretch, absorb the sunlight, take the energy and store it to produce the fruit we'll harvest in late fall.

Before my eyes, Summerhill blossoms, the same as it does everyday.

But not totally.

Today, a woman lies in my guest room.

Summerhill might look the same, and so do I in my typical work uniform, but inside my chest something shifts.

Most notable, perhaps, is how much I don't fear the movement.

Chapter 22

Mallory

I NEEDED YOU OUT OF THERE AS SOON AS POSSIBLE.

I try not to look too deeply into his words, but it's nearly impossible not to.

They traipse across my mind. Wander into my heart.

I fall asleep to them.

Chapter 23

Mallory

BIRDSONG AWAKENS ME.

Sunlight, full and strong in a swath of bright yellow, pours through the window. A slight breeze runs through the tall tree outside, ruffling the tightly wound purple buds. In the distance, the olive orchard runs on and on, endless.

This bed is more comfortable than the inn, and possibly more comfortable than my bed back home.

I stretch out, starfish, point my toes. Allow myself to enjoy this bliss. I refuse to think about the photos on my phone. My middle of the night exodus from the inn, the danger that lurked while I slept. A few more moments of peace is all I'm after.

My eyes close, and I listen to the quiet, punctuated only by the melody of the birds in the tree. It's—

My hand flies to my stomach, neck craning to see down to my midsection.

A flutter, once more. Like a fish swimming, or the jerky movements of a butterfly.

"Hey, Peanut," I whisper, smile shaking. Tears burn my eyes. "I'm here." My hands run over my belly, head dropping back on the pillow. "We had a scary night, didn't we?" My gaze finds the window, the natural beauty beyond. "But we're ok now, aren't we?"

Thanks to Hugo.

One more flutter, and a tear leaking from the corner of my eye.

I wait and wait, hoping for another movement, but that's it. Peanut is finished with the somersaults.

Reluctantly, I tear myself from the bed I could luxuriate in all day. I don't know what time it is, but based on how sunny it is outside, I'm guessing it's somewhere around midday.

Once I'm in the bathroom, I take a long, hot shower under water pressure that is just right. The towels are fluffy, soft. Perfect. I'm like Goldilocks, except I've been invited to stay.

I dress and add moisturizer to my face, letting my hair air dry. Finding my phone in my purse, I see that it's a little after noon. I also have a missed FaceTime call from Jolene, but the hunger I'm feeling supersedes a return call for now. She is going to lose her mind when I tell her what happened.

I was so tired when we arrived early this morning, I didn't spend any time looking around myself.

The hallway where the bedrooms are opens up to a dining room on the left, and a living room beyond that.

It's an open floor plan, with tall, large windows allowing incredible views of the orchard. The floor is a light-colored wood, with a large dining room table, and beyond that, two cozy-looking couches oriented in an L-shape. There is a stone fireplace, and above it, four swords on four separate display racks. They all have different shapes, and now I'm making a mental note to ask if they have different names.

My growling stomach propels me out of the living room in search of the kitchen.

When I find the kitchen, I'm stunned. It's gorgeous, something out of a magazine. Matte black cabinets with copper handles, four of them with glass fronts to show off the dinnerware inside. The counter is one solid piece of finished wood, long and gleaming, with a live edge at the far end. The whole vibe is upscale masculine.

I open up the fridge, anticipating a selection of food fit for a bachelor. Just because the kitchen surfaces are stunning doesn't mean what's happening on the interior matches. A loaf of stale bread and a jar of outdated salad dressing wouldn't have surprised me, but Hugo has a fridge like a home chef. It appears he's perfectly capable of using this fancy kitchen.

Fresh herbs, wrapped in bags and placed in jars of water. Cut vegetables in a bin with separate compartments. Soda waters lined up like soldiers. Cuts of raw meat wrapped in paper and plastic, stored in a separate container. I half-expect his cheese drawer to say *Fromagerie* on it. It doesn't, but he does have a wedge of real parmesan, and feta imported from Greece.

This is not the fridge of a bachelor enjoying his bachelorhood. This is the fridge of a real man. An adult.

How is it after all this time, Hugo is single? He's... well, he's *everything*.

I perform a quick discovery of the kitchen, opening drawers and cabinets, familiarizing myself with where things are located. After that, I whip up a veggie omelet with sourdough toast and breakfast sausage. The only thing missing is decaf coffee, and I'm already jonesing for the vanilla latte Sal made me yesterday.

Was it really only yesterday? So much has happened since then. I officially reversed the 'Vivi hates Mallory' train, kept up my yearly tradition on Maggie's birthday, had my privacy violated by an unknown person, and woke up here this morning, in Hugo's home.

It's enough to make my head spin. Pouring myself an ice-cold glass of water from the fridge, I settle onto a stool tucked under the overhang of the kitchen island.

Time to call Jolene.

I take a big bite of my lunch and pull a three-wick candle closer, propping my phone against it. The call rings and rings, and I stare out at the olive orchard beyond the picture window over the sink. Hugo's home is beautiful, like a little slice of a fairy tale dropped in the middle of the Sonoran Desert.

"Hey," Jolene says, voice snapping my attention back to the screen. "Where are you?"

I swallow. "Hugo's kitchen."

Jolene's eyebrows cinch. "You're in Hugo's kitchen with wet hair because...?"

I explain in detail what happened last night, alternating getting the story out with eating my food while it's warm. When I'm finished, Jolene hammers me with question after question, lawyer mode activated.

What time did this occur? Where did you go prior to the inn? Who did you see when you went to those places? Did you speak to anybody when you arrived at the inn?

Jolene has her notepad out, recording my answers.

"Do you clearly remember locking your door?" she asks.

"I wish I could say I remember, but I don't. I tripped when I walked in and everything went flying, and I was so concerned with catching myself and not hurting Peanut. I have no specific memory of locking the door."

Jolene nods, pen moving across the paper.

The possibility that I did not lock the hotel room door, that it's me who exposed myself and my baby to potential harm, makes me sick. "Jolene, I am a terrible mother. Last night could have been one hundred times worse. How could I forget to lock the door?"

"You don't know if that's what happened," she reminds me. "But also, please cut yourself some slack. Yesterday was Maggie's birthday. I've known you for a long time, so I can confirm that you are a basket case on that day. Now," she says, adopting her stern tone. "Let's keep going. Focus on facts. Not feelings. Who else had access to the room besides you?"

"Everybody, if I left the room unlocked." The idea makes me want to tear my hair out.

"For argument's sake, let's assume the room was locked. Who has access?"

"The hotel manager, I suppose. Whatever key housekeeping uses to service the room." As I say it, I picture Braxton. He was working last night. He didn't have a single word to say to me when I returned to the inn, arms full as I walked through the lobby. And then later, he tried to tell me I needed to check out, and Hugo shut him down. "The night manager probably has access to a master key. I got a weird vibe from him the first time I met him."

The top of Jolene's head moves like she's nodding, pen scribbling. "What behavior did you find objectionable?"

I love Jolene in lawyer mode. She is such a boss.

"He looks at me longer than is socially acceptable. He's unfriendly. His whole vibe is very off-putting. It's probably why he works at night."

Jolene finishes writing down what I'm saying, her gaze refocusing on the screen. "Those are opinions."

I blow out a breath. "I know."

She's biting the side of her lip, thinking. "Why take pictures with your phone? Let's assume whoever did this is sexually perverse. Taking photos of a woman sleeping may arouse them. If that were the case, he would've taken them with his phone. Unless," she holds one finger up, "he took them with both phones. Maybe he gets off on picturing you being scared when you find the photos."

"Ugh," I groan. "This gets worse the longer we talk about it. I'm never leaving the house again."

"I know, I know, it's disgusting, but stick with me here. I think you have two possibilities. One, he took photos with both phones, in which case he's likely a pervert. Two, he only took photos with your phone, in which case—"

"It's a scare tactic," I finish.

"Exactly. Now, who would want you scared? And scared enough to do what, exactly?"

"Someone who knows why I'm in Olive Township."

"Yep. Maybe someone who has information and doesn't want it discovered, or—"

"The person who killed Simon De la Vega."

We stare at each other, her caramel eyes looking meaningfully into my chocolate color. "You know what this means. You're onto something. Someone played their hand."

"Maybe," I hedge, because if there's one thing I've learned, it's to err on the side of caution. We might deal in facts, but emotions are rarely far behind. Emotions can alter stories, exaggerate events, place hope where none should exist.

"Maybe," she agrees. "And maybe that means we can start using this to create episodes. We need them," she reminds me, not that I need reminding. I am all too aware of our download stats, our decrease in podcast subscribers.

"I'm going to begin working on backstory, on creating the story around what happened. But also, I'm bringing in a digital marketing agency."

My eyes bulge. "Jolene, we've talked about this. We can—"

"No, we can't. I mean this with all the love in the world. Get out of your own way."

"That did *not* sound loving."

"Tough love, toots. Now, listen. I did some work for a company called P Squared Marketing. Legal stuff. A majority of their business is focused on brick and mortar concepts, but I asked if they ever work on promoting podcasts or other forms of media. The owner, Paisley, told me they have experience creating a social media campaign for an aspiring author, and he now has a publishing deal." Jolene pauses, giving me a chance to react.

"That's really cool, but I don't see what it has to do with us."

"I asked if she'd have a meeting with us. Over the computer, obviously, since you're in Olive Township."

My first inclination is to decline, but I can't stand to dash the pleading hope on Jolene's face. "One meeting," I concede. Jolene has been by my side since college, indulging me in my crazy dream to start a podcast. I owe her at least a meeting with a marketing company.

Jolene breathes a sigh of relief. "I'll text you the details and email over the meeting link. I better skedaddle, my lunch break is up in a few."

"But you didn't eat lunch."

"I run on coffee, legalese, and the occasional cigarette that I fucking hate but everyone else does it so I do it, too." She grins at my shaking head. "I'm not happy that you're choosing not to tell the police about your photos. Stay there with Hugo, alright? Don't go back to that hotel."

"Obviously. But I can't stay here. There's another place in town. A lot nicer than the inn."

"Why can't you stay here?" Hugo's voice curls over my shoulders.

Chapter 24

Mallory

I WHIP AROUND, SUDDENLY PAINFULLY AWARE OF MY bedraggled wet hair, my belly peeking from my cropped tank top. I didn't think I'd see him this early, so I hadn't considered him when dressing. Didn't he say he had a full day today? I could swear that's what he told me this morning before dawn had dared to crack.

Any preoccupation with how I look disappears the moment my eyes find Hugo. He's a little dirty, and a little sweaty, and he's wearing a backwards baseball cap. He walks closer, pushing up the sleeves of his long-sleeve shirt, palms gliding over muscled forearms.

Good thing there isn't a doorway anywhere nearby for him to grip the top of the frame. I'd be a goner.

What happened to the pregnant lady?

Oh, she melted into the floor. Don't mind her, step over the large puddle.

My eyes track Hugo as he approaches, stopping right behind me. I look up at him, into the dark brown eyes fringed in sooty lashes, the sharp arc of his generous eyebrows. So unfairly thick and shapely. Lost on a man.

"Hey," I say, swallowing around what can only be described as cactus needles in my throat.

"Why can't you stay here?" he asks again, looking down at me. His eyes burn with intensity, as if this is the most important question he can possibly ask me.

"She can," Jolene pipes up. "And she will."

Hugo looks over my head, finding my outspoken best friend on the screen.

"Hello. I'm Hugo."

Jolene grins. "I know who you are."

I turn around on the stool, shooting a stern look at Jolene. *Act right* I say with my eyes. "This is Jolene. My best friend and producer of Case Files."

"Nice to meet you, Jolene. Are you aware that your best friend is incredibly funny and has a knack for alliteration?"

Jolene's lips purse, I think so she won't grin like a loon. "I've noticed this about her once or twice."

Hugo's standing behind me, and even though there's a back to the stool, it's like I can feel him through the upholstery. His nearness is hypnotizing. Distracting. Makes me curl my bare toes around the bottom rung on the counter stool, my body looking for a place to put the tension.

"So," Hugo says, "you think Mallory should stay with me?"

"Either that or find the perv who took photos of her sleeping and castrate him. Can she borrow one of your swords?"

I glance up at Hugo to gauge his reaction. He's showing no horror or shock, face straight as he plays along. "A sword is too much weapon for a job like that."

Jolene shrugs one-shouldered, eyes glimmering with mischief. "I guess she'll have to stay with you."

"She's welcome here. Her and Peanut." Then he touches my shoulder, the lightest, kindest connection, and my body responds by throwing tiny flamethrowers all over the place.

"I promise we won't overstay our welcome," I assure him. I don't miss the way the corners of his eyes squint like he has words balancing on the tip of his tongue but he's not sure he should say them.

"I knocked off early so I could take you into town for your car, and lunch." He cranes his neck at my empty plate, an inch of sourdough crust the only evidence there was ever food on it.

"I thought you said you had a full day?"

"I made room," he answers. "Let me grab a shower and we can leave when you're ready. Jolene, it was nice to meet you."

He retreats from the kitchen, entering the hallway I came from awhile ago. His pants are work-softened, tight in all the right places. Just before he disappears from my sight, he reaches behind his head, gathering his shirt at the neck. One more step and he's gone, taking what was sure to be a spectacular view with him.

"Mal," Jolene fans herself with her hand. "Are you kidding me? My ovaries volunteer as tribute."

Hugo

"Give me three more seconds and I'll be out of earshot," Hugo shouts.

"Way to go," I mutter.

"No, no. Way to go, to you. You probably put your phone on timer and took those photos yourself so you could weasel your way into Hugo's bed."

"Guest bed," I correct.

"Not for long," she counters.

"You're a pill, you know that?"

"But you love me."

"I do. Now go subsist on your sad and concerning diet and send me all the info for our marketing meeting."

Jolene blows me a kiss and ends the call.

I wash my plate and the cooled frying pan, drying and replacing them where I found them. Walking to the guest room to get changed, I hear the muffled sounds of the shower coming through the inch of space under a door at the end of the hall.

Hugo's in there. Naked. Soapy. Slick. I bet his hair darkens to pitch when it's wet. Does he have a tattoo? Freckles on his upper back that resemble a constellation? An interesting scar? Wounds from all those years fencing?

I dart into the guest room before I can do anything foolish. There will be no giving in to the fantasy playing through my mind right now. Maybe I should find an icepack and place it in my underwear, because that ho at the top of my legs is parched, and my temporary roomie is looking like water.

Firmly, I close the door behind myself. I spend a few minutes changing into one of my loose dresses and brushing out my mostly-dried hair, then wind it into a bun at the nape of my neck. Grabbing my purse and a pair of slip-on sandals, I make my way to the living room to wait for Hugo.

He's already there, standing near a window, holding a sandwich in one hand and a can of soda water in the other. He wears a fresh pair of jeans and a white T-shirt. My stomach rolls at the sight of him. How am I going to stay here and not spontaneously combust?

I must make a noise as I enter, because he turns to find me. His gaze lowers to my stomach, followed by a fleeting look of disappointment.

I stop at the far end of the room beside the couch and look down at myself. Am I not dressed appropriately? "We're only running errands, right?"

"Yeah," Hugo answers, eating a quarter of his sandwich in one bite.

"You had a weird look on your face when I walked in." Has he changed his mind about letting me stay here? That must be it. He's second-guessing our proximity, the way we've been steadily getting closer every day since I arrived. "Are you thinking we should put some professional distance between us? I get it. I'm here to maybe connect and possibly solve our loved ones' murders. Not be your roomie."

Maybe. Possibly. I hate the way these words come with caveats. Just the sound of them has me envisioning a person opening their mouth and raising one finger in the air, as if they're reminding me none of this is concrete. It could all be for nothing, and I'll have to figure out another way to forgive myself, and face raising my child in a world where my sister's murderer roams free.

Hugo finishes chewing his bite, takes a sip of his water, and wipes his hands with a napkin he pulls from his back pocket. Then he places the napkin on a side table and lays the remaining sandwich on it.

He walks closer, eyes on me. Stops directly in front of me. He's close enough I smell his bodywash, or maybe it's deodorant, or hell, maybe it's simply *him*. Between that scent and the way he's looking at me, my toes are curling, pressing into my shoes to keep me from swaying.

"Mallory." Hugo wears a look of utter seriousness. "It seems you need to keep hearing me say this, so I'll do it again. *I want you to stay here*. I promise you, I have never invited a person into my home who I did not want to be there."

My teeth strum my bottom lip as his words work over me. Words are nice and all, but action says so much more. Dylan gave me words, and when it came to facing the reality of the life we made, he couldn't run away fast enough.

But last night, Hugo raced to me. Wrapped me in his arms and took me from the inn and whatever danger may have still been lurking. He caught me when I fainted. What more do I need? He's spoken, and he's shown.

"Alright," I nod. "You had a look on your face when I walked in, and I guess I'm defensive. It's not easy being a pregnant woman, staring down the reality of becoming a single mom in only a handful of months."

A muscle along Hugo's jaw tics. "Mallory, you can keep your fists in fighting stance against the rest of the world, but when it comes to me, you'll have no need." He reaches for my hand, wraps it in his. The scrape of a callus has my breath quickening. "You're here to work, and my compliance, and even my participation, makes that easier for you. And maybe I'm one-sided here, and if I am, that's ok, but this doesn't feel like it's only a working relationship. It feels like maybe we're..." He struggles to find the right word, and his thumb rubs over the top of my fingers. "Friends?"

My heart is busy melting over his words, and that spot below my navel is busy distracting me. If his thumb weren't running circles over my hand, I could focus.

"Friends," I manage to say. "Definitely."

Chapter 25

Hugo

FRIENDS.
Seriously?
I friend-zoned myself.
May as well kick my own ass while I'm at it.

Chapter 26

Hugo

MALLORY, MY *FRIEND*, SITS A FOOT FROM ME. THE car window is down, the wind swirling those dark locks around her face. Her brows are furrowed, her cheekbones taut. I wonder if she realizes she is chewing the side of her bottom lip. Is she thinking about what happened to her last night? I know I haven't been able to go more than a few minutes without having it invade my mind. Not only the events, but the possibilities.

The second I sat my ass in the desk chair at the Summerhill on-site office, I called Penn. He was huffing and puffing when he answered my call, out on a run with Slim Jim, his Belgian Malinois. Penn lives closer to town, and closer to the Olive Inn. For Daisy's safety, I wanted him to know what happened to Mallory. I also called Vivi, made sure she knew.

Penn, being the person he is, suggested he pay Braxton a visit. "If it wasn't him, he would have seen somebody walking through that lobby."

Hugo

I told him Mallory is trying for as little disruption to the town as possible, and he had some choice words for her decision. "I'm not making any promises. If I see that fucker so much as sneeze near Daisy, it's on." I can't deny him that, especially when it's exactly what I want to do.

"What are you thinking about over there?" I ask Mallory.

"Last night," she answers, her eyes finding mine. We share a long look before I redirect my gaze to the road. The look may have only lasted a few seconds, but I saw fire in her eyes.

"What about it?" I ask, a tightness to my tone. My fingers curl on the steering wheel, the same way they did early this morning when the event was fresh. Mallory isn't the only one furious at the idea of her and Peanut being encroached upon.

"Too many emotions to name, honestly. And I have thoughts... many thoughts. Namely, what if whoever did this isn't simply a perv looking to—" she cuts off, grimacing. "I don't want to finish that sentence. What if someone's sending me a message?"

A message? I hadn't considered that. My thoughts started and ended with a sicko.

"What kind of message?"

"Maybe somebody found out what I'm doing here, and they don't like it. Maybe they were trying to scare me into leaving."

My fingernails scrape against the scruff on my jaw. I hadn't bothered to shave after the shower I took, I was too antsy to get back out to Mallory. To take her anywhere she might need to go. "Why would anybody in this town care what you were doing?"

Using extra care, I take the turn off Summerhill Road, heading for town. Mallory is quiet, almost as if she doesn't want to answer me. Almost as if she would prefer I reach her conclusion on my own.

When I don't have anything to say, Mallory drums her fingertips on her thighs and says, "My job is kind of like putting together a puzzle. I try different pieces to see if they fit, and eventually that means enough pieces fit together to form a picture. That also means I try a lot of pieces that don't fit together. Solving an unsolved crime, or any crime, really, means there are usually many failed attempts to fit enough puzzle pieces together to reach the truth."

"Got it." I nod. "Why do I feel like you're setting me up to receive bad news?"

She shakes her head, and the gold hoop earrings she wears swing. "I'm laying down a foundation of knowledge. It won't do either of us any good if I tell you what I'm thinking without preparing you."

"Consider me prepared." I'm not though. In truth, I feel a little bit sick to my stomach. Mallory's been at this for a long time, but every step is new to me.

"I think it's worth considering that whoever took those photos of me last night was trying to scare me into leaving because they found out I'm here to learn about your dad, and that would only matter if—"

The lightbulb goes on in my head, the answer screaming at me. "If there was something to learn."

Hugo

A wedge forms in my throat as I do my best to grapple with a possibility I wish were impossible. "That would mean someone in Olive Township either has information about what happened, or—" I cut off, blinking hard. I can't keep driving.

Slowing, I pull over onto the shoulder of the road and shift to Park. Propping my elbow on the car door, I press a fist to my mouth, and say, "Or it means the person who killed him still lives in Olive Township. And if that were true, it would mean I have been living around them my whole life." My voice wobbles. Cracks.

"Hugo," Mallory murmurs. She unbuckles her seat belt, tenderly touches my face. I turn toward her, letting her cup my cheeks. Her touch is soft. Soothing. "All of this is an attempt to put the puzzle together. We're talking out loud, seeing if the pieces fit. I know this is asking a lot of you, but try to remember these are queries, not conclusions."

She's right. Lord, she's smart. Balanced. Levelheaded. Strong.

"Alright," I answer, my gaze falling over her face. She's so beautiful it hurts. No makeup face. And those shoulders, exposed by yet another loose-fitting sundress.

I get a sudden idea. "What do you think about going somewhere a little further than Olive Township?"

"I'm game," she answers, a question in her eyes.

"I think you should go shopping."

Her eyes narrow at me. "You don't like my clothes?"

"That's not what I said." I point at her waist. "Buckle up."

"I have clothes, you know." The click of her buckle connecting is the only sound, then she says, "I bought a few more things when I extended my stay the first time."

"You're going to need more clothes. More everything."

She scoffs. "And why is that?"

"Because I'm going to ask you to stay longer. Keep trying puzzle pieces."

She fights a smile. "Is that right? When do you plan on asking me?"

I fight the same smile. What is it about this woman that has me feeling ok even though there is the looming possibility that something terrible may have been happening under my nose all these years? It's like the terrible thing can still exist, but facing it with Mallory makes it bearable. Makes it into something that won't take me down.

"When the time is right," I tell her. And ok, yeah, I'm flirting. Friends can flirt, right?

MALLORY COMES out of the dressing room in a dress that shows off her pregnancy. Or maybe it doesn't show it off as much as it doesn't hide it. In fact, everything she has tried on for the last two hours we've been shopping has highlighted the small bump she sports. As a bonus to me, everything she's tried on has also shown off her perfect ass, round and generous, and begging to be touched by me.

It is absolutely, one hundred percent not *my* hands that are begging to touch *her* ass. Not at all.

Mallory seems to prefer dresses and skirts, and when the saleswoman approaches with maternity skirts, Mallory balks. "There's a pouch," she says, nose scrunching as she pinches the draping fabric on the front of the skirt.

"That's for your belly, dear," the woman says sweetly. "Just wait until you really pop. These non-maternity stretchy skirts you've been trying on won't cover you."

Mallory's jaw drops. The woman retreats, and Mallory turns her disbelieving eyes on me.

"Did Vivi wear stuff like this?" She holds up the skirt the saleswoman brought her. She pulls away the loose fabric, and it really does resemble a pouch. "I could put my joey in here and hop away."

Laughing, I point at her belly. "I think you are supposed to do exactly that."

"I'm not a marsupial," she huffs, holding the skirt out in front of her. She examines it, sighing. "I guess I'll need stuff like this eventually. It's hard to believe I'll be big enough to fit into it." She retreats into the fitting room with the new items.

I sit back in the upholstered chair, crossing one leg over the other, trying to figure out what has me taking a pregnant woman shopping for maternity clothes on a Monday afternoon when I have a business to run. And, the even bigger question, why do I like it so much?

"Hugo?" Mallory calls from behind a closed door.

I sit up, glancing around. The sales attendants are busy helping other people, and besides, Mallory did not call for them. She called for me.

"Yeah?" I ask, coming to stand outside her door.

"I feel supremely stupid, but I need some assistance."

I swallow. The teenager in me perks up, recalling fitting room fantasies that most definitely will not be taking place today.

"What can I help you with?"

"Can you come in?"

"Uh." I look again at the saleswomen. Only one is in my line of sight, and she is busy. "Sure."

There's the turn of a lock, and the door opens an inch. Mallory says, "You'll have to open it the rest of the way. I need my hands."

What? She needs her hands? For what?

Pressing a palm flat to the door, I push it open just enough so I can slip through, but not so much that anybody else can see in.

Mallory stands with her back to me. Her gaze is on the ground, long, dark hair falling over her shoulders in two separate waves. I close the door and lock it behind me, then turn to face her. The mirror on the opposite end of the fitting room allows me a full view of Mallory's front. She lifts her head to look at me, causing her hair to follow, revealing inch after inch of skin. From the top of her rib cage down, she is covered by the dress she was just in. From the top of her rib cage up, she is covered only by her hands. Except her hands are too small to do the job adequately, and round flesh spills out on all sides.

Force my eyes to stay on hers in the mirror. That's what I have to do right now. And even though I'm focusing on her like my life depends on it, guess what I can still see in my central vision?

"What's the problem?" I croak. This is it. This is how I die. A half-glimpse of Mallory's breasts were enough to do me in.

"The zipper is stuck." Mortification twists her tone, makes her sound pained.

Grateful to have something else to look at, I search out the zipper running down the middle of her back.

Yep. It's more than stuck. It's broken. "I'm going to have to rip the dress off you."

"What?" she asks, alarmed.

"The zipper is totally broken. You must have really been fighting with it."

She blows out a frustrated breath. "Like wrestling a hyena."

I take one side of the hanging fabric in each hand, getting a good grip on it. "I think you won the match," I say, giving the fabric a forceful yank. The sound of ripping fabric fills the air, but it's only an inch. I repeat the motion, using more force this time. The tear of fabric sounds different this time, longer and somehow *sexy*. The rip goes down the seam, all the way to the top of the red thong Mallory wears. Because of course she does.

I rake a hand over my face. "Your favorite color is red, isn't it?"

She nods. "Red like my face right now."

I meet her eyes in the mirror, noting the embarrassment, but something else, too. A blossoming heat. Our locked gazes persist, time slows. My voice comes out like gravel. "Red is my favorite color, too." Then I slip out, giving Mallory her privacy. Basically, I run away.

I don't know much about life. I'm a guy who won a gold medal in a sport most people know little about, and I've retired to live a quiet life carrying on my family's legacy. But I do know one thing for certain.

When it comes to Mallory, I am so fucked.

She emerges from the dressing room a few minutes later, flustered. The red has not faded from her cheeks. Not one bit.

"How did everything work out for you?" The saleswoman's saccharine voice cuts in.

"Good," Mallory says. "Mostly. I had a problem with a zipper, but, um"—her eyes laser in on me—"I worked it out."

The saleswoman's smile falters. "Oh no! I hope I didn't miss your distress signal."

Mallory looks at me again. "You didn't. I had a knight in shining armor."

The woman takes the stack of clothes from Mallory, marching to the register.

I can't help my smirk. "I'm a knight?"

Mallory holds up two fingers. "Two saves in fewer than twenty-four hours."

Together we walk to the register. "Let's hope there aren't any more ever again."

"I don't kn-ow," she warbles the last word. "I will definitely be needing help reaching things on top shelves. And if I see a spider, all bets are off. I'll be requiring the services of my knight, pronto."

My chest swells. My shoulders straighten. Perhaps I walk with a bit more swagger.

She called me her knight.

Her knight.

We reach the counter where the woman stands, ringing up Mallory's stack of clothing.

"One of these items is in very bad shape," she says, suspicious gaze darting between me and Mallory.

"That would be the zipper problem I had," Mallory says sheepishly.

"We have tools for zipper problems." The woman eyes me before returning her gaze to Mallory. "Looks like you had your own tool for solving your *zipper problem*."

She says it in a way that's part amused, part *I know what you did.*

Mallory laughs, but it's not her real laugh. She thumbs at me. "He's not just a pretty face," she jokes.

Mallory hasn't caught on that the saleswoman thinks we got busy in the fitting room, and since her cheeks are still pink (adding to the evidence of our escapade) I'm not planning on telling her.

The saleswoman recites the total. I grab my wallet, brandishing my card before Mallory can say a word.

"What? Hugo. No."

"Too late." I shrug, and then there's the electronic sound of a payment accepted.

Mallory frowns. "I wasn't expecting that."

"I know you weren't." I take the two large bags off the counter, heading for the exit. "I made a lot of money fencing. First the gold medal, and then a lucrative cereal box brand deal, among others. I bought my car, and remodeled my house into a place that feels like home, and now there's nothing more I need. Really."

"Well, thank you. I'm not used to being around a person who does nice things so easily."

"That's too bad, Mallory. Because you deserve it."

She does. She really does. Mallory wants to solve my dad's murder. Her sister's, too. She's not here making money.

I hold open the door for her, and we step into the cool early evening. It's that odd time of year in the desert, when the day is warm but drops to chilly the moment the sun disappears. "How does a podcast make money?"

"Sponsorships. Advertising. But how many of those we get depend on how many downloads we receive." Mallory worries her bottom lip with her teeth. "Our numbers have been steadily decreasing. Jolene wants to bring in a digital marketer. Her goal is to get picked up by a podcast network, but right now we don't have the numbers for it."

We arrive at my car, and I open her door. Mallory slides in, and I place her bags in the trunk. "How did you get into podcasting?" I ask, when we're exiting the parking lot.

"I took psychology classes when I first got to college,

and I was fascinated. But instead of going toward psychology, I got a degree in journalism and became an investigative reporter. Then I wrote an article about a true crime case that helped to exonerate the woman who had been found guilty and imprisoned. After that, Case Files was born."

I stare at her in awe. "That's one of the coolest things I've ever heard. You should walk around telling that story to everybody you meet."

"Right, the same way you tell everybody you meet that you're a gold medal Olympian?"

"That's different," I argue.

"How?" she shoots back.

"One is bragging, the other is just a really cool story."

Mallory looks south as I take the on-ramp for the freeway. "Do you see that little mountain over there?" She points at a large hill in the near-distance. "My mom and her husband have a house at the base of it."

"Do you want to stop and visit?"

Mallory shakes her head, sad but determined. "We don't talk much. After Maggie died, my mom couldn't bear to look at me. Fourteen years later, and she still can't."

"Because she's so fucked up over what happened?"

Mallory goes silent. Just when I think she's finished talking, she says in a voice so full of pain it rips my heart out, too. "Because it was my fault."

That makes me mad. Not *at* Mallory, but *for* Mallory. I understand her thinking that way when she was a kid, because I did the same. It's not abnormal for a child to find a way to blame themselves. But it has been fourteen years. Has nobody stepped up and told Mallory she's not to blame? And is Mallory really going to sit there and shoulder the blame? The guilt alone must be eating her alive.

"You are not responsible for what happened to Maggie. At all."

"I left her alone that day. I took her to the water park, and I was supposed to watch out for her, but I didn't."

If what Mallory needs is for me to defend her to herself, I will. I'll take her away from skeezy night managers, I'll rip dresses with broken zippers, and I'll keep her from continuing to play this unhealthy narrative she's spent far too long believing.

"Mallory," I say with every ounce of seriousness in my body. "If I wasn't driving in five lanes of traffic going seventy-five miles an hour, I would look you in the eyes while I say this: your sister died because a crazed lunatic decided to end her life. The same way my dad died. You didn't cause that. You didn't make it happen. You didn't ask that psychopath to make that choice. And the way your mom has acted since it happened is reflective of her, not of you. She's missing out on you, and that's really fucking sad."

Tears roll down Mallory's cheeks, and she dashes them away with the backs of her hands. Fucking traffic. Fuck this freeway. I want to hold her. Wipe her tears.

"Thank you," she says. "That's three times." I feel her

eyes on me, the warmth of her gaze seeping into me. "Three times you've rescued me."

If my heart had biceps, it would be flexing them right now. That is how much I feel like Mallory's hero.

I am so far beyond fucked, I can't even see it in my rearview anymore.

Chapter 27

Mallory

I'VE BEEN LOOKING FOR MAGGIE. I WENT TO THE LAST *place I saw her, those plastic beach chairs. Cold panic set in the longer I looked.*

There was a scream, and it drew me here.

To this bathroom on the far end of the water park, shaded by fake palm trees, beside a Sno-Cone hut with a Closed sign hanging unevenly.

I push my way through the small crowd blocking the entrance to the bathroom, women in shorts and one-piece swimsuits, some turning away to cover their children's eyes.

The tile floor of the bathroom is old. Cracked. Worn from years of parkgoers. The smell inside is unpleasant, like the chemicals they use in the water but also of sulphur from the drains.

Three stalls, and a fourth at the end, larger than the others. Door flung open.

My heart and my stomach drop out of me, replaced by

sickening dread.

Don't let it be Maggie. Don't let it be Maggie.

Hot pink shorts come into view first. A lime green swimsuit. A neck with red, angry marks. The sweetness vanished from her eyes.

My Maggie is gone.

I drop to my knees and scream. The same women who shielded their children's eyes pull me away. One drags me back, she is tall and strong, and she presses my face to her chest, covers my ear with her palm. The whispers, the shouts, they muffle. Drowned out by my silent screaming.

I wake with a start. Press a hand to my belly. It grounds me, reminds me where I am.

The seconds tick by. My bladder becomes insistent now, as does the dryness in my throat. It's as if my body is saying *you're alive, and you have needs.*

Rolling over, I push myself up to seated. My phone lies on the nightstand, and I tap the screen. It illuminates, showing me the time. 1:17.

I pad sleepily to the bathroom, take care of my bladder first. Quietly I walk to the kitchen for a glass of water. A motion sensor night-light flickers on as I walk down the hall, and I'm grateful for it. The full moon from a few nights ago has disappeared, and the night outside is an endless black shot through with stars.

The kitchen is dark, and I pause at the threshold, getting my bearings. Behind me, the motion sensor nightlight goes out. My eyes adjust, and I see the outline of a figure near the sink.

"Hey," Hugo says, sleep curling into his deep voice.

"Hi," I answer. The room is coming into focus now. Outlines of appliances, the window over the sink, the fruit bowl on the island laden with crisp green apples.

"Are you thirsty?" Hugo asks. He doesn't wait for my answer, he's already moving for the fridge. He opens it, and it bathes the front of his body in light.

My throat, already dry, now rivals the sandy desert in the distance. Hugo wears nothing but shorts, and his body is something someone would paint. Long muscles, shaped and chiseled. I can't see everything in full relief, but the light illuminates just enough to make it hard to see anything but him. He turns away with a bottle of water, and the light disappears with the close of the door.

Hugo reaches me in two strides, hands me the bottle. I open it and sip. Hugo steps away, leaning over a section of the kitchen counter. He pushes a dimmer switch, and now a faint light stretches from underneath the cabinets. Low, but enough that I can see the way his eyes rake over my body. I'm wearing my nightgown, a slip of red silk. It's not lined in lace with a slit up the thigh or anything overtly sexy like that, but it's comfortable and loose and most importantly, not what I was wearing when the creep took pictures of me. I saved the yellow pajamas, just in case, but I will never wear them again. A shame too, because they were new.

"Couldn't sleep?" Hugo asks, his gaze finally landing on my face. A warm glow spreads through me, knowing he was drinking me in. I want to be what quenches him.

He leans back against the lip of the counter, crossing

his arms. The stance makes his biceps pop, his shoulders flex.

It makes me need to cross my legs.

"I had a bad dream," I answer. "You?"

"Same," he responds. "Do you have bad dreams often?"

"A few times a year," I confess.

"Me too," he answers. "The same dream?"

I nod. "You?"

"They differ, but it's the same handful on rotation."

We fall quiet. We've confessed what keeps us up at night, but neither of us feel the need to describe it, because we already know. It is a dubious honor to understand one another this well.

"Do you want a hug?" Hugo asks.

I hadn't thought to want a hug. To even need one. I've been shouldering my grief and pain and sadness alone for a long time. In the beginning, I wanted hugs. To be held and soothed. Over time, that stopped. I wasn't getting it, and I learned to survive without it.

Hugo's offer brings that need screaming to the surface, makes me realize it was there all along, unmet and never truly going away.

"Yes," I whisper, setting my water on the counter and taking a step toward him. He pushes off the counter, meets me more than halfway. He doesn't slow or stop, falter or question. He wraps me up, pulls me against his chest. My arms wind around his back, his hand works up into my hair, cradles my head. His other hand splays against my back, holding me in place.

We stay that way, silent and unmoving. Breathing one another in. Relaxing into each other. It's the best hug of my life.

A tiny moan escapes me. My eyes blink open, and I open my mouth to blame it on my exhaustion, but there's a rumble in Hugo's chest. His throat. He's groaning, too.

And then his fingers move in my hair. The tiniest contraction. A second moan from me.

Involuntary, I swear.

He does it again, almost a massage. A tiny sound in my throat, as if he holds a switch and flips it. My hands on his back begin to move. A faint touch over his smooth, muscled skin.

Higher, to his shoulders. His neck, my fingers curling, nails lightly scratching.

A deeper groan from Hugo, reaching between my legs.

These touches are soothing, and stoking the flames that flickered to life that first day we met. The flames we've been denying ever since.

Hugo's face dips, lips pressing against the middle of my forehead. He is hard and thick against my hip.

This is it. The precipice. We both know it. Neither of us expected the other person. He was doing his own thing in Summerhill. I was navigating life in Phoenix. But were either of us really living?

Is that what we're doing now? Waking up? Living? Were we waiting on each other, needing one another to awaken the other?

"Mallory," Hugo says, agony twisting my name.

Hugo

"Hmm?"

"I'm unbelievably close to kissing you."

"I'm even closer to letting you."

He spins me around, lifts me like I weigh nothing, and sets me on the kitchen counter. Without a thought, I open my legs, allow him to step between. He gazes at me, dark brown on dark brown, the understated glow from the light revealing the need in our eyes.

Hugo reaches for me, hand landing on my collarbone, gliding up my neck. He fingers my jaw, positioning my face. Another tiny moan from me.

"Those fucking moans," he whispers. "They're killing me."

"So many more where those came from," I taunt.

He growls, something low and animal and so sexy it makes me swallow. My hands find his shoulders, and he reaches around my back with his free hand, hauling me flush against him. Now my center is pressed against his rows and rows of abs, and it's everything I can do to not get greedy. I'm dying to grind against him. I wore underwear because it felt indecent to sleep in someone's guest bed without them. Now I'd be lying if I said there isn't a little part of me that wished I hadn't.

Hugo's face hovers closer to mine, and I tip mine up, offering. He obliges, dipping lower, lips touching mine at long last.

Fire. That's what I feel. A zinging electricity, shooting out to my limbs. Our lips move, pressing and yielding, and I hold onto his shoulders while his tongue parts my lips. A groan from both of us.

We kiss and kiss, taking sips of air when necessary, but we don't let up. He holds me close, and there is such sweetness to it. I know this kiss must end, but I never want it to.

We slow, tongues receding, but I nip his lower lip gently, sucking it into my mouth to soothe. It elicits a frustrated growl from him. He likes that.

We part, gazing at each other once again. Coming full circle. I prop my hands behind myself, steadying me. Hugo's gaze drops to the edge of the counter, where he stands between my legs. More specifically, where my center presses to his stomach. His eyes move over the small space, a lazy perusal, followed by a deep breath.

"We should probably go back to bed," he chokes out.

I know what I'll be doing the second I hit those sheets, and it won't be sleeping.

"Yeah," I wheeze.

Hugo steps back, helps me off the counter. I grab my bottle of water, the only reason I came out here. Hugo slides the lights off, and then I feel his hand on the small of my back, and I shiver at the memory of his lips on mine. He guides me down the hall, and that motion sensor light illuminates.

We pause at the guest room door, and I look up at him. Muscled and tousled and so handsome it hurts. I want to keep making him feel good. I want him to do the same to me.

He grips the top of the doorframe. Looks down at me. His muscles pop, and I die a thousand hot and sex-starved deaths.

"Mallory..." he says, having no knowledge of the way I'm melting on the inside.

I'm already shaking my head, and he stops to let me talk. "Don't say that was a mistake."

A pleased smile tugs up one corner of his mouth. "Never. I was going to tell you that was the best kiss I've ever had."

I smile, too. Unabashedly. "Me, too."

He leans down. Brushes a kiss on my forehead. "Get some rest, Beautiful."

I practically purr. "Right back at you, Handsome."

Two minutes later with a hand between my legs, I lie in bed and envision him down the hall, doing the same.

Chapter 28

Mallory

For the rest of the week, the inner workings of Summerhill keeps Hugo busy.

There are no more kisses, and we don't talk about it. We're not pretending it didn't happen, or at least I'm not. But Hugo is cautious now, careful. More than before. Like I'm made of glass.

I'm not allowing myself to dwell on it, and honestly, I'm busy too, poring over my notes, determining what could be made into episodes for the podcast.

It was a kiss that outshone all others, but I'm a woman with things to do.

On the way into town after our shopping trip, Hugo took me to my car so I could drive it back out to Summerhill. I used it earlier today to run to a store in town and find an oversized whiteboard and colorful markers. Putting everything in front of me visually helps me see things in a different way. Details that sit in the background get the chance to present themselves, and sometimes, it's the details that make all the difference.

Hugo told me to commandeer his dining room table, and that is precisely what I've done. I'm sitting here now, comfortable in a new pair of buttery soft leggings and matching tank top, sipping at my second decaf vanilla latte of the day.

I'd mentioned to Hugo in passing that I saw his sister at Sweet Nothings, and how Sal had made me the coffee drink. Now there's a fancy, sleek silver coffee machine on the kitchen counter. Decaf organic beans and vanilla syrup in the pantry. Whole milk in the fridge.

It's what friends do, right?

He made it clear we're friends, but the way his eyes drank me in in the fitting room says otherwise. And that kiss. Kisses that are mistakes don't feel so earth shattering.

I've learned enough about attraction to know oftentimes it has a mind of its own. The attraction we feel toward another person doesn't always make sense. Sometimes, it doesn't appear to fit. We think we have a type, and then out of nowhere, we're blindsided, inexplicably drawn to someone.

Hugo is my type. Hugo is every woman's type. Two short weeks with that man, and I already know the kind of person he is. A defender, protector. Generous, and kind. Loyal. He wouldn't be back at Summerhill, taking the reins of the family business, if it didn't require a little bit of all those traits.

Sitting back, I draw my legs up into my chest. Or I try to, at least. My stomach prevents it, so I have to splay open my legs, prop them against either arm of the chair. It's not a good look, but it's comfortable. Coffee in hand, my eyes wander over my computer screen. I'm brainstorming concepts for episodes ahead of this afternoon's meeting with the marketers. I have no idea what they're going to want from me, but I can't show up empty-handed. I don't want to waste anybody's time.

At precisely noon, Hugo strolls into his house. This has been our routine over the last few days. He is out of the front door by seven in the morning, returning midday for lunch. That's when I take a break from my work and join him in the kitchen. The domesticity of it, the ease with which we assumed this ritual, should scare me, right? Maybe what I should fear is how much it doesn't scare me. Everything with Hugo feels easy. Good. He might be a relaxing sigh in human form, but he's also sex on legs. Some days when he walks in the door, dirty and sweaty from work, it's everything I can do not to pounce. Keeping myself from overheating has become a second job these days.

With envious eyes, I watch him assemble an Italian sandwich. Pepperoni, salami, capicola. I could close my eyes and taste the salty spice of the lunchmeat, but I settle for making a face at Hugo as I stir my chicken salad with diced celery and walnuts.

He grins knowingly. "I can eat on the porch if it's too much temptation for you."

Plating my sandwich, I say, "I can control myself." Am I only talking about the food? Definitely not. Maybe

Hugo

I'm saying it to remind myself. And if I say it enough times, it must be true, right?

"What's the first thing you're going to eat after Peanut is born?"

"A boatload of sushi," I answer without hesitation. "And then an Italian sub."

"Screaming Eel," Hugo says around his bite.

"Come again?" I ask, pulling out the island stool and taking a seat. Hugo grabs two soda waters from the fridge, pops the tops, and slides one over to me.

"Screaming Eel is a sushi restaurant." He stands on the other side of the island, facing me. "Normally I'd say to never trust a sushi restaurant in the middle of the desert, but that rule does not apply to Screaming Eel. I can take you there, after Peanut's born." We lock eyes over the island. A conversation happens in the silence.

Why would I still be here after Peanut's born?
You can come back.
For what reason?

The conversation is one I don't want to have, even in the quiet. Even when it's not real. I don't want to face the eventual end of my time in Olive Township. Here at Summerhill. Everyday I've napped in the swing bed on Hugo's porch, and gone on a long walk in the late afternoon, soaking up the sun and the surroundings. Hugo has been so busy, and I don't want to interrupt him while he's working, so I stay away from the office where I know he goes every morning. I focus on what I can see, and it's enough. The view takes my breath away and soothes the savage beast within, the one that guards my heart holding a banner that reads *It's your fault.*

Out here, in a place so beautiful, in a home so cozy, with a man so kind, I consider forgiving my fourteen-year-old self. It's difficult, and I'm not there yet, but the fact I am considering it feels momentous.

"I'd like that," I answer, accepting his offer for a future outing for sushi. We don't need to talk about my departure. If Hugo wants to make a plan, far be it for me to rain on his parade.

By the time Peanut's born, I should be long gone. I don't really know why I'm here now. Planning for podcast episodes can happen anywhere, and I tell myself I'm here to keep interviewing, keep digging, but is that true? Olive Township is a couple hours from Phoenix. If I had an idea and wanted to talk to people, it would only be a day trip for me to do so.

So why am I still here? Let's call a spade a spade. I'm here because I don't want to go.

Eventually, I'll have to. My recording equipment is in Phoenix. Maybe I can push that aside for now. Pretend it doesn't exist. Live here, in this moment, on this heavenly olive mill, where the sun feels extra sunny, and the birdsong is sweeter.

We finish our lunch in a companionable silence, and Hugo clears our plates.

"What do you think about taking a tour of the mill tomorrow?" he asks when he's standing by the front door fitting his feet into his work boots.

"Yes, please." I clap my hands together excitedly. "I

have to warn you, I'm already in love with this place. After tomorrow, it might escalate to an obsession."

Hugo looks like the idea of this makes him happy. "Then there is probably something I should warn you about also."

"What's that?"

"It's likely I'm going to nerd out really hard about olives."

I laugh. "Uh-oh. Nerd alert."

Hugo offers me the sexiest grin. He snags a ball cap from a peg near the door, performing a move that sends a tingle to the top of my thighs.

He puts it on backwards.

I look away. I have to. I can't be held responsible for what happens next if I allow my eyes to continue to drink him in. I look at my toes instead. I could really use a pedicure.

"I'll see you for dinner," he says.

"Mm-hmm. Yeah. Sounds great," I manage, forcing my gaze up so I don't arouse suspicion.

Too late. His eyebrows pinch in the center. "I hope your meeting with the marketing company goes well."

My heart lurches. He remembered. We hadn't even talked about it this morning. The last time I mentioned it was yesterday when he came back for lunch.

"Thank you," I say, doing my best to only look in his eyes. The way he did for me when my breasts were covered by little in that dressing room.

With a dip of his head he retreats from his house. I watch him through the front window. Long-legged stride, confident. Returning to finish out his day on an orchard he loves. The same land his dad tended. And his dad before that, if what I read online is correct.

Hugo climbs into his company truck, turning back to glance at his house. He catches my gaze in the window. I've been caught staring.

I raise a hand, waving. He does the same, adding his crooked grin. The combination is lethal.

He's a backwards-hat wearing, lower back touching, doorframe gripping, sword wielding owner of an olive orchard.

My next thought is a sucker punch to the solar plexus.

Some day, some other woman is going to strike gold with him.

I've made myself presentable in time for my call with Jolene and the marketing company.

I follow the link in my email, joining a meeting for which I am one minute late. My scant tardiness can be blamed on Peanut for making me need to pee. *Again.*

"Hello," I greet after checking to make sure my microphone and camera are turned on.

"Hi," a cheerful, stunningly beautiful blonde woman says. She sits on the long side of a gleaming wood desk, a dark-haired woman by her side. "Jolene was just telling us a little about Case Files. I'm Paisley, the owner of P Squared Marketing. This"—she motions to her right—"is my social media strategist, Cecily. I've asked her to join us today because she is a wizard when it comes to growing and finding the right followers on social media."

"Is this where I act demure and say something to negate your compliments?" Cecily grins mischievously at Paisley.

Paisley shrugs. "Not unless you want to, but if you did I'd have to pinch you and make sure you're really you."

Do I like these women already? Yes I do.

"It's nice to meet you both. I'm Mallory. Thank you for meeting with us today."

"We're more than happy to, especially after working with Jolene and hearing about your podcast." Paisley opens the laptop sitting on the desk in front of her. Cecily does the same. "Now," Paisley says, "I want to be certain upfront that I understand your needs. Jolene says that in the three-year run of Case Files you've had a higher than industry standard subscriber count, but in the last eight months you've seen a steady decline in downloads and subscribers. This impedes your ultimate goal of being picked up by a podcasting platform."

"Great summary," I respond.

Paisley turns to Cecily, giving her the floor. Cecily launches in, saying, "Low subscriber count and fewer downloads are not your real problem." Cecily is no-nonsense, something I appreciate. "Those are only symptoms of your issue. A quick peek of your social media accounts showed me you post infrequently, and when you do post, the content isn't attractive. If a true crime podcast is storytelling, then so is social media. It's not a whodunit, but more of a *I bet I can make you want to know who did it.*"

Cecily's way of talking about the intersectionality between true crime and social media has me feeling enthusiastic. Peanut, too, based on the bubbles tumbling around my belly. My midsection isn't visible on screen, so I give Peanut a stroke in response.

"Love it," Jolene says, practically vibrating with excitement.

The front door opens suddenly, and Hugo strides through. He holds his left wrist, hand in the air. From where I'm set up at the dining room table, every lady on my screen has a full view of him.

"Pardon the interruption," he says apologetically. "I cut my hand on a piece of machinery. Couldn't find the first aid kit at the office, so I had to come back for the one I keep here."

"It's ok," I assure him, fighting the urge to go to him and inspect his wound.

Jolene says hello, and before I can introduce the women on the screen, Cecily says, "Hugo?"

She wears an expression of familiarity, like she's seen a long lost friend. Inside me, a little green monster rears its ugly head.

Did they date? Did he care for her? Were they intimate?

Hugo comes closer, and I see it now, the blood trickling down the inside of his palm. He stands behind my

Hugo

chair, and I'm struck by the two of us on the same screen. I've noticed our image in storefronts before, but we're usually moving, and it's too fleeting to get a proper look. This is a reminder of what I saw that day in the dressing room, how good we look together.

"Cecily," Hugo says, sharing her tone of friendly wonderment. "It's been a long time since you've been home. It's nice to see you."

Home must be Olive Township. Definitely an ex, then. High school sweethearts, maybe?

She laughs uncomfortably. "It's not home I'm avoiding. It's a few certain someones who reside there."

Hugo nods knowingly, lifting his hand. "I better tend to this cut."

He waves with his good hand and walks away slightly faster than his usual gait.

"Mallory, you're in Olive Township?" Cecily asks.

I nod, about to answer when Jolene says, "She went for the spa but stayed for—"

"A possible story," I cut in quickly. Jolene could've been about ready to say anything, and I fear it was a word starting with the letter D. That joke is better for girlfriends sipping margaritas. Jolene might know these women well, but I don't.

"Something for the podcast?" Paisley asks, steering us back on course.

"Uh, yes." I glance down the hall to check for Hugo. I don't like saying what I'm about to say so plainly in front of him. "I'm looking into the unsolved murder of Simon De la Vega."

Cecily takes a sharp breath. "Hugo must be ok with that." Her eyes grow wide. "He knows, right?"

"Yes, yes," I rush to say. "Hugo, Vivi, everyone. I have Sonya's blessing."

Cecily looks relieved. "Good. I'm surprised, though. They've always been very"—she mimes zipped lips—"about it."

"Sonya told me it was time." That's all I'll say about that. If Sonya wants people to know the full extent of her reasoning, she can be the one to reveal that.

"It looks like," Paisley pauses as she scrolls her computer, "you haven't started talking about that case yet. Nothing on socials, no episodes. Is that right?"

"Correct. I spent the morning writing out ideas, working through how to structure it for episodes. Deciding if what I have is enough to begin."

Paisley's nodding. "I won't pretend to know anything about podcasting and the work that goes into it, but what I know is the only way you're going to get subscribers and downloads is if you tell new people the content exists. Are you willing to do that? You have the support of the family, but do you have their blessing to take it to socials?"

Hugo appears at the hall entrance. His socked feet kept his return quiet, and now he stands still, looking at me. Then he nods his head deliberately, leading me to my answer. He wants me to take his dad's story outside of Olive Township, bring it out into the world.

I look back at the screen. "All systems go."

"Cecily will create a plan and reach out to both of

you. She'll be your point of contact, but I am available at any time, also."

Jolene's nodding. "Thank you, Cecily and Paisley, for meeting with us."

The call ends, and the screen goes dark.

Hugo still stands at the entrance to the room, but now his arms are crossed, and he leans one shoulder against the wall. It's only now that I notice he hasn't bandaged his wound.

"Are you ok?" I ask tentatively, nodding to the towel wrapped around his hand. In his other hand, he holds a first aid kit.

"Fine," he assures me, but I'm not having it. He's done such a good job caring for me, he needs to let me take care of him for once.

"Sit," I instruct, leading him to a chair at the dining room table. He settles down, and I take the first aid kit from him, laying it out on the table and opening it.

"Let's see what we're working with here," I say, gently unwrapping the towel.

The cut isn't deep, and it's no longer bleeding. It was good that he returned to wash it.

Carefully, holding his upturned palm with my own, I apply an antibiotic ointment. I'm fighting my senses now, the way I want to launch myself into his arms. His nearness and the smell of earth and sweat and Hugo. It's overwhelming.

Hugo is still, and quiet, but I can tell he likes it. Being taken care of.

I'm applying two bandages when Hugo says, "It's one

thing to talk about making what happened to my dad into podcast episodes, and another to watch it happen."

I toss the trash from the bandages on the table. Step back so he can stand.

As soon as he's upright, I step into him. Put my hands on either shoulder. "I'm not going to sensationalize anything. I promise you, I will give your dad's story the respect and care it deserves." The trust not only he, but his whole family, has placed in me, sits heavy in the center of my chest, guiding me.

Hugo's left hand reaches up, wraps around my right forearm. "I know," he says, on a slow downward stroke. "I know you will."

It's silly and juvenile, but I cannot calm my curiosity about how well Cecily and Hugo might know each other. Schooling my voice into a tone of vague interest, I ask, "So, Cecily is from here?"

"Yeah. A little younger than me, by a few years if I'm remembering accurately."

My head tips sideways, and I pretend to adjust my earring. "How do you know her?"

Hugo's gaze tapers. His lips twitch, like maybe he wants to tease me. "Do you remember my friend Duke who showed up late to the Olive Festival?"

"The guy with good hair who Daisy almost married?"

Hugo nods. "He has two sisters. Cecily is one of them."

"Hmm." I can't adjust my earring again, that would look too obvious. I settle for picking an invisible piece of lint from my top. "Were you and Cecily ever involved?"

Hugo makes a face, like the question is abhorrent. "She's my friend's sister."

"So?"

"Friends don't date their friend's little sisters."

"Umm, I think you are very wrong about that."

Alarm widens Hugo's eyes. "Why? Did Vivi say something?"

"No, but I don't think it's uncommon." It's cute watching him be a protective big brother.

So cute, I decide to needle him some more. "Vivi is a grown woman though. She can do what she wants. With *who* she wants to do it with."

Hugo has caught on, and he inspects my face with a shrewd gaze. "You're messing with me, aren't you?"

I can't help the grin spreading across my cheeks. "Maybe."

Hugo reaches out, pinches my hip bone. "Troublemaker."

I wiggle my eyebrows. "I solemnly swear I am up to no good."

Hugo laughs. The phone in his pocket dings with a text message. He drops the hand from my hip so he can read the message. He frowns at the screen, and the private bubble we're in pops. "The mill manager is asking where I am. I better get going."

Hugo strides for the door, pausing once he reaches it. "Mallory, I think you should know that green is a great color on you."

He chuckles and walks from the house.

Maybe green is a great color on me, but right now, my cheeks are nothing but red.

Chapter 29

Hugo

"Mom?" I pop my head into the kitchen at the big house.

"Back here," she yells.

I'm walking through the living room to find her when she emerges from the office. Aunt Carmen follows behind, wearing her eyeglasses and holding a pad of paper, pencil poised above it.

She reads out, "... Proud owner of a sexy cardigan collection, Ralph spent his Friday nights country dancing with two left feet and romancin' the ladies."

"Cute," my mom compliments about my aunt's latest obituary. She turns an appraising eye on me. "Hugo, are you here to tell me about the young lady you have staying in your home?"

Aunt Carmen whistles. "Busted."

"It's Mallory," I explain to my mom.

She gives me a droll look. "I know."

My eyebrows raise teasingly. "If you know, why are you asking?"

"To my knowledge, Hugo, you have never brought a woman to your home."

I rock back on my heels. "You would be right about that."

Her eyebrows lift too, imploring me. "The man who hasn't allowed a woman to step foot in his house, has one staying in it?"

"She's a guest, Mom." A guest whose back I want to curl my fingers against. Lean in after her showers to smell her bodywash. Typical guest behavior, yeah?

"So she's staying in your guest room?"

"Yes. She needed a place to go after..." I falter, unsure how to phrase it. We don't know who took pictures of her, or their motive, and Mallory said emotions can cloud the clear head a person needs to objectively see a case. "Someone entered her hotel room while she was sleeping and took photos of her with her phone. She found them and called me, terrified."

"What?" My mother shouts. "Where was she staying?"

Oh no. I know where this is going. This is the same woman who marched into my elementary art teacher's classroom and asked her how she'd like it if someone told her she's not allowed to go potty when she needs to.

"Mom." I say it calmly, hoping to demonstrate a cool head. Not that I had one the night it happened. I raced into town like it was the Indy 500. But that was different. Mallory was in a dangerous situation, and I had to get to her.

"Hugo, it'll take me two seconds to find out on my own," my mom warns.

Aunt Carmen sighs. "For the love, Hugo, just tell her."

"Olive Inn."

My mom taps a finger on her chin. "Is that why you left in the middle of the night earlier this week?"

"Yes."

"And you brought her here? To your home?"

"Yes."

"Instead of one of the other hotels in town?"

"She's safer here."

"With you."

"Huh?"

"She's safer here with you."

"Well, yes."

"Interesting."

"What is?"

"She called you when she needed help. Not the police. And you responded by not only taking her away from harm, but giving her a safe place."

I nod. "Yes, Mom."

"You turned toward each other, Hugo. She turned to you for help, you turned to her to provide it."

"I did what any decent person would do." Why am I arguing? I know how I feel inside. The way my blood flows hotter, faster when Mallory is present. The way I've thought about her every day this week while I'm working, envisioned her lying in the guest bed across the hall.

"Of course you did. That's how I raised you to behave.

But Hugo, you're doing yourself a disservice by thinking you did the bare minimum."

A disservice? I don't know if I want to dissect that comment.

"You two are almost painful to watch," Aunt Carmen says. "What your mother means to say is that you have a pregnant lady shacked up at your house and you need to spend a little time thinking about why." She dusts off her hands, congratulating herself. "There. You're welcome."

My mom laughs. "Bet you didn't come here to have that conversation."

I scratch the back of my neck with two fingers. "I came here to ask where that old picnic basket is. The one we used when we were kids."

"Why?" My mom crosses her arms, staring me down. "Are you taking someone on a picnic?"

"No, I'm planning to climb inside and wait for people to pass by, then jump out and scare them half to death."

"You do that to me," Aunt Carmen says, "and I'll hit you with whatever I have in my hands at the moment."

Mom spends a handful of seconds staring me down, then decides to let me off the hook. She hunts down the picnic basket, and a few minutes later I'm on my way, basket in hand, rattled by her questions and commentary.

Hugo

SATURDAYS ARE the busiest day at Summerhill. The store brims with shoppers, the restaurant packed with hungry patrons.

We're closed on Sundays, because as my mother says, even the Lord rested on Sunday. If my vote were the only one that counted, I'd be open seven days a week. Sunday is when people are off work, and would distribute the weekend crowds a little more evenly. My mother and I have equal share in Summerhill, so we compromised by expanding the hours we are open on Saturdays. Vivi has a small share of the business, but she has little to do with the operations beyond overseeing the on-site restaurant we opened in the last couple years.

This leaves me no choice but to show Mallory around Summerhill on a Saturday, with the masses.

She meets me in the kitchen at my house at eleven. She slept in today, and honestly, good for her. That woman is always working, her mind never stopping. She's either reading a book, listening to a podcast (not a fellow true crime podcast, I learned when I asked, but one on wellness), writing something, poring over her notes, or internet sleuthing. At this point, I think she knows more about the people of this town, and its history, than I do.

"You look nice," I tell her, glancing over from where I'm standing in front of the high-end coffee machine I purchased this week. It's a big upgrade from the drip coffee maker I had, and I didn't know what I was missing out on. I tell myself I would have bought it eventually, but let's be real. I bought it for Mallory after she mentioned those decaf vanilla lattes at Sweet Nothings. I love Sal, but there's no way I'll let him have a leg up on me. Not where it concerns Mallory.

"Thanks," she answers, looking down at herself. She's wearing that tan suede skirt she got at the mall last weekend. "It's a little big on me, but probably not for much longer."

I have to turn away from her to keep my face from showing my true emotions. I can't understand a man who walks away from the woman carrying his child. I'd be honored if a woman like Mallory used her body to bring my child into the world. I'd cherish her, and care for her, and do everything in my power to show her my gratitude.

Getting my bearings, I turn around with her coffee in hand.

"I was hoping that was for me," she grins impishly, taking the cup I'm offering. "I smelled the vanilla."

"And this, too." I move to the fridge, coming away with the chocolate cherry chia seed pudding I made yesterday. "I added a scoop of protein powder. Should keep you full and your blood sugar regulated."

She takes the jar from me and spins away, but it's too late. I've seen the moisture in her eyes.

"Are you ok? Did I do something wrong?" Is she allergic to chia seeds? Did she tell me, but I forgot?

"No," she says, pained. Frustrated. She grabs a spoon from a drawer and closes it with her hip. "I cry at the drop of a hat. It's *annoying*."

At that, I smile. I remember that about Vivi. And if there's one person who doesn't like to cry in front of people, it's my sister.

She blinks away the tears and lifts her cup to her lips. Her gaze meets the ceiling, and she moans in a way that sends a straight shot to a part of me I'm trying to ignore. "So," she says, sliding onto the counter stool. "What did you do while I was a lazy bones this morning?"

"Accomplished a few tasks around the house. Paid bills. Answered emails. Worked out."

She perks up. "Worked out?"

"I made the fourth bedroom into a gym."

"I didn't know what that room was. The door is always closed."

"You have professional level curiosity and you haven't opened that door?"

She shrugs, cup poised at her mouth. "I'm not poking my nose into your things, Hugo. A closed door means you shouldn't open it."

"Funny you should say that, considering you came to Olive Township to figuratively open a closed door."

Realization dawns.

That's what my mom meant this morning when she kept pushing about how I brought Mallory into my home. I literally opened my door to Mallory. Is that what I'm doing with my heart, too?

Mallory wiggles her eyebrows. "I guess I'm selective about the doors I open."

I lean back against the lip of the counter, regarding her. She's beautiful. "You seemed interested when I said I worked out this morning. Is that something you do when you're at home in Phoenix?"

She nods vigorously. "I'm a regular at my Pilates

reformer class." She absentmindedly strokes her stomach. I've noticed she's been doing that more often now. "I was, anyway. My center of gravity isn't going to be able to handle the reformer for a while. Definitely no inversions."

"Now I understand why you have such strong legs." The words are out of my mouth before I can stop them.

Mallory is pressing her lips together, looking at me with mirth. "You've noticed I have strong legs?"

"Yeah," I say, playing it off. "What else was there for me to look at in the fitting room when you needed my help with your stuck zipper?"

Mallory's teeth graze her lower lip, her cheeks turned up in a smile. "I can't think of a single thing. Or two things."

"Nope," I say, palming the back of my neck.

I want to kiss her again. Wrap her up, run my hands through her hair, cup her cheeks, taste those pink lips. It's only been a few weeks since the day I met Mallory, but something about this feels... *special*. Like she was delivered to me. As if there's some sort of magical force making this happen.

"You're welcome to use the gym," I tell her. "No reformers in there, but it should be able to cover all the basics."

"I appreciate that," she says. She finishes her coffee. "And I appreciated my latte. And now, I would appreciate the tour of Summerhill."

Chapter 30

Mallory

SUMMERHILL IS *EVERYTHING*.

Earthy, beautiful, unpretentious but luxurious. I regret that this is not the first place I came when I arrived in Olive Township. Sammich is a local treasure, but this... *Wow*.

The first stop on our tour is what Hugo simply refers to as the 'shop.' The large sign on the front reads Merry Little Market.

"It was my mom's job to name it," Hugo says, holding the door open for a stream of people. Some say thank you, some say nothing, and none of them know the person holding open the door for them is the operator of this whole business. "I think she was high on Christmas cheer at the time."

"It's cute," I defend.

"Better for a Christmas tree farm," he gripes.

The doorway clears, and Hugo places his hand on the small of my back, urging me inside.

Backwards caps, and small of the back hand placement. This man knows just how to get this girl riled up.

The interior of Merry Little Market veers toward industrial. The floors are a finished gray concrete, and in lieu of a ceiling is exposed ductwork. Row upon row of six-foot-tall rolling carts hold jars of what I'm sure are olives and many other types of goods. There is a section for olive oil soaps, a wall of local wine, and a refrigerated grab-and-go section of food from the restaurant. Near the back of the large space is an adorable coffee shop with cases of baked goods.

"This is amazing, Hugo," I say in awe, watching people mill around, choosing their items. We walk in deeper, and I start on the first aisle.

Vinegars. A classic balsamic with traditional pairings turns into a white balsamic with prickly pear, blueberry, and peach, and even specialty bourbon flavors in bottles that resemble bourbon casks. I keep going, perusing each aisle, taking it all in. I've always felt in awe of what the earth provides for people in terms of nourishment, and this is a bit like that. It's made even better knowing a family like the De la Vegas have a hand in it.

Hugo is quiet as he stands beside me, letting me soak it all in. "Bacon olive oil?" I ask, pointing at a bottle.

"One of our best sellers," he answers. "The olive oil sommelier I'm working with right now is creating a vanilla bean oil."

My eyebrows raise. Lips purse. I say nothing.

His eyes narrow. "You still don't believe an olive oil sommelier is a real job."

Hugo

I shrug, teasing him. "There are all kinds of weird jobs. Professional mourner," I point out.

Hugo's eyebrows draw together. "Come again?"

"They go to a funeral with low attendance, so it won't look empty. Or someone might hire them to attend a funeral and make a scene. Wailing, sobbing, all the theatrics."

Hugo's hands slip into his jeans pockets. "That sounds fucking terrible."

I laugh, looking over a bottle of jalapeño oil. I keep going to the next aisle, where there are stuffed olives and selections of olive wood kitchen utensils. "You don't have to look at all this," Hugo says. He sounds almost...shy?

"Hush." I give him a reproachful look. "This is my friend's store and I won't have you interrupting me while I look over each and every item. He puts his heart and soul into this place, he deserves to have people appreciate it."

Hugo's lips purse, nodding, and then, slowly like the dawning sun, his mouth relaxes into a smile.

I elbow him lightly. "Is this the part where you nerd out about olives?"

"I promised myself I wouldn't."

"Why?" I tug at the hem of his shirt. "I was ready to learn about all the things."

He looks uncertain.

"Don't self-censor now," I tease.

I watch as he makes a decision, a resolve forming in those dark eyes.

"We're going to need the ATV," he says. "But first, food. I need to make sure you and Peanut are fed."

Without another word he grabs my hand, marching me out of the store. We stride across the grass lawn where people sit at picnic tables, and others play shuffleboard and bocce ball, and a group of children play an oversized game of Connect Four. Hugo's leading me to another building perpendicular, similar to the store in exterior design, except for the windows on three sides of the second half of the building.

In a beautiful copper sign is the word *Simon's*.

That stops me short. How have I not noticed that? I haven't been by here on my daily walks, but I have driven through on the road that leads out to town.

"The restaurant is named after your father?"

"Recent development," Hugo answers. He gazes at the sign. "Vivi, my mom, and I had the hardest time choosing a name, so we kept calling it Summerhill." He rolls his eyes. "Not very original."

"But last week I had the idea to name it after my dad. And when I ran it by my mom and my sister, they loved it."

"That's beautiful, Hugo. Truly."

My hand is still in his, and now he gives a quick tug, bringing me closer to him. His dark eyes burn, intense and beautiful and focused on me. Stubble darkens his jaw, and I have the urge to run my fingertips along it.

"I have you to thank." His voice is deep, falling over me. In the middle of this mayhem, the chatter of strangers and the shrieks of children, Hugo makes me feel like I'm the only person here.

"Me?" I squeak.

He tucks a lock of hair behind my ear. A lone fingertip travels the shell of my ear, sending a cascade of desire rippling through me. If he dipped his face a few inches, we'd be kissing. I wish he would.

"You," he confirms. "For a long time, my father was a subject I didn't dare broach. But Mallory, you being here, asking questions, I know I was hesitant about it at first, but you've made him feel accessible again. I didn't know how badly I needed that."

Emotion surges through me, and my body responds by crying. Hugo grins like he finds me adorable. He starts for Simon's, and when we walk inside, he reaches one long arm behind the hostess stand and plucks a tissue from a box. I move to take it from him, but he dodges me, running the tissue over my cheeks. Tender. Sweet. Our breath hitches in tandem.

Hugo takes a step back, tosses the tissue in the trash.

Every table at the restaurant is occupied, the atmosphere jovial. Happy chatter and the sounds of the open kitchen fill the air. The view of the olive orchard beyond is spectacular. I spot Vivi in the kitchen, wearing a white chef's coat. She's not cooking, but she's overseeing every dish produced.

At that moment, Vivi turns around, spots us, and gives us a harried wave. "I thought Vivi had a restaurant in town," I say, my eyes on her as she yells through the open window to someone deeper in the kitchen.

"Dama Oliva is her place in Olive Township, but she helped create the menu here. She's filling in today because the head chef called in sick. Which probably means my mom has her kids at the big house. We can go there later. Say hi."

"I'd like that."

A teenage boy hurries through the kitchen carrying the most adorable wicker basket. Vivi stops him, peeks inside, and tosses in something else. The kid skids around the corner and hustles out to Hugo.

"Mr. De la Vega, here's your picnic."

"Thank you, Leo," Hugo says, and the kid's eyes widen.

"You know my name?" he croaks, then immediately follows it up with, "I mean, you're welcome." Then he spins on the heel of his bulky black tennis shoe and hightails it back to the kitchen.

"I don't think he expected you to know his name," I murmur.

"I know every employee's name," Hugo says, like it's nothing. But it is something, and it doesn't even surprise me. That's Hugo, being Hugo.

Hugo takes my hand again, leading me around the backend of Simon's, across an expanse of grass where two Adirondack chairs sit at the far end. We keep going down a slope, and arrive at a small garage.

Hugo sets the picnic basket on the ground, dropping my hand so he can remove his keys from his pocket. He selects one and unlocks the garage.

Hugo

"Never know who might decide to take these for a joyride," he quips, lifting the garage door. Inside are three side-by-sides, gunmetal gray with the Summerhill logo on the doors. They look like buggies, but more all-terrain with the deeply grooved tires and sturdy frames.

I wink at him. "I might, now that I know they're here."

He laughs. "I'll look out for your trail of dust going across the orchard." He situates the picnic basket on the floor in the back seat, then swings around the small vehicle and opens the passenger door. Grandly, he gestures inside. "Your ride."

"My chariot," I tease.

"Your wagon," he adds. "Or hooptie."

I love having this inside joke with him, just a little something silly and special, only for us.

Hugo reverses carefully from the garage, putting the buggy in Park to close and lock the door behind him.

Hugo drives slowly. Carefully. Like he carries precious cargo. He skirts the outbuildings, the restaurant, the store, favoring a circuitous route that takes us past his house. My gaze falls over the tidy outside with the rich green front door. It's the most at home I've felt in years. Almost since I can remember. My apartment in Phoenix is nice, and it's a home, but this feels different.

He drives up to the edge of the grove, pausing at the tree line. Using a flat arm, he motions out in the distance. "Do you see that mountain range out there?"

Far away but looming are the Arizona Mountains, followed by the Superstitions beyond. Legend has it, the

Lost Dutchman's Gold Mine is somewhere in the Superstition Mountains, holding vast amounts of gold. I believe in legends of lost treasure about as much as I believe in magic, which is to say, not at all.

I nod, keeping my eyes trained where Hugo is pointing. "Those mountain ranges make Summerhill possible. They create a microclimate, giving the valley below a slightly different temperature than the rest of the desert. They also serve as a barrier for wind, and provide the soil with additional water from rainfall runoff."

Hugo shifts into Drive. The ride is mostly smooth, this part of the desert has been tamed. More sand than rocks. Olive trees instead of towering saguaros.

The breeze rolls through Hugo's hair. It's a little long, the brown-black tendrils curling over his ears. His posture is relaxed, muscles loose. He's not humming, but he wears the face of a man happy and carefree enough to do so.

"Summerhill is one thousand acres," he says, then winks at me, "or 404.6 hectares."

He's nerding out, and I love it. The way his eyes become bright and animated, an edge of excitement to them. The passion he feels for what he does makes him that much more attractive.

There's a break in the trees ahead, a dirt path to enter. Hugo turns with care, so much care that I know it's for me. For Peanut.

We enter the grove, and I can't stop my mouth from dropping open. We're surrounded by silvery green leaves, small white blossoms exploding on every side of us. The air is sweet, like apricots, with a spicy undertone.

"Did we go through a portal?" I ask, and Hugo beams with pride, and happiness. I don't think I've seen him this alive. This passionate.

Was he this way about fencing? He rarely talks about it. Now I have a new mystery to solve, something else to be curious about.

"We're in Narnia, aren't we?"

Hugo tosses me a smile. It takes a seat beside my heart.

We drive the path on and on, until we come to a clearing ahead. It's the perfect place for a picnic.

Hugo pulls up beside the expanse of grass, and I don't know how big it is except to say it's large enough to comfortably seat a few dozen people. Fewer if they lie back and let the sun warm their bodies.

"How did this get here?" I ask as we climb out, and Hugo reaches into the back seat for the basket.

"I had them put in."

"Them?"

He nods, opening a little compartment on the back of the side-by-side and producing a blanket. "There are four around the orchard. I wanted places for the employees to relax. Take a break from work and enjoy themselves. One of the other green spaces has a trunk with lawn toys. Frisbee, Koosh, some of those soft footballs." He leads the way to a spot in the middle of the grass. "Happy employees make better tasting olives."

I didn't know it was possible to be more impressed by Hugo, but here we are.

Taking the blanket from where it drapes over Hugo's arm, I shake it out and lay it down. Hugo bites the side of his lip and looks at the ground. "Do you need help sitting down?" he asks me.

"I'm not that pregnant yet," I sass. "But I might need help getting up."

My belly has grown in just the past few days. According to the app I downloaded last month, Peanut is nearing the size of a banana.

Hugo sits down beside the picnic basket, while I navigate gracefully sitting down. It's not really possible, and I end up deciding not to care how I look.

"I asked my sister to put together a picnic basket, and when I tried to tell her what I wanted, she told me to shut up and let the chef work her magic." Hugo shakes his head. "Let's hope she remembered your diet restrictions."

"I'll make do," I assure him. I'm not worried. I don't think there's much that gets by Vivi.

She's sharp, and she's quick, and it's evident how much she cares for people.

Hugo makes a show of removing items from the basket, announcing them. "Arancini," he says. "Stuffed olives with a note from Vivi that says they have feta, not bleu cheese." He huffs a smile. "Sometimes I forget my sister is a professional. Anyway." He goes back to announcing food items. "Panko-crusted chicken." There's a note attached to it. He reads it quickly, balling it up and throwing it back into the basket.

"What did that say?"

"Nothing."

My eyes narrow. "You think I'm going to buy that? I'm a curious person. You know it, and I know it." My finger circles the air. "I wouldn't be here if I weren't."

Hugo fishes the paper from the basket and tosses it to me. Catching it, I unfurl the small square.

No garlic in any of this in case you want to smooch.

I dissolve into laughter.

Hugo rolls his eyes. "Vivi's a lot."

"She's great," I assert.

"She's both," he compromises. "I hope you're hungry."

"Always," I answer, because it's true. Sometimes I'm hungry, sometimes I'm ravenous, but I'm always on the spectrum of being ready to eat.

"Almost forgot," Hugo says, reaching back into the basket. He comes away with a bottle of something dark orange and sparkling. "Blood orange Italian soda."

He pours the drinks, and we munch on the picnic Vivi packed us. Unsurprisingly, everything is delicious.

"This is gorgeous, Hugo," I comment, popping a stuffed olive in my mouth. "But I'm sure I don't have to tell you that. You get to work here every day."

He lies back, propping himself up on one elbow, and looks around. "I'm in the fields less than I thought I would be. Taking over as the operator means a lot more office time. Sometimes I grab a side-by-side and come out here during the day, just to be out in nature. Vivi and I used to run through here as kids. Pick up the fallen olives and pelt them at each other." He smiles at the memory.

He looks at me with careful, considerate eyes. "Did Maggie ever do anything like that to you?"

"No. Maggie was an angel on earth. Sweet nearly all the time. Maybe she would've been a hellish teenager." The idea of it puts a rueful smile on my lips. "Something to balance her out and make her seem typical. The truth is, she was anything but. She was gentle and kind. She held funerals for bugs." Usually these memories hurt, but right now they feel...*ok*. What is that about?

"My dad, too. I mean, he didn't have the innocence of a child of course, but he was a better human than many others." Hugo smoothes out a ruffle in the blanket, eyebrow furrowed. "The police said he likely didn't see his attacker. I've always hoped that's true. If it was somebody he knew, he would've felt confused. Hurt. Disappointed."

I shift on the blanket, lying down and mirroring Hugo. "Sal told me that not only did your father not have enemies, but he only had friends."

"It's true. So it must've been a random crime, right?"

I picture my notes, spread out around Hugo's dining room table. The way I've been toying with the possibility that Simon might have known his killer. "Maybe," I hedge. "Anything is possible."

Hugo shifts to lie on his back. I do the same, my hands naturally falling to my stomach.

Hugo

"Oh," I say, as Peanut twirls and jumps.

"What's wrong?" Alarm puts an urgency in Hugo's tone.

"Everything is fine. Peanut likes Vivi's food."

"You can feel the baby?"

"Only recently. The first morning at Summerhill, actually." Where I was safe, in Hugo's guest bed.

Peanut somersaults again. Right now, it feels like something swimming, but everything I've read says that before long, it will look like an alien stretching inside me, an elbow and a knee and the heel of a foot passing over, visible from the outside.

Hugo props himself up on his elbows, gaze zeroed in on my stomach. "What does it feel like?"

"A flurry of bubbles, but stronger. Almost like a darting back-and-forth."

I prop myself up on my elbows too, looking down at my belly. It's still relatively small, especially compared to what I know it will grow to be, but its profile is taking up more space now. Protruding, making itself known.

"It's cute," Hugo says. "Your bump."

I smile down at it. "I happen to think it's pretty cute, too."

"Can I touch it?"

I glance right, and find his eyes are already on me. He looks hopeful, but also shy.

The only other person who has put their hands on my stomach, besides my doctor, is Jolene. When I chose to have Peanut on my own, I never could have guessed how it would feel to do everything by myself. Nobody to tenderly run a hand over my stomach, or coo and read to my bump. I can do all that myself, but it would be nice to share it with another person.

Never in a million years would I have guessed Hugo might be the person to ask if he can touch my belly, but it doesn't feel weird.

"Yes," I hear myself say.

Chapter 31

Hugo

CAN I TOUCH IT?

Did I really ask that?

It's not a puppy at an adoption fair. I wish I could rewind the moment, take it back, but it's too late now because the question is out there. There's no use berating myself.

Mallory said yes, but odd questions require a double check. "Are you sure?"

Instead of answering, Mallory says, "Sit up."

I do as she says. From her propped up on her elbow position, she motions her chin toward her stomach. "Peanut's waiting."

Tentatively, I reach out. I didn't touch Vivi's belly when she was pregnant. What reason would I have? She was married, and as much of a jerk as her husband turned out to be, that guy was all over her belly. I never asked because she looked like she had enough from him. Also, she's my sister. I'll hug her all day long, but touching her stomach felt too intimate.

Too intimate, yet here I am, pressing my uncertain fingers against the fabric of Mallory's clothing. Mallory sits up, covering my hand with her own. She takes over, sending my touch on a path across the top of her stomach, traveling down the other side and under, then back up and across the top.

"It's...firm," I finish lamely. I don't know what else to say.

"It has to be, to protect Peanut. Wild, right?" She keeps her hand on mine, running it in a small circle. Mischievous glint in her eyes, she asks, "You don't have a breeding kink, do you, Hugo?"

Shock sends my head back an inch. "I don't know what that means exactly, but I can use context clues. The answer is no."

She chuckles. "I'm not one hundred percent certain, either. I was just wondering if a pregnant belly is, like, a *thing* for you."

My hand stills under hers. "Uh, no." Then I realize how I've said it, and now I'm doubling back to fix what I said. "It's not a *thing* for me, but it's not *not* a thing, either." Fuck. I've bungled this whole conversation. So I sigh, grab a metaphorical shovel, and dig myself even deeper. "It's more the person the belly is attached to. I mean—"

Mallory's shoulders shake with suppressed laughter. "You can quit while you're behind."

Hugo

I slip my hand out from under hers. That's enough belly fondling for today.

Mallory tips her face up to the sun with eyes closed, propping herself up with a hand flat behind her. Her other hand absentmindedly strokes her belly.

The sun dapples her skin, presses into her shiny, dark hair. That suede skirt rides up, showing more of her toned thighs. She mentioned my gym earlier, maybe I should learn some exercises safe for her and Peanut. We can work out together. Already I can picture her on my treadmill, ponytail swinging, face flushed.

"You know, Hugo," she says, eyes still closed, "nobody has ever done something this nice for me unless they wanted to get in my pants." Her eyes open, gaze slicing to me.

I'm not sure what to say. After the breeding kink debacle, my mouth is better off closed. But I can't deny or hide the shade of crimson flashing over my neck. I remember every second of what she felt like in my arms in my kitchen in the middle of the night, and every night I've thought of her. What it would be like to hold her again. Hear those tiny little moans of hers. Make them louder.

Mallory shakes out her hair, gives me the fuckin' cutest look I've ever seen. "Are you trying to get into my pants, Hugo?"

My breath comes quicker. There's an easy answer to this question, but it's not simple. Within that answer are many other thoughts, emotions, considerations. And I should probably say no, though that would be a lie.

Mallory grins lightly. Teasing. She's playful. Flirting. I think I know what she wants my answer to be.

My fingers find her ankle, fall over her skin. Lightly I stroke with my fingers, run circles with my thumb. She swallows, and I know she's trying to appear unaffected.

"I'm not trying to get in your *pants*." My light touch travels north, up her calf. Behind her knee.

Her breath hitches.

"This skirt, though? That's a different story." My touch climbs. "I don't need in. Only"—I glance at her, my fingers hovering at the hem of the fabric—"under."

Mallory's tongue slips out, presses against the center of her top lip. A pink flush sweeps over her cheeks. "Yes," she whispers.

Over soft skin my fingers travel, blazing a trail up the inside of her thigh. The heat coming off her warms my hand, makes me hungry for her.

"Lie back," I tell her. I want her comfortable, enjoying my touch. She lowers herself, and I lay out beside her. Her lips are pouty and perfect, and I capture them in a searing kiss. Like last time, it's unbelievable how good it feels. How right.

I find the silk edge of her underwear, my touch slipping beneath. She arches into me, rubbing her hand over my neck. My fingers split her, locating my target, and she gasps when I slide inside. Against her neck, I whisper, "I brought you out here to show you my favorite place, because I knew you would find it special, too. And this?" I curl my finger. Add my thumb and turn circles. "This is because I've spent too much time thinking about your little moans, and how good they would sound if they were louder, and for me."

On cue, she groans. More emphatic than in my kitchen. I kiss her neck, her collarbone, her shoulders. She hangs on and whimpers, nails dragging through my hair.

"You're so beautiful," I murmur. "Always, but especially like this."

She grows slicker, hotter, and then she clenches around me, eyes closing and head tipping back. "Hugo," she moans my name, and it sounds better than when my name was announced during the medal ceremony at the Olympics.

My lips press to the hollow of her throat, not letting up, making sure she's squeezed every drop from her orgasm. When I pull away and find her eyes, her cheeks are bright red.

"I wasn't expecting that," she says. "I...I don't know what to say."

I'm adjusting her skirt, gathering myself and my thoughts. Then I press a kiss to her forehead, because I have found that I like doing that. I don't think I've ever done that before.

"I like you, Mallory, and I'm tired of pretending I don't, or that I shouldn't." Honesty is best, right? I have no interest in playing games with this woman.

"I feel the same, Hugo." Her chest still heaves as her heart rate slows, her eyes glassy with post-pleasure glow. "I have since the first time we spoke. But—" she falters, glancing with concern at her stomach. "Does this not bother you?"

"Should it?"

"I don't think most men would be thrilled about it."

I shrug. It's hard to explain, but I'll try. "I like you, and that's right about where the thought process ends. Not because of your baby, or despite it. I like you, period. Full stop."

She smiles. Not a beaming grin, but something slower. "I'll accept that response."

We finish the picnic Vivi packed us, including the shortbread cookies I didn't notice. Mallory's flush on her cheeks dissipates, but I smell her on my fingers. It makes me hard.

Mallory asks me more questions about fencing, and what it was like to qualify and compete in the Olympics. I ask her about previous podcast episodes, and where she records.

It ends up being one of the best afternoons I've had in a very long time. I'm not surprised.

With Mallory in the picture, everything feels better. Brighter.

Chapter 32

Mallory

Jolene: One month, Mal. You've officially been gone one month.

Mallory: Little longer than I expected...

Jolene: Have you seen a doctor?

Mallory: Yes. I set up an appointment with the ob-gyn Hugo's sister used. My appointment is tomorrow.

Jolene: Are you going to learn the sex?

Mallory: I haven't decided.

Jolene: I expect you to call me THE VERY SECOND you step out of that office.

Mallory: Pinky promise.

Jolene: On to other topics. Are you hooking up with Hugo?

> Mallory: We're not hooking up.

> Jolene: You're such a liar. Does he make you wear his gold medal while you ride him?

> Jolene: Are you there?

> Jolene: Hellooo??

> Jolene: Mallory!!!!

When I mention in passing to Hugo the next morning that I have an appointment, he offers to go with me.

"I can drive you," he says, smearing avocado on a slice of toasted sourdough. He piles a mountain of scrambled eggs on top. This plate is for me, and the only reason I know that is because he was finishing his when I walked in the kitchen a minute ago. "I'll sit in the waiting room, if you'd prefer."

"You have a full day of work," I argue. I don't know why I'm protesting. It would be nice to have somebody there. It's a reflex, this urge to do everything on my own.

"I can make time," he counters.

"Don't worry about it," I say with a wave of my hand, when what I really want to say is something along the lines of *I'd love to have you there with me.* But the words are already out there, and I'm not sure how to retract them, and Hugo's already changing the topic.

"My mom has asked if you will be joining us at family dinner tonight. It'll be worth your while, I promise. Vivi cooks."

I feel bad for turning down his offer to come to the doctor with me, so I go to him where he stands at the sink, wrap my arms around him. "It would be worth my while even if the food was terrible."

He lowers his face, drops a kiss to my lips. We haven't done anything except kiss since that day on the blanket surrounded by olive trees. It's not that I need to rush anything, but at the same time, my hormones are in high gear. I know he doesn't regret what we did, he wouldn't kiss me the way he does if that were the case. But there are moments, when his lips are on mine and I'm burning up with desire, that I want to be manhandled. I want his weight, the slap of skin, beads of sweat forming on both of us.

"I'll see you this evening," I tell him. "I have an errand to run before my appointment, and I'm going to grab lunch in town."

"Errand?"

"Police station," I explain.

Confusion tugs at his eyebrows. "You changed your mind and decided to tell the police about the pictures?"

I hesitate. Hugo knows I'm doing work, and he knows what my work is about, but he doesn't ask very many questions. He may have given me his blessing, but that doesn't automatically mean he wants to be involved in every detail. I can't lie to him, though, especially not when he's asking me a direct question. "I'm hoping to sweet talk my way into your dad's file."

A little bit of the light in his eyes goes out. I hate that. I wish it never had to happen.

With a second, parting kiss, Hugo leaves for work, and I get ready for the day.

THE POLICE STATION is a brick building in the center of town. Two flagpoles fly an Arizona state flag, and a United States flag, but nothing else about it is remarkable. It doesn't seem like a lot happens in Olive Township, but then again I've been ensconced in a safe bubble at Summerhill.

Admittedly, I've been there due to something I would've normally reported to the police.

"Hello," an older woman snaps when I walk in. She sees my belly and softens her tone. "What can I do for you, dear?"

It's amazing how people melt when they see a pregnant woman. Almost as if the presence of my belly is magic.

"Hello, Mrs. Black." I read her name off her desk, and offer my winningest smile. "I was hoping to ask someone a few questions about an old case."

She pulls her glasses lower on her nose, peering at me

over the frame. "I've been with this department longer than you've been alive. What case are you referring to?"

"Simon De la Vega."

She *laughs*.

"Sure, hon." The glasses return to the bridge of her nose. "Let me open up the coldest case file in this town's history to a complete stranger."

I smile sweetly. Bees are attracted to honey, not vinegar. "Mrs. Black, I'm certain you know which officer was with the department during that time. If I could have a teeny, tiny conversation with them, it would be very much appreciated."

Her fleshy arms cross over her generous bosom. "Does the family know you're here poking around their business?"

I admire the loyalty of small towns, the way they fiercely protect their own. "They do. In fact, I can give Hugo a call right now."

Her mouth opens to respond when a portly older gentleman walks through the door. He's wearing slacks and a long sleeve, crisp shirt. Tie. Holding a large paper cup and a white bag printed with the Sweet Nothings logo.

"Detective Towles," Mrs. Black greets, sounding like she's already done with the day even though it's not yet halfway over. "This young lady is asking questions about Simon De la Vega."

Her words send the detective up short, coffee sloshing through the pill-shaped hole in the mouth of the cup. "Is that right?" He looks at me, head tipped. His dark hair has salt and pepper creeping up on all sides. Wrinkles pull at the corners of his eyes, crease his forehead.

He regards me for a few seconds before he says, "Come on back with me."

I'm expecting to follow him through metal detectors, or at least a security guard taking a peek in my purse, but there are zero safety measures. Small town, I guess.

Detective Towles leads me past a row of occupied desks. Every man and woman looks up as I pass. At the far end of the room, the detective ducks into an office. He steps behind a desk, placing his coffee and breakfast on top. He motions for me to take a seat at one of the two chairs in front of his desk. "What can I do for you, miss?"

I don't like the idea of sitting while he's standing, but hopefully compliance from me will beget compliance from him. I settle in a chair, crossing my legs at the ankle. "I was hoping to ask a few questions about the Simon De la Vega case."

Detective Towles's eyebrows climb up his forehead. "That case is nearly twenty years old."

"Correct," I nod.

"Let me guess. You read about the case on some obscure message board and now you're curious?"

"Not quite. I host a true crime podcast—"

His palm shoots out, stopping me. "Do you know how many true crime junkies I've had call me over the years? Someone runs an old episode of *Unsolved Cases* and my department gets flooded with tips." He grimaces as he wrestles with the knotted tie at his neck, attempting to loosen it. "This department does not have the funds to deal with it. I'm stretched thin as it is. When Olive Township grows, the police force must grow alongside it. I'll let you guess which one has grown, and which one hasn't."

"I'm not asking for any of your resources," I assure him. "Only the case file."

"I thought you had a few questions, and now you're asking for the case file?"

"You're busy," I remind him. "Your time is valuable."

"If you want the file, you'll have to make a public records request."

Asshole. I know exactly what he's doing. "That'll take weeks."

"Maybe even months," he adds, reaching for his coffee.

Cool. A detective on a power trip. This is fun.

"It would be a lot easier if you could simply hand me the file. I'm sure it's in its physical form. I doubt you were electronic back then."

He takes a sip of coffee. A few drops dribble out from the lid, land squarely in the center of his white shirt. "And you think you're going to find something in there our entire department missed? Simon was one of our own, and we did everything we could to find out what happened."

It's mostly ego keeping the detective from cooperating, but perhaps it's a pinch of disappointment, too. In himself, in his department. He wanted to be the one to solve the murder, find justice for the beloved Simon.

"It doesn't hurt to have a fresh set of eyes after all this time."

"Do the De la Vegas know you're poking your nose into their business?"

"I'm staying at Summerhill."

He flinches at the admission. "I can call Sonya or Hugo right now and verify that."

I smile serenely. "So can I."

He looks down. Notices the coffee on his shirt. With an aggrieved sigh, he removes a packet of stain wipes from the top drawer of his desk. Wiping at himself, he says, "I'll get one of my desk sergeants to find it. Might take a couple weeks. It's in archives."

I wince at the idea of Simon's case sitting in archives, collecting dust. Forgotten. Somewhere in Phoenix, Maggie's file does the same.

"I appreciate it." I stand up, removing a business card from my purse and placing it in the center of his desk. It was Jolene's idea to have them made. "Have a nice day, Detective Towles."

"Same to you," he peers at the card. "Miss Hawkins."

I exit his office, retrace my steps back to the front. "Have a lovely day, Mrs. Black," I say on my way by. Her eyes burn with curiosity. I'm sure she thought I was on a well-traveled boulevard of broken dreams.

Even though I don't have the file in hand yet, this feels like a win. When I have dinner with Hugo's family tonight, I'll be able to tell them I'm making progress.

The development with the case file makes me happy, and I reach for my phone, pausing outside the doctor's office.

Hugo

I want Hugo. Here, with me. I want to do all this with him.

"Excuse me, miss, are you new in town?"

My head whips to the voice. Deep, rich, curling into my bones. My grin is automatic, reaching my eyes. I think it may reach down into my heart, too. "What are you doing here?"

Hugo steps in beside me. No hesitation. His arm goes around my waist. Right here on the street for all to see. "The more you see someone show up for you, the more you'll let them." He drops a kiss to my forehead. "So, here I am."

I reach up, palm his cheek. My heart becomes more than a life source, it's a conduit for happiness. How does Hugo do it? So readily, so generous. No reservation.

I know the answer. His mother didn't quit, like mine did. The circumstances weren't identical, so the comparison isn't completely fair. I don't want to think about that right now. I want to bask in Hugo.

"You are so good to me, Hugo."

"You are so deserving, Mallory."

And then he kisses me. On the lips. Right in front of the doctor's office, for anyone and everyone to see.

"Hugo," I admonish softly. "People are going to ask you questions. They're going to think you're the father."

"I don't care what anybody thinks," he all but growls.

What people think of me means little to me, but I do care what they think of Hugo. This is his town. His home. I'm a guest, a visitor.

"Don't," he says softly, smoothing out the furrow

between my brows. "I know exactly what you're thinking. I'm a grown man, and this is my choice. *You* are my choice."

He takes my hand, and leads me into the office.

People stare. The women in the waiting room, the receptionist. Even if Hugo doesn't know them, they know Hugo. Operator of Summerhill, winner of Olympic medals. A local celebrity, though I admit I hadn't fully considered that until now.

When the nurse calls me back, Hugo stays seated. I stand, looking down at him, and decide in that moment to include him. All he wants is to support me, and it's well past time I allow someone to be there for me. The truth is, I can do all this on my own. But that doesn't mean I have to.

Chapter 33

Olive Township

WHISPERS OF THE TOWNSPEOPLE WEAVING THROUGH my palo verde trees, slipping around my agave.

My happiness spills through in the sunshine, the white olive tree blossoms, the most brilliant purple flowers on the jacaranda. The hot pink and yellow blooms on the cacti are me, smiling. I send the sweet scent of citrus flowers through the air.

Long have I waited for him to find a safe place for his broken heart.

And he has.

I've put on a show for her. Displayed my brightest colors, brought forth a pageantry.

Her smile tells me she likes it. Her eyes tell me he's healing her broken heart, too.

Chapter 34

Hugo

"It feels like an ice cream kind of day," I declare on our way out of Dr. Connolly's office.

Mallory is still crying. Happy tears, I know, but I'll do anything to make sure she keeps smiling.

"Mom and baby girl are healthy," Dr. Connolly had announced, rolling on her round stool. Mallory gasped, looking to me. A smile lit up her face, more brilliant than the sunrise. I didn't know what to do, but Mallory took over. She grabbed my hand, leaned into my side. I dropped a kiss onto her forehead. She'd smiled up at me, said, "I'm so glad you're here. Thank you for challenging me when I said I didn't mind coming to this appointment alone."

Now we have two reasons to celebrate. Mallory is having a girl, and I do believe I've broken down one of her walls.

I feel a jubilation that's been elusive to me. It's impossible, but Olive Township feels different. The sun burns brighter, warmer. The flowers are more vibrant, the air scented with orange blossoms.

I think I know what it is. I'm not in love, because it's only been a little over a month since I first set eyes on Mallory. It's too soon, right?

I can see it, though. Love. In the distance, but not that far. If we keep going on this way, that is most definitely my final destination. It's invigorating, not something to be afraid of. It's something to look forward to.

Mallory pauses on the sidewalk outside of the doctor's office, hands on her belly. "Well, little girl, what do you think? Vanilla ice cream?" Mallory pretends to listen, then she looks at me. "Baby girl says it's a brownie batter day. Two scoops."

I take Mallory's hand, pull her in close. "We better not delay."

Mallory video calls Jolene on our way to the ice cream shop. They speak in high-pitched tones, there are watered down screams, and Jolene announces plans to spoil the little girl rotten.

"Hey wait," Jolene says once the excitement has simmered. "What car are you in?"

Mallory trains the phone on me. I give her a quick wave before putting my hand back on the steering wheel. Something tells me I just became best friends with precautions and safety.

"Hugo went with you to the appointment?" Jolene asks, as if I'm not eighteen inches away.

"Moral support," Mallory explains.

Jolene isn't buying it. "Uh-huh. Be honest with yourself, Mal. You two are a thing."

Mallory opens her mouth, and I can tell by the set of her jaw she's getting ready to argue.

Or deflect.

So I get there first. "I'm still working on wearing her down," I tell Jolene.

A devilish grin curls Mallory's lips. "He has a breeding kink."

I shake my head. Pinch the bridge of my nose. I should have known Mallory would go toe-to-toe with me.

"I don't know what that is," Jolene sings out, "but I like it."

Mallory rolls her eyes playfully. "Of course you do."

"Jolene," I say, and Mallory turns the phone toward me. "For the record, I don't have a breeding kink, but I am craving ice cream."

"Hang up with me and get your ice cream," Jolene commands.

Mallory repositions the phone so it faces her. "I'll talk to you later, ok? We need to chat about work stuff." She blows Jolene a kiss, and ends the call.

Olive Township's hidden gem ice cream parlor is off the beaten path, tucked away in an eclectic shopping center called The Village. There's a post office, an antique store, a yoga studio, and various other stores all facing an outdoor courtyard with a large water fountain in the center.

"This is such a cute little space," Mallory says, stopping to inspect an old wagon wheel. "Very rustic." She

Hugo

peers into the window of the antique store, walking along slowly until we reach the ice cream shop.

I hold open the door for her and we step inside. It smells exactly as it always has, like fresh waffle cones, and sugar. Mallory points at the neon sign on the wall, a dripping ice cream cone with the words *It won't lick itself.*

I lean down, my lips ghosting her ear when I whisper, "I was in seventh grade when I realized that sign had two meanings."

"Who is the owner of this place?" she whisper-hisses.

As if conjured, Ruth dances from the back of the store. She stops, realizing the music isn't on. She goes toward a little box on the wall, presses a button, and '50s music fills the air.

"That's better," she says, and her dancing resumes.

I wave at the old woman. Vivi told me Ruth turned eighty-two on her last birthday. "Hi, Ruth."

"Thought that was you, Hugo. Who's your girl?"

My arm winds around Mallory's waist, my palm making its way to the side of her belly. I pull her in close. "Ruth, this is Mallory."

Ruth squints over the cold case holding rows of ice cream. "Are you having a baby?"

One thing about the old bird, she doesn't pull any punches.

Mallory beams. "A girl."

Ruth points at me. "Hopefully she'll have his eyebrows. Never thought it was very fair of God to put eyebrows like that on a man. Been drawing mine on my whole life, and he gets those shapely caterpillars?"

I can feel the way Mallory shakes with repressed laughter.

I could correct Ruth, but is it worth it? Like the afternoon we visited David Boylan, it's easier to allow Ruth to assume I'm the father of Mallory's baby.

We order our ice cream, and on our way out the door Mallory snaps a photo of the sign on the wall. "That's going to make Jolene cackle."

We sit outside under the shade of an umbrella, and as absurd as it sounds, it feels like today was made just for us. Mallory pushes her toes past the umbrella's shade, into the sunshine.

She wiggles her toes, and damn do I like seeing her this way.

Just looking at her makes me want to take her back to my house, back to my bed. The only reason I haven't is because I'm nervous about the baby. I have questions, none of which I'm willing to enter as a search query on the Internet. My best bet was to ask the doctor, and I almost did, but then I froze. The last thing I want Mallory to think is that I'm expecting sex from her.

What happened in the olive grove was amazing, but it was a far cry from all the things I want to do with her. To her. But I don't want her thinking I expect it, and asking questions about the safety of having sex while she's pregnant might make her feel that way.

Looks like I have another night of fucking my own hand in the shower to look forward to. The thought is depressing enough, but then it's followed up with a voice that elicits from me the same response as nails on a chalkboard.

"Mallory! There you are!"

Mallory straightens up as Liane Rooney stops in front of her. "Hi, Liane."

"I haven't seen you around town recently. I was wondering where you've been keeping yourself."

Mallory glances at me. She looks unsure of how to respond.

We've already set tongues wagging by being in the doctor's office together and kissing on the sidewalk. Might as well go all in. "Mallory is staying with me out at Summerhill."

Liane's eyes grow to the size of salad plates. "Is that right?"

"It's lovely out there," Mallory says.

"It sure is," Liane says, adjusting her purse on her arm. "I'll have to come out to visit you. I need to stock up on the prickly pear white balsamic. Wouldn't dare dress my arugula without it."

"Ooh, I'll have to try that," Mallory responds. She looks at me. "Can you bring a bottle home with you?"

"He has to check with the boss, right Hugo?" Liane taps my shoulder and laughs too heartily at her own joke.

I muster up a smile and nod.

"Speaking of things I wouldn't do, I better pick up the vanilla bean the mayor loves so much. Can't serve a warm butter cake without that ice cream."

Liane disappears into the ice cream parlor. As soon as

she's safely inside the store, I push back my seat. "Let's get the hell out of here before she comes back."

Mallory is already pushing back her seat, falling in step with me as we hurry away. "She's nice, but she can be intense."

"Small doses," I say as we arrive at the passenger door of my car. "I can only handle her in small doses."

Mallory waits for me to climb in the driver's side, then she says, "Promise you'll tell me when I've worn out my welcome? I don't want to become someone you can only handle in small doses."

As much as I would love to get the hell out of here, her comment needs to be handled immediately. Setting my ice cream down in the drink holder, I reach over the console. I tuck her hair behind her ear, stroke my knuckles over her jaw. "The doses I want of you don't come in a big enough serving size."

Her lips tremble before breaking into a shaky smile. "You know eventually I'll have to go back to Phoenix. Eventually, I'll have this baby."

The reminder isn't necessary. I think about her, and everything it means to be with her, all the damn time. I drive myself crazy trying to figure out how to make all this work.

"I know. So can I please enjoy you now, while I have you?"

The look Mallory gives me is vulnerable. Fragile. She's tough and she's strong, and has survived unimaginable pain. I only want to be good to her. For her.

Hugo

Her tongue darts out, swipes over her bottom lip. "I keep waiting for you to enjoy me."

Eyes on me, she palms my thigh. Her hand slides up higher.

I'm painfully hard in an instant. It's a familiar feeling these days. Everything Mallory does drives me up the wall. I walked in my house last week and there she was sitting at the kitchen table, one knee pulled up to her chest, while the other leg stretched for the ground. She looked cute as hell, not to mention the spectacular view. Now every time she wears those leggings, that's what I think of. I'm above pilfering them from her laundry and having my wicked way with them, but only barely, and not for much longer.

Mallory's fingernails graze the front of my jeans. "Every time we kiss, I come out of my skin. At this point, I'm desperate for you."

"Remember our picnic in the olive grove?"

"How could I forget it?"

My touch skims Mallory's throat, feathers over her collarbone. "The smell of you was on my fingers, and as soon as I got home that day I used that hand on myself and came in an embarrassingly short amount of time."

"I love that." She makes pass after pass over the tightened fabric of my jeans.

On a groan, I ask, "Mallory, are you trying to get in my pants?"

Chapter 35

Mallory

Low laughter trips from between my lips. It's my question, turned around on me.

His length presses against his jeans, and as much as I'm dying to get to him, I have some sense. It's the middle of the day, in a low-slung sports car. Kissing on the sidewalk for the entirety of Olive Township to see is one thing. My head bobbing in Hugo's lap where any passerby can spot us is another.

Looks like teasing him with my words is my only option. "I don't want *in* your pants. I want you out of them. I want to get on my knees and put you in my mouth. I want your face to disappear between my thighs. Then I want you to bend me over the kitchen table and make it so you'll never eat there again without remembering me."

Hugo gapes at me before his brow sets in determination. "I can have us home in twenty-five minutes."

Home.

Hugo

Not *I can have us back to my house in twenty-five minutes.*

But, *home.*

My physical attraction to this man is already nearing nuclear, but the way he gives himself to me without reservation might be one of the sexiest things about him.

WHO KNEW twenty-five minutes could feel like twenty-five years? The tension in Hugo's car is thick, syrupy.

We're on the long stretch of Summerhill Road, a few miles from the turnoff and the sign announcing the olive mill. I reach out, drift my fingers along the front of his pants. I've done this every so often during our drive, just to tease him. But this time, I'm switching it up a little.

A flick of my fingers undoes the top button of his jeans. I look at Hugo, find his gaze on mine. His eyes squint, only slightly, as he tries to figure out what I'm doing. What I'll do next.

Between pinched fingers, I pull on his zipper.

"Mal," he breathes.

My fingertips meet the soft fabric of his underwear. "Swordsman?" I ask, eyebrows raised, voice soft. When he doesn't say anything, I say, "Teasing is fun, but I need just a little bit more." My chin dips, and I ask, "Can I have more?"

He swallows, clears his throat. Adjusts himself on the

seat. "The last thing in the world I will say right now is no."

My fingers dig into the opening at the front of his boxer briefs, wrapping around warm skin. Hard and thick in my hand, I pull him out. He's big, bigger than I've been with before. Wrapping my hand loosely around him, I glide upward.

He groans through tight lips. It's so sexy, so enjoyable, I find myself pressing my thighs together.

The pad of my thumb finds the bead of dew at the top, swirling it.

Hugo's right hand leaves the wheel, covers mine. He pumps slowly, once, twice, three times. The muscles in his jaw are snare drum tight.

"That has to be it," he says reluctantly, releasing his grip over me. "You have to stop. I have no intention of this being over anytime soon."

"Noted," I say, and I plan on listening. But not quite yet.

Using my elbow, I prop myself up, loosening my seat belt the tiniest amount to allow for a little wiggle room. Leaning over, I lower my face and take Hugo into my mouth. Not completely, just enough that I can gather his moisture on my tongue.

Above me, the sound of a heavy exhale.

And then I wrap around him with my lips, one slow release. For good measure.

I pull off and sit back, sending him a satisfied smile. He looks dazed, one hand on the wheel while the other rubs his jaw. He's still stiff and punching the air, defined ridge and veiny.

Reaching over, I help him back into his jeans. Zip and button. Like it never happened.

He's looking at me, and he shakes his head almost imperceptibly. "You just might be the death of me."

I shrug, rubbing at the corners of my lips. "I was curious. I had to see it."

He breathes an incredulous laugh, taking the turn for Summerhill. He is forced to drive slow, mindful of the employees, the guests.

When we pull up to his house, he says, "Don't move."

Through the windshield I watch him unlock his front door, open it, and leave it open. Then he comes to my side of the car, opens the door, and offers his hand. The second I'm on two feet, he lifts me.

"Wrap your legs around me," he instructs. Once I'm situated, he says, "I expect to have these legs pressed against my head in less than five minutes. Understand?"

I wiggle my core against him, as much as I can with this belly in my way. "Understood."

Hugo walks me into the house, kicks the door closed with his foot. "And I will definitely be paying you back for that little move you pulled in the car."

I capture his mouth, say against his lips, "All part of my master plan."

He marches us into his bedroom, lays me down on the bed. Around the room he treads, lowering the Roman shades. When he turns back to me, his eyes are heated.

He stalks forward, to the edge of the bed. Offers me a hand. "Stand up."

Bossy.

I love it.

With my hand in his warm palm, he helps me off the bed. Stands me upright, and takes a step back.

"These sweet little dresses you favor." His eyes rake the length of me. "I like them, too. But right now, I want you naked." He gathers the hem in both hands, and I lift my arms in the air. So eager.

Hugo works the dress over my head. Tosses it across the room. It's just me, my bra and panties, and my belly. For the briefest second I feel shy, and then I decide I don't want to feel that way. This is me. My body as it is right now. If I feel anything less than confident, it will detract from this experience. And I refuse to have a less-than-enjoyable experience with Hugo. This is too important. Too special.

Reaching behind my back, Hugo unclasps my bra. My breasts, swollen and heavy from pregnancy, tumble out. Hugo flings the bra somewhere around the room, eyes glued to me.

"I thought I was going to melt into the dressing room floor that day," he says, standing back to admire me. A low growl rumbles in his throat as his hot gaze swallows me whole. He leans in, wraps a hand around my neck, guiding my mouth up to his. He devours me, pulling at my tongue, sucking it into his mouth. One hand is in my hair, the other riding the length of my body, cupping my breast. Gently he squeezes, massaging circles. Thumbs my nipple.

I arch into him, moan into his mouth. Wrap my hand around his neck.

He breaks the kiss, moves it lower. Peppering my neck, my collarbone. My chest. Finding my nipple with his tongue. My hands run through his hair, scratch over his scalp.

He lowers himself to his knees. Kisses my belly.

My heart.

His nose presses to the V at the top of my thighs. He inhales deeply, says, "You can't possibly know how often I've thought about spending time down here."

Looking down at his thick head of dark hair, I say, "Me and my lady part are very happy to bring your daydream to fruition."

His chuckle against me is warm. "You think you're so funny, Mallory." He hooks his fingers into the straps on my thighs, pulls my underwear to my ankles in one swift motion. Leaning forward, he presses a kiss to me. "Let's see how funny you can be when I make it hard for you to speak."

With a gentle push, he guides me back onto the bed. Grips my hips and hauls me to the edge. His dark-eyed gaze is on my face, hungry.

"You're so beautiful." Hands on my knees, he peels them apart. Gaze drops, attaching to the center of me. "This part of you? A totally different kind of beauty."

His fingers touch me now, spread me apart. Lazy strokes, up and down. Slow. Luxurious.

Almost like he's *playing*.

"Hugo," I whimper. I need his mouth, his tongue.

"A tease for a tease," he murmurs.

Throwing a forearm over my eyes, I playfully pout. "You are so mean."

His finger slides into me. Curls. "Is that mean?"

"Yes."

He breathes a chuckle. Then there's the swipe of something warm and wet over me. "Is that mean?" he asks, his deep voice pressing into my sensitive part.

I let my forearm drift back over my head. Eyes on the ceiling. "That was very nice."

The softest, sweetest kiss over that little bundle, and I stiffen.

"Should I keep being nice?" The vibration of his words rolls over me.

"Yes, please."

"So polite," Hugo teases. His tongue takes the place of his fingers working those slow, lazy strokes. "Let's see how impolite I can make you be."

Two hands slide under my ass. My hands find his dark hair, fisting. His pace is unhurried, like he could spend all day where he is.

Behaving as if he doesn't just like it down there, he loves it.

My nails find his back, scratch. My hips bow off the bed. Groaning and mewling, I say, "Just like that, Hugo. Just like that. Don't stop."

When I come, it's like a freight train barreling down

the tracks. A body-wide experience. Hugo stays where he is, softly lapping at me, as if he's bringing me down the same way he brought me up.

Planting soft kisses on the insides of my thighs, he says, "You taste amazing, you smell incredible, and I could listen to you come everyday."

Living on a beautiful olive orchard with a man like Hugo, and coming every day? That's my idea of utopia.

Hugo stands, and that's when I realize he's still clothed. I sit up, reach for him. He thumbs his glistening lower lip while I unbutton and unzip his jeans.

"Take off your shirt," I tell him. He reaches behind himself, gathers the fabric, removes the shirt in one fell swoop. It's backwards-hat-level sexy.

He helps me work his jeans and boxer briefs over his hips, and then he kicks them away. And here he is, naked and glorious and mine to do with what I please.

My fingers trail over his abdomen. "It's criminal how muscled you are." Placing my hand on his hips, I haul him forward to me. Lick his abs, tongue tracing where my fingers were. His length brushes my breasts, and he fists it, gathering the wetness like I did on the drive, runs it over my nipples. My head dips, and I take him in my mouth.

His moan is strangled, and I love it. Love the way I can make him sound like that. This man who operates a huge business, who cares for his employees, who's been so hurt and covers it so well.

He hits the back of my throat, and I gag.

"Are you ok?" He brushes the hair back from my face.

I pull back, let him sit in my mouth while I look up at him and nod.

"Fuuuck," he groans.

I let him go with a loud, overdone *pop* and ungracefully roll over onto all fours. Sticking my rear into the air, knowing he can see every part of me, I say, "Now, please."

Hugo palms my ass with one hand. Lines himself up with me. "I don't need a condom?"

"Pretty sure I'm already pregnant," I joke. "And I'm clear."

"I am, too, but..." He runs his length through me, hesitating.

I look over my shoulder. He looks like a pornographic version of a Greek god, naked with rippling muscles, holding himself from underneath, poised to split me in two.

Over my back he meets my eyes. "Will I hurt the baby?"

If that isn't the sweetest thing. "No," I assure him. He looks so worried.

"Are you sure?"

Because he's already pressed to me, I only have to move back an inch to capture him. His eyes are trained on where we're marginally connected. I press back further, taking in another inch of him. "I am one hundred percent certain. Now, Hugo, please fuck me."

"Can't deny you a thing when you talk like that." He buries himself inside me in a measured pace. Maybe one day he'll manhandle me, but for now, he needs to do this

his way. I don't care how it's done, only that it happens. I want this man more than anything, his heat and his weight and his strength.

Hugo gathers my hair, holds my shoulder with his other hand. "You're gorgeous, Mallory. Beautiful and luscious." He releases my hair, hand wrapping over my breast. "Here." He flicks my nipple, hand descending over my belly. "And here." Back up to my hip, where his fingers curl, holding me in place. "I want to take care of you, Mallory. You, and your baby."

Steadying, he creates a rhythm. There is a slap of bodies, heat generated by us. His tempo breaks, becoming frenzied. He moves on from my hip, only to dip his hand between my legs.

"One more from you," he growls, working me.

I love it. The way he fills me, leaves me empty, fills me again. It's heady, and lusty, and sweet, and this man is almost too much. Too good.

My thigh muscles ache, that slow burn, and soon I'm constricting. Jerking and clenching. Hugo cups my sex, holds onto me. Thrusting harder now, losing his grip on that easy pace. He's beside himself, chasing his pleasure. And then he shouts something, a sound not a word, raw and animalistic. Grips me hard, and comes.

"Fuck, Mallory," he pants, leaning over me, kissing down my spine.

"Same," I gasp, grasping for my senses.

He pulls out, but doesn't leave me. I feel him, slipping around. Covering me in his spend.

I drop to my elbows. Give him better access. "Are you marking me?"

"Yes," he answers. "The same way you've marked me."

"I most definitely have not done what you're doing right now."

"Your marks aren't visible," he replies, the answer quick and ready. He stops, sits on the bed, urges me to sit up. "But I promise you, I'm covered in them." He captures my mouth, kissing me with a ferocity I would've expected before the mind-blowing sex. "Let's get cleaned up," he says, when he pulls back. "I want to take a nap."

"I can go back to my room," I say, pushing off the bed.

He grabs my hand, spins me back to him. "Don't you dare. I want you in my bed, curled into me."

My answer comes without reservation. "Yes."

We go into his bathroom and get cleaned up, then we settle back into his bed. He fits me up against him. Runs his hand over my stomach. It's not that I've forgotten I'm pregnant, it's that I spent the last hour feeling like a woman. With Hugo's touch on my belly, it brings reality into stark relief.

Here I am in his bed, carrying with me proverbial suitcases of baggage. I don't want him to feel like he's taking me on. Or worse, that I'm a charity case. Though if I have to be someone's charity case, I don't mind if it comes with orgasms that make my toes tingle.

My hand falls over Hugo's, stilling it. "I know I'm a lot. I won't hold you to anything you said when you were, you know."

Hugo

His mouth, near my ear, takes a little nip. "When I was what? Between your legs? Buried deep inside you? Kissing your back?"

Heat unfurls in my belly at his words. "I was going to say *in the throes*."

Chapter 36

Hugo

My lips hover in the space behind her ear. "Hold me to it."

She stills. "What?"

Urging her onto her back, I brace myself on a forearm so I can look down at her. Dark hair fanning my pillow. Rosy-cheeked and pink-mouthed. "Hold me to every word of it."

"Hugo..."

I hate that she doesn't believe it's possible for me to want her this badly. And Peanut, too. "My words aren't empty, Mallory. I don't say things I don't mean."

Maggie's death was a tragedy, and a second tragedy was the way Mallory was treated afterwards. Cast aside, blamed, forgotten. Grief makes people do terrible things, but it's no excuse. Only a reason.

And then there's Peanut's biological father, leaving Mallory and his child behind. I'd hate him, but the truth is, I'm thankful. His selfishness, my blessing.

Hugo

"You're going to let me be there for you, ok? You're going to hold me to my words, alright?"

It's crazy, and it's fast, but it's everything I've been standing in place for. I wasn't frozen.

I was waiting. For Mallory.

Chapter 37

Hugo

"Have you heard I'm going to be a grandmother again?"

I stop short in the entrance to the kitchen. Mallory stumbles against my arm, and I immediately wrap it around her waist, steadying her.

My mother stands in the middle of the room, her hands on her hips, staring at me expectantly.

Vivi strides in from the living room, Everly and Knox in tow.

"What?" Vivi demands when she sees my expression.

"You're having a baby?" I ask.

"What the...? No."

"Mommy's having a baby?" Everly looks up at Vivi, then down to Knox. "Mommy has a baby in her tummy."

Vivi looks at me like she's prepared to take her meat cleaver to my neck. "Hugo, what the hell is wrong with you?"

"You, Hugo," my mom says loudly, drowning out

Hugo

Vivi's assurance to Everly that there isn't a baby in her belly.

"Ohh," Mallory says. "Hugo went to my appointment with me today."

"That, and he kissed you on the sidewalk for all the world to see." Mom crosses her arms and gives me a defiant look, like she's waiting for me to feed her a bullshit excuse.

What's the use? I can't deny a thing, not when it comes to Mallory. There really is only one option at this point.

I spin Mallory, hold her in both arms, and dip her backward. She gasps in surprise for a brief moment, and then my lips are on hers, drinking the rest of her surprise. Her arms go around my neck, holding on.

"We get it," Aunt Carmen says as the kiss continues.

I draw Mallory upright. Her cheeks are pink, her hair is askew. She clears her throat and I fix her hair.

Then I look at my family. Everly has her hands covering her eyes, two fingers spread out over her right eye so she can peek. Vivi swings Knox into her arms, looking pleased.

My mother is beaming. "Knew it," she calls out. "Come here," she motions to Mallory. "The last time I saw you I didn't know you were pregnant. I want to hear everything."

Mallory steps into my mom, who places an arm around her shoulders. "Tell me about the idiot who let you go. Just kidding, I don't care about him. Tell me how my son has cared for you."

Mom leads Mallory away, toward the living room. Aunt Carmen takes Knox from Vivi, and asks Everly if she'd like to see the new coloring book she bought recently.

Vivi begins pulling vegetables from the crisper, chicken thighs from butcher paper. We get to work, and Vivi is quiet. She's working her way up to saying something to me, so I wait.

She's lifting the skin off the chicken thighs, rubbing seasoning under it, when she finally breaks.

"I like her, Hugo. As a person, and for you."

"But?" I'm peeling carrots, watching the peels go everywhere except the garbage can I'm aiming for.

"But what are you getting yourself into? She's pregnant."

My back teeth gnash. "I noticed."

"Are you signing yourself up to be this child's father? Because if you're not, you need to think long and hard about what you're doing."

"It's sweet of you to be concerned about me, but—"

"I love you, Hugo, but I'm not concerned about you. I'm worried for Mallory. Being a new mom is hard even with a partner. And here you come, bringing adrenaline and oxytocin, playing house. Playing *family*. What happens if one day you decide you've changed your mind? You've realized you don't want to raise another man's child?" Vivi's squeezing a chicken thigh, mangling it. I don't think she knows she's doing it. "That woman knows she's going to be a single mom. Don't make her be a single mom with a broken heart."

Hugo

I could be mad at my sister's words, her lack of faith in me. I'd be justified. Instead, I wrap my arms around her. She is stiff, and then she softens.

"Why are you hugging me?" she asks, in a defeated voice.

"Because you need it," I answer. If it's not me who gets the pleasure of knocking out my sister's ex, I hope I can shake the hand of the man who shows Vivi she's worth more than what she's received.

"Sometimes, everything really hurts," she admits, her head on my shoulder. "I don't want Mallory to hurt, too."

"I will be the last person in the world who will hurt her."

Vivi sighs. "You give me hope. Maybe I'll meet someone one day, a man who doesn't mind that I have two kids and some untended trauma."

I give her an extra squeeze before releasing her. "Whoever he is, I'm going to have to vet him."

"If you scare him away, you'll have to accept the fact that I'm moving into your house with my two kids."

"If it's possible for him to be scared away, he didn't deserve you in the first place."

Vivi smiles gratefully at me. She notices the crushed chicken thigh on her cutting board and tosses it in the trash. "I might want to take up kickboxing, or some other sport where I can get out my aggression."

She washes her hands with hot, soapy water, saying, "Don't worry, I didn't touch you with these hands."

Vivi and I work side by side preparing dinner. At some point Mallory returns, jumping in to set the table.

Everly entertains us during dinner, Aunt Carmen regales Mallory with her personal favorites from the obituaries she has authored, and Knox makes it clear he'd like to be held by Mallory when dinner is finished.

My mother, undeterred by my groans, brings out a photo album of me growing up. "Get over it," she tells me. "I've been waiting my whole life to show you off."

Mallory is game to play along, sitting next to my mom on the couch while she flips through the album. School pictures and holidays, Mallory patiently listens to my mom talk. "I was so proud of him that day," my mom brags, pointing to a photo she took of me at the medal ceremony. It's not a good photo, I'm not looking at the camera, but she took it, and she loved it enough to place it in an album.

The second Mallory yawns, I usher her from the house.

"We'll see you soon," I remind my mom when she frowns. "I live just over that slope."

I've been waiting all evening to get Mallory home. I want her again. Need her, really. She is a sun I never want to set, a wave I hope always crests.

I take her to my bed. Strip her down. Love her with my hands, my mouth, my body. Afterward, we take a shower. I take my time washing her, running my hands over her stomach. Vivi's words from this evening skip along my mind. *Are you signing yourself up to be this child's father?*

Chapter 38

Hugo

"I have a confession to make," Mallory says out of nowhere.

We're lounging on the porch bed, letting the afternoon sun warm our toes. She's tucked under my arm, head heavy on my chest. Mallory loves it out here, staring out at the cloudless sky, and I love anything that makes her happy.

"Lay it on me." My fingers graze her arm, bringing chill bumps to her skin.

"Your fencing costume was...sexy."

I look down at the top of her head. Take a moment to compose myself. "Because the mask covered my ugly mug?"

Mallory shifts, pushes up on her elbow so she can look at me. "You looked hot, Hugo."

I do my best not to laugh. She's being open and honest with me right now. "I have to say, nobody has ever called me hot wearing breeches."

"Not to your face."

"Or at all."

She grins. "Bull riding has buckle bunnies. What does fencing have?"

"Trails of dust from women running the other direction."

Mallory slaps my chest. "Stop. I said what I said. Hot."

I palm her lovely cheek, stroking her soft skin with my thumb. "You're just saying that because you found out I'm good at making you come."

"*Great* at making me come," she clarifies, and my chest puffs with pride. "But no. I'm not. You looked powerful. Strong. In control. Not to mention how muscled your thighs look in those white pants."

"Don't even think of asking me to wear that outfit for you."

She giggles. "Actually, I was wondering if you'd give me a beginner's lesson."

"I take umbrage with thrusting sharp objects at you."

She gives me a look.

I sigh. "I heard it."

She laughs. "Come on. I looked it up. Fencing swords have blunt edges."

"They can still hurt you. That's why fencers wear protective gear."

Mallory pouts. "Can you give me a little show, then?"

"No costume."

"No costume," she agrees.

Hugo

We're standing in the living room. I've pushed the coffee table out of the way to give us more space.

"These," I start, pointing at the weapons above the fireplace, "are the swords. They are the foil, épée, and saber." I point at each in turn. Mallory nods studiously. I bet she was a star pupil in every class.

"What is the name of that one?" she asks, nodding her chin at the fourth sword, closest to the fireplace mantle.

"That's a sword."

"Yes, but what is it called in fencing?"

"That is not a fencing weapon. In fencing, there are only three." Gingerly, and with great caution, I lift the sword off its hooks. "This is a real sword. I purchased it when I was in Bern, Switzerland, and I walked into a knife shop. There was a secret room at the back with swords and other weaponry, and a knight's armor. I'd been fencing with blunt edge weapons for so long, I decided to spring for the real thing." I direct the tip at the ground, and Mallory looks over the intricate handle. "It's unbelievably sharp. In case you're wondering, I have cut myself on it. Not badly, but still." I replace the sword on its hooks.

"Here's what I know about fencing," Mallory says, taking a step back with one foot. She lifts a hand, raising a pretend sword. "On guard."

She looks so cute, so playful. First she let me nerd out over olives, and now this? It doesn't get better than this woman.

"That's your starting position," I indulge her, mirroring her body posture. "You could retreat to create space or dodge an attack." I demonstrate a simple step back. "Or lunge, to step forward and reach your opponent." I do this as well, arm extended.

Mallory presses a hand to her arm. "You got me."

"Good," I tell her, advancing. She lets me wrap her up in my arms. "Not letting you go, either."

"I have another confession to make." She bites the side of her lower lip, eyes lively.

"And that would be?"

"Jolene made a joke about me wearing your gold medal and riding you."

That has never been a fantasy of mine...until now.

I let her go, taking her hand, leading her down the hall.

"Where are we going?"

"To my closet to get my gold medal."

An excited giggle behind me. The cutest sound.

Hand in hand, I take her to my closet, to the small fireproof safe where I keep both medals. When I have it in hand, I turn to Mallory. "Strip," I tell her. Eyes locked on me, she listens. When she's naked, all womanly curves and soft skin, I place the medal over her head. Settle it between her full breasts.

She looks down, admires it. "It's not as heavy as I thought it would be. But it is cold."

Hugo

I can't focus on the weight of the medal, or the temperature. A goddess, a siren, an American wet dream stands before me.

"This image will live on in my mind. In infamy."

Mallory smiles in this sexy, coquettish way. "I should be wearing spike heels. Then it would be perfect."

I'm shaking my head before she can finish her sentence. "It's perfect because it's on you." I point at my bed. "That's where we're headed." I make short work of my clothes. For a fantasy I've never had, I'm pretty damn excited about this.

Clothing shucked, I climb on the bed. Mallory hoists one leg over me, bracketing my body with her thighs. The medal lies against her creamy skin, looking one thousand times better on her than it does on me.

Her hand wraps around me, pumping, like she's getting me ready for her ride. And as much as I love it, I have a different ride in mind for her first.

"Up here." I nudge, lightly smacking her behind.

"What?" she asks, confused.

"My face. That's your ride."

"Hugo, I"—her head shakes—"I've never done that before."

Something possessive in my chest unfurls. We're at ages where we can't give each other many firsts, but I love knowing this isn't a road she's traveled with anybody else.

I wink at her. "Guess I'll have to break you in."

With my hands I encourage her to move up my body. She rises up on her knees, makes her way up me with my assistance.

"I feel shy," she admits, sitting down on my chest.

"Don't be. You're going on two rides today, this is the first. Now, listen. I'm hungry, so get yourself up here and let me have my fill."

She's not convinced. "Promise me you won't let me suffocate you?"

"I can think of far worse ways to go."

"That's not funny."

I can't help my smile at the stern look on her face. She's gloriously naked, sitting on my chest, and wearing my gold medal. Not sure life gets better than this.

But then she relents, comes up over me, and settles in.

I take back what I said. Life does get better.

"Grab the headboard," I instruct, getting to work. I can't see much because of her belly, but that's ok. My imagination does the job.

Before long she's gripping the headboard and tipping her head back, crying out. It takes her a moment to come down, but when she does she's scrambling down my body, leaving a wet trail.

"Need you so bad right now," she groans. She leans down, gives me a few quick bobs of her head, and positions me in place. I hold onto her hips and watch her slowly impaled by me.

"Yes," she hisses, head tipping up.

I give her my hands, let her use them as leverage. She grips me tightly, lifts herself up and down. Faster now, she picks up the tempo. Her breasts sway, my medal

Hugo

along with them. Her body undulates, taking what she needs, hitting the perfect spot for her.

Heat licks up the base of my spine, my orgasm not far off.

Mallory looks at me with a heavy-lidded gaze, slides down until she's fully seated. "Do you like the way I look wearing your gold medal?"

"Core memory," I answer. "It'll be hard for me to close my eyes and not see this." My words send Mallory over the edge, and then I follow her down, into that carnal place.

She collapses on the bed beside me.

I lean over, kiss her forehead. "That was..." There are no words.

"I know," she says.

We lie that way for a while. I bring her a warm rag and clean her up. We dress, and end up in the kitchen where I make her an early dinner while she sits at the island and peppers me with questions about the inner workings of an olive mill. Like last night, I hold her hand and take her back to my bed for sleep. A fog of bliss covers us, that heady feeling that harkens to big things to come, but there's a softness to the peak. Something slow, steady, and stable. Me, Mallory, and Peanut.

Living just like this, in our perfect, little life.

Chapter 39

Mallory

I'm sore in places I forgot existed. It's a good kind of sore, the delicious ache that comes with even better memories. Sex served every way I like it. Tender, sweet, rough, intense. Hugo feels like a piece of my life that's been missing. A piece I'd always known was vacant, but never believed I could fill. Without realizing it, I'd resigned myself to a life where I'd forever feel a little bit broken. It hadn't occurred to me someone could come along and fill in those cracks.

I never saw myself in a place this beautiful, with a man so incredible, but now that I've experienced it, I don't see myself being able to let it go.

Cecily has emailed me her unbelievably detailed and incredibly organized social media content plan. She's going to spend the next two weeks listening to previous *Case Files* episodes, and create content around those. My marching orders are to go through all those episodes and supply her with my favorite parts, anecdotes, and details. All future episodes will follow the same format.

I haven't given up on the original reason I came to Olive Township, but for a moment, I'm slowing down. If Jolene was serious enough to bring on a marketing company, I want to give it my best effort.

Hugo and I fall into a rhythm that involves great conversation, meals prepared together, laughter, and incredible sex. He learned exercises safe for pregnant women, and we've incorporated time in the home gym into our routine.

The domesticity of it is great, but it's so much more than that. It's healing. Filling me up, sliding into my crevices. We haven't talked about the future, but a conversation is inevitable. There's a time bomb in the form of a human living in my body.

But maybe we can live in this bliss a little longer. Linger here, in this fairy tale of a situation. I'll close my eyes, willfully blind, and let all those sweet words he murmurs in my ear when he's inside me be my sustenance. For now, they are all I need.

THREE WEEKS of living in our perfect little bubble on Summerhill, interrupted by a knock on Hugo's front door.

I look up from my spot on the couch, a book about

child brain development open on my lap. Hugo looks at me on his way to the door, winking and saying, "It's probably my mom asking for her picnic basket. She's watching Everly and Knox today."

Hugo pulls open the door, and I hear him say, "Detective Towles? Is everything alright?"

The answering voice is quiet, and I can't make it out. Hugo widens the door, steps aside, and the detective walks in.

I wave from my place on the couch, placing a bookmark between the pages and sliding the book on the coffee table. I'm wearing loose, comfortable pants and a cotton tank top that shows my belly. A few days ago, at my twenty-four week appointment, the doctor said, "Looks like you have a little basketball in there."

I stand up and round the couch. Hugo comes to stand beside me, and I say, "Hello, Detective."

"Miss Hawkins," he replies. "I thought, given the nature of your request, that I would hand deliver this."

He holds out a bulging folder. In an instant, I know what it is, and I'm already searching Hugo's face. He's nodding slowly, tugging on his earlobe in a way I've never seen him do.

I reach for him, tightening my grip on his arm. "You can still change your mind."

"You know," Detective Towles interrupts, voice gruff, "Just because I'm giving you this to look through doesn't mean something big is going to happen. You don't have to get worked up. The boys and I gave this case everything we had."

Hugo

"Understood," Hugo says woodenly. He takes the file.

"Thank you for coming all the way out here," I say, because Hugo seems to be at a loss for words.

"I'm not that nice," the detective admits, scratching at his brow. "I wanted to make sure you're staying out here like you said."

I smile. "I know."

He gestures at my midsection. "Congratulations, Miss Hawkins. Hugo."

I keep waiting for the moment Hugo will correct somebody's assumption, but even now in his distressed state, he does not deviate. "Thank you," he says, voice rough.

We walk the detective to the door. He steps through, pausing to look back and say, "I'm going to need that returned to me."

"Yes. Thank you."

Hugo and I stand on the front porch, watching him drive away in an unmarked police car.

The trail of dust plumes, and then his car disappears over the slope.

"How are you?" I ask, turning into Hugo, wrapping my arms around his waist. In one hand, he still holds the folder. The other comes up, cups my cheek.

"I'm ok," he rasps. "Like Towles said, he and his guys pored over everything. There's probably nothing new in here."

"Yep," I agree readily, knowing where Hugo's coming from, because it's the same way I feel.

Ultimately, we want to know what happened to our

loved ones. But alongside that desire is fear of finding out. Even the possibility of knowing sparks a shred of apprehension. A person can want something desperately, but also fear having it.

My arms run the length of Hugo's back. "What do you think about tabling the folder for a little bit? We don't have to dive into it. It's been two decades, what's a few more days?"

Hugo nods thoughtfully, stepping out of my arms. He extends the file to me, and I take it. It is thick, and heavy, smelling of dust and old paper.

"That file should be in your care. You're the professional here, not me. And I think, if you wanted to tear it open right now and spend the next seven hours inside it, I would support you." He leans in, kisses my forehead. "I'm going to finish the salsa I was making when Towles showed up. Then I'm going to make the guacamole, and we're going to sit on the porch with our virgin margaritas like we planned. You can read the book you've been reading, or"—he glances at the folder—"you can read that."

He retreats into the house. I stare down at the nondescript folder, feeling its weight in my arms. Inside, the blender starts up. I walk inside, deposit the folder on the dining room table next to all my other work. Pinching my lower lip between two fingers, I stare down at my notes. The whiteboard. And now, the case file.

The whole point of me coming to Olive Township was to gain the De la Vegas trust and receive their blessing to look into Simon's murder, and the possible connection to my sister. Now that I'm one step closer, something is holding me back. I'm not sure what it is, only that it's creating a hesitancy. I came to town with fire, a fervor. I had an end goal, but the more time I spend around Hugo, the more my fully formed and concrete end goal begins to waver. As if spending time around him, getting to know him, and sharing our grief is poking holes in my plan. Months of emailing him, hanging my hopes on his response, and now I'm here, right in the middle of where I thought I wanted to be, believed I needed to be, and I'm waffling.

I was desperate to learn the connection between the two murders, and solve the riddle. My heart needed to know there was one less evil person in the world with my baby, but am I really driven by that anymore?

Hugo announces the food is prepared, and I help him carry everything onto the porch. We sit in the warm sun, me with my book, and Hugo with his. It's almost criminal how much I enjoy living in his orbit.

When my belly is full of salsa and guacamole, and my thirst has been quenched by the citrusy nonalcoholic margarita, I put down my book and climb on the swing bed.

Lying back on the pillows, with the afternoon sun tickling my toes, I say, "There's room for one more up here."

Hugo smiles, and makes short work of the distance between us.

We settle on the swing bed together, adjusting the pillows. My head tucks into the space of his neck, my right leg thrown over his thighs. His fingertips graze my back as we watch dark clouds gather in the distance.

"I noticed you weren't poring over that folder," Hugo says after a while.

"I'm conflicted," I admit.

"Tell me more," he says.

My hand finds his chest, runs over the soft fabric covering hard planes as I assemble my jumbled thoughts into coherent sentences. "I thought coming here and investigating, getting an answer once and for all, would be what I needed. But meeting you wasn't like I thought it would be. I thought I would be healed by facts. By truth. By justice. Instead, it was so much simpler than that." My touch leaves his chest, runs up his neck. I lean back so I can look at him. His strong jaw, his expressive eyebrows. Those soulful brown eyes gazing back at me. "It was a man on an olive orchard, with a heart just as broken as mine."

Fire lights in his irises, burns hot. "You're everything, Mallory. You take me out. You take me down." His hand runs through my hair. "I never saw you coming. Had no idea you existed. And now I can't exist without you."

He smiles at a tear that streaks from my eyes, flicks it away. My mouth closes over his, our lips yielding. Tongues tasting. My hand dips lower, slides into his sweats. I want this man. Every inch of him. I need him like air. Water. Food.

"Bed," he says on a groan. "Now."

"We're on a bed," I argue, delivering a few leisurely pumps.

Hugo

"I'll bring you out here when it's dark, and I will fuck you ragged. But for now, I can't have anybody seeing you like that. You're mine." He nips at my jaw. "Nobody sees you being pleasured but me."

Well. That will do.

My hand leaves his sweats. We disentangle ourselves, and he helps me from the swing. On quick feet we hurry through the house, all the way to his bed.

It's there, with rain clouds approaching and Hugo moving inside me, that he dips his lips to my ear. Whispers, "I'm in love with you, Mallory."

Words that heal. Words that energize. From Hugo's lips, and his heart. It couldn't be more perfect.

Every emotion I feel for this strong, protective, generous man comes rushing forward. An intensity that overwhelms, makes me so ready, so happy to return the words. My fingernails rake his back, my face turns to capture his mouth. "I'm in love with you, Hugo. I think I have been all along."

Chapter 40

Mallory

The days turn into weeks, and the case file remains untouched.

I still want to know, I want to figure out what happened, but it doesn't feel like my ability to bring Peanut into this world is contingent upon one fewer bad guy existing in it. Especially now that I know one incredible man exists.

It's a good feeling, not being driven by something dark.

But there is still my podcast, and as they say in the entertainment industry, *the show must go on*.

Cecily's efforts have revived *Case Files*. My listens and downloads have increased, as has the subscriber count.

I talk with Jolene and Cecily every other day, tweaking posts and captions, coming up with new ideas. So right now, when my phone lights up with Jolene's name, I don't think much of it.

Hugo

"Hey," I answer on speaker, swallowing a bite of toast.

"*Ohmygosh* you aren't going to believe what I'm about to tell you!" Jolene's high-pitched voice bounces around the kitchen.

"What?" I ask, taking a sip of water.

"Foundry emailed me. Foundry!"

I cough on the water. Foundry isn't simply a podcast network, it is *the* podcasting network. They sign big names, bring in smaller shows, nurture careers. "What did they say?"

"They want a meeting! The email says *'We'd like to discuss Case Files and the future it could have at Foundry.'* Mallory, this is it. I can feel it!"

I sit back on the island stool, rub a hand over my forehead.

"Where did you go?" Jolene asks.

"I'm still here. Just in shock."

"I should respond, right? Do you want me to set up a meeting?"

"Of course. Why? Don't you want a meeting?"

"More than anything, but, Mal..." Jolene sighs. "You've been really on top of getting Cecily everything she needs, and turning around our social media game. But when it comes to Simon De la Vega and creating new episodes? You're kind of failing."

"I know, I know. I'm sorry. It's hard to explain."

"Let me give it a shot," Jolene says, clearing her throat. "You fell in love with Simon's son, found what you've been looking for since you were fourteen, and no longer feel the same urgency."

Hugo chooses this moment to come around the corner, fresh from his morning workout.

Sweat beads at his hairline. He's shirtless, covered in muscle. A male smoke show.

I blink hard a couple times before saying, "Bingo."

Jolene has no idea Hugo has walked into the room, and keeps speaking. "Mallory, if we take this meeting with Foundry, we need to come to it with future ideas. They need to see a podcast that is not in short supply of episodes. And, not to sensationalize what happened, but this cold case would be an incredible pitch. Hugo was an Olympian. There's rich backstory, personal interest."

My forearms press the edge of the island, and I survey Hugo's response to Jolene's words.

He works his lower lip between his teeth, nodding slowly.

"What's Foundry?" he asks.

"Hugo?" Jolene says, volume raised. "Is that Hugo?"

"It's me," he answers, crossing the kitchen. Coming closer. Quickly, I explain Foundry, and their email.

"Hugo, I'm sorry," Jolene says. "I don't mean to make this awkward. For you, or for Mallory."

"It's not awkward," he answers, stepping in to me. He grabs the stool, turns me toward him. Leans down, and now we're eye to eye. "Mallory has a job to do, if she still wants to do it. I gave her my blessing months ago, and it still stands."

"Are you sure?" I ask, forgetting Jolene's listening. "Once it's done, that's it. It can't be taken back."

"When you first came here, I said yes because it felt like even though I didn't want to heal, I should. Now I'm saying yes because it feels like the right thing to do."

"So, we're saying yes to a meeting, then?" Jolene's voice interrupts the moment.

"Yes," I agree. Hugo brushes a kiss over my lips. He smells like salty sweat, and whatever it is that makes him so delectable.

"Your appointment is in an hour," he reminds me.

"Twenty-eight weeks," Jolene reports. "Are you free next weekend? I need to put my hands on my best friend and her preggo belly."

"We're free," Hugo answers for me. "You can stay here, with us."

He walks away to grab a shower before we need to leave and Jolene tells me how happy she is for me. And Peanut.

"I knew this would happen," she brags.

"You did not," I argue.

"Ok, I didn't, but it's seriously so perfect. Who better to understand what made you who you are today?"

"It feels very right," I admit.

Jolene and I spend a few more minutes talking about the podcast, and she tells me she'll see me next weekend. "Let me know if there's something you want me to bring from Phoenix. Anything you need that you can't get in Olive Township."

I tell her no thank you. Everything I need is right here.

Off the phone with Jolene, and with Hugo in the shower, I compose an email to David Boylan. If we're going to move forward creating episodes around Hugo's dad, David would be an ideal person to interview.

> To: DaBoy72@gbt.com
> From: Mallory Hawkins
> Hi David,
> Thank you for taking the time to meet with me and Hugo. During our conversation, I did not get the chance to tell you that I am the host of a true crime podcast called Case Files. With the blessing of the De la Vega family, I am looking into the possibility that the murder of Simon De la Vega may be connected to a murder that took place in Phoenix fourteen years ago.
> Although I haven't begun recording episodes yet, I wanted to check in with you and see if you would be open to an interview that I would use as an episode.
> Again, I am thankful for the time you gave us already, and for giving my baby her first gift.
> Best,
> Mallory Hawkins
> Host of *Case Files*

Hugo walks out, ready to go. I hit Send on my email.

Hugo

"Baby is measuring exactly where she should be. Your fasting glucose looked great. All in all, Mom is healthy, and so is baby." Dr. Connolly gives me a reassuring smile.

Music to my ears. As if Peanut can feel my happiness, she delivers a swift kick.

I grab Hugo's arm, place his hand on the spot on my belly. He's been wanting to feel her, but so far he hasn't been able to.

The seconds pass, and Hugo frowns when nothing happens. Dr. Connolly laughs, and on our way out of the door says, "That's kids for you. They rarely do what you want them to do. Just wait until she's a teenager."

After we get checked out and I've made my next appointment, Hugo calls Penn to see if he and Daisy are available for lunch.

We meet them at Good Thyme Café, where Hugo requests a table on the back patio. "It's going to get pretty warm starting next week," he says, and Penn teases him for watching the weather like an old man.

"Like an olive farmer," Hugo retorts, clapping Penn loudly on the back.

The hostess leads us to a gorgeous little space behind the restaurant. It backs up to a greenbelt of grass that could only be kept that green with the use of sprinklers. Beyond it is wild desert, palo verde trees and saguaros as far as the eye can see.

Ambrose video calls Hugo after we place our order. Hugo answers, corralling the salt and pepper shakers and propping the phone against them.

It's my first time meeting Hugo's best friend, though I've heard enough about him. His shoulders are so wide they fill the screen, making me ponder his wingspan. Everything about the guy is massive, from his chest to his arms, but it's his smile that's the most disarming. There is kindness in the corners, a humble curve to his lips.

"It's nice to meet you, Mallory," Ambrose says. "I've heard enough about you by now, it's good to put a face to all the yammering Hugo's been doing."

"Alright, alright, before you two start trading funny stories about me," Hugo cuts in, "what's going on, Ambrose?"

Ambrose's gaze roams the group of four staring back at him. "No Vivi?" he asks.

"She's prepping dinner service," Daisy says. "But I'm sure she'll be bummed to know she missed you."

"I thought you should hear it from me, instead of ESPN. I hurt my knee in practice this week, and—"

Daisy gasps. "Nooo, Ambrose."

"Dude," Hugo says, but with a tone of *oh no*.

"Fuck," Penn murmurs. "How bad?"

Ambrose sighs. "Pretty bad, unfortunately. Torn ACL. Ligament damage. Meniscus, too. I'm looking at a surgery for sure, I just don't know when. I'm seeing an orthopedic surgeon in Phoenix in a couple weeks. Once that happens, I'll know more."

"You'll be convalescing…here?" Hugo's eyebrows are raised, hopeful.

"Why?" Ambrose asks. "You want to wait on me hand and foot?"

Hugo

Hugo laughs. "My bedside manner is impeccable."

Our food arrives, and Ambrose says goodbye.

"He's in the NFL, right?" I ask, popping a fry in my mouth.

"Linebacker," Daisy says.

"Ohh, so that's why his shoulders took up most of the screen."

Daisy laughs. "All through school the teachers called him *Gentle Giant*."

"Until he got on the football field, anyway." A worried look pulls at Hugo's features. "I wonder what this injury will do to his career?"

Penn wipes his mouth with his napkin. "Good job, bud. Way to think positive."

As the group chats, I glance out across the green lawn, toward the desert beyond. It's almost beautiful, except for a break in the spindly palo verde trees. One is dead, the green a sad, dried out gray-brown, and up through it grows a saguaro that hasn't yet developed limbs. The younger cactus stands tall, looking out of place.

"Did you spot a coyote?" Hugo teases me, gazing out where I'm looking.

"Just that dead tree with the saguaro growing up through it. Only that tree is dead when all the others around it are thriving. It's odd."

"I don't make it a habit to know the history of the local cacti," Penn says, "but I did overhear Margaret talking about the way a rogue Saguaro was growing up under the shade of a palo verde, only to eventually rob the tree of the rainwater and nutrients in the soil."

I stir my straw in my iced tea, thinking this over. "It killed the host."

"Exactly," Penn nods. "Saguaros are federally protected, so it's not like anybody's going out there with a machete and hacking it down."

"Saguaros can be moved," Daisy chimes in. "Carefully though, keeping their roots intact, and they have to go to a new home in the ground."

I stare out at the crestfallen limbs, the way the cactus stands proud. It seems so wrong, the way the cactus was in the shade stealing from the only reason it was able to live there. The guest choked the host.

And then it hits me.

"Hugo," I grip his arm.

His carefree expression is wiped away by my alarm. "Are you ok? Is Peanut ok?"

"We're fine," I assure him, loving the way he checks on the two of us. "How was your dad at keeping records?"

"Not sure. Why?" His dark eyes narrow. Across the table, Penn and Daisy lean forward.

"I want to see the employee records from the time leading up to when he was killed." I think of the police report, sitting on the table next to my computer. "And then I want to check the police file and cross reference them with your dad's records."

Hugo's nodding, already looking at Penn. "I keep a tab open here. Tell the server to add our lunch to it."

I grab the second half of my BLT. Penn and Daisy

Hugo

wish us luck, and we weave our way back through the restaurant.

"Mallory, Hugo!" The call of our names brings us up short. Liane waves from a table of women right in front of us. No chance for us to continue, claiming we didn't hear her.

"Hi, Mrs. Rooney," Hugo says, polite smile in place.

"I keep meaning to make a trip out to Summerhill, but something is always keeping me from visiting. It's either a board meeting, a conservation society luncheon, or—"

"Kissing babies," Hugo supplies. Normally a comment like this would be a joke, but his tone does not fit. It's as if his mind has gone where mine went when I saw that victorious saguaro and its victim hanging brokenly around it. Suddenly we both need to explore a possibility. And Liane Rooney is keeping us.

Liane laughs off Hugo's comment. "One of my many duties. I promise to make it out this week."

"Sounds great," Hugo says, pulling me along. "There's a new shipment of vanilla olive oil arriving tomorrow. You should be the first to add it to your collection."

"It was nice to see you," I say as we pass her table. The interaction is so harried, I don't notice who it is she's having lunch with.

Hugo helps me into his car, and when he slides in the driver's seat, says, "That woman has the worst timing."

"Forget about her," I say. "Is your mind where my mind is?"

"I'm sure the police questioned all the Summerhill employees. But, yes."

We pass Sweet Nothings as we drive down Olive Avenue. It brings to mind my last conversation with Sal. He'd said something about how not only did Simon not have enemies, he only had friends.

What about his employees? Were they more like friends?

And then the question. Did one of them kill the host?

Chapter 41

Hugo

OUR FIRST STOP IS MY HOUSE FOR THE POLICE FILE. Mallory makes a stop at the bathroom. Just this week her gait has evolved to include a side to side sway as her center of gravity shifts with every step.

I never saw myself in love. I never saw myself with a pregnant woman. I never saw myself in love with a woman pregnant with a baby we did not create. But here I am. Atypical and impossibly perfect.

Mallory comes to me where I stand next to the dining room table. Her arms wind around my waist. "Just because we had this little epiphany doesn't mean we have to roll with it. We can stand here and decide not to look into the employee records."

I appreciate how kind she has been every step of the way. How accommodating. She needs this story for the future of her podcast, but she's willing to let it go if it becomes too much for me.

Knowing she cares that deeply makes me want to give

it to her more. So I touch her face, cup her cheek the way I know she likes. Capture her mouth in a kiss because I won't miss the opportunity.

Pulling back, I look deeply into her beautiful eyes. "Let's go see if we can find something the police missed."

It's the middle of the day, and every Summerhill employee is hard at work. Claudette, the mill manager, emerges from her small office when we walk in. She's a stout woman with lips that turn down at the corners, which is really too bad because she's nice as can be. Claudette knows how she looks, and, in accordance with her good-natured personality, jokes it keeps the riffraff away.

"This is Claudette, my right hand at Summerhill. Claudette, this is my girlfriend, Mallory."

Mallory's eyes widen, cheeks tugging with a suppressed smile. She weaves her hand in mine, squeezes hard.

"I've always known Hugo keeps a tight lid on his personal life." Claudette's grappling with the metaphorical fastball I've thrown her, but she recovers well. "It's nice to meet you, Mallory."

"You as well," Mallory responds. Tucked under her arm is the folder holding every piece of known information relating to my father's murder.

Hugo

Claudette retreats into her office, and I take Mallory into mine. I close my door with my foot, because I don't want interruptions or curious glances while we're digging through records. Or the police report.

Mallory stands in the middle of the small room, looking around. There's a desk with an ancient computer, a small bookshelf, and a chair.

"I've been so busy updating the website and expanding what the mill offers, I've neglected my office," I explain, going to stand behind my desk. Beside it is a small metal filing cabinet. Knowing my dad, that is our best bet for finding old records.

"Except the mini-fridge." Mallory points at the black rectangle in the corner, humming along.

"That's usually where I keep my lunch."

Mallory stands at the bookshelf, poking through titles. "But you've been coming home for lunch every day since the day you brought me there." Confusion crosses her face. "That's not what you always do?"

"Sandwiches were suddenly my favorite lunch, and they're better fresh."

"You know what?" Mallory selects a book on olive oil extraction techniques, turning it over in her hands. "As your *girlfriend*, I am not surprised."

I wince. "Was that ok? We didn't talk about it."

Mallory crosses the small space, sets the book on my desk as she rounds it. Her hands start at my chest, slide up my neck and into my hair. "I'm still wrapping my brain around why you want to take on me and Peanut."

I run a hand through her hair, and she tilts into my

touch. "I'm still hacking away at what's inside you that makes you think it should be a problem for me."

"You're too good to me, Hugo."

"No, Mallory. For you, I am just right."

Mallory lifts on her tiptoes. Angles her face up for a kiss. We're here in my office for a specific reason, but we seem to have momentarily set it aside.

"This is so confusing," she whispers as I brush my lips over hers. "I came here with all this adrenaline, ready to pore over old papers, but now..." Her hand trails down, finds the front of my pants.

"I'm equally confused," I confess, growing into her hand. I'm starved for this woman, always. It doesn't matter when I've had her last, I'm in a perpetual state of wanting her.

A mischievous twinkle enters her gaze. "Our questions won't go anywhere if we spend five minutes engaged otherwise."

Mallory sinks to her knees. Pulls me from my jeans.

"I swear I didn't plan this," I mutter as she swallows me down.

Her cheeks lift into a smile. "Mm hmm," she says, the sound vibrating.

My hands find her hair, fingers flexing. "Hold still."

She listens.

"Put your hands on my thighs. Squeeze them if this becomes too much."

She listens again.

Hands on her head, I feed her slowly, inch by inch. Careful with her. Because I love her.

Mallory whimpers, but she doesn't give the signal. "You like it?" I ask.

She nods slightly.

"More?" I ask.

Another slight nod.

I listen. I give her what she wants. And then when the sensation builds to a crescendo, and I move to pluck a tissue off my desk, Mallory's hands travel to my backside, holding me in place.

My back teeth grind together, jaw flexed, and silently I fall apart.

Mallory pulls back, stands. Smiles at me as she grabs a bottle of water from the mini-fridge.

"You," I point at her after I get myself situated.

"I swear I didn't plan that," she says playfully, drinking the water.

I stride to the office door, turn the lock. Nobody would've barged in, but still. I need the door locked for what I'm about to do.

"Get on my desk," I instruct.

Mallory blinks at me, doesn't move. "We have work to do, Hugo."

"I know," I answer, stalking toward her. "I need you sated."

Mallory doesn't move. So I move her. Even twenty-eight weeks pregnant, I lift her. Put her on the desk, haul her forward. "Pull my hair," I tell her. "And give me those soft little moans of yours."

I could stay with my lips on Mallory's thighs until the end of time, but she's so ready, so turned on from being on her knees for me. It doesn't take long before she's threading her fingers through my hair, doing her best to quiet those moans.

"Attagirl," I tell her, coaching her through it as she squirms on my desk, back arching while I lap at her.

I don't stop until her legs are shaking, until she's begging me to give her a break. Pressing a kiss to the inside of her knee, I pull her panties up, and her dress down. Help her into my desk chair, because her muscles are too weak.

Pulling the second chair from around the front of my desk, I settle in beside Mallory. She leans over to kiss me, and I more than happily oblige. We taste salty and indecent. I love it. I love her.

"Now I feel ready to dig," I say when we separate. "How about you?"

Mallory smiles at me. She's so gorgeous, it's almost painful. "I feel ready for a nap, to be honest. But I'll work, instead."

Chapter 42

Mallory

It's not easy sitting beside Hugo after what we did. Especially because after the buzz wears off, I'm ready for more. Maybe it's the pregnancy hormones, but I'm not so sure. In fact, I'm positive that's not it at all. Perhaps it never was.

It's him. Hugo. I want him with an unbelievable ferocity, in every way. Even sitting here, smelling his scent, makes me soft. Warm. Gooey. I am basically a s'more for this man.

"My dad was not the most organized keeper of paperwork," Hugo admits. He sighs and rubs at the pleat between his brows. There's a mountain of papers to sort through, sitting in a spot on the desk my ass only recently vacated.

"All these old invoices? Why keep them?" He shakes a handful. "Some of these are from twenty-five years ago."

We work for a solid two hours. Not surprisingly, I need to pee. Hugo tells me where the office bathroom is, and I go in search of it. I locate it easily, and run into Claudette on my way in. She sends me a polite smile, one I return when an idea strikes me.

"How long have you worked at Summerhill? Just out of curiosity," I add, hoping she doesn't take it as anything but a simple query.

"Going on ten years. I took over for my father when he had his stroke. He was the mill manager for as long as I can remember."

"I'm sorry to hear that happened to him."

"He's ok. Lost some motor function, but it was well past time for him to retire. If he didn't love the De la Vegas like family, he would've stepped away sooner."

"The Summerhill community seems like a close one."

"We really are." She smiles proudly. "Aside from those who come here for seasonal work, we have very little turnover." Thumbing behind herself, she says, "Speaking of work, I better get back to it."

She heads the opposite way. I finish up in the bathroom, hurrying back to Hugo.

"Tell me about the people who come here for seasonal work," I say, whirling into his office and closing the door with a flourish.

Hugo looks up from the papers he's sorting through. He sits back in the desk chair, rakes a hand through his hair.

"They arrive in the fall and winter months. Here in the desert that means October through January."

"They come during that time because it's—"

"Harvest season."

Hugo

I'm nodding as I think this over. "We're still looking for old employee records, but I think we should also keep an eye out for a list of seasonal people."

"Seasonal people would've been gone by the spring," Hugo points out.

"True. But did your dad ever keep people on following harvest? Somebody who wanted to stay, and was a good employee?"

Hugo shrugs. "It's not impossible, but I don't know of anybody off the top of my head. I was really young."

We continue the search, stopping only to eat some of the protein bars and almonds I tucked away in my purse earlier when we stopped at Hugo's house.

My focus remains steadfast, for the most part, but I'll admit to being distracted by the way Hugo bites the side of his lower lip. And the way his big, callused hand palms his thigh, elbow stuck out to the side when he leans down for a closer look at a paper.

"I found something," he says, excitement poking at the corners of his tone. "It couldn't be more informal." He slides the paper across the desk to me. "It's literally a list of names, with a date."

Hugo's dad wrote in all caps, the letters clear and precise despite the age. At the top of the paper, underlined, are the words CHRISTMAS BONUS. The year listed is only one prior to the year he was killed.

"See that?" Hugo stabs at a name on the paper.

Jimmy Esteban.

"That's Claudette's dad," he explains. "He worked alongside my dad for years. I don't recognize any of the other names. My mom mentioned once that there was a large exodus following what happened to my dad. The employees were really upset. But those who've been hired since have stayed on."

"Jimmy stayed when all those employees left?"

"Yes. Claudette took over for him eventually."

"I ran into her in the bathroom. She told me as much. She's the one who mentioned the seasonal employees."

I reach for the police file, flipping open the folder. I locate the list of all the people the police spoke with, including every Summerhill employee. Down the list I go, reading out a name as Hugo confirms they are on his dad's list.

At the bottom of the police list is a black rectangle. "This one appears to be recently redacted." My finger slips over the ink. It doesn't leave a mark on my skin, but it looks newer. Not nearly as aged as the rest of the document.

"What reason would the police have for redacting the name of someone they interviewed?"

"Protection. Usually it's done to keep someone's personal information from getting out. It's odd, though. Why this name, and not the others? What is it about this name that needs protecting?"

Hugo sits back. His lips purse, and he rubs his thumb and his forefinger together. Suddenly he's up from the desk, crossing the office in two strides. "I'm going to ask Claudette to call her dad."

"I'll wait here for you."

Hugo halts with his hand on the door handle. He

Hugo

looks back at me, shaking his head. "Wherever I am, you are welcome there, too."

My heart trips over itself. None of this is by design. He's not *trying* to say the right thing, but it happens because of who he is.

I get up, and he holds out his hand. Together, we make our way to Claudette's office.

The friendly smile falls from her face when she sees Hugo's serious expression.

"Everything alright?"

"I need a favor, Claudette."

She nods, encouraging Hugo to continue.

"Can you please call your dad and ask him if he remembers any new employees from around the time my dad was killed?"

The request obviously takes Claudette by surprise. "Umm," she blinks hard. "Sure. But, Hugo, how do I explain this to him?" Claudette's eyes flicker to me, like maybe I'm the reason for all this.

Hugo squeezes my hand. "Tell him Simon's son waited too long."

Claudette takes her phone from her purse. She taps on the screen a few times, and then a ringing sound fills the air.

A man answers. "Hey, hon."

"Dad, hi. Listen, I have a question for you, and I know you're not expecting it." She glances at Hugo. "Like, at all. I have Hugo in my office, and he would like to know if you remember any new employees from around the time Simon was killed."

"Hugo? Hello there."

"Mr. Esteban, it's nice to hear your voice."

"Likewise, son. You have a question about employees?"

"Recently I came into possession of the police file from my dad's murder investigation. There's a list of Summerhill employees who were interviewed, but—"

"All of them," he interjects.

"Excuse me?" Hugo says.

"All of the employees were interviewed. Every single one. Myself included."

"Mr. Esteban, I'd like to know if there were any newer employees around that time period. Anybody who might not have been included on an employee list. Someone who maybe wasn't in the system yet?"

"Hugo, I wish I could give you the answer you're seeking, but it's been a really long time. Everything I told the police back then is still true today. I didn't leave anything out. I'm the one who gave them the names of every Summerhill employee. Even the guy who kept coming around trying to buy a parcel of Summerhill land. Every name, I gave it to them."

"That must be the redacted name," I whisper, and Hugo nods.

"Do you remember his name?"

"Well, I, uh..." A few seconds pass. "I'm sorry, I don't. It's been so long."

"That's ok, Mr. Esteban. It doesn't sound like he was all that important anyhow."

Hugo

"I don't think he was," the old man says. "Wasn't around much, or for long."

Hugo's nodding, looking at Claudette to let her know he's done. "Thanks for your time, sir. We'd love to see you sometime."

"Love you, Dad. I'll see you and Mom for dinner tomorrow." Claudette waits for her dad to respond, then hangs up. "I'm sorry that wasn't more fruitful," she says to Hugo.

"Thanks for giving him a call. I know it's one of his least favorite subjects."

Claudette taps her desk with the side of her thumb. "It's one of everybody's least favorite subjects. The whole town loved your dad."

If the whole town loved Simon, why would somebody kill him?

It's this question that sticks with me when we leave the Summerhill office. Stays with me as Hugo and I make dinner that evening. Pokes at me when we lie on the porch bed and star gaze.

Hugo is far away, too, in some distant land in his mind. He chopped green onions with a look like he was a thousand miles away. Kissed me with restraint. For the first night since I can remember, his hands did not stray when we laid down in bed.

I fall asleep safe in Hugo's arms, only to be awakened later by his pained whispers.

"It's him." His voice is strained.

"Hugo?" I run a gentle hand over his shoulder. He's still sleeping. Still dreaming.

Jennifer Millikin

"It's him," he croaks.

Chapter 43

Hugo

Twenty years ago...

MY KNEES PUSH INTO THE DIRT AS I CROUCH DOWN. I roll the olive between my fingers, ready for the moment Vivi walks by. Last week she hit me right in the eye, and it hurt so bad I cried. I won't get her as bad as she got me, because she's my little sister and I'm not allowed to, but I'm still going to get her good. She's not as sweet as my mom and dad think she is.

It's only a few minutes before I hear voices. Definitely not my little sister.

They come closer, and I recognize my dad's deep voice. He steps into the clearing, and he's followed by a man I've never seen before. The man wears a brown leather jacket and jeans. Boots. He has red hair, and pale skin.

I know I shouldn't be eavesdropping, but I'm also not supposed to be lying in wait for my sister so I can pelt her with an olive. My dad's lips form a hard line, an expression he makes when he's angry. There's no way I'm exposing myself now.

"I told you no," I hear my dad say.

The man looks angry, and now I feel afraid.

"I don't think you understand. You don't have a choice," the man says to my father, menacing. "He's in charge now."

My father straightens his shoulders, pulls himself up to full height. "You are the one who doesn't understand. There is always a choice."

The guy looks so angry. What if he starts beating up my dad? Maybe I can hit him in the eye with this olive. Maybe that will be enough to distract the guy, and then my dad can throw a punch. I've never seen him hit anyone, it would be kinda cool.

The guy turns around, walks away.

So much for seeing my dad turn into an action hero.

My dad tips his face to the sky, lips moving. He's praying. He prays a lot, tells me we have much to be thankful for. Reminds me to say my prayers, because we never know when God will call us home.

I look down, feeling guilty about hiding out here in the grove. I don't understand what I witnessed.

My fist is still clenched around the olive. I open it, look down.

The weirdest sensation flies through me as I take in the split skin, the mess.

The olive, crushed.

Chapter 44

Mallory

"It's not the first time I've had this dream," Hugo admits.

We're sitting up in his bed, cross-legged and facing each other. The night is dark, and still. Hugo's hair is mussed on one side. He is shirtless, wearing only the soft pants he prefers to wear to bed.

"Tell me everything. Every detail, even if it seems inconsequential." My notebook balances on the inside of my knee, pen poised. I'd waddled out to the dining room table for my things as soon as Hugo was awake and articulating what he'd dreamed.

Hugo talks and talks. He paints a picture of what his nine-year-old self saw, adding his adult view here and there.

"Over the years, I've had a lot of dreams about my dad. Sometimes I daydream, too. I was never sure what was real, or imagined. So many of my memories are brief, or high-level. I wasn't certain if it was the way things really happened, or if my brain wanted to fill in the picture because it wasn't detailed enough for my adult self."

"That's not uncommon," I say, still writing what he said. It's my own personal shorthand, circles and arrows, abbreviations. "Has the memory of seeing your dad in the orchard with that man ever changed? Or is it always the way you saw it just now, in your dream?"

"It's never changed," he says, confident. "It's one of a handful of final memories I have of my dad."

Hugo's head droops, and I toss my notebook aside, crawl to him.

Placing my fingers under his chin, I guide his gaze up to meet mine. "What is it?"

"Why didn't I tell somebody about that? I didn't tell my dad I saw him. I didn't tell the police." Emotion thickens his tone. "What if he was the murderer? What if I saw the guy who murdered my dad? What if me not saying anything helped him walk free? And then—" Alarm rakes over Hugo's face. "Maggie," he whispers.

"We don't know if they're connected. They might not be." I can't stand the way he's blaming his nine-year-old self.

"Two people are murdered the same way, in towns only two hours apart."

"Six years apart," I remind him. "Please don't blame yourself."

He nods, and my fingers under his chin move with him. "Promise me you won't think that anymore."

He holds silent for a beat before he says, "I promise."

Hugo

Together we slide back down into bed. Hugo pulls the covers up over us. I turn away, my back pressed to his front. His hands wind around me, finding my belly.

"I love you both, you know that? You and Peanut."

"We love you back, Hugo."

"How do you know she loves me?" He's inserted a playfulness into his tone, a sure sign my words have soothed him. "She never lets me feel her kick."

"Because—*oof*."

Hugo stills. "Was that *her*?"

Another kick. Strong, like the one prior. Hugo makes a sound, a heavy breath like he can't believe it.

"She feels what I feel. All these chemicals of happiness, and love, she feels those. She hears your voice."

"I read about that," Hugo says, his voice suddenly sounding shy. "I've been looking through your baby books."

Of course he has. He's *Hugo*. The sweetest man I've ever met.

"We haven't talked a lot about the future, but we need to. I know you have a life in Phoenix, and my business is here. I can't move the olive orchard."

My breath hangs in my throat, and I wait.

"Mallory, will you stay here at Summerhill? Will you and Peanut move in with me? Permanently?"

My heart dances. Tears burn my eyes. But my brain has a hard time accepting his words. Peanut's father literally signed away his rights to her. How can it be that another man wants her so desperately? And me? "Do you know what you're asking, Hugo? I didn't think I could get pregnant in the first place, there's no guarantee I can get pregnant again. Do you really, truly understand what it is you're giving up?"

Hugo's hands move lower to my hips, and he urges me to roll over. When we're facing each other, our heads on the pillows, Hugo runs his fingers through my hair. "It seems that you, you beautiful, infuriating woman, are the one who doesn't understand." He takes my hand, places it over his heart. "You and Peanut are enough. You are everything. I won't be going without. In this situation, I am only gaining."

So many times I've cried the past few months, and it felt unnecessary. The tears that flow now deserve a place on the pillow they're landing on.

"You don't think it's too soon?"

He lifts my hand, lips skimming my knuckles. "If you don't mind, I'd rather skip the long beginning."

"You are so good to me, Hugo."

"I'll never stop being good to you, or Peanut. Never. You're my girls."

We are, aren't we? Hugo's girls.

I've never felt this perfect. This whole.

We fall asleep holding each other, my belly between us.

Chapter 45

Mallory

I AWAKE THE NEXT MORNING, INVIGORATED. I can't wait to get my hands on my notes, and my whiteboard. Hugo makes us breakfast, and my decaf vanilla latte. He mentions he'll be late coming home for lunch today, he has a meeting at noon. I kiss him goodbye at the door, something good and sloppy that promises more later.

Settling at the dining room table with my latte, I check my email before getting started with work. David Boylan's response to my email jumps out at me, and I open it.

> To: Mallory Hawkins
> From: DaBoy72@gbt.com
> Thank you for your email. I'll admit, I looked up both you and Hugo following your visit. I was surprised to learn about your profession. As much as I would prefer to keep the past in the past, I recognize

the importance of seeking truth, and justice. Especially for someone like Simon. Yes, I agree to be interviewed for your podcast.

Best,

David Boylan

P.S. A thought occurred to me after you and Hugo left my house. What if the police could solve the murder after all this time? It always stood out to me that they were able to gather my blood at the crime scene from that small cut on my hand. Imagine what they could do if they used all their new technology?

Excitement zips through me, the thrill of making progress. Interviewing David will be huge for the podcast.

I set that aside, and for an hour I work on going through my notes of everything Hugo told me last night.

I add the red-haired mystery man to my whiteboard, drawing an arrow to Simon's name, connecting him to the redacted name from the file. It's not a certainty, but Jimmy Esteban said he'd given the man's name to the police. It's reasonable to assume it was his name redacted.

Cecily calls me midmorning, and we have a long planning conversation. I'd decided to take her phone call outside on the patio, and by the time we hang up, I'm regretting that choice. The sun has risen higher, tightening its grip on everything in sight. It's only May, but it's feeling like July all of a sudden.

I'm gathering my water, my phone, and my notes when a car bumps over the gently sloping hill. A

Hugo

Mercedes sedan, white and sleek. It pulls up to a stop, and Liane Rooney steps out.

"Mallory," she calls, smiling in that regal way of hers. "Just the woman I was hoping to see."

"What can I do for you?" I ask. Summerhill is a good twenty-minute drive from Olive Township, and Hugo's house sits far enough back from the restaurant and store that people don't venture this way. This was Liane's destination.

Oh, no. I hope she's not here to ask me to serve on a board with her.

"First of all, allow me to apologize for showing up here unannounced. I was at the Summerhill store buying a few bottles of that vanilla olive oil Hugo talked about. I love to give things like that away as gifts."

"It's no problem. I just got off a phone call, so I have a little free time."

"Lovely. I won't take up too much of your time. I was just wondering if you have someone planning your baby shower?"

"Oh." My fingertips drum my lower lip. "I hadn't thought about it."

Liane gives a half-suppressed chuckle. "Then I suppose nobody else has either."

Now that she's mentioning it, the number of things I'm going to need to buy fall over me like an avalanche. I've done very little in preparation for Peanut. To be fair, I thought I'd be in Olive Township for the weekend, and now it's looking like my stay might be indefinite.

"What would you say about me getting together with

Vivi and Daisy and planning a little party for you? It doesn't have to be a full on baby shower. Think of it like a...*sprinkle*."

A sprinkle. I like that. "I think that sounds amazing, Liane. And so thoughtful. Thank you."

"Of course. Every baby and mommy deserves to be celebrated." She smiles.

I'm sure a part of her wants to be the one who hosts my *sprinkle*, but it's still sweet, even if it's not totally altruistic.

Liane fans herself, tenting her hand as she looks up at the sunny sky. "I was wondering, Mallory, if you wouldn't mind getting me a glass of water? I was not anticipating this heat wave, and I'm not dressed for it." She gestures at her tweed skirt and matching jacket before fanning herself.

"That does look like a hot outfit," I concede. "Come on in."

I lead the way into the house. Behind me, Liane asks, "How is your final project going?"

"Final project?" I ask, before remembering the story I gave her at Sammich the day I passed out at the Olive Festival. It's only been a few months, but it seems so long ago now. "It's going great. I've learned a lot."

"Looks like it," Liane says, drifting over to the dining room table. She's looking over all my notes, perusing my whiteboard. It's not that I don't want her to, but it's also sort of that I don't want her to. I'm not ready to share it all with the world.

Liane glances up at me. "You're like a detective."

Hugo

"Or a criminal justice major," I say with a smile. I make my way to the kitchen, hoping she'll follow. I hear her heels behind me, and she comes to a stop at the kitchen island. "Hugo did a beautiful job with his kitchen remodel. Stunning."

"I agree," I say, handing her a cold bottle of water. She uncaps it and drinks. "Thank you," she says gratefully. "The desert is so dehydrating. Though I guess I don't have to tell you that."

"Nope," I chuckle. "Learned that lesson the hard way. Plus, I grew up in Phoenix."

"Did you? I didn't realize you were from the valley. I took my son there a lot when he was younger. He loved the big water park."

Over time, I've become a master at controlling my reaction when the water park is mentioned. I've had plenty of practice, thanks to the place being a big attraction. Per usual, I nod and smile. "Along with every other kid on a hot summer day. I loved going there, too."

Liane's eyes light up. "You know, Mallory, the oddest thought just popped into my head. Have you thought about collecting and storing your baby's stem cells? There's a company that sends out a kit, and the doctors collect the stem cells at birth. I'm a huge proponent of it."

"I hadn't considered that. Why are you a proponent?" It doesn't seem like Liane's going to be leaving anytime soon, so I go to the pantry, looking for small bites I can make into a platter. If I'm not going to be able to keep working for a little while, I may as well be a good hostess.

"There's so much they can do with stem cells," Liane

says. "I've always been a little worried that if something ever happened to me, I don't know if there'd be anybody who could help me out. Especially since I'm adopted."

Chapter 46

Hugo

Since I told Mallory everything about my dream in the middle of the night, I've been unable to think of little else. It has consumed my morning. I wish I could travel back in time, shake my younger self. Is it possible my dad's killer has been living in my memories all this time?

"Hey," Claudette says, stepping into my office. "My dad asked if you can call him when you get a chance. He thinks he might've remembered something."

I perk up, reaching for the phone.

Claudette's outstretched arm has me pausing. "Keep in mind, my dad might not be the most reliable source of information."

"Thank you for the heads-up," I tell her. Even if that's true, like Mallory said, the smallest, most insignificant detail can be consequential.

Jimmy Esteban answers on the fourth ring.

"Hugo," he says, in lieu of *hello*. "I was hoping you'd

be able to call me soon. I had a memory, and at my age, you never know how long those will last."

I breathe a laugh. "Hit me with it."

"The redhead guy. Your dad said he was there trying to buy land, and he wasn't taking no for an answer. But when it came time for him to be questioned by the police, he told them he was an employee. Only reason I know that is because the detective let it slip. Not Towles, the other one who retired and moved to Alaska."

"Hmm," I answer, because I'm not sure what to say.

"Here's the thing, Hugo. I don't think he wanted to buy land. I think your dad was just saying that."

"Why would he do that?" Last night's dream comes back to me. The same as it always is, the words never changing.

I told you no.

You don't have a choice. He's in charge now.

There is always a choice.

What does it all mean?

"I think your dad was trying to keep somebody from doing something on his land. With his business."

I spend a moment absorbing that before asking, "Do you mean money laundering?"

"I don't know what I'm implying, exactly. But I know"—he pauses—"*knew* your dad. There was no way he was going to let anything illegal happen. Assuming that's what the red-haired guy was there for."

"Why didn't my dad go to the police?"

"Maybe he was silenced before he could. Or maybe he didn't feel like they could help him."

Hugo

I think back to Detective Towles showing up at my house, case file in hand. The redacted name, and how Mallory pointed out the age of the ink didn't match the age of the document.

He's in charge now. I've never focused on those words before, never given them consideration. They press at me now, demanding closer examination.

I shift my weight, lightly brushing two knuckles over the desk as I think. "Mayor Rooney was the mayor at the time my dad was killed, right?"

"Yes, I believe so."

Thoughts turn over in my mind, rapid and hard to decipher.

My dad is dead, and then what? For what? Who benefits?

"Thank you, Mr. Esteban. You've given me a lot to think about."

We say goodbye and hang up. My mind races, flitting through everything Mallory and I have learned.

At this point, there is only one person I can think to call.

Chapter 47

Mallory

"You're adopted?" I ask, coming away from the pantry with an arm full of snacks. "That's neat. So was—"

The words freeze in my throat, and a shiver skates down my spine.

In his email this morning, David Boylan said his cut had been small. He's amazed it was enough blood to have been found on a dusty road.

"Who else was adopted?" Liane asks.

"Oh, um," I stutter, thoughts slamming into one another. "Just this other guy I know."

"What other guy?" she asks. She sounds different now. On edge. Excited, almost, but that doesn't make sense.

I dump the boxes of crackers and cookies on the counter. Force myself to turn around.

Face her.

It's the same Liane, but different. Watchful. Like her image is no longer her first priority.

Hugo

I force a smile. "Someone I know from Phoenix. I don't know why I said that." I tap my head with one finger. "Baby brain."

Liane nods slowly. Deliberately. "I've always wondered if I have a sibling out there in the world. What if I have numerous siblings? Wouldn't that be something?"

"It would be wild," I agree. My heart rate is soaring. What is the matter with me? People are adopted all the time. Liane and David both being adopted means nothing.

Except they appear to be around the same age. They aren't replicas of each other, but they aren't totally dissimilar.

David had many people to corroborate his whereabouts the day Simon died. According to him, he was at the Olive Festival hoping for prickly pear lemonade that was late.

"You know what I just had a crazy pregnancy craving for? Your prickly pear lemonade. Now that..." I shake my head like I just can't believe it. "That is some delicious lemonade. Maybe you can serve it at my sprinkle."

"I'd be happy to," Liane responds. The edge to her voice has receded. She sounds like her usual self.

"How long have you been serving it up at the Olive Festival?" I'm arranging snacks on the plate, keeping her in my line of sight. I'm being paranoid. It must be a mothering instinct.

Protect the cub.

"Why don't you ask me the question you're really thinking?"

"Hmm?" I ask, letting my eyebrows cinch in the middle. "What do you mean?" My voice is forced. Even I hear it. There goes my heart again. Hammering my breast bone.

"Mallory." Liane pushes off the island. Steps closer to me, then stops. "Ask me why David Boylan didn't get lemonade the day Simon died. It's written right over there, in your notes."

Alarm bells ring in my head, but I do my best to keep cool. "I hardly think that detail matters."

"You're lying." Liane's voice is calm. Cool. She doesn't take a step closer, because she doesn't need to. I'm boxed in.

"Lemonade doesn't seem like something to lie about," I say, putting on my best unaffected tone. I'm failing. It's impossible. Panic races through me, hot and cold at the same time.

"See the way you're standing right now?"

I glance down at my stomach, my hands stretching protectively over my belly. No matter how unflustered I'm trying to keep my voice, my defensive hands have told a different story.

Liane continues. "That tells me everything I need to know. You would do the same things I've done."

I stare at her, almost serene in that fancy tweed skirt and smart matching jacket.

Unperturbed, she says, "When it comes to protecting

Hugo

my family, there's nothing I won't do. No limit on the number of times I'll do it."

"You've said that to me before. On the day of the Olive Festival. You said I'll love this baby so much there's nothing I won't do for them."

"Brava," Liane trills. She has a lilt to her voice. As if she's victorious.

What has she won?

"You're very smart, Mallory. Not smarter than me, of course."

The mask Liane has worn every time I've seen her is slipping. The unhinged woman she is on the inside nudges the disguise, yearning to get through.

My phone lays on the far side of the island. I make a casual step right. Barely noticeable. "You must not be very smart if you're here, gloating."

She makes a high-pitched, pinched sound in her throat. "I couldn't help myself. Nobody has come so close to figuring me out. And not just one, but two! Two times I had to protect my family. Never thought somebody would connect them, but here we are."

That brings me up short. Rips my heart from my chest. "Maggie," I sob.

"I didn't know her name. Not until last week when I looked you up on the Internet. But yes, *Maggie*." She waves her manicured hand, diamond ring glinting in the overhead kitchen light. "It was one of those summer heat waves, and I couldn't take it anymore. I drove my son to Phoenix to go to the water park. Let's just say he made some *unfortunate* choices in how he treated your sister, and—"

"What do you mean by that?" I demand, hot anger coursing through me. "What did he do to her?" My stomach turns over, my imagination galloping out ahead of Liane's confession.

"This isn't about what he did, Mallory. I won't discuss my son with you."

A haughty lift of her chin. She looks like she's losing steam, her euphoria over her crimes waning a tiny bit. I have to keep her talking. As agonizing as it is, I need to hear it all.

"So you hurt her?" I ask, my lips curling over my teeth. Rage like I've never felt singes my veins.

Liane shrugs. "She was looking for you to tell you, and well, I couldn't have that."

My fingers itch to wrap around her throat, to do to Liane what she did to Maggie. "You strangled her?"

"Mallory, I did what I needed to do to protect my baby." She shakes her head, speaking to me as if I'm being insolent and she's delivering reason. "And then I helped you up off the ground when you found her. I didn't know that child was you, of course. I went back when I saw a crowd gathering. Had to make sure there was a reason for my DNA being there if they came across it."

I sway. From shock, I think.

"Learned my lesson from Simon. I cut my hand on that stupid road, and it was simply dumb luck that David Boylan turned out to be my twin brother." She laughs, but the sound is empty. "That's how I knew it was meant to be."

Through the front window, behind Liane's back, rises the faintest trail of dust.

"You're sick," I say, anything to keep her talking.

"I've never been more sane. But you? It's very sad. You went a little"—her head tilts furiously side to side, her eyes widening manically—"cuckoo." She warbles the word.

Outside is the roar of an engine.

Liane hears it, knows it's Hugo. "Time to die." She lunges for me, wraps her hands around my neck. A homicidal maniac stares into my eyes, using a singsong voice. "No sprinkle for you."

My pulse pounds, my blood boils.

Air. I need it.

I claw at her hands, dig into her skin.

How can this be? How did I not see this coming?

My baby, my baby. My perfect little Peanut. She needs oxygen. I'm her mother. My only job was to protect her, and I failed.

Somewhere in the house, there's a door coming off its hinges. A bang. The sound of something metallic.

My hands fly out, punching at Liane. This cannot be it. I punch everywhere I reach. Her head. Her stomach.

A blade pierces Liane's arm. I watch it come through her skin, slide out, the sound unforgettable.

Liane screams and lets me go. I drop to my knees, crawl away. My throat burns.

"Call the police," Hugo commands, nudging his

phone to me with his foot. I scramble for it, my hands shaking so badly it takes me two attempts to pick it up.

"Don't bother," Liane laughs, her back against the fridge. Blood pours from the wound on her arm, darkening her tweed. "My husband is the mayor, remember? And your dad wouldn't let him run his money through Summerhill. So it was buh-bye to Simon." Hugo presses his sword tip against her throat, and blood trickles, blossoming through her silk blouse. "I had to protect my family," she cries, as if it's a perfectly reasonable excuse. "Couldn't let him live with what he knew about the mayor. Or the man who worked for us. Can't leave any strings untied!" Her voice rises higher, more crazed. Like she's been waiting all these years to brag about her magnificent plan.

I look down at the phone to dial for help, and see it's recording.

Hugo. So damn smart.

Suddenly there are shouts. People bursting through the open front door. Sonya, then Carmen. Penn.

For the first time, Liane looks afraid.

"Hugo, what's going on?" Sonya demands, coming closer. With wide eyes she glances from Hugo to Liane.

"She killed him," Hugo says, voice vibrating with rage. "Dad. She killed Dad."

Sonya gasps. Her face twists in horror, hand covering a single sob that escapes her mouth. Carmen comes up behind Sonya, wraps her arms around her.

Penn rounds the far side of the island, offers his arm and helps me stand. Swallowing my own saliva feels like

Hugo

a thousand thorns in my throat, but the adrenaline carries me through, keeps me upright. That, and Penn's steadying arm.

"Killed...Maggie," I croak, chest heaving. The truth sharpens the pain anew, makes it burn in my chest.

A sound tears from Hugo's throat, a roar and a growl and a snarl all at once. He wants blood. He wants retribution. He wants *revenge*.

"Hugo," Sonya says softly, shrugging off Carmen. She lays a gentle hand on the arm Hugo's using to keep his sword trained on Liane. "Don't do it. Think of your father. What would he do in this moment?"

"I know what he would do," Hugo grits out, gaze never wavering from the woman trapped against the fridge.

Sirens in the distance. Many of them.

"But I'm not him. And I know what I've been waiting a long time to do."

"Would you really kill your mayoress?" Liane's eyes grow wide. A monster, presenting as a doe.

"Fucking ribbon her already," Penn mutters.

Hugo presses harder, more blood flows. "When you murdered my father, you created the day you would die by his son's hand."

Everything about this situation is scary and painful, but when I hear those words, I'm transported to the day Hugo told me he daydreamed about saying that very sentence to his father's killer. The look of pain in his eyes.

"You're lucky I didn't find out about you before I met Mallory. Because my sword would've already pierced your heart." Hugo presses the flat side of the sword under her chin, forcing it to lift. Her wild eyes are on him, and he looks at her with unparalleled intensity. "When you took my dad, you left me scarred. So here is a matching set for you." With barely a flick of his wrist, he slices each of her cheeks from the corner of her lips to the tops of her ears. "You are a clown, and now you will look like one."

Red bubbles at the cuts, slides down.

Sirens blare. Uniformed officers rush inside. Hugo lowers his weapon, steps to my side.

Penn releases me, and Hugo is there, pulling me and Peanut into his body. I don't know how, but Hugo no longer holds his sword. Penn must've taken it.

"Mallory, Mallory," Hugo chants into my hair. The emotion pours off him, his voice thick with it. With urgency he kisses my forehead, my cheeks, my lips. "That was the worst image I've ever seen. I was terrified. It took everything I had not to gut her while her hands were on your throat."

I nod, shock wearing off. I try to talk, but I can't find my voice. My vocal cords throb.

The police are hauling Liane up, cuffing her, making sense of what happened. Sonya does the talking, until Hugo says, "I recorded everything she said." He finds Detective Towles among the uniformed men.

The detective shakes his head at Hugo. "I told you to wait for me. You hung up."

"I saw her car parked out front. I couldn't wait for you. She had Mallory and my baby."

My baby.

Hugo

I wish I could use my voice, tell Hugo how grateful I am, how much I love him. My eyes are working just fine, and the tears are flowing.

Detective Towles hauls a bleeding Liane away. She has gone utterly silent. Hugo slicing her face seems to have stolen her ability to speak.

"Hugo," one of the police officers says. "This is an active crime scene. We need everybody out, and we're going to need to take statements."

Hugo's shaking his head. "I want Mallory and my baby checked out by her doctor. Everything else can wait."

Hugo declines the offer from the officer to drive us into town to see the doctor. "I'm not letting you out of my sight," he murmurs, pulling me in close. His tone is gruff from rescinding fear, weak with relief.

As if I'm made of glass, he helps me into his car.

An officer approaches, and Hugo rolls down his window. "Bring her by the station once she gets the all-clear from her doctor."

"Will do," Hugo responds, hitting a button to close the window, shutting us out from the world beyond.

He shifts into Drive, taking me away from the swirling lights of the police cars.

"I'm dying to hold you," he says as we crest the small hill. "But first things first. I need to get you to Dr. Connolly. You and the baby."

"My baby," I clarify, using my voice though it hurts.

"Your baby," Hugo says, jaw tight.

My head shakes, hair swirling. "Your baby...too." It's

the voice of someone recently deprived of oxygen, the sound of it bringing back what it felt like to have my airway cut off.

Hugo glances at me. "I know what I said back there. I heard it. I didn't mean to presume, I was beside myself."

He still doesn't get it, and I can't speak the words I want to say. So I point at my belly, then at him, and I nod.

He points back at his chest, a grin better than a sunrise splitting his face. "My baby?"

I nod again, vigorously this time. "Yours," I manage.

"My baby," he says again, eyes flickering over me. "My girls."

Chapter 48

Mallory

Dr. Connolly was waiting behind the front desk when we walked in. The police called ahead and told her what happened at Summerhill.

"Baby girl looks great," she says, running the wand over my belly. The sound of Peanut's fluttering heartbeat fills the room. "Healthy. Heartbeat is perfect." She takes the wand away, and the sound in the room ceases. I wish I could listen to it all the time, a background to my day. Like white noise. I wipe the gel from my skin with the paper towels she has given me.

"No kicking," I choke out, sounding like I've sat beside a campfire while chain smoking.

"She'll start up again soon," Dr. Connolly assures me. "What I'd like to know is how you're doing?"

"I'm ok." The tears falling down my face say otherwise.

She frowns. "How could you possibly be ok after

what you went through today?" Gently she prods my throat, my vocal cords. I wince.

"Rest and hydration," she says, "but I'm not a general practitioner, so please, if you're feeling anything you're concerned about, don't hesitate to call Dr. Murray. He makes house calls."

I nod, while Hugo thanks her.

The office staff stares at us when we leave. So do the people in the waiting room. Could news have made it out and around Olive Township that quickly?

Hugo makes a stop at Sweet Nothings for a chamomile tea with honey.

Sonya calls and says the police are having a special team come out to clean up the kitchen. "You can stay here tonight," she offers.

Hugo agrees, and reminds his mom he has to take me to the police station.

"You ready?" he asks, a hand on my thigh.

Blowing across the top of the tea, I whisper, "I'll do my best."

My hand hurts from writing. It's hard to speak more than a few words at a time, almost impossible, so they brought me a pencil and paper.

I've done my best, writing out everything I can remember. There are some holes in my memory, small

Hugo

pieces of what happened I can't recall in sequential order. Some things I know aren't verbatim.

I try to tell them this, and they assure me it'll come back over time. "Your brain is still protecting itself," Detective Towles says.

I also write down everything that happened at the Olive Inn, and send the photos of me sleeping to Detective Towles. I have no idea if it's connected to Liane, but they should know about it.

"Why didn't you tell me about this when it happened?" he asks, clearly unhappy. Hugo explains my reasoning, and the detective makes it clear he's not in agreement. "I'll look into it," he says gruffly.

I point at the detective, then at Hugo, raising both hands as if to ask *How?*

"I'll tell you everything," Hugo promises me. "For now, I'd love to take you home."

Sonya has homemade chicken noodle soup simmering on the stove when we walk in. Hugo tells her he's going to his house to pick up some of our things. Sonya takes over, caring for me in a way only a mother can. She sets me up on the couch in the living room, turns on her favorite cooking show. She brings me ice water, heats another cup of tea, and asks me what else I need.

"I'm fine," I whisper.

Sonya sinks to the couch beside me. Her eyes fill with tears. "You sweet girl. You almost died figuring out who killed the people we love. I'm grateful, please believe me, but a part of me is frustrated with your curious nature."

If it didn't feel like needles in my throat, I'd laugh.

Sonya brushes hair back from my face. "My son loves you fiercely. Please be careful with yourself."

She's looking at me with such tenderness, how could I do anything but nod my agreement?

Hugo walks in holding two bags. He carries them upstairs, returning immediately. We eat dinner together, me and Hugo, Sonya and Carmen.

Hugo explains to all of us how it came to be that he was coming home today when he said he'd be late with a meeting. "After I talked to Jimmy Esteban, I had a weird feeling. Nothing was sitting right. So I decided to call Towles, ask him why he'd redacted that name before he gave Mallory the file. It was obvious neither one of us trusted the other, and it made for a conversation that wasn't going anywhere. Then this odd feeling came over me, and I decided to trust him. I told him everything Mallory and I had learned, and he told me Mallory had piqued his curiosity in a case he'd resigned himself to never solving. He'd redacted that name because he knew there was something off about it, and he'd wanted to protect the man's information so he could do his job properly and follow a hunch."

Hugo looks at me with a stare I can't decipher. "I don't know if I'll ever understand it, but something told me to go home. I got up from my office chair and ran to my car. Thank God I did."

The most unusual sensation trickles over me. A feeling of safety. Like someone whispered *I've got you.*

"How did you know to come to my house?" Hugo asks his mom. "How did Penn get there?"

Hugo

"Carmen and I were standing in Merry Little Market when Penn walked in to buy the vanilla olive oil for Daisy. We were talking when we saw you driving fast up to your house. We knew something was wrong."

"It's good you were there," Hugo admits, glancing at me. "I don't think I would've left her alive."

"I guess we'll never know," Sonya says.

She and Carmen hover after we eat, watchful of everything I do. Hugo must take notice, because he says he'd like to watch the sunset just the two of us.

Sonya and Carmen share a look before retreating.

We go outside, and Hugo helps me onto the porch bed. He arranges pillows, and has me lie back. He settles in beside me, his hand rubbing over my stomach.

"Have you felt Peanut yet?"

I shake my head. *No.* If I hadn't been to the doctor, if I hadn't heard Peanut's heartbeat for myself, I'd be going out of my mind with worry.

Hugo works his way down to my midsection. He lifts my top, and the warm air drifts over my skin.

"Hey, Peanut," he says, voice low. Deep. His fingers caress the hardness of my belly.

"Pretty scary what happened to your mom today, huh? I don't blame you for going into hiding." Hugo's eyes find mine. He looks so good with his lips beside my skin. So perfect. So right.

"If you wouldn't mind giving us a little push of your heel? Maybe a knee, or an elbow. Just a little something to let us know you're hanging in there." Hugo's fingers flex, and he palms my belly, letting it roll over the expanse.

A press from the inside. A dragging feeling. Hugo and I gasp at the same time.

"Look at you go," Hugo says, wonder clear in his tone. He sends a message through my belly with a push of his hand. Peanut pushes back.

I make a noise, marveling at this wonderful thing happening in front of me. Hugo looks up, eyes wide, astonished.

"It's like she's communicating."

I swallow, and it hurts. "She is."

He presses a long kiss to my stomach. Reverent. "Mallory, I want her. And I want you. Forever. Will you be my forever girls?"

Peanut kicks. *Hard.*

Hugo laughs.

"She said yes," I croak.

Hugo crawls up my body. He kisses the space below my ear once, twice, three times. "I love you. I love you, I love you. I could say it a million times. Let me be your husband. Let me be the man who shows you how incredible you are."

"Can't...do better...than that."

Hugo chuckles against my skin. "You were designed for me, Mallory. I can feel it."

"Yes," I murmur.

Hugo takes me to bed in his old room. He explains it's more of a guest room now, that he's taken most of his childhood memorabilia with him to his house.

We climb under the covers, and I whisper something I've been thinking about since everything happened this morning. I've been drinking nothing but tea all evening, and it's helped soothe my vocal cords.

"Sounds crazy, but watching you with that sword today..." I bite my lip, reluctant to say what I've been thinking.

Hugo catches on, smiling provocatively. "Did you like what you saw, Mallory?"

"Not in the moment, but later when I thought about it...yeah."

His hand finds my breast in the dark. His thumb flicks over my nipple, making me arch into him. "Do you have a sword kink?"

"Perhaps. Choking is definitely not on my sex menu, ever."

Hugo groans. "Too soon."

The only communicating we do after that is with our bodies.

Chapter 49

Mallory

In the weeks following the event with Liane, I pore myself into *Case Files*. If I thought it was personal before, now it's tenfold.

Jolene came to visit, hell on wheels when she learned what Liane did. "I wish I'd been here, Mal. I would have stuck her through the chest, Inigo Montoya style." She mimed using a sword.

Jolene helped me write episode scripts, and schedule interviews. Liane's arrest and confession galvanized everybody, and they are more than ready to share their experiences. Mayor Rooney resigned following his wife's arrest, and after being interrogated by a relentless Detective Towles who brought a lot of emotion with him into the small, dark room, was determined to have not known about his wife. His finances however, are all being investigated due to Liane's rant in Hugo's kitchen that day. Something tells me there will be a lot for the police to find. Liane has, not shockingly, claimed to have been

Hugo

lying about her son and what he did to Maggie. He lives in Baltimore now, a world away from his insane mother, and also denied any wrongdoing when contacted by authorities. Even behind bars, Liane is turning herself inside out to protect her adult child.

As broken as I feel over everything that happened, I'm doing my best to stay calm. Peanut needs me to be emotionally healthy.

Cecily and I have been in constant contact, creating content to stir up interest in the podcast and the forthcoming episodes. The local media attention on the solving of not one, but two, long-cold murder cases has helped everything we're doing. The De la Vega family has refused media interviews, stating they will be exclusively working with a true crime podcast.

Hugo's home, specifically his kitchen, has been scrubbed and bleached. I had a hard time standing in it at first, but I've decided to reframe the situation. Instead of thinking of it as a place where I nearly lost my life to strangulation, I think of it as the place where we took down my sister and Simon's murderer. When I look at it that way, I am empowered and no longer a victim.

Most surprising of all was the phone call from my mom after the detective who worked on Maggie's case called to tell her about Liane.

"You ready for this?" Hugo asks, taking my hand in his. We're sitting out front of my mom and stepdad's house.

There's no making up for lost time, but forward progress is all we have. I won't miss out on that because I want to protect myself, hold a grudge, let past pain guide future behavior.

"I'm ready. Thank you for coming with me."

"By your side is right where I want to be." His voice, his words sink into my chest.

My mother steps out front. Her hands are at her mouth, as if she can't believe it. Then her arms open wide.

I go to her, step into her embrace. She let her torment grow thorns, keeping others away. I don't know what that was like for her. How much a person must be hurting in order to hurt others.

"You are so beautiful," she whispers into my ear. "And I am so sorry."

There are tears. Handshakes as I introduce Hugo.

"We're marrying in Olive Township next weekend," I tell my mom once we're settled in her living room. "It'll be small. In the orchard. Family, and close friends." Hugo and I share a smile. We know it's fast, but nothing about us has been typical. No other person in the world could possibly be as right for one another, and waiting is unnecessary.

"Is that an invitation?" my mom asks tentatively.

I nod. "Yes."

"I wouldn't miss it."

We spend the afternoon with my mom. My stepdad makes an appearance, but not for long. It's the way he's always been, and I don't expect anything different from him.

"She has closure now, you know?" I say to Hugo when

Hugo

we're on our way back to Olive Township. My head rests against the car seat. "Maybe things will change."

Hugo takes my hand, kisses my knuckles. "It's looking like they will. She's coming next weekend."

I hum happily. "Next weekend... when I get to become your wife."

He nips the knuckle on my middle finger. "You're already my girl."

A slow smile curves my lips. "Good thing I didn't let it deter me when you ignored all my emails."

He chuckles. "I thought you were a nosy little podcaster who wanted to stir up trouble."

I shimmy my shoulders. "I am a nosy little podcaster, and I most definitely want to stir up trouble."

"Just wait until I get you home, Mallory. I'll show you trouble."

"Promises, promises," I tsk.

He laughs. "I love you."

"I love you, too."

We drive east, the sunset in the rearview, bidding us farewell with its brilliant pinks and purples. I may have called Phoenix home for the first twenty-eight years of my life, but Olive Township beckons me.

My hand finds the back of Hugo's neck as he drives, my fingers curling over his warm skin, gliding up into his hair. He groans, a sound of contentment.

Peanut and I are the luckiest girls in the world.

Chapter 50

Hugo

I married Mallory, not in the wedding hall we built recently, but among the olive trees, where my dad walked. A place where I can close my eyes and hear the rich baritone of his laughter. Feel his gait beneath me as I sat atop his shoulders.

When I look into Mallory's brown eyes and pledge my everlasting love and devotion to her, I know he is present.

"I felt him today," my mother says later, eyes shiny with unshed tears. "When I was getting ready. I looked in the mirror, and I felt his hands on my shoulders."

"I believe it, Mom." I kiss her on the cheek. "I've never given much thought to how it all must've been for you when he died. You were devastated, but it didn't keep you from taking good care of us. How did you manage that?"

"Hugo, my boy," she reaches up, pats my cheek. "I could see your father in your faces. My broken heart came second to my responsibility to you and your sister."

Hugo

"Thank you, Mom. I mean it." I hug her, spot my *wife* over her shoulder. Mallory smiles wide. Happy and beautiful. I send her a wink.

I'm not a gambling man, but I'd bet someone had a hand in bringing her to me.

Chapter 51

Olive Township

THE CONCLUSION OF A DECADES-LONG MYSTERY brings a satisfaction to these old bones. There is no pleasure in knowing a truth, in watching a wolf prance around dressed as a sheep.

Justice has been served. Old wounds will heal.

Hugo has found the one with whom he can settle. I yearn for the same to be true for his sister.

Not much longer now.

What was sown a long time ago will soon be reaped.

Epilogue

Mallory

"I'm telling you, get the blood orange margarita. Forget your tequila and soda nonsense." Vivi slams a palm on the table at King's Ransom.

I tip my head, survey her reddish-orange drink with the sugar rim. "Fine," I concede. "Next drink."

Vivi slides her fresh drink to me, nudging mine out of the way. "This drink."

I look out, find my hot husband's eyes. Send him a wink. It's our first night out since little miss Simone Maggie came screaming into the world. Sleep-deprived and knee-deep in infant clothes, Hugo and I are in love with each other, and our sweet girl.

The healing in my heart started by Hugo has been amplified by Simone. She's a reminder of something beautiful and good and true. Splendor born from agony.

She looks nothing like her biological father, an unexpected bonus. Where he was fair-skinned and light-haired, she is olive-toned with hair that matches my mahogany. She looks like me, but really, she looks like Hugo.

Vivi's waiting on me to sip my new drink, to tell her I love it. I think it's the chef in her. She wants people to love what she loves, to share with them what makes her happy.

I oblige, sip my tart sting of tequila and citrus, and nod. "Ok, yeah. You win. This is my new drink."

Daisy gives a ladylike snort. "Champagne or bust."

Vivi pretends to gag.

I catch Hugo's eye again. He's sitting with Duke and Penn at the next table. Vivi was adamant we spend the first hour having conjoined guys' and girls' nights. She'd said it was no fun being the fifth wheel, and she didn't want to be forced to make conversation with Paper Towel Duke while the couples canoodled. I'd had to ask for clarification on the less-than-kind nickname for Duke, and Daisy explained it had something to do with Penn saying a wet paper towel can't fulfill its intended purpose, and that's what Duke is.

Daisy swallows down her drink, glancing at Penn with hearts in her eyes. "It almost feels like everything that happened with Duke and Penn was a dream."

"Not for the rest of us who lived it with you," Vivi grumbles.

Daisy rolls her eyes. "She's still mad because she made a lot of food for my reception and then I didn't get married."

I laugh. "I really wish I could've watched all that go down."

Hugo

"You can," Vivi says dryly. "It's on YouTube."

Immediately I pull my phone from my purse and watch the video. I cackle, and gasp, and ogle my husband in his suit. He wasn't the focus of the video, and he only makes a brief appearance, but in my opinion he stole the show.

Sonya texts me a picture of Simone sleeping in her arms. She reports Simone's last feed, how many ounces, her most recent diaper change. Sliding off my stool, I slip over to Hugo and present my phone to him. He gazes lovingly at our daughter, reading the text from his mom. "That's one ounce more than she had at three o'clock this morning," he notes.

Penn and Duke share a look. Hugo notices, and says, "You fucks can fuck right off."

Penn points a stiff finger across the table. "There's the man we know and love."

Now that I've infiltrated the guys' table, the separation is null. Penn matriculates to the bar, where he orders a refill for Daisy and delivers it to her. She rewards his thoughtfulness with a long and slightly obscene kiss.

The speakeasy's false wall opens, and a brick wall of a man steps through. He has a mop of curly, dark hair, and a round face. Shoulder to shoulder, I think he'd outmeasure a yardstick.

"Ambrose," Hugo booms. He's off his stool, arms open, lumbering toward his best friend. Hugo is a big man, but when he hugs Ambrose, it's almost comical. Penn and Duke follow, greeting Ambrose with hugs and masculine back slaps.

Daisy and Vivi hang back, and when Ambrose approaches he pauses, smirking at Daisy in a friendly, familiar way. "My lady," he says, sweeping his arm to the side. Daisy grins, hopping off her seat and jumping into his arms.

"They have a running joke," Vivi explains, eyes on Daisy as she touches Ambrose's forearms, asking him questions. "Daisy says Ambrose is like the giant from The Princess Bride."

I squint my eyes and cock my head. "From the right angle, I can see it."

"But, like, one hundred times hotter," Vivi adds.

I turn a sharp glance at Vivi. "Um, what?"

"You have eyes," she sasses. "Use them."

Playfully, I cross my arms in front of my chest. "I only have eyes for your brother."

"Perfect answer," she murmurs, gaze staying on Ambrose.

Daisy steps back and Ambrose looks to the table, at me and Vivi. The only two people who haven't greeted him yet.

He extends a hand my way. "Mallory, it's nice to officially meet you. Congrats on Simone."

My hand is swallowed up by his. "It's nice to meet you in person, finally. Thank you for agreeing to be Simone's godparent."

He glances at Vivi. "Me and Vivi, godparents."

"We'll teach her all we know," Vivi jokes.

"This should be good," Ambrose adds, the corner of his lips turned up when he trains his eyes on Vivi.

Vivi finally slips from her seat. "Come here, you big lug. What do you think you're doing, making me wait to say hello to you?" She steps into Ambrose's embrace, dwarfed by his size.

"Saved the best for last," he says, fumbling for an appropriate place to set his big, meaty hands on Vivi's body.

Their reunion feels different than everyone else's. It's hard to describe, but the word *tender* comes to mind. Makes me think of the way Hugo said Ambrose was like a brother to him, and therefore a brother to Vivi.

I'm not so sure about that.

Ambrose melts into the dynamics of the group. With him present, Vivi doesn't have to feel like a third wheel. They chatter, and I listen. Just like I prefer to do.

Hugo brings me another margarita. I've been preparing for this night, pumping breast milk so Simone has plenty to eat while I wait for the alcohol to leave my system. He stands beside me, rubs circles on my back. Places a kiss on my forehead and whispers, "I can't wait to get you home."

We've only been cleared for sex for a couple weeks, and it's been slow going. We're enjoying each other, the process, the forced slower pace as my body adjusts following birth. Hugo is patient, and I never feel like he wishes for more, or different. He meets me where I am, always.

Soon, Simone will legally be Hugo's. But our family is already a happy one.

Ambrose is answering question after question about

the NFL, and his knee surgery. "Dr. Cordova—the doctor who did my surgery—isn't confident I'll ever play the same. He's seeing evidence of arthritis." Ambrose says it like he's reading off a grocery list, but his eyes sweep to the beer in his hands. I'm betting he has a lot of complicated feelings on the matter.

I finish my drink, and Hugo announces we're taking off. "Simone will be up approximately three hours after I fall asleep," he says, but he's not complaining. Honestly, he sounds giddy.

"Get out of here, Mom and Dad," Duke jokes. "Tell my sister I said congratulations the next time you talk to her."

"You could call Cecily yourself," I say gently. There are some odd family dynamics there I don't understand.

"Nah. She's doing her best to forget Olive Township exists. I won't interrupt that."

Duke's well-wishes for Cecily are regarding her contribution to the recent success of *Case Files*. Without her, we wouldn't have been able to wrangle the content and package it in bite-sized, interesting pieces.

Liane was recently moved to the state prison, where she will serve a life sentence for the murders of my sister, Simon, and the red-haired man we learned was named Brigham McNealy. His body had been discovered at the bottom of a canyon not too far from Olive Township only eight years ago. Mayor Rooney is currently in jail as he awaits trial for money laundering, fraud, and tax evasion.

As for the photos of me sleeping, Braxton the night manager may have deleted the footage from the security cameras that night, but he got blackout drunk at a local sports bar and confessed his perversion. By his own admission, he has a thing for the pregnant form. The pictures the police found on his phone confirmed it, and he's currently sitting in jail, waiting to have the book thrown at him. It's probably better than what would've happened to him had Penn and Hugo found him first, but I wouldn't mind Braxton getting a helping of prairie justice. I felt violated all over again when I found out, but I've done my best to move on. Putting any more emotional energy into it only prolongs the situation.

After a handful of margaritas, I'm supremely grateful Hugo does Simone's night feedings. When she wakes in the morning, I get up with her. I'm hungover, but the sweet baby in my arms makes me feel better. Hugo finds us in the rocking chair he placed next to the fireplace in the living room.

"How are my girls?" he asks. He's sleepy and squinty-eyed. And so handsome.

"Better now that you're awake." I smile up at him. He drops a kiss on my forehead.

"I was thinking, today is the day I trade in my car."

"What?" I stare, shocked. "You love that car."

He shrugs. "It's not practical. I want a car seat in both of our vehicles."

That afternoon, with Simone sleeping in her stroller, Hugo says farewell to his precious, bright red sports car.

He glides a palm over the hood. "Goodbye, Welcome Wagon. Caio Chariot. Home Hooptie." Then he glances at the sensible SUV he has chosen. "Hello, Dad-mobile."

I kiss his cheek. "Fatherhood looks good on you."

That night, with Simone sleeping peacefully on Hugo's chest, I lay out beside them on the swing bed. So much of my life spent searching for things. And to think, it was all only two hours away. Waiting for me out here, on an olive orchard.

The End

Acknowledgments

Readers. The first acknowledgment must go to you for coming along on this journey with me. I am constantly amazed and honored you spend your precious time in the worlds I create. Thank you, thank you, thank you.

My editor, Nicole Purdy. You always make me look harder at the characters, go deeper into their minds and motivations and thoughts. Thank you for helping me shape Hugo and Mallory and their story.

My beta readers for this book: Crystal, Brittany, Danie, Catherine, Katie, Chelsea, Mindie, Paramita, Lillian, Natalie, Amanda, and Erica. THANK YOU! The insight of early readers is invaluable, and I'm eternally grateful you helped me make Hugo shine.

About the Author

Jennifer Millikin is an Amazon Charts best-selling author of contemporary romance and women's fiction. She is the two-time recipient of the Readers Favorite Gold Star Award, and readers have called her work "emotionally riveting" and "unputdownable." Her third novel, Our Finest Hour, has been optioned for film/tv. Jen lives in the Arizona desert with her husband, children, and two dogs. With nineteen novels published so far, she plans to continue her passion for storytelling. Visit www.jennifermillikinwrites.com to connect.